Mail Order Bride
SIX HISTORICAL ROMANCE NOVELLAS

Mail Order Bride
SIX HISTORICAL ROMANCE NOVELLAS

Stacy Henrie
Kristin Holt
Annette Lyon
Sarah M. Eden
Heather B. Moore
Sian Ann Bessey

Mirror Press

Copyright © 2016 by Mirror Press, LLC
Paperback edition
All rights reserved

No part of this book may be reproduced in any form whatsoever without prior written permission of the publisher, except in the case of brief passages embodied in critical reviews and articles. This is a work of fiction. The characters, names, incidents, places, and dialogue are products of the authors' imaginations and are not to be construed as real.

Typeset by Rachael Anderson
Edited by Julie Ogborn, Jennie Stevens, and Lisa Shepherd

Cover design by Mirror Press, LLC
Cover Photo Credit: Elizabeth May/Trigger Image
Cover Photo Copyright: Elizabeth May

Published by Mirror Press, LLC
http://timelessromanceanthologies.blogspot.com

ISBN-10: 1-941145-84-1
ISBN-13: 978-1-941145-84-5

TABLE OF CONTENTS

Written in Her Heart   1
by Stacy Henrie

Wanted: Mail Order Bride   59
by Kristin Holt

The Sound of Home   131
by Annette Lyon

For Better or Worse   195
by Sarah M. Eden

An Inconvenient Bride   255
by Heather B. Moore

The Price of Silver   319
by Siân Ann Bessey

MORE TIMELESS ROMANCE ANTHOLOGIES

Winter Collection
Spring Vacation Collection
Summer Wedding Collection
Autumn Collection
European Collection
Love Letter Collection
Old West Collection
Summer in New York Collection
Silver Bells Collection
All Regency Collection
Annette Lyon Collection
Sarah M. Eden British Isles Collection
Under the Mistletoe Collection
Road Trip Collection
Blind Date Collection

Written in Her Heart

by Stacy Henrie

OTHER WORKS BY STACY HENRIE

Lady Outlaw
The Express Rider's Lady

Of Love and War Series
Hope at Dawn
Hope Rising
A Hope Remembered
A Christmas Hope

One

Woodland, California, 1884

"I've decided to place an advertisement in the *Matrimonial News*," Georgeanna Fitzgerald announced, tapping her pen against her desk. A tremor of excitement, mingled with nerves, bolted through her at voicing her plan aloud. Surely, this was the answer to several of her problems.

From the desk adjacent to hers, Clayton Riley, her financial advisor and personal secretary, snapped up his chin. "You're what?"

"Going to place an advertisement in the—"

He waved his hand impatiently. "I heard what you said, Georgie. I'm trying to deduce what in the world you meant. An advertisement for whom?"

Georgie set down the pen and maneuvered her bustled skirt around her chair in order to stand. "For me, Clay."

"Why?"

He ran a hand over his frown, drawing her attention to his chiseled jaw and masculine mouth. She still thought him quite handsome. A few years back, she'd even fancied herself in love with Clay, but that girlish infatuation had been rebuffed. He'd seen her as his employer's daughter first, then as his employer after the death of her father. Perhaps he even felt brotherly affection toward her, but he hadn't ever seen her as someone of romantic interest.

"Your father's money will provide for you. We've been over this." Clay placed his folded hands on top of the desk and leaned forward. "Why then, would you need a husband? Especially one who might only want to marry you . . ." His voice faded as a chagrined expression passed over his face.

"For my money?" she countered with more triumph than irritation. She'd hoped to make him understand. "That's why I want to place this advertisement." Georgie paced across the Turkish rug, her skirts rustling behind her. "I'm tired of only being found attractive to men because I inherited my father's fortune. Which is why I don't intend to mention my wealth in the *Matrimonial News*."

She shot him a victorious smile, but Clay shook his head, his brows drawn down in confusion. "Why become a mail order bride then? If not to be provided for?"

"There are many reasons why a woman would wish to marry." Georgie circled the rug again. "Companionship, love, the hope of a family."

Clay cleared his throat, though his eyes had strayed back to the stack of papers before him. "And you want these things?"

"Well, yes." She bit her lip. "Sort of."

"You aren't making sense."

She went to his desk, splaying her hands on the wood surface and bending toward him. "It's the perfect solution," she explained. "If I marry, not only will I have a companion, someone who doesn't want me simply for my money, but I will also receive the rest of my inheritance. The part Father stipulated would be mine when I married."

He looked up again, his blue eyes sharp. "Do you mean to say that your annual income is insufficient? If that's the case, then we can certainly adjust—"

"No," she said, interrupting him. She placed her hand on his arm, though she wasn't sure why the muscles underneath his jacket sleeve felt taut with concealed tension. "My annual income is more than adequate. But it won't be enough to build a new orphanage for those sweet children in Sacramento. I want them to have every convenience, and I can't do so without that reserved money."

Clay leaned back, breaking her hold. "So you would marry a complete stranger," he asked as he crossed his arms, "in order for the orphans in Sacramento to have a better home?"

Why did he seem angry? Georgie fell back a step, raising her chin in defense. "It isn't as strange as it sounds. Women have chosen to be mail order brides for centuries—and for far less compelling reasons," she added. "Age being one of them. I'm twenty-two years old." She turned away as a feeling of longing welled up within her. "In many people's eyes, I'm practically a spinster, and yet, I'd like to be a wife and mother."

Her cheeks grew warm at admitting such hopes to Clay. But he needed to know her mind was made up, especially since he would no longer be using her home as his office once she married.

The thought of not seeing Clay on a daily basis caused an ache of a different sort. Their longtime friendship would have to be sacrificed in order for her to marry. But, if she could help other orphans, now that she was one herself . . . Ones not so fortunate as to have been born to a father who'd made his fortune during the California Gold Rush and who'd loved his wife, Georgie's mother, every single day, even after she'd passed away.

"My mother was a mail order bride," she tossed over her shoulder as she approached her desk.

"Yes, but your father told me that she did so in order to better her station in life. To keep from being a lady's maid forever."

"And I'm hoping to better the orphans' stations in life." Georgie picked up the picture sitting on her desk's front corner. Her parents and her ten-year-old self smiled back. She and her mother had shared the same honey-colored shade of hair and hazel eyes, but Georgie's height was all from her father. Would any man want a tall woman with more angles than curves as a wife?

Georgie replaced the picture. "It's true. Mother wanted more than servitude for her life, but Father said he fell in love with her the moment she climbed out of the stagecoach. Mother said it only took her another hour to realize she could love him for always too."

Of course, Georgie didn't expect instant love, even if her parents had found it. Mutual respect and affection would do for her, with the hope that love would grow over time. If her parents could make marriage to a stranger work, she certainly could too.

Clay pushed back his chair and stood. "As your personal advisor, Georgie, I can hardly recommend this as a solution to . . ." He gestured around the room. "To help young orphans or fight loneliness."

She drew herself up, though she still stood a head shorter than Clay. "That is why you are my financial advisor. Not my advisor in matters of the heart."

His frown deepened as he ran a hand through his brown

hair. "Be that as it may, your father charged me to look after *you*—not just your money."

"Precisely." Georgie flounced into her chair and slid a clean sheet of paper in front of her. "Which is why I want you to narrow down the selection process."

"I beg your pardon?"

She pointed her pen at him, emphasizing each word. "I want you to choose the most suitable men out of those who respond."

"Me?" he choked out. "I thought you said I'm not to counsel you on matters of the heart."

"You also said Father made you promise to look out for me." She smiled sweetly at him. "Which, in this endeavor, means I need your unbiased, objective opinion as to whom I should begin correspondence with."

Clay raked his hand across his face and turned away, stalking toward the bookcases on the other side of her father's study. "Georgie," he warned, hidden frustration leaking into his voice.

"Please, Clay." She perched forward on her chair, hoping he sensed her eagerness and sincerity. "I could honestly use your help."

He halted before the bookshelves, his hands inside his trouser pockets. Tense silence filled the space between them. At last he emitted a grunt of acceptance. "What would you have me do?" He didn't turn around.

Georgie ignored his obvious display of annoyance. "If you would kindly run this advertisement to the post office when I'm finished, that would be lovely." She nibbled on the end of her pen. "Now, what to write?"

She studied the piece of stationery, then began to dictate out loud as she wrote. "Educated, amiable lady of twenty-two, with blonde hair and hazel eyes, seeks intelligent, witty, kindhearted gentleman of twenty-five to thirty-five years of age."

Though she heard a scoff from Clay's direction, she chose not to comment. Thirty-five might be a bit too old for her, given that Clay was twenty-nine and believed that seven years between their ages was too many. But she was no longer an exuberant seventeen-year-old.

Georgie read through the words once more, smiling at what she'd written. This was the perfect solution, practically an answer to prayer. She'd been asking the Lord for weeks about how to supply the children with the new, larger home they so desperately needed, and then, she'd overheard someone at church mention the *Matrimonial News*.

Now, her life and the life of each of the dear orphans she was patroness over was about to change for the better.

Clay scowled at the sidewalk, his derby hat doing little to shade his eyes from the warm afternoon sunshine. If only it would turn cloudy and stormy, something more in keeping with his present mood. An annoyed growl, as much at himself as at Georgie, filled his throat. This matrimonial advertisement scheme of hers was foolhardy, irrational, illogical . . .

"Afternoon, Mr. Riley," an alto voice intoned.

Lifting his eyes, he found old Mrs. Huckabee seated on her veranda. The woman lived to be "in the know" of the comings and goings of Woodland's residents.

"Afternoon, ma'am." Clay tipped his hat to her.

"Heading into town, are you?" she asked. "Or are you going home at this early hour?"

He hoisted the envelope in his hand. "Actually, I'm posting a letter."

"For the lovely Miss Fitzgerald?"

Lovely, yes. But also young and stubborn and rash . . . He reined in his thoughts long enough to answer, "Yes."

"Such a shame she's all alone in that big house," Mrs. Huckabee said with a heavy sigh.

Clay decided not to remind the woman that Georgie wasn't entirely alone. She had a cook, a maid, and a man-of-all-work. Not to mention Clay was there every day, typically only returning to his room at the boarding house in the evenings.

"Do you think she'll ever marry, Mr. Riley?"

Sooner than you know. "Perhaps, ma'am."

"Such a sweet-tempered girl."

Most of the time.

Clay quickly retracted this thought as unfair. While he didn't like Georgie's idea of becoming a mail order bride, she had always been kind, lively, and full of optimism. Except when she'd spoken earlier of being seen as a spinster. The memory of her crestfallen expression plagued his mind. She'd all but admitted to being lonely.

Was that what had bothered him the most about their earlier conversation? Clay had come to find peace and contentment in their daily, tried and true friendship. But to hear that Georgie was still lonely . . . Was that what grated at him? Or why he felt as if he'd been punched in the stomach?

"I shan't keep you, Mrs. Huckabee." He dipped his hat a second time.

"Of course. Good day, Mr. Riley."

Clay smiled and walked on, though the curve fell from his mouth half a block later. If only he hadn't insisted Georgie visit the orphanage in Sacramento last year. Then she wouldn't feel compelled to marry a complete stranger in order to further help those innocent children.

But, no, he didn't mean that either. Georgie had blossomed as patroness of the orphanage, and so had her young charges. As an orphan himself, Clay had done what he could for the children over the years. But involving Georgie had proven to be a blessing for her and for the children. He wouldn't wish that away, not even to avoid her scheme to post this matrimonial advertisement.

Eyeing the letter again, Clay frowned. Why should it bother him if Georgie married or how she went about finding a husband? The answer came swiftly. He liked his current life. It was predictable, comfortable. Had been for the last seven years. And while he wasn't working for Patrick Fitzgerald any longer, Clay enjoyed advising and working with his daughter. Georgie and her parents had long since become the family he'd lost when his grandfather had passed on.

"Then I should be overjoyed," he reminded himself. If Georgeanna Fitzgerald was like family, then he ought to be happy helping to secure a good match for her. But the feeling roiling in his gut didn't resemble happiness at all.

He didn't particularly like the image that rose in his mind of Georgie speaking with and spending time with another man. Or another man ardently kissing her. Clay's jaw tightened at the notion.

He could choose not to mail the advertisement. His feet ground to a halt on the sidewalk, his mind spinning. But Georgie's sad expression danced before his eyes again, compelling him forward once more. She'd sounded so hopeful when she spoke of marriage and a family of her own. How could he deny her that? Even if he did think her methods for obtaining a husband and children were completely unorthodox.

Lord, give me the courage to do right by her. Help me to let go of my annoyance.

As his silent prayer ended, numb resignation settled over him. He would mail her letter and weed through the replies to find a man worthy of Georgie. That was the best he could do.

But Clay couldn't help thinking, ten minutes later, as he relinquished the envelope to the postmaster, that his peaceful, unchanged life was about to be forever altered by the outcome of Georgie's scheme. For good or ill, things would never be the same for either of them.

Two

1877: Seven years earlier

Hands behind his back, Clay observed the Fitzgerald's well-manicured lawn from the drawing room window. Everything about this place oozed tasteful opulence, but opulence nonetheless. The plush carpets, the marble-inlaid hearth, the expensive vases of freshly cut flowers—this mansion's furnishings made his grandfather's nice home in Sacramento seem like a crude cabin by comparison.

Clay swallowed, hoping to bring moisture to his dry mouth. The last financial advisor to work for Patrick Fitzgerald had been much older than Clay's twenty-two years. Would he be viewed as too young and inexperienced by comparison? He hoped not. From what his grandfather had told him, Mr. Fitzgerald had once been young and eager to prove himself too. Instead of making it rich from gold-hunting, he'd made his money by providing supplies to the miners. And now, his million dollar fortune was tied up in various stocks.

Which had fared better than Grandfather's had.

Thoughts of his maternal grandfather, Clay's only family, squeezed his lungs with grief. Grandfather had taught Clay everything he knew about life and banking. Clay's earliest memories were of sitting beneath his grandfather's desk, counting pennies. He hadn't wanted for anything growing up, except to have remembered his parents better.

The Panic of 1873 had changed everything. The bank had folded, bringing Clay home from college without a diploma. A year later, his grandfather also succumbed to their financial ruin. The doctor told Clay that it was the shock of everything that had ultimately killed Grandfather.

Still in shock and grieving himself, Clay sold the only home he'd known and had taken a job at a newspaper. But now he needed to go back to his roots—to banking and finance and to advising others to make sound decisions about their money. This position with Patrick Fitzgerald would not only put his longtime banking skills to use but also help him feel closer to his grandfather.

The squeak of shoes in the entryway pulled Clay's attention away from his thoughts. Beyond the open door, a lanky girl of fourteen or fifteen skittered to a stop on the marbled floor. Her honey-colored hair was pulled back in a childish pink bow, but the long lashes fanning her greenish-brown eyes and her perfectly bowed lips suggested she would likely grow into a beauty someday.

"Are you the next applicant?" she asked.

Clay chuckled, surprised she would address him so directly. "If you mean for the position with your father, then yes."

Her gaze swept over him from head to toe. "You look rather young, at least in comparison to the man in Father's study right now. How old are you?"

"Twenty-two. How old are you?" he countered good-naturedly.

"I'm fifteen." She drew herself up to her full height, which was rather tall for a girl her age. After a moment, she blew out her breath. "All right, fourteen and a half. But still."

He couldn't help laughing again. "I remember feeling the importance of that half myself."

"Really?" She waltzed into the room, her hand outstretched. "It's nice to meet you. I'm Georgeanna Fitzgerald. But everyone calls me Georgie."

So, this is Patrick Fitzgerald's only child, Clay thought as he shook her hand. "Clayton Riley."

"Have you been to college, Mr. Riley?" Georgie plunked down onto the sofa.

"I have. A few years, at least." Clay threw a look toward the doorway. If he'd expected to meet any member of the Fitzgerald family, it would've been Patrick's wife, not his precocious daughter.

As if sensing the direction of his thoughts, Georgie waved him into a nearby armchair. "My mother's not feeling well, so I'm playing hostess today. Now, where did you go to school?"

Hostess or juror? Clay held back another chuckle. If nothing else, talking to Georgie would keep his mind off of how badly he needed this job.

"I went to Yale," he said, taking a seat. "I'd planned on going into banking."

"Planned?" Georgie cocked her head. "What happened?"

Clay cleared his throat. How much did she know about the world at large? he wondered. "Let's just say, things changed with our financial situation four years ago, and I wasn't able to continue."

She bobbed her head solemnly. "Oh, yes, the Panic of '73."

"Yes." Clearly she knew more than he'd given her credit for.

"Do you know anything about finances?"

Leaning back, Clay regarded her with a half smile. "Why do I feel as if this were the interview?"

Her cheeks went pink, but she kept her chin up. "Because, if I like you, Mr. Riley, I might share a few secrets to help you get this job."

He studied her with new interest. "Very well. My grandfather was a banker and taught me everything he knew about managing money. I was set to take over his bank after I graduated, but it folded during the Panic."

"Good," Georgie said with another nod.

"Pardon?" Maybe she wouldn't prove to be as helpful as he'd hoped.

"No, no." She waved away the question. "I don't mean good about your grandfather's bank but good that you know so much about banking and money."

"Ah."

"Where is your grandfather now?"

"He . . . uh . . . died. Three years ago."

"I'm so very sorry to hear that, Mr. Riley." The compassion in her voice, coupled with her sad expression, eased some of the pain those words had cost him.

He dipped his chin in acknowledgement as he found himself admitting, "I miss him every day."

"Do you have other family?"

"Afraid not," he replied. *Time to move onto a different topic.* "So, have I passed your inspection?"

Georgie pursed her lips before a full smile lifted them. "Yes, you've passed."

A funny sense of relief washed through him. "Now,

what are these secrets to getting the job?" He bent forward and rested his elbows on his knees.

"Are you religious?"

"I am." Another trait he'd inherited from his grandfather.

She clapped her hands. "Perfect. The last man wasn't at all. Of course, he didn't bother to answer any of my questions..."

Clay stifled a retort, afraid that he'd offend her if he pointed out the irregularity of being interviewed by an employer's teenage daughter.

"Let Father know you're religiously inclined and about your grandfather and his bank." She scooted forward, lowering her voice as she added, "But don't drop any names unless he asks. He likes a man who's self-made, who can stand on his own two feet."

Or her own two feet, he mused, thinking of her. "Duly noted. Anything else?"

"Tell him that you realize you're young, but you've had plenty of experience already, and college was the finishing touch even if you didn't graduate."

A door opened elsewhere in the house, followed by the murmur of voices. Georgie jumped to her feet.

"You're up. Good luck, Mr. Riley." She rushed toward the door where she paused. "I hope you get the job. I liked talking to you."

Clay smiled fully. "I liked talking to you too."

She disappeared only moments before her father commandeered the doorway with his tall figure and impressive bearing.

"Mr. Riley, I presume?"

"Yes, sir."

"Come with me."

Clay followed Mr. Fitzgerald across the entryway and through an open door into the study. His nervousness spiked anew as the millionaire shut the door behind them and indicated that Clay should take a seat in the chair opposite the large desk. But Clay reminded himself that he had a few tricks up his sleeve care of Miss Georgie Fitzgerald.

Sometime later, he emerged from the study triumphant. He'd been offered the job. After collecting his hat from the stand and shaking his new employer's hand, Clay walked outside. He hadn't gone far when he heard someone call to him from behind.

"Mr. Riley?" He turned, frowning in confusion when he didn't see Georgie. "Up here," she added.

Clay looked up to find Georgie leaning over the railing of the second-story balcony. "I got the job," he announced with a smile, glad for the chance to tell someone the happy news.

"You did?" A full grin brightened her face.

"Thanks to your help."

She shrugged her thin shoulders. "I'm glad to do it. So, when will Father have you start?"

"Tomorrow."

"See you tomorrow then, Mr. Riley." She straightened and waved.

"Bye, Georgie."

He resumed walking up the sidewalk and began whistling a jaunty tune. There would be quite a few things to express gratitude for in his prayers tonight: gratitude for this new job, for his grandfather's training through the years, and for the clever, spirited Georgie Fitzgerald.

Three

Knowing Clay disapproved of her decision to become a mail order bride, Georgie decided not to broach the subject again for at least a week or two. But ten days had passed since he'd dutifully mailed her advertisement, and she couldn't wait any longer to learn if she had any replies or not.

"Any letters come this week?" she asked as they sat in the dining room. Clay usually joined her for dinner, preferring Mrs. Shaw's cooking to that served at the boarding house.

He grunted a yes without pulling his gaze from his plate.

Georgie rolled her eyes. "I meant letters for me, Clay. Has there been any . . . interest . . . in my advertisement?" That word did the trick.

He lifted his head to look at her. "Yes, actually. You've had four interested parties."

"Four?" Georgie sat back, a bit surprised. She'd hoped for at least one or two. "Any of them promising?"

"I don't rightly know," he said, an expression of consternation passing over his face as he trained his focus on his meal once more.

"Haven't you read their replies?"

He shook his head. "I've had a busy week, Georgie. I'll get to them soon."

His irritable tone stung her. "Don't trouble yourself." She set down her fork and placed her napkin onto the table. "I can read through them myself. Just tell me which pile or drawer you've put them in."

She rose to her feet, but Clay stayed her exit from the room by placing his hand over hers. A thrill shot through her at his touch, even though she tried to tell herself such a reaction was silly and pointless. He didn't see her as anything more than his employer or the sister he'd never had.

Instead of speaking, though, Clay gazed down at her hand as if seeing it for the first time. His thumb traced the back of her palm, intensifying the flurries up her arm and down into her stomach. Then, just as suddenly as he'd captured it, he released her hand.

"I'll read them tomorrow." He glanced down at his dinner again. "You asked me to help, and I will, I promise."

"Very well." She resumed her seat.

An unspoken tension cloaked the room, but Georgie couldn't identify its source. Was Clay angry with her? Or was it resignation she felt radiating from him? Shouldn't she be happy that he'd promised to help? Instead, she wanted to weep or to ask him to hold her hand again.

No, she firmly told herself about both. She'd wasted more tears than she could count, pining after Clayton Riley through the years and wishing he'd see her as a woman he could love. She'd finally locked her heart against feeling anything more than sisterly affection for him, and she didn't plan to unlock it only to be hurt again. But something had to be done to dispel the gloomy cloud hanging over them.

"Will you stay and play chess?" she asked, not daring to meet his eye for fear that he'd refuse. She didn't want him to leave now, still frustrated with her.

Clay cleared his throat. "A game of chess sounds wonderful."

She threw him a grateful smile. "Good. Because I plan to beat you tonight." She wagged her finger at him. "And no letting me win, either. You know how that annoys me."

His answering smile brought Georgie an inward sigh of relief. They were back on familiar ground, old friends once more. "I would never," he said, throwing her a mock look of solemnity, "dream of letting you win, dear Georgie."

Dear Georgie? Clay thought. The words had slipped so easily off his tongue. Too easily.

He shifted his weight in the armchair and stared hard at the chessboard between them. What was wrong with him? He'd surprised himself by caressing Georgie's hand at dinner, which had felt delightfully soft and smooth, then he'd up and called her by a term of endearment.

He gave an emphatic shake of his head. It hadn't been an affectionate term. He'd only been teasing her, nothing more.

"Clay," she said, arching her eyebrows. "It's your move."

Pushing aside his muddled thoughts, he took his turn, but his mind wasn't on the game. It had strayed to the four envelopes stowed inside his desk drawer. He'd put off reviewing these replies to Georgie's advertisement, though his week had been every bit as busy as he'd said. There'd been his usual work to complete. But he'd also taken the time to visit several buildings in town in hopes of finding a new office since, once Georgie married, her future husband wasn't likely to appreciate Clay sharing a study with his wife.

He frowned, drumming his fingers on the chair arm with irritation. The idea of Georgie marrying still rankled, especially knowing one of the letters in his desk likely represented her potential groom. He lifted his gaze from the chessboard to Georgie's face and found her brow furrowed with concentration.

As he'd predicted all those years ago, she had grown into a real beauty. Her hair, swept up off the nape of her neck, gave him a clear view of her creamy throat where it met the lace of her collar. Her nose sloped perfectly over pursed, pink lips. *Kissable lips,* he thought.

He sat back with a start, suddenly fearful of what he might think or do next. His foot tapped with frustrated impatience beneath the table. Impatience at himself and his clearly addled brain. When had he begun to think of Georgie as kissable? They *had* kissed once, four years ago, but he'd regretted his foolishness almost immediately. Now, a part of him wished to turn back the clock and create a different outcome.

Georgie had looked so beautiful that night, a beauty she still possessed. Though it was more than her outward appearance that he'd begun to take note of the last week. He liked her sincere smile, her passion when she spoke of the orphans, and her ability to converse with him on any topic.

"The intense looks and finger tapping will not throw me off," she murmured as she bent forward and moved one of her knights. "As I said, I intend to win tonight fair and square."

Clay stopped fidgeting long enough to make his next

move, though he didn't check his staring. How ironic that he'd shared a study with her for two years now and seen her every day the preceding five but only now felt as if he were really seeing her. He didn't want to imagine someone else sitting at his desk, talking or laughing or good-naturedly arguing with Georgie. He wanted it to still be him.

To still be him...

This thought ricocheted through Clay, filling every corner of his mind with its declaration. Could he possibly... have feelings for Georgie? Feelings that went beyond brotherly affection or dutiful protection? Reeling at the possibility, his next move proved sloppy. Georgie was quickly gaining ground.

Clay ran a hand over his face as he debated what to do with this new insight. He couldn't very well declare himself at least, not yet. He was sure he had hurt Georgie in the past, even if she hadn't ever said as much. But he'd never considered that their friendship could change into something more. Now, only time and effort could prove to her that he felt differently than he once had. And time was not something he had in abundance. Not when he'd told her that he would read over the *Matrimonial News* replies tomorrow.

Too bad he couldn't throw his own response into the ring with those desiring to correspond with her.

The sudden idea made Clay sit up straight. Why couldn't he converse with her? Let her see he had changed when it came to matters of the heart? Per her request, he would choose the best of the four who'd replied and add his own letters to the mix. Of course, he would have to disguise his handwriting and assume a different name. But, then Georgie would be able to choose for herself.

And if she doesn't choose you? he asked himself.

His jaw tightened at the prospect as he took his next turn. The idea of having her reject him sent sharp regret lancing through him—regret that he'd been blind for too long. But he had to try. Surely, he could be convincing in his letters, and perhaps it wouldn't be too difficult. After all, he had no idea of the caliber of the men who'd already written to her.

"Checkmate," she announced in a victorious tone. "I won!"

He grinned. "Yes, you did."

Georgie narrowed her gaze at him. "You usually don't take to losing this easily. You didn't let me win, did you, Clay?"

"No." *At least, not on purpose.* "Congratulations," he added. "You played splendidly." Unlike he had. But he didn't care. He had a plan now, a way to win her over. And that move was far more important to him and to his heart—than any game of chess.

Four

1879: Five years earlier

"Georgie, who is that," Clay asked, "talking with your father?"

Seventeen-year-old Georgie whacked the croquet ball with her mallet, then turned to see whom Clay was referring to. An older gentleman and a stunningly beautiful young woman had joined her father on the veranda.

"Oh, that's Roger Holley and his daughter, Marian. They're old family friends. They've come to stay the week with us." Georgie strolled across the shaded lawn toward her ball. "They came to Mother's funeral last year. Don't you remember?"

The memory of her mother's death brought a twinge of deep sadness. How she missed her, though Clay's continued presence in her life had helped. It was nice to have someone else, besides her father, to talk to.

"I think I would have remembered *them*."

Clay's awed tone brought Georgie up short. She glanced at Marian again and found her watching Clay with unmistakable interest on her porcelain face. A surge of jealousy soured Georgie's stomach. Marian Holley was a twenty-year-old heiress from San Francisco, who had dark eyes and ebony hair. The young woman was only three years Georgie's senior, but they had never been bosom friends. Marian struck Georgie as snobbish and unfriendly. But somehow, the older girl had succeeded, in less than five minutes, in obtaining the one thing that had eluded Georgie for the last two years: Clay's interest.

"She's very beautiful, don't you think?" Georgie moved to stand beside Clay, their croquet game abandoned. He cleared his throat, his telltale sign that he was uncomfortable or didn't wish to answer.

"Uh, yes," he finally admitted. "She is nice-looking."

Georgie gave a light laugh, though it was laced with pain. "It's all right, Clay. You haven't stopped staring at her since she came out onto the porch."

"That obvious, huh?" He turned his back to the house and ran a hand through his hair in agitation. "Whose turn is it?"

"Never mind." She dropped her mallet on the grass. "Come on, Father can introduce you."

She led him to the porch, where she greeted Roger Holley and Marian. Mr. Holley was all smiles and exclamations over how much Georgie had grown the last year, while Marian offered a simple hello without taking her eyes off Clay. Georgie's father made the introductions, then Mrs. Shaw brought out bowls of ice cream for everyone's enjoyment.

To Georgie's consternation, Marian took the porch swing, and Clay asked to sit beside her. The two men occupied the only other chairs, which meant that Georgie had to perch on the porch steps like a child. Irritation warmed her skin. Every few seconds, she glanced at Marian and Clay, who were deep in conversation.

If only I could have inspired that look of enthrallment on his handsome face.

"Where shall we play chess?" Georgie asked him when she'd finished her ice cream. She couldn't even say what flavor it had been.

Clay glanced her way, his expression full of chagrin. "Don't you think we ought to forgo our game, Georgie? We shouldn't leave your guests to fend for themselves."

His subtle reprimand made Georgie wince inside. She was still learning how to play hostess in her mother's absence Clay knew that.

"Oh, I would enjoy watching you play, Mr. Riley," Marian cooed.

Georgie resisted the urge to roll her eyes. The thought of playing chess with Clay while Marian hovered nearby sounded as fun as a toothache.

"It's all right," Georgie said, standing. "I think I'll go read." Guests or not, she wasn't about to stay on the porch and watch Clay bask in Marian's presence. She walked away from the group toward the front lawn, her chin up, willing back tears of hurt.

Clay would never see her as anything more than the fifteen-year-old girl he'd met two years ago. But she wasn't that girl anymore. Though she might not be able to compete with Marian in age or beauty, Georgie was still a woman herself—with a heart that yearned for the one man she feared would never return her love.

Five

For a second time, Georgie read through the two letters Clay had selected—one from a Mr. Strauss and the other from a Mr. Harris. She liked Mr. Harris's open, humorous style of writing. And while she could tell Mr. Strauss was educated, he had admitted to being thirty-six, even though her advertisement had asked for someone no older than thirty-five. She did appreciate his frank manner, and yet, she also sensed a measure of loneliness behind his words.

"What do you think?" Clay asked, folding his arms over his chest with an air of self-satisfaction.

"I like them both," Georgie said, lifting a reply in each hand. "Mr. Strauss sounds intelligent and polite. And Mr. Harris strikes me as witty and friendly." She threw a smile at Clay. "You chose well. Thank you."

He nodded, though his triumphant manner of a moment ago quickly vanished. "So, with whom will you correspond?" He directed the question to the piles of papers on his desk.

Georgie studied the two letters again, thinking. Each man possessed qualities she liked. But which one would make a good husband, someone she could be happy with? To know for certain, she would need more time and correspondence with both men. Her gaze snagged on a line in Mr. Harris's letter. He'd mentioned having a close relationship with his grandfather, the man who'd taught him everything about life and love.

"This Harris fellow sounds a bit like you, Clay."

"What?" The word sounded strained. "What gave you that idea?"

"No need to get grumpy," she countered, setting the letter on the desk beside the one from Mr. Strauss. "I only meant he was close to his grandfather like you were."

Clay cleared his throat. "Ah. Well, surely many people are close to their grandparents."

"Do you miss him? Your grandfather, I mean?" She hadn't thought to ask him this question in some time. "I miss my mother and father . . . very much." A sadness she hadn't felt in months swept through her. She was every bit as orphaned as the children she wanted to help. But then, so was Clay.

"I miss all three of them," Clay said, setting down his pen. "Your parents were kind enough to allow me to feel like more than an employee."

"They loved you like a son," Georgie murmured. Both her parents had said so, although she had loved him as something more than a brother.

How strange her days would be when Clay was no longer a significant part of them. Was she ready for such a permanent separation from the life she'd known for the last seven years? An unsettling feeling crept into her stomach.

I'm doing the right thing, aren't I, Lord?

She wanted the peace and excitement she'd felt the other week, when she'd first concocted her plan. And yet, she also wanted to put off saying goodbye to Clay, the man she'd once loved and who'd become her dearest friend.

"I'm going to write to them both." Georgie pushed aside the letters and removed two blank sheets of paper from the desk drawer.

"Both?" Clay echoed, his eyebrows shooting upward.

She gave him a decisive nod. "I want to get to know each one a little better before making any decisions." *And before you have to leave*, she thought, throwing one more look at his handsome face. Then, ignoring a twinge of regret, she began writing.

Six

1880: Four years earlier

The cold night air froze some of Clay's irritation as he stepped out onto the veranda. Patrick Fitzgerald's New Year's Eve party was in full swing inside the house. Prominent citizens of Woodland, as well as wealthy guests from Sacramento and San Francisco, had come to ring in 1881 with the millionaire and his daughter, including Marian Holley and her father.

Despite exchanging regular letters with Clay since their first meeting last year, Marian seemed to have little to say to him tonight. Instead, she'd flirted with every other man at the party.

Clay relaxed the tight muscles of his jaw as he stared at the glittering stars above. He felt the fool, and he hated the gutted feeling that brought to his stomach. But he couldn't let go of his admiration for Marian. She was beautiful no question—but he'd discovered a certain vulnerability about her that she didn't show to everyone, a measure of loneliness and self-doubt, that had compelled him to be her friend.

And, as he'd hoped more and more the past six months, something more than just a friend.

He sniffed in derision. He'd convinced himself that 1881 would be the year for an engagement between them, even if he had little money to bring to the marriage. And yet, Marian's cool behavior tonight had dashed his hopes.

A sound from behind made him turn. Georgie had exited the house.

"In need of some fresh air?" she said, moving toward him, her cream-colored dress rustling.

Clay nodded. "You?"

"Yes." She wrapped her gloved hands around the railing and leaned forward. "The stars look beautiful."

Instead of looking up, though, Clay found his attention caught by Georgie's rapt expression. When had she grown from the gangly teenage girl he'd met that first day? Tonight, she looked every one of her eighteen years and quite stunning in a gown that hugged her trim figure and hinted at her feminine curves. Her hazel eyes appeared especially bright in the moonlight, her cheeks flushed slightly from the heat indoors.

"Quite lovely," he murmured, thinking not about the stars but of Georgie. As she turned toward him, he glanced away, fearing she'd notice his staring.

"Are you glad that Marian will be staying the week?"

Clay coughed. "Yes, it's been some time since she was last here."

"Do you . . . still favor her?" Her voice sounded uncharacteristically timid.

He wanted to deny the sentiment, especially in light of Marian's actions tonight, but he couldn't. "Yes, I believe I do."

Georgie lowered her chin. "I thought so."

Before he could comment further, loud voices from inside declared the hour to be nearly midnight. He and Georgie turned to face the open doors of the house, though she seemed as reluctant as he felt to return to the party. Patrick and his guests counted down to the New Year, then began toasting each other and offering perfunctory kisses on the lips or cheeks.

Georgie met his eyes and smiled, though the gesture seemed to leak sadness. "Happy New Year, Clay." She placed her hand alongside his jaw and offered him an innocent kiss on the cheek.

"Happy New Year, Georgie," he returned softly as he took her other hand in his, intent on giving it a friendly squeeze and then releasing it.

But he didn't.

Perhaps it was the moonlight, caressing her pretty face, or the fact that she stood close enough that her rosewater perfume pleased his senses. Or perhaps it was her warmth in contrast to Marian's coldness that made him hold her hand longer than society would deem appropriate.

Whatever the case, he lingered. And in the next moment, Georgie leaned forward and pressed her lips to his. Her kiss, feather light but sweetly ardent, stirred a longing within him. He let go of her hand, bringing his to the nape of her neck as he returned her kiss.

Several glorious seconds passed, her lips yielding to his. Then, from inside the house, Marian's throaty laughter reached his ears, the sound dousing him like cold water and jerking him back to reality. He shouldn't be kissing another woman, not if he intended to wed Marian someday.

Another dreadful thought pushed its way forward. *What would Patrick say if he discovered me kissing his eighteen-year-old daughter?*

Stepping back, he released Georgie. "I'm sorry," he said, running a hand over his face and trying to catch his breath. "I shouldn't have done that."

She crossed her arms and looked away, cloaking her thoughts from him.

"Look, Georgie . . ." He put a reassuring hand on her arm as he tried to get his jumbled mind working again. What could he say that wouldn't further hurt her feelings?

"I'm fine." She shrugged off his hold and tipped her chin upward. "Don't trouble yourself on my behalf. It won't happen again." Turning away, she stepped toward the house, but Clay caught the rare glimpse of unshed tears in her eyes just before she disappeared among the guests.

The rawness in his gut intensified. He'd suspected for some time that Georgie felt more than friendship for him, and tonight, he'd spurned those feelings. Worse, he'd let her believe, if only for a moment, that he might share such feelings.

He turned back to the darkened yard, his hands strangling the railing. He didn't want to hurt Georgie; she was his best friend. But there couldn't be anything more between them. Not when she was still so young and her father was still his employer.

Hopefully, she can forgive me, Clay thought, stepping back toward the noisy house. *Hopefully, tomorrow, everything will be back to normal between us.*

Seven

Clay leaned back against his headboard, reading Georgie's latest letter to "Mr. Harris." Harris was his mother's maiden name, one of the few facts about his life that he hadn't discussed with Georgie over the years. Only here, in his room at the boarding house, after work, did he dare read her replies.

Over the last few weeks, she'd kept up regular correspondence with him and Mr. Strauss. Thankfully, she simply handed Clay the letters, leaving it to him to address and mail them. Those for Mr. Strauss went to the post office, while those for Clay were stowed beneath his mattress to keep the boarding house matron from discovering them when she cleaned.

He hadn't read any of Georgie's replies to Mr. Strauss, though he'd very much wanted to. But he wouldn't add insult to injury by prying into all her personal affairs.

In her last letter to Mr. Harris, she had asked his opinion on love and whether he'd ever been in love before.

Knowing her, Clay guessed that she'd likely asked Mr. Strauss the same question. She'd even followed up the inquiry with an answer of her own:

> *I once fancied myself very much in love with a young man of close acquaintance, but time and wisdom eventually cured me of such girlish fantasies. Now, I feel only affection in that regard, and my heart is free to love another.*
>
> *I don't pretend to believe that love will automatically come from a union of strangers— or near strangers, since I've come to know you better with each letter—but I can't help but hope that love will someday make itself present. I hope you don't find this notion silly, for I will move ahead as my heart and God dictate, even in the absence of such love.*

Raking a hand through his hair, Clay read through her haunting words a second time. Georgie had admitted to loving him in the past, but he'd been too blind at the time to see it. Could he still convince her to give him a second chance?

Sooner or later, she would learn the truth about the letters from Mr. Harris. Would she be grateful or angry at him for attempting to win her heart? Either way, he'd never forgive himself if he didn't at least try.

He swung his legs over the edge of the bed and stood. Then, crossing to the small desk, he sat to write his reply. Sometime later, he knocked on his neighbor's door. Peter had agreed, for a small fee, to rewrite Clay's letters.

"Come in," Peter said, after opening the door. Clay thrust the letter at him as he entered. He hated having his friend read the personal lines, but he couldn't risk having Georgie recognize his handwriting.

"Let me know if there's anything you can't decipher." Clay sank onto the unmade bed, while Peter took a seat in the only chair.

His friend read the letter through. "Looks fine," he said, glancing up. "But why not just confess to the girl? Why the secrecy?"

"Because it's the only way I know to make her believe that I've changed, that my feelings for her . . . have changed." Clay glanced down at his hands, the weight of his unknown future pressing down on him. "I only hope it'll be enough," he added, "to convince her that my intentions are sincere."

Eight

1881: Three years earlier

Nineteen-year-old Georgie glanced up from her book at the sound of Clay crumpling a piece of paper. He tossed the paper ball onto the rug, where it landed near her chair. It was just the two of them in the drawing room tonight. Her father had gone for a walk, leaving her and Clay to entertain themselves after dinner.

"Bad news?" she inquired as she set aside her reading material.

Clay grunted in agreement, his gaze boring holes into the cold hearth.

"Care to elaborate?" She didn't like seeing him upset or his usually affable, easygoing manner disturbed.

"Marian's gone to England." He pushed at the wad of paper with the toe of his shoe.

"For how long?" Georgie asked, not trying to mask the surprise in her voice.

"At least until the London social season is over." His words were tinged with bitterness. "Probably longer, though.

She has an aunt there, and her father is hoping to marry Marian off to some English nobleman."

"Is that what she wants?" Georgie prompted gently.

He ran his hand over his jaw. "She says it's not, but she's acted differently ever since New Year's Eve."

Georgie needed no reminder of that holiday—the one when she'd kissed Clay. Did he think of that moment at all? There'd been so many times over the last five months when she had recalled their kiss, holding it in her mind like a jewel too precious to wear. But she doubted Clay remembered it. This realization pricked at the defenses she'd built, starting that night, around her heart.

"I'm truly sorry to hear she was unkind to you, Clay." She picked up her book, doing her best to ignore the foolish hope attempting to sprout inside her. Would things be different between them, now that Marian was out of the way?

It doesn't matter, she scolded herself.

"It'll be all right," Clay said, scooping up the wrinkled letter from off the floor. He stood and shoved the paper into his pants pocket. "I think I'll take a turn around the block myself. Care to join me?"

She glanced up, her heart beating faster. Had he changed his mind about her already? Did he see her any differently? But his blue eyes and open expression conveyed only friendship, not romantic interest.

Reality crashed over her with the force and shock of an icy wave. Even with Marian gone, Clay still only saw her as family.

Better to keep my heart locked tight then, instead of allowing myself to be hurt again.

"No, you go ahead." She forced her gaze to remain on the open page before her. "I believe I'll stay behind."

Nine

Georgie tossed Mr. Strauss's latest reply onto her desk with a sigh. The man had been candid with his response to her questions about love: *I've never agreed with the starry-eyed notion of love, nor have I ever been "in love." I much prefer the idea of mutual tolerance and affection.* While she appreciated his frankness, she did find his answer rather unromantic.

"But I'm not doing this to find romance," she murmured out loud.

Clay was away, so she had the study to herself. Although, it had felt particularly large and empty this afternoon without him. Was that because she knew she must reach a decision soon on which man to marry? Once she did decide, Clay would be gone, and the room would feel like this permanently.

Pushing aside such unpleasant thoughts, she picked up her letter from Mr. Harris. She liked the relaxed style of honesty and kindness he conveyed in his replies. A funny story from his youth had her chuckling before she reached his answer to her questions regarding love:

> *Like you, I thought myself to be in love once. But I've come to realize I was very much mistaken in that regard. Love is more than a passing fancy, in my opinion. I believe it is something born of thousands upon thousands of moments of quiet connection—a force that burns brighter over time instead of diminishing.*
>
> *Do I hope to find love still? Do I think such a thing is possible between two people who've only just realized such a connection? Unequivocally, yes.*

Tears swam in her eyes, blurring the penned words. If only Clay felt the same about love as she and Mr. Harris clearly did. There was no use dwelling on what might have been, though. Instead, she would continue to hope that one of these men would turn out to be as kind, dependable, and funny as Clay but with one added quality: he would return the love she came to feel for him.

Blinking back the tears, she finished reading Mr. Harris's letter. By the time she reached the end, she had a good idea which man she was ready to commit to. Of course, she would need to make the question of whether to marry Mr. Harris a matter of prayer first. But her heart told her that she could surely find happiness and, hopefully, love—as his wife.

She located a clean sheet of stationery and wrote a reply to Mr. Strauss first. While she felt certain he would be fine, she still felt bad at having to tell him that she'd chosen another man. She did reassure him, though, that he would make some woman very happy one day with his practical perspective and heartfelt integrity.

With that task completed, she removed another piece of paper from the drawer. She would inform Mr. Harris that she would only be corresponding with him from now on. A smile pulled at her lips with the thought of meeting him in person for the first time. Perhaps he would even agree to come to Woodland so that if they married that day, those people closest to her could be in attendance.

Like Clay.

She frowned. Her feelings for Clay were buried, gone. Weren't they? He hadn't rushed to woo her after Marian Holley's abrupt departure and subsequent marriage to an English lord.

The past is over, she told herself. *It's time to look to the future.*

Before Georgie could begin writing her letter, someone knocked at the front door. Mrs. Shaw was in the kitchen, preparing supper, and Gertie, the maid, had the afternoon off. That meant Georgie would have to see who was calling.

She set down her pen, walked into the entryway, and opened the door. A dark-haired young man stood on the stoop, his hat in hand.

"Can I help you?" Georgie asked.

"Is this where Clayton Riley works?" He glanced past her.

"Yes, but he isn't here right now." She motioned for the man to come inside. "Would you like to wait for him? He shouldn't be long."

Frowning, the young man shook his head. "I've got to catch the next train—urgent business out of town. Could you give him a message for me?"

She nodded. "Certainly."

The stranger shifted his weight. "Will you tell him," he said, lowering his voice and forcing Georgie to lean forward so she could hear, "I can't rewrite anymore of those letters for him not until I get back in a fortnight or so. Tell him I'm real sorry."

Letters? she thought. The word echoed through Georgie's mind as loud as a gong, prickling her skin with confusion and a touch of alarm. Clay wouldn't be corresponding with someone else who'd also placed an advertisement in the newspaper, would he? He'd abhorred the idea of her doing so.

"What letters?" she asked, hating how her voice squeaked, betraying her growing concern.

"The letters he's been writin' to some girl named . . ." He squinted, seemingly unaware of the dread his words had churned anew inside her.

So Clay is writing another woman. But who and why? A sudden roaring filled Georgie's ears.

"Uh, her name is . . . Georgie," he finished. "Yes, that's it."

Georgie reared back as if she'd been slapped. Her hand rose to her heart, which was pounding like a bass drum.

Did Clay know another woman named Georgie? *No,* she thought. *My nickname is too unusual.* But she hadn't received any letters from Clay. If he had something to tell her, he would have simply handed her a note or, better yet, told her in person.

"I'm afraid I don't understand." The entryway seemed to drain of air the longer she stood there.

The young man glanced over his shoulder. "Look, I gotta go, miss. All I know is that he was corresponding with some girl who had placed a mail order bride advertisement, but he didn't want her to recognize his handwriting. Just tell him what I said." With that, he put his hat on and turned away, muttering, "Nosy secretary."

Georgie stood staring after him until he disappeared from view, her legs unwilling to move. She'd been corresponding with Clay for the last month? She shut the door and sagged against it.

"He's Mr. Harris," she whispered. The man displayed the same easygoing manner, even in writing, that Clay possessed, and he *had* mentioned being very close to his grandfather. Then she recalled Clay's defensive reaction when she'd said that Mr. Harris sounded a bit like him.

Forcing her feet to move at last, she returned to the study. She made her way to her desk chair and sank down onto the cushioned seat, her bustled skirts ballooning around her knees. Why the subterfuge? she wondered. The thought that Clay would deceive her into believing him to be someone else made her insides twinge with hurt. Hurt that was quickly followed by anger.

What was he trying to prove? That she hadn't a clue about who she was marrying? That she was simply being foolish? Or, was this his way of sabotaging her venture, one that he'd objected to from the beginning? Perhaps his motives had more to do with her money or with not wanting to give up his place in her household.

No, Georgie thought, resting her forehead on her hand. She knew Clay too well to believe his actions had been motivated by money or position. But she'd also believed him to be forthright and above deception. She needed to see him, to speak with him, to discover the real reasons for what he'd done.

She picked up the letter from Mr. Harris and read through his thoughts on love once more: *Do I hope to find love still? Do I think such a thing is possible between two people who've only just realized their connection? Unequivocally, yes.*

Her anger began to soften. Was he thinking of her when he wrote those words? Of them? Hope sprang to life, almost painfully, inside her. And this time, Georgie couldn't uproot it with the memory of her past hurts.

If there is a chance that Clay's feelings for me have changed...

"You're looking rather deep in thought."

Georgie jumped at the sound of Clay's voice, her pulse pounding in her throat. She watched him as he crossed to his desk and sat down, a whistle on his lips.

He looked every bit as handsome as he had the day she'd first set eyes on him as a teenage girl. But today, in this moment, the gap in their ages no longer felt like a barrier to her heart's desires. She'd been given a glimpse of Clay's feelings, and for the first time in years, they appeared to match her own. This realization frightened her to her very core, and yet, it also made her feel lighter and happier than she had felt in a long time.

What would it be like to sit here, together, not as employer and employee but as husband and wife? Georgie cleared her throat of emotion, pushing the remnants of her hopeful vision aside for now.

"You're cheerful," she said, infusing nonchalance into her tone.

Clay shot her a smile. "A friend of Mrs. Huckabee's has asked me to help her with her finances."

"Another client? How wonderful," she managed to say.

"You don't sound as if it's wonderful." He chuckled. "Is something wrong?"

She found herself staring at him again. That boyish grin and his earnest blue eyes, directed straight at her, succeeded in melting away any remaining irritation she may have harbored against him for his secret. She didn't understand his reasons for corresponding with her as Mr. Harris. But, if he wished to remain anonymous, she would oblige him a little longer.

"Actually," she said as she straightened, "I'm doing well. I believe I've determined which of the two men I intend to marry."

The merriment drained from Clay's face. "Is that so?" he asked, his voice sounding tight.

Georgie pushed out an exaggerated sigh. "Yes, I think so. Though it wasn't an easy decision." She stood and approached his desk, her letter to Mr. Strauss in hand. "Will you mail this letter of apology to Mr. Strauss for me?"

A flicker of triumph lit up Clay's gaze before he shadowed it behind a passive expression. The brief window into his thoughts was enough, though, to set Georgie's heart galloping wildly. He hadn't wanted her to choose the other man; he'd wanted her to choose himself.

He took the letter from her and glanced at it. "Apology?" he echoed. "So, it's this other fellow who won you over?"

"Yes, Mr. Harris is the one. And I should thank you, Clay." She studied him from beneath lowered lashes as she continued. "I know you didn't wish for me to go about marriage in this way, so I appreciate your help all the more."

He shifted in his chair, his eyes on everything in the room but her. If he had nothing to hide, he would have stoically congratulated her or held onto his initial annoyance at her plans. But his silence betrayed him most of all.

"We'll need to discuss later," she added, lifting her chin in a feigned show of determination, "what arrangements must be made to move your things to a new office. But first, I'd like to send Mr. Harris a telegram. Before I lose my nerve." She gave a light laugh. "So, if you'll just give me his address."

"You want his address . . . now?"

She pressed her lips together to keep herself from crowing over his panicked expression. "That would be helpful, yes. I assume you've been writing my address on the envelopes, apart from that first exchange of letters through the paper. So his address should be on his envelopes, too, shouldn't it? I'd like to know if and when he wishes to meet me in person."

Clay ran a hand over his jaw, his entire manner agitated. "I . . . um . . . don't mind sending a telegram for you."

Frowning, Georgie shook her head. "I don't know. It's a rather personal message. It might be best if I sent it."

"No, truly. I insist." He offered her a smile, but she could tell it was forced. "After all, I did promise to help you."

"Well, if you're sure."

"Of course." He brandished a pen while Georgie swallowed a laugh at his eagerness. "Just dictate what you want me to say."

She began pacing the rug, pretending to think long and hard over what to say in the telegram. "Am I correct in assuming he lives in San Francisco or Sacramento?"

Clay grunted agreement without offering more information.

"Perfect," she said. "Then ask him if he can meet me for lunch at the hotel this Friday, say one o'clock. A pity we haven't exchanged photographs yet. But tell him I'll be the one in the pale blue dress." She arranged her expression to look innocent and hide her amusement as she spun to face him. "I suppose if we suit each other, we can walk down to the church and have the marriage performed right away. That is usually what mail order brides do, isn't it?"

"Yes," he said, strangling the single word.

"Wonderful. Thank you again, Clay—for everything."

On impulse, she moved around the desk and placed a quick kiss on his cheek. Perhaps the touch would remind him of what he might have missed and of what lay in store if he cared as much for her now as she did for him. She caught sight of his wide-eyed response before she bolted from the room, her cheeks stained with a blush she feared would give her away.

Only three more days to go, she reassured herself. *Three days until I learn the whole truth about Clay and his heart.*

Ten

1883: One year earlier

Clay covered Georgie's eyes as he followed her at a slow pace into the dining room. "No peeking," he directed.

A full and genuine laugh escaped her lips. The sound warmed him more thoroughly than the hearth in the study. It had been days since he'd last heard her laughter. Too many days.

He hated the helpless feeling in his gut during the last month each time he had found Georgie staring at nothing or quickly brushing away tears. The anniversary of her father's death had come and gone, and with it, some of her brightness for life. But Clay was determined to help her get it back.

"All right," he said to Georgie. "You ready?" He grinned over her head at the three members of her household staff who watched with amused expressions on their faces.

Georgie nodded her consent.

Clay cued Chester, Georgie's man-of-all-work, to light

the single candle on the cake's top tier. Then Clay lowered his hands from her eyes. Georgie stared at the cake as another enchanting laugh bubbled from her.

"It's beautiful, Mrs. Shaw," she said, reaching out to touch the arm of her housekeeper in gratitude.

The older woman beamed. "It did turn out rather nice, didn't it? Gertie helped me frost it." Mrs. Shaw and the maid exchanged a smile.

"But only one candle?" Georgie twisted to face Clay. "Not twenty-one? Are you trying to remind me how much younger I am than you, Clay?" She pushed a finger into his chest, but her pretty hazel eyes betrayed her mirth.

He held up his hands in surrender. "Mrs. Shaw wouldn't let me."

"Didn't want that many holes ruining the effect," the housekeeper muttered.

"Go on now. Blow it out," Clay said, nudging Georgie toward the table. "I'd like a slice before I head home."

"But you don't like chocolate cake," she countered.

"For your birthday, I'll make an exception." And he meant it. He'd eat every bite of the three-tiered cake if it meant seeing Georgie happy again.

"Very well." Smiling, she leaned forward and blew out the candle in a single breath. Chester, Mrs. Shaw, and Gertie joined Clay in clapping.

"Take it into the kitchen, Chester," Mrs. Shaw ordered, "and we'll slice it up for everyone. You can help serve, Gertie." The three of them trooped out of the dining room, leaving Clay and Georgie alone.

"I have one other surprise." He pulled out a chair for her at the table.

"You do, do you?" She sat down and allowed him to push her chair in. "What is it?"

"You'll know in just a minute." He hurried to the study and removed the pile of cards and letters that he'd stowed in his desk the last week. Returning to the dining room, he took the chair next to hers and set the stack before Georgie.

She glanced down at the letters and back up at him. "What are they?"

"Have a look." He couldn't help grinning as she removed the twine holding the pile together.

Picking up the first letter, she unfolded the page and began to read the child's large script. After a moment, she lowered the letter, her expression one of shocked delight. "They're from the orphans?"

"Yes. And all of them were more than happy to wish their patroness a good birthday." Her eyes sought his, and the warmth within them brought a strange twinge to his heart.

"You organized all of this?" she asked.

Nodding, he shuffled the cards closer to her, but Georgie clasped his hand, staying his movement.

"Thank you, Clay."

He squeezed her hand, anxious for her to understand he would help her with anything. She wasn't just his employer; she was his closest friend.

"You're welcome, Georgie."

She released his hand to pick up another letter. And as he watched her read each one, the smile on her face growing larger, he silently thanked the Lord that the sadness clinging to her had faded away. *At least, for tonight.*

The future looked bright and happy again, and there was nothing greater he could wish for than that for his dearest friend.

Eleven

The night before he was to meet Georgie at the hotel restaurant, Clay paced his room, circling the small space over and over again. Tomorrow, he would have to tell her the truth about his letters. The idea tightened his gut with apprehension. She had seemed hesitant but happy two days ago, when she'd announced her decision to meet Mr. Harris. Although, he was sure the kiss she'd given him on his cheek that afternoon had held more than friendship in the gesture. Or maybe that was only what he wanted to believe.

"Ahh," he groaned, yanking his tie free and tossing it to the floor.

Would Georgie be thrilled or disappointed when she learned that he and Mr. Harris were one and the same? *Perhaps I should never have pretended to be someone else,* he thought. But if he hadn't, he would have missed the chance to let her know his feelings had changed. He loved her—he had for some time now—and this knowledge filled every part of his heart. He was only sorry he'd been blind to that fact for so long.

Clay slowed his frantic pacing and sat on the bed. Though he still felt justified in and even compelled to do what he'd done, he hadn't consulted the Lord. And now, he needed His help more than ever.

Lowering his chin, Clay whispered, "Lord, forgive me for charging ahead without Thy blessing. Please help good come from this, if possible. And if not, I only ask that I don't hurt Georgie further. I love her . . ." He inhaled a shaky breath. "But I want her to be happy, first and foremost—even if it's not with me. Amen."

Then he lifted his head. Those last words, sincere as they were, had gutted him. And yet, while he didn't know what the outcome of tomorrow's meeting would be, he could face it now with more confidence. Whatever happened, he would do everything in his power to help Georgie—even if that meant stepping aside and denying his heart of its greatest desire.

Georgie fiddled with the hem of the table linen as she waited for Clay's arrival. Sleep had eluded her for most of the night as she had vacillated between hope and fear.

What if Clay's feelings hadn't changed? What if she was simply setting herself up for more hurt? And yet, if he did love her as she loved him . . .

There was no denying he'd breached her heart's defenses after she'd discovered the truth about his letters three days earlier. She'd always enjoyed conversing with him on any topic, but for the past few days, she'd become keenly aware of the respectful way he treated her opinions, even when he disagreed with them. He also appeared to take great pleasure in making her smile or laugh and in offering her sincere compliments. Those simple gestures had melted her insides to honey over and over again. There'd even been moments when she'd caught him staring at her, a hopeful longing in his blue eyes that matched the one growing inside her.

She'd become aware of other things too: like the way his hand brushed her sleeve when he pushed in her chair at dinner, igniting her pulse, or how his full smile made her want to kiss his fine, masculine mouth—not as she had as a foolish young girl but as a woman fully and ardently in love. There was no one else she wanted to spend her life with than Clay. But did he truly feel the same about her?

Some of the peace she'd felt last night, after praying, returned and stilled her restless fingers. *Just hear him out,* and move forward from there, she reminded herself. *And, whatever happens, you're not alone.* That had been a recurring thought during the wee hours of the morning, when she'd awakened.

"May I have this seat?"

Clay's voice washed over her like soothing rain, cleansing away her fears. She looked up, and her throat went dry at the sight of him in his Sunday suit. His handsome face and tall frame drew the attention of several other women in the restaurant.

Ignoring her rapid pulse, Georgie peered innocently up at him. "Clay? What are you doing here? I told you this morning I wished to meet Mr. Harris alone."

He sat down, tension radiating from his stiff frame. "Georgie, there's something I need to tell you."

She feigned an impatient look. "Whatever it is, you'll have to say it quickly, or Mr. Harris will take one look at you and me together and think I chose someone else."

"That's what I'm trying to say." He glanced away, then back again, his expression tortured. "*I'm* Mr. Harris. Harris was my mother's maiden name."

He cleared his throat, drumming his fingers against the tablecloth, his eyes lowered. "I've been writing to you this whole time," he continued. "A friend of mine rewrote my letters so you wouldn't recognize my handwriting. You can't know how sorry I am for deceiving you, Georgie. Truly, I am. And I'll understand if—"

"Clay?" she interrupted.

"What?" he half growled as he lifted his gaze.

She smiled sincerely and leaned forward, placing her hand over his. "I know about your letters."

His brow furrowed with apparent disbelief as he sat back. Then a frown pulled at his mouth. He curled his fingers tightly beneath hers, then relaxed them.

"Since when?" he asked.

"Since three days ago." She blushed and dropped her chin, directing the rest of her words to the tablecloth. "Your friend came to tell you that he'd been called out of town and couldn't rewrite the letters for you. But you were out, so he left his message with me."

The answering silence made Georgie raise her head. She found Clay studying her. Her blush deepened beneath his careful scrutiny until a half smile brightened his face. The amused look and the way he intertwined his fingers with hers filled Georgie's stomach with butterflies.

"Did you ask him about the letters?"

She exhaled a sigh. "Yes. And I'm sorry that I didn't tell you. To be honest, I was hurt and angry at first. But then I started to wonder about your motives. I thought I'd play along until I learned what they were."

Even if they weren't what she wanted to hear, she would still listen. She'd decided as much last night. She and Clay were too good of friends to harbor contention or secrets between them any longer.

"Why did you do it, Clay?" She kept a level gaze, ready to read whatever emotions filled those blue eyes. "Especially when you didn't seem at all interested in marriage? Or in my method for finding a husband?"

He rubbed his thumb over the back of her palm, causing a pleasant thrill to skip up her arm. "I did it," he said as he bent toward her, "because I love you."

The breath left her lungs in a soft whoosh. These were the words she'd dreamt of hearing him say to her for so long. The words that echoed those written in her heart.

"Really?" This moment felt almost too wonderful to be real.

He laughed lightly. "Yes, really." His expression instantly sobered. "I know that I've hurt you in the past, Georgie, and I was a bullheaded fool for not realizing what's been right in front of me all of these years. But, will you forgive me?"

She wanted so much to kiss him in reassurance but not here. Instead, she settled for squeezing his hand. "I already have."

The evident relief and admiration on his face made her want to sing. "I had hoped for a less crowded spot to ask this," he said, his eyes taking in the nearly full restaurant, "but it'll have to suffice."

He cupped her hand between both of his. "Georgeanna Fitzgerald, will you do me the honor of being my mail order bride, my wife, and the woman of my heart?"

Tears sprang into her eyes. "Yes, Clay. I will."

"Then I say we skip lunch." He grinned and stood. "Let's go get the rest of your household, instead, so we can meet the preacher at the church."

"I can't think of a more splendid plan," she announced as he pulled her to her feet.

He guided her out of the hotel, her hand securely tucked inside his. Georgie felt as if she were floating down the sidewalk as they headed for home.

"Was Mr. Strauss really the best of the bunch?" she teased. "Or, did you purposely pick the worst candidate so that you would come out the winner?"

Clay clapped a hand to his chest as if wounded. "I promised I would pick the best, Georgie, and I did." Raising their joined hands, he kissed her knuckles, setting her heart pounding again. "Although, I did hope I would win out over the stoic Mr. Strauss."

"Perhaps I ought to read the other replies, just in case." She threw him a mischievous smile. "After all, we haven't said our vows yet."

Giving her a mock frown, he tugged her behind a giant flowering bush. "You may read the others," he said, pulling her close, "as long as you promise not to change your mind about us."

She looped her arms about his neck. "Never," she promised. "I believe you and I were meant to be, Clayton Riley, even after all these years."

His blue eyes softened. "On that, I couldn't agree more."

He bent toward her, his lips claiming hers. Georgie's heart beat double time. She leaned into him, enjoying the firm press of his mouth and the solid warmth of his presence.

Like her mother, she too would be a mail order bride. After all, it had been her advertisement and Clay's replies that had brought them together at last. And today, she would marry the man who she had loved for years and who, wonder of wonders, now loved her back.

Her last coherent thought as Clay deepened their kiss was that the long wait had truly been worth it.

ABOUT STACY HENRIE

Stacy Henrie graduated from Brigham Young University with a degree in public relations. Not long after, she switched from writing press releases and newsletters to writing inspirational historical romances. Born and raised in the West, where she currently resides with her family, she loves the chance to live out history through her characters. In addition to writing, she enjoys reading, road trips, interior decorating, chocolate, and most of all, laughing with her husband and kids. You can learn more about Stacy and her books by visiting her website.

Find Stacy online:
Website: StacyHenrie.com
Facebook: Stacy Henrie
Twitter: @StacyHenrie

Wanted: Midwife Bride
by Kristin Holt

OTHER WORKS BY KRISTIN HOLT

The Husband-Maker Series
The Menace Takes a Bride
The Cowboy Steals a Bride

Prosperity's Mail Order Brides
The Bride Lottery
The Cowboy Steals a Bride

Holidays in Mountain Home
Home for Christmas
Maybe this Christmas

One

WANTED: Midwife Bride

Frontier town bachelor doctor, age 30, seeks experienced midwife for business partner and marriage. Must be pleasant, cooperative, companionable, and prepared for long hours. Midwifery training and experience more important than age. Prefer age 35 or younger, as children are desired.

Reply to Doc Joe, Evanston, Wyoming Territory.

Two

1888, New York City
Residence of Dr. Ernest Walter Thornton III

On the twenty-first of June, Naomi Thornton's marriage ended softly, quietly, simply. Entirely opposite its highly celebrated beginning.

In fact, her husband of one year and eight months didn't yet comprehend it was over.

They'd lasted a good while longer than most critics believed, for female physicians made horrible wives. Everyone said so.

Perhaps that's why Ernest had taken up with a mistress.

She'd seen them together, sharing a quiet luncheon at a stylish café.

Through the stream of passersby, she'd witnessed Ernie's kiss upon the woman's temple, his touch at her waist. Evidently, the two were lovers and had been for quite some time.

High fashion masked the woman's thickening waistline, but Naomi's trained eye noted the pregnancy with clinical detachment. She'd wager her annual income the child, if male, would be named Ernest Walter Thornton the Fourth.

Agony over the demise of their marriage seemed a natural response, yet she could rouse nothing more than disappointment.

The grandfather clock chimed half-past seven. A key scratched into the lock at the front entrance. Ernest, an hour late for the supper Cook had prepared in honor of Naomi's thirtieth birthday.

In the center of their brownstone's entryway, she stood tall. He'd purchased the stylish brownstone with her inheritance. She held all the cards, therefore he wouldn't stay another night.

The latch opened, and her husband's vibrant conversation filtered in with warm summer air, the sounds of carriage wheels rolling past and horses' hooves clattering.

Late evening sunlight flooded the entryway, gleaming on the polished hardwood floor. Two male silhouettes. Ernie's companion spoke, revealing his identity before the door shut.

Dr. Isaac Krenn, lead physician at Fairchild Memorial. A narrow-minded fellow who believed medicine a man's world.

Ernie removed his top hat and spun it playfully toward Charlesworth.

The butler caught the hat as if Ernie had handed it off with dignity. Charlesworth bowed, accepting walking sticks and Krenn's hat. The butler retreated without so much as a nod of acknowledgment for Naomi.

When her husband left for good that night, his man, Charlesworth, would go too. She'd hire new house staff, loyal to her and none else.

"Isaac." Ernie opened the door into the parlor. "I'll pour you a drink."

"Thank you, Ernest." Dr. Krenn clapped Ernie on the back.

Despite Krenn's unwelcome interruption, Naomi would address her husband the moment their hospital supervisor left. The best way to keep him from staying long would be to join them.

Krenn held Naomi's gaze, conveying distaste. He didn't like a female practitioner at his hospital. She didn't like the idea of him dictating what went on at Fairchild Memorial.

In the morning, after she filed for a divorce, she'd engage an attorney to see what could be done about her grandfather's hospital . . . and removing Krenn from the board of directors and the premises.

Ernest poured expensive single-malt scotch into two Bavarian crystal tumblers. He handed one to Krenn.

"*Mrs.* Thornton." Dr. Krenn seldom referred to her by the hard-earned title, Doctor. "I've just come from a meeting of the board of trustees."

Krenn never addressed her without purpose. "Oh?"

"The Board"—he slid a glance at Ernest—"delved into the unfortunate demise of Mayor Barnard Brown and reached the unanimous, professional conclusion that you, Mrs. Thornton, are to blame."

Of all the *ludicrous, ridiculous, falsified—*

Defensive arguments rose to her tongue. "The chief surgeon said Brown died of natural causes." *I wasn't in the vicinity.*

Naomi ignored her husband, whose silence condemned him. The louse.

Hands clasped at her waist, she vowed she would not lose her composure. These two believed women unstable, emotional, and incapable of rational thought. She'd learned this too late . . . after Grandfather's death and her marriage to Ernest.

Under no circumstance would she prove them right.

She'd respond with logic and reason. "I never met the mayor nor had occasion to be in the same room. My signature is not on his records. I ordered no treatments nor consulted with those who did."

"Your silly arguments won't sway a soul." Krenn tossed back the remainder of his scotch. "The board's decision is final."

Anger fueled her racing pulse. She flicked a glance at Ernie and found him pouring another drink. The cad's satisfied, smug expression told her all she needed to know.

Both men—the whole board, for that matter—*knew* she was innocent.

Cruel pleasure lit Krenn's fleshy features. "The newspapers will run the story tomorrow. I cannot protect you."

She wanted to shriek, rip his thinning hair from his scalp, rake her close-cut nails down his pockmarked cheeks. Instead, she took a pair of measured steps nearer her accuser. "I'll fight this. I'll contact my attorney."

Ernest swirled the amber liquid in his tumbler. "I've already engaged him, darling, to protect me from your scandal."

The attorney had been Ernie's, first. Once Grandfather's estate had been settled, she'd had no lawyer of her own.

Surely that didn't matter. Despite Krenn's lies, truth would prevail.

"I'll hire another attorney."

Ernest raised his tumbler in mocking salute. "Who would take your case?"

Mayor Brown, adored by most, had left a widow and four small children who'd won public sympathy. Once the papers reached every influential New Yorker tomorrow morning, she'd be ostracized.

She'd never again work in the city, the state, perhaps all of New England.

"*My* attorney," he intoned, every inch the Ernest Walter Thornton the Third she'd come to loathe, "has prepared divorce papers, my dear. I cannot have you . . . blemish my reputation."

Divorce papers.

Exactly what she wanted, but not like this.

He would win. With an influential judge as an uncle and the Thornton money and name behind him, she hadn't a snowflake's chance in July. She hadn't a hope of salvaging her reputation or the fortune she'd brought to their union.

Within weeks of their nuptials, he'd seen to it he had full control of the money. He'd presented his manipulative behavior as simply doing his husbandly duty—managing the finances so she wouldn't have a worry.

The law gave men entirely too much power.

Ernie glared. "To murder the mayor, you *must* be insane. You should rot on Blackwell Island."

First, blame—as if she were incompetent. Now accusations of *murder*?

Fear collapsed her airway. She'd read the horrors exposed last year by *World* reporter Nellie Bly. To enter Blackwell's Madhouse meant torture, unsanitary conditions, privation of every sort. Whether forced into the inescapable asylum or incarcerated, pending a murder investigation and trial, her life was *over*.

With chilling dread, she knew he *would* incarcerate her if she didn't disappear, *now*.

Could she slip out the door, melt into the crowd? She had several dollars in the purse at her belt—where was her reticule?

The man who'd vowed before God to cherish her looked her in the eye. "Goodbye, Naomi."

Three

July 6, 1888
Evanston, Wyoming Territory

Thirteen days after her life in New York shattered, Naomi stepped off the train in Evanston. *Two thousand miles from home.*

She drew a deep breath, squeezed the handle of her secondhand valise, and held her hat in place as a brisk breeze threatened to tear it loose.

Miss Naomi Fairchild. She'd scrubbed Ernest Thornton's name from her own and sworn never to use it again.

Most fitting to begin anew the week of Independence Day.

She scanned the clearing platform for any sign of Doc Joe, the man she would wed.

For two years, since the time she'd become enamored of Ernie and prepared to marry him, she'd read Doc Joe's advertisement for a midwife mail order bride in *Midwifery Circular*. She'd occasionally paused to wonder what kind of man would specifically seek a midwife for his bride.

Today, she'd find out.

This marriage would be different, better. Theirs would remain a business partnership and marriage of convenience. He'd advertised for a midwife, and that's exactly what he'd get.

She'd learned her lesson. Insisting upon a male profession had cost her everything. Ernie had thrust her head into the gaping jaws of hell. She'd barely escaped with her life.

No one need know she was a fully credentialed physician. Especially not Joe.

She wanted this fresh start. And financial support. All of five dollars, twenty-three cents remained in the purse at her belt—all of it the excess funds Doc Joe had wired to generously cover travel expenses.

Without him, where would she go? Without him, she'd never have had money enough to escape the city. Without him, she'd have gone hungry or perhaps been detained by police.

She'd fled the brownstone with *nothing*. The little purse at her belt had contained coin enough for a night or two in a low-rent boarding house, a little food, and the all-important telegram to respond to Doc Joe's advertisement.

She'd dared spend precious coin on worn, out-of-date, working-class clothing only after Doc Joe had wired a generous sum for train fare and meals along the way. The clothing had been necessary. Wearing them, she looked nothing like herself, and had easily slipped from the city.

Folks saw what they expected to see.

She drew a deep breath, scanned the busy train platform, watched passengers claiming trunks and railroad employees offloading merchandise crates.

The station gradually cleared, and Naomi stood on the

platform alone but for a few railroad men refilling water and coal.

Doc Joe hadn't come for her.

For the first time in months, she smiled big and broad and with relief. He'd no doubt found himself unable to get away from a medical emergency and trusted she'd have her wits about her enough to find his place of business.

She rather liked the idea of getting a good look at the neighborhood, perhaps at him, before introducing herself.

Squaring her shoulders, she headed inside the station to ask where she might find the local doctor.

Four

"Doc Joe, I swear, that Chinaman better live."

If Joe could spare a second, he'd glare at the sheriff. This gunshot had pierced the patient's left shoulder, broken his clavicle and two ribs.

And that was the less severe of two bullet wounds.

The second had struck the young man in the neck. He bled profusely.

Somewhere, too near the carotid artery, the bullet kept slipping beyond his reach.

"I'm doing the best I can." Joe pressed a bandage against the entry wound long enough to slow the torrent of blood, then explored with forceps once more. If his patient would have the slimmest hope of survival, Joe had to remove that bullet, fast.

"This captive's got to survive," Sheriff Lloyd Preston repeated for the third or fourth time, "long enough to question."

Railroad switchman or varmint, didn't matter. This man was a human being—the only reason Joe needed.

He doubted the sheriff would get one word out of this victim. At this rate, the patient would bleed out before regaining consciousness. He'd lost one cork-soled shoe somewhere between the shooting and the clinic's door. Its mate hung askew from his narrow foot.

Too young to die. Innocent or perpetrator, *much too young to die.*

Damn, but Joe needed twice as many hands.

He needed better lighting.

He needed a fighting chance.

Sweat ran into his eyes and stung like the dickens. He swiped his sleeve across his forehead as his hands and forearms were smeared with blood.

The sheriff strode closer, blocking the afternoon sunlight through the south window. "Ain't that an awful lot of blood, Doc?"

"Step out of the light, won't you?"

"Oh, yeah, sure."

"Hand me that towel." Joe gestured with a tip of his head, concentrating on the delicate movement of his forceps . . . and lost the slippery lead.

The lawman complied. Joe dried his face and hairline, then tossed the cloth away.

Less than five seconds passed before a long shadow blocked the strong July sun.

"*Sheriff*—" Joe glanced up, irritation immediately squelched by the fine figure of a lady in his doorway, lit from behind.

Not uncommon to have folks drop by, needing his care. Best he could tell, he'd not met this woman. No lady could tolerate seeing a Chinese man, blue blouse torn open to reveal a naked chest and dual wounds gushing blood.

No obvious signs of trauma, so she could wait. "It'll be a while—"

She dropped a valise and, quick as could be, pulled off her hat and jacket.

"Might as well come back." But his direction fell on deaf ears.

Before he'd finished shooing her, she'd rolled up her sleeves and slipped his spare apron over her head.

He swallowed hard. "Naomi Fairchild?"

She pumped water into the sink to scrub her hands. "Yes. I trust you are Doc Joe."

Relief as welcome as rain in August washed through him.

Hallelujah.

This woman, his midwife bride, somehow ordered the sheriff out of the way with her mere presence. "Put me to work, Doctor."

His forceps finally found solid purchase on the slug. He eased the culprit out of the man's neck to ping in the pan just as he finally got a good look at the face of his bride-to-be.

Smooth, porcelain skin, eyes so blue it hurt to look at them. Golden-blond hair, thick and wavy, swept up and away from her face, pinned into an arrangement both practical and feminine. Apparently, she thumbed her nose at fashion because she hadn't cut a fringe of bangs about her forehead that would take time to curl.

Most important, she hadn't fainted at the sight of him bloody to his elbows. And she hadn't run back to the depot. Nor refused to help when she saw a Celestial on the table.

A confident, competent, down-to-earth woman.

He liked her already.

Her eyes, the color of a Wyoming summer sky, held his gaze.

His bride wasn't merely lovely. Pretty wasn't accurate, either.

He'd never seen a woman, not on the congested streets of Chicago and not in Wyoming, who could hold a candle to her. Attraction seared through him.

She blinked. "Doctor?"

"Naomi?" His gut tightened.

"Doc." The sheriff thumped him on the shoulder, yanking his attention to the here and now. "Your patient's bleeding."

Palpitations ensued at the sensation of her slender forefinger sliding over his own. He glanced down to find her competent, feminine touch inside the no-longer gushing entrance wound, pinching a nick in the artery.

Maybe she'd grown up the daughter of a country doctor and learned at his elbow.

Maybe this midwife knew a great deal about surgery.

Or, could be, she was a whole lot more than a midwife.

Elation bubbled within him as he forced his focus onto the damaged vessel, stitching it closed the best he could.

She dropped a saturated flannel square into the waste basket and picked up another from the tray, knowing when to apply pressure and when to allow him room to work.

This was all gonna work out fine.

Once this crisis was over, he'd interview young Naomi Fairchild. If the discussion went well, he'd ask her to marry him.

He had the minister on notice and the marriage license prepared in case she actually arrived and turned out to be as useful as the telegram implied.

Within a couple hours, Doc Joe would find himself a married man.

He couldn't wait.

Five

Naomi washed dried blood from her hands with more force than necessary.

She'd failed, spectacularly, and ruined everything.

Despite her determination to hide her advanced medical training, to meet Joe's request for a midwife and only a midwife, she'd given herself away in under thirty seconds.

For *what*? Her attempt to assist Doc Joe in saving their patient had proved fruitless. The Chinese immigrant had died without regaining consciousness. Joe had gently washed the man's body of all traces of blood, bagged his clothing and personal effects for the sheriff, and personally carted the man's sheet-wrapped body to Chinatown on the other side of the tracks.

Joe's compassion had been evident throughout.

She'd been affected so strongly, she'd thrown herself into scrubbing the surgery upon their return to keep from thinking too hard.

How could she not feel profound respect?

Doc Joe was so unlike any man she'd known in medicine.

Disappointment made her ache marrow-deep. She sighed and whisked the scrub brush harder beneath her fingernails. Working here, living here . . . it could have been so good.

No sense dwelling on might-have-beens.

She hadn't survived years of college and medical training to lose her practicality when she needed it most.

Now that the situation had passed, and the deceased cared for, Doc Joe would send her on her way. He'd paid her train fare believing her to be a midwife, as she'd confirmed via telegram. She'd accepted his money, arrived, and immediately exposed herself as a liar.

He'd ask for the train fare he'd spent in good faith. She didn't have the money.

If she didn't spend much on meals, she had enough for train fare as far as Ogden. She'd find work, scrubbing floors if necessary. Eventually, she'd save enough to wire him the funds and repay him in full.

Maybe she could hang her shingle in town, accept patients, *if* they'd have her, and if Joe wouldn't mind her encroaching on his work. She'd have better luck finding a job waiting tables or cleaning the hotel. That might be a wiser plan, given the sorry state of her finances.

"Dinner's here." Doc Joe's warm, heavy hand settled gently upon her shoulder. "I order meals from the restaurant through the block, and luckily I remembered to tell them there'd be two of us from now on."

He squeezed before withdrawing.

She'd not expected him to feed her before sending her away, but he was uncommonly kind.

Like antiseptic to a laceration, realizing all she'd lost here, with him, stung. This man might have been her partner in life. The perfect kind of arrangement with a man she could respect, but where love didn't ruin things.

"Come." He handed her a fresh towel to dry her hands. "Let's eat."

"Thank you." She followed him into the back room where a small dining table and two chairs sat tucked beneath a window overlooking the alley. Light from neighboring windows puddled on the dry, weed-strewn space. Dusk still lit the sky with hues of purple and navy blue. Splendid, to look out a window and see the sky.

She would have loved Wyoming Territory...

He emptied a crate onto the table. A crockery jug. A cut-down flour sack contained rolls, and a Dutch oven released steam when he removed the lid.

Roast beef, baked potatoes, summer vegetables.

Her mouth watered, and her stomach grumbled.

Dishes, silverware, and cups came out of the crate too. He made quick work of filling two plates, then poured lemonade from the jug. Setting the crate on the floor, he made room for them to eat comfortably.

Without a moment's hesitation, Joe offered his hand.

Her breath caught. The simple gesture looked like...

Acceptance.

No one needed it more than she. No one deserved it less.

Refusing to think about it, she slipped her fingers into his. Warm, large, solid, unfamiliar. So different than Ernest's.

He prayed, asking a blessing on their meal, for their lost patient and those who loved him, and on their forthcoming union.

Just like that.

Forthcoming union.

As if it were already agreed upon. It had been, with the exchange of two telegrams. Just enough to agree they would marry. But then she'd arrived, and that plan had dissolved in the immediate need to save a man's life. Hadn't it?

Did Joe realize she'd deceived him, or not?

He ate, like a man who'd not seen a meal since breakfast. His plate was piled high, with twice the portions Ernie consumed. But Ernie was slight of build, lean, only a few inches taller than she. Doc Joe was broad, thick, heavily muscled. He didn't look so much like a surgeon as a dock worker. Musculature such as his came by hard work and nothing less.

Naomi learned long ago to eat when the opportunity presented itself. She'd often missed meals due to rounds at the hospital, new admissions, crisis patients. So she ate, despite her stomach's rebellion.

No sense asking him if he'd like her to leave until she'd filled her stomach. She couldn't afford to pay for a meal like this, not until she secured employment.

Doc Joe slowed once his meal was nearly consumed. "You did very well today. Far more skilled and knowledgeable than I'd hoped."

She blinked, half expecting sarcasm, but his tone matched his complimentary words.

Next, he'd lecture. Warn her to tread lightly. Remind her who was in charge. *Wait for my decision, Naomi. I'm the resident physician. This is my patient.*

She shoved Ernest back into his drawer and turned the key.

Joe wiped his mouth with a napkin, then sighed as if trying to find the words to tell her they didn't suit.

She'd make it easy on him. "It's all right. No need to spare my feelings."

Confusion compounded the weariness etching his features. "My compliment was most sincere. Your skill in surgery is..."

"More than you wanted." She slid her chair back, prepared to go.

He locked a gentle hand around her wrist. Something she couldn't decipher shone in his hazel eyes. "*Everything* I wanted."

Somehow, she simply couldn't trust that to be true. He'd think about it and come to distrust her before they had so much as a chance.

"I have to go." She tugged free, and he had the courtesy to release her.

He pushed to his feet but made no move to block her exit. "Why? Where will you go?"

"I'll be fine." Far easier to focus on the deep cleft in his chin than risk meeting his eye. "Don't worry about me."

"Wait." He raised two hands as if to gentle her. "What did I do wrong? What did I say?"

"Nothing." He'd done *nothing* wrong. She was the problem, not him.

His brows drew together, obviously struggling to understand. "You saw the result of a young man caught in the crossfire. Our patient." He spoke rapidly. "It's not safe for you to be out on the streets. Let me walk you to the hotel. Or you stay here and I'll go."

Regret warred with embarrassment, and humiliation came in a close third. Why hadn't she been honest with him to start with? He'd paid for her travel, and the good man hadn't mentioned her lies nor demanded she repay him.

The shakes had taken hold. Surely he saw her trembling.

Why had her mask of imperturbable woman, entirely in control, deserted her now?

"I'm a doctor." The confession tumbled out of her mouth, unguarded, regurgitated with zero self-mastery. "A medical doctor. I graduated valedictorian of my class in '85."

He took a careful, single step closer. "This is not a problem."

"You wanted a midwife, not a doctor. I didn't tell you I'm a doctor." Now her voice trembled too. He'd think her hysterical *and* a liar.

Ernie's threats of incarceration in a madhouse came rushing back, and all at once, her desperation to remove herself from Doc Joe's presence became a fight for survival.

"I know." He touched her, just a gentle cupping of her elbow, but the contact sizzled as if it'd been a caress.

"Of course you do." Self-recrimination returned with the force of a nor'easter.

"Not your year of graduation, didn't know you were first in your class—congratulations, by the way."

She stared at him, the shakes worsening. Why didn't he demand his money back, then order her out of his clinic? "I'm sorry."

His grip slid down her arm, and he took her hand in the gentlest of holds. "Don't be."

"I should be sorry. I deliberately misled you. You didn't want a doctor. You wanted a midwife."

"Just because I advertised for a midwife doesn't mean I didn't hope for something better. Do you have any idea how hard, how long I've worked to find *anyone* willing to move to this corner of the territory to work with me?"

He slipped his fingers between hers and cradled their joined hands against his broad chest. The pad of his thumb raised tingles where he stroked.

He leaned a little closer. "I'm thrilled with your performance under pressure. Your skills . . . You'll help me save lives. Together, we can make a real difference."

"You—" He truly meant what he said. "You don't care I misled you?"

His smile, so strong and sure, so handsome—she couldn't look away. "I'll repay the train fare, eventually. I'll honor my debt."

His brow quirked, and he shook his head. "You are able to deliver babies?"

"Yes."

"I imagine you can diagnose, treat, suture, set broken bones?"

"Yes."

"Fate couldn't have dealt me a better hand than sending you to me."

How could she possibly respond to a statement like that?

He led her back to her chair. "Please sit. Finish eating before your meal grows cold. If you don't mind, I have a few more questions."

Somehow, after all she'd done, he still wanted to consider a future together. His kindness left her shaken, his smile stole her breath, and the warmth in his eyes almost convinced her to trust him.

Six

Joe needed to comprehend this beautiful, complex creature he had every intention of wedding. She'd been prepared to bolt, and he couldn't let that happen. He had to make her understand, then he could ask further questions.

"I need a helpmate—a woman I can trust implicitly. A business partner who's also my wife, so it's easy to roust both of us at the same time." He held her gaze. "I need a woman who thinks clearly in a crisis, who's more concerned about saving lives, aiding the sick, than newest fashion and gossip about town."

She nodded with hesitation.

"Forgive my bluntness." He touched her hand. "*I need you.*"

She startled. "But you don't know me. The one key element you advertised for I misled you—"

"And gave *triple* the value. You're a physician." A grin spread over his face, and he leaned closer. Couldn't she see his honesty? "I couldn't be happier."

That rendered her speechless.

Why hadn't she simply stated the facts in her telegram? He wouldn't have turned her away. That topic would need to wait until they'd developed much more trust between them.

"Enough about me. Tell me all about you."

As if she removed an apron of insecurities and put on a fresh one representing confidence, her demeanor changed. Apparently, she could handle the business side of their arrangement with ease. He'd have to remember that.

"I turned thirty years of age last week."

Bewilderment socked him in the gut. "Thirty?" He'd seen her features by full daylight. Flawless skin, no lines to speak of. Thick, lustrous hair. Slender, youthful figure.

"You don't believe me."

"Honestly, I had you pegged at twenty-five."

"I assure you I'm thirty."

"From my advertisement, you know I'm thirty, as well. Thirty-one, November first."

He gestured with a rolling motion, urging her to continue.

"I've delivered approximately seventy babies. Most with excellent outcomes."

Too good to be true: lovely, experienced, and from all he'd seen, knowledgeable. A tad frantic over stretching the truth in her telegram, but that only spoke of her innate honesty, right?

It seemed she had nothing further to offer, so he'd need to ask a direct question. Asking about her marital situation was awkward without first disclosing his past. "I've never married. Medical school was my entire focus for so long I never had time for courting or marriage. What about you? Have you been married?"

Pain flashed in her eyes, and like a flower closing its

petals at night she seemed to curl in on herself. "I was married, but..."

Emotion strangled her voice. He felt her pain, knew it had to be fresh, recent. This same pain marred the faces of a dozen widows he knew. The loss of a husband explained so very much. Her willingness to uproot herself and move nearly two thousand miles. Leave her practice, associations, friends, and family to start somewhere new.

She hadn't touched the remainder of her supper, so he pushed the plate aside and offered his hand. For a moment, he thought she'd refuse to take it. But she slipped her hand into his.

He squeezed her cool fingers, hoping to convey compassion and honesty. He truly didn't care she'd been someone else's first. He just wanted her to be his from now on. "It doesn't matter. It's all right that you have, that you were..."

Where had the words gone?

He'd never had trouble consoling widows in the past, never found it hard to speak of death or loss. But now, it had become personal. He wanted to know more, to ask how much time had transpired, but couldn't. Maybe one day, once the pain of her loss had lessened.

He brought their joined hands to his mouth and kissed her knuckles.

With marriage, issue generally followed. He deserved to know if she had offspring, if said little ones would be joining them. "Children?"

"No."

"Forgive me for asking," he murmured, leaning closer. He braced himself with an elbow on his knee. "I want children. You're able, as far as you know?"

"Y-Yes." She'd leaned toward him too. Her cheekbones

had taken on a tint of pink, and her pupils slowly encroached upon blue irises. Evident signs of attraction, just as his certainly were to her.

He didn't care if she knew he wanted her. Might be better if he said so, outright.

"I don't mind admitting I'm attracted to you, Miss Fairchild. Marriage to you won't be a burden."

A strangled croak of laughter slipped past her lips.

"That didn't come out right, did it?" He grinned, couldn't help it. Her attention settled on his mouth and his pulse accelerated. He couldn't wait to kiss her.

"No."

"This interview requires only one more focus." As far as he was concerned, Naomi Fairchild had turned out to be more than he'd needed and wanted. He'd marry her this very second. But he wanted to kiss her. Right now.

"Oh?"

He stood, drew her by the hands to stand with him. He brushed thumbs over her cheeks, all the while holding her gaze. Heat flared in her eyes, lamplight reflecting in the perfect blue of Lake Michigan on a calm summer day in Chicago. "I want a real marriage, full disclosure, honesty."

Did she understand? He searched her expression for evidence of agreement.

"You?" he asked when he couldn't be sure of her feelings on the subject.

"Yes. I want all that."

He knew so little of the circumstances of her husband's death, how long ago she'd buried him, but he knew one thing for sure—she'd welcome his kiss.

He drew her close and reveled in her little shivers.

"I intend to kiss you, Naomi. If you want to say no, now is the time."

Seven

Oh, how she wanted his kiss.

But he seemed in no hurry. His gaze traveled from one cheekbone along the line of her jaw to her mouth. He lingered but made no further advancement.

As if savoring the anticipation.

Warm, effervescent excitement made her feel more alive than she'd been for two long years. Had she ever experienced this magnitude of attraction?

She'd met Doc Joe mere hours earlier. Immediate appeal had grown into appreciation, which had become genuine attraction.

The nickname would no longer do. Not if they'd whisper promises to one another in the form of a first kiss. Kisses meant something, at least to her.

She swallowed, attempting to moisten her mouth. "Doc Joe?"

"Hmmm?" His eyelids had lowered, his expression one

of unmistakable male interest. Dipping his head, he drew near.

"What is your name? Your full name, if you don't mind."

Honest pleasure echoed in his chuckle. "Madam, my name is Joseph Henry Chandler."

"It's a pleasure to meet you, Dr. Chandler." He stood near enough now that the warmth of his much larger body, the brush of his trouser leg against her sturdy navy blue skirt, and the tantalizing friction of his thumb along her jaw had her tingling from crown to toe.

"Call me Joe."

"If you insist."

"I do." He inched nearer. His pupils dilated.

She'd arrived in Evanston without a glimmer of confidence in herself as a woman, and Joe's genuine attraction to her had nearly restored it. She could kiss him, for that gift alone. "When do you intend to kiss me, exactly?"

"In a moment."

"Why the delay?" She chuckled.

"It's the final step in the interview. It should be allowed a position of honor on the agenda."

"You believe one kiss will complete this interview?"

"Undoubtedly. It will lend certain scientific proof." He skimmed the pad of his thumb over her cheekbone.

"Proof?"

"Proof of mutual compatibility. Interest. Passion."

Nerves tingled in the wake of his touch. *Delicious.*

"I see."

"Understand, I *want* spark in my marriage. It's time for children, family, permanence. I want it all."

Her stomach quivered with the most delicious sensation.

"I must determine if you are as perfect a fit as you appear."

But she wasn't perfect. No good at kissing, either. She'd failed to please her husband. Her romance with Ernie had been lukewarm at best, and they'd both known she was the source of the problem.

But Ernie and Joe were two very different men.

By evidence evaluated with her own senses, he was undoubtedly attracted to her, far more than Ernie may have ever been. And she was far more attracted to Joe than she'd ever been to Ernie.

Suddenly, she had to know. "Did you kiss other applicants and find them lacking?"

He chuckled again. This man, so easily amused, drew her. She found her hands cupping his elbows. In a bold move of an empowered woman, she slid her hands to his narrow waist. Lean, strong, and healthy.

Sharing the marriage bed with this handsome fellow would be glorious.

"So, how 'bout it?" He nuzzled his nose across the hollow of her throat.

"I asked you a question, Joseph. I asked how many applicants you kissed and then sent away."

He eased back, allowing her a glimpse of his broad, appealing smile. "Not one. Twice in the past two years I carried on a correspondence with midwives who said they'd travel to Evanston, but both failed to actually make an appearance in town."

"Ah." To many, this railroad town on the Wyoming Territory border would seem too far away. For her, not far enough.

"I'll never know why. I wrote once more after each lady's arrival date came and went, but never heard a word."

"I'm sorry." But she wasn't. The other women's choices had brought her to Joe.

He shrugged as if past experiences were irrelevant. "Consider yourself warned, Miss Fairchild. I intend to kiss you."

"So you said."

"Consider it my final warning."

"I'm quite forewarned." She chuckled. "I believe the moment may be passing us by."

He laughed and, still smiling, lowered his mouth to hers with such tenderness and barely-there pressure, her heart rate spiked.

He lingered. *Glorious.*

His simple choice to take his time, to dally, swept through her. Had Ernie ever once taken more than a perfunctory second? Already, Joe's kiss far surpassed all she'd ever known.

Gradually, he increased the weight of his lips upon hers, the drugging friction lighting up her body. A frisson of electric intensity coiled in her belly and seemed to radiate to all four extremities.

He slid one hand into her hair and brought her closer with the curve of an arm about her waist. He pulled her flush against his solid body.

So tall. So broad. So much better than—

He broke their kiss, leaving her floating. Dazed. Dizzy.

She wanted more. She wanted *him.* For keeps.

But he wouldn't want her, not if word of her alleged guilt eventually reached Evanston. Would anyone listen before exacting vigilante justice and hanging her? Or turn her over to the authorities for return to New York?

Why would he trust her word in light of her accusers' inflammatory statements?

Why would he defend her?

But that wasn't all. In that moment, captivated by Joseph's warm hazel eyes, she realized the awful truth. Dr. Krenn and Ernie had stripped her bare, destroyed her reputation, stolen her career, pilfered her inheritance, gambled with the hospital Grandfather had founded.

They'd left her with nothing but the one thing Ernie hadn't been able to steal.

Her heart.

She'd *never* loved Ernie. She could see that now.

One kiss with Joseph Chandler, and her heart was in serious danger for the first time.

This man had the potential to hurt her, far more than Ernie ever could.

How could she risk trusting her faulty decision-making ability, or another husband—even the unusual likes of Doc Joe Chandler?

He tucked her up tight against him, hugging her close. "You pass."

He rocked her back and forth, and she fought to hold on to tears that threatened. Happiness warred with terror. The dark side nearly won.

She heard him swallow, as if he needed a moment to catch his breath. He eased back and pressed another firm kiss to her mouth. "Allow me to propose in person. Naomi Fairchild, will you do me the great honor of becoming my wife?"

Tears filled her eyes.

Joe mistook the emotion as happiness, for he swept the tears away with his thumbs, kissed both cheeks.

The risks were tremendous. But she wanted to stay. She wanted the life he offered. Maybe, *maybe* her past would never catch up with her, and she could build a life of peace and happiness in this little city on the far side of nowhere.

Maybe Joe would never break her heart. Maybe she could hold back her heart and prevent herself from falling completely for him.

Maybe, just maybe, she dared take the leap.

The alternative was safer, but offered very little as compensation. No life at all.

Warmth lit Joe's remarkable hazel eyes from within. Emotion filled his eyes with tears she doubted he'd allow to escape. Such hope. Hope and anticipation and desire.

Desire for *her*.

Just once in her life, she wanted to know what a good marriage was like. However long it lasted. "Yes."

He whooped with joy, picked her up, and spun her in a circle, crowing with happiness. Her laughter mingled with his.

Three more spins and he finally allowed her toes to touch the floor. He stole another quick kiss.

Grabbing her hand, he put out the lamp and tugged her toward the door. "Let's go. The minister's waiting on us, marriage license in hand."

"Now?" He didn't want to sleep on the decision?

"Yes, now."

"I have travel dust on my skirt and a blood splatter on my sleeve." But the legal attachment of his name—*Mrs. Chandler*—would be a shield. She wanted his protection. Who would ever find her?

"You're gorgeous. You can bathe when we go home after the ceremony."

A swell of emotion made her esophagus constrict. "You want me, as I am?"

"Yes. One thousand times, yes."

Eight

Naomi stood with Joe in the minister's parlor, the preacher's wife and grown daughter ready to serve as witnesses. Joe laced his fingers with hers, as if he wished to hold on to her.

Endearingly sweet.

In a matter of sixty seconds or less, she'd be Mrs. Joseph Chandler. Dr. Naomi Chandler, MD, had a lovely ring to it.

The handsome, genuine smile on Joe's face was so *real*. It shamed any citified curvature of the lips on her former husband's face.

You honestly think this is a good idea? Ernest's criticism. Again. *You've not thought this through, Naomi. You never think things through. He'll find out you murdered Mayor Brown.*

I did not. I'm innocent.

She wrestled Ernie's pompous voice into submission and realized Mr. Drescher, the minister, had asked her a question. "Pardon me, Pastor. Do repeat that, please?"

Drescher glanced at Joe, his expression hinting at confusion. His eyeglasses reflected lamplight as he held her gaze. "I asked, Miss Fairchild—*Doctor* Fairchild—do you solemnly swear you are free to be joined in marriage?"

A twist of sharp panic cut through her even as adrenaline flooded her system. She'd thought she was prepared for this, had convinced herself over the many days of train travel, after struggling to decide what to do and ultimately sending a telegram to Doc Joe.

She'd already determined her answer would be yes. Absolutely. She was *completely* free to marry.

Her heart rate accelerated, chugging faster than a cross-country locomotive on the flat expanse of prairie.

She'd always been a poor liar.

She sucked in breath. She'd give herself away if she didn't control her breathing.

Honesty had always been on her side. A trait she'd prided herself on throughout her training.

Joe cupped her elbow. His warm touch through her sleeve anchored her, steadied her.

Almost against her will, she turned to him. He'd see the truth in her eyes, words she couldn't bring herself to say. Her breathing rasped too loud.

Concern marred Joe's expression. "Naomi?"

She fought to moisten her dry mouth. Nodded, because she didn't trust herself to speak.

Joe slipped a strong, broad arm about her shoulders. With him she felt safe. Sheltered. Protected.

She trembled against him. He'd feel her quaking—he'd *know*.

These precious, long-awaited sensations and affection would disappear.

How many times could he forgive her half-truths, fibs, and outright lies before he turned on her?

Longing, deep and poignant, opened an old ache inside her. She wanted so badly for things to be right with Joseph Chandler. He represented everything she'd wished for the first time around and *still* wanted. Marriage to him had the potential to become a splendid partnership in every way.

Joe addressed the minister. "Helmut, she's a widow." His warm, soothing grip on her deltoid muscle spoke volumes. He honestly believed her free, available, and stepped in to say so, assuming she was still so deep in mourning over her recent loss she couldn't speak of it.

She ought to nod and sign the paper declaring her sworn statement of her single status. She had no doubt Ernie had already married his pregnant mistress. His uncle, the judge, would have pushed through the paperwork, freeing his favorite nephew to marry the love of his life. If Ernie was free, so was she.

If *only* she had proof the divorce was finalized. Proof would erase her agony and ensure her union with Joe would be valid.

She nodded with as much confidence as she could scrape together.

"Very well." Drescher nudged his spectacles into place. He signed a line on a form labeled *Marriage License*. It already bore Joseph's signature and a date—the same day he'd wired his reply to her first telegram.

His certainty, intention, solidity—it all added to his appeal. How could she resist falling for him?

To live a lie, cross her fingers, and *hope* he'd understand seemed foolish.

Joe kept his arm snug about her. Her shoulder pressed against his solid ribcage.

She really ought to tell him about her circumstances. Lies and secret purposes had been the cause of death in her first marriage.

No way could she allow him to continue with his misunderstanding.

"Joe?" Adrenaline spiked. She breathed deeply, fighting for control. She'd never lost consciousness, not once in her life. She refused to entertain the thought of fainting now. "May we have a word in private?"

Nine

Disappointment, sharp and bitter, swamped Joe as he shut the Dreschers' back door. He held Naomi's hand securely and headed for a garden bench twenty yards from the house. Her stark pain had cut him to the quick.

Whatever she had to say, he didn't want the minister overhearing.

The cooling night air swirled around them, and the buzz of crickets would have been soothing in any other circumstance.

He'd seen Naomi's expression, felt her trembling against his side.

The preacher's question as to her freedom to join in marriage had doused her happiness, sure as a candle's flame pinched into a whisper of smoke.

Diagnosis: intense love for her deceased husband and inadequate time to grieve.

Now that the moment arrived, she couldn't go through

with marrying again. No matter she'd thought herself ready upon leaving New England.

Or perhaps not ready, but otherwise desperate.

Desperate for protection? Financial support? To separate herself from everything that reminded her of a lost love?

He seated her on the bench, lowered himself into place at her side, and immediately put his arm about her shoulders. He linked his hands, the better to cradle her in the circle of his arms.

The last rays of daylight had faded beyond the mountains, leaving them in shadows, with only distant light from nearby houses. A mere sliver of moon hung in the sky. He couldn't read her features, so he might as well hold her while he could.

How would he let her go when she said the words, admitted she couldn't marry him?

He wanted to fight for her, beg her to stay, offer to allow her whatever time she needed to grieve her lost husband. He'd set her up at the hotel, pay for her lodging, and court her slowly. Most important of all, he'd wait.

And he'd tell her so, just as soon as the knot in his throat loosened.

He sounded like a man in love.

But that was crazy. He wasn't the type to lose his heart. He'd never been in love, so what did he know?

But he'd had two long years while running his advertisement in *Midwifery Circular* to fall in love with the idea of loving her.

She sniffled and wiped away tears with her fingertips.

Automatically, he reached into his pocket for a handkerchief. Despite the day's work, it remained clean. She pressed the linen to her face, and her pain became his.

His throat constricted even tighter. Tears threatened. Shoot. He hadn't shed tears over a woman—*ever*.

Before he paused to think it through, he lifted her onto his lap and turned her into his embrace.

He'd thought to hold her but found her holding on to him, every bit as tight.

Without hesitation, he soothed his hands over her back. Tried to communicate patience and understanding and calm. He pressed a kiss to her temple.

Couldn't she sense how very right this was? She fit in his arms, filling the emptiness in his life, the niche he'd carved out for the ideal bride.

The uncomfortable thought—that his touch reminded her of her lost love, and she thought of him instead, flitted past. He squashed it like a pesky fly.

Part of him didn't care if she was still in love with another husband. He wanted to take her to wife. Eventually, she'd come to love him too—*instead*.

Wouldn't she?

What if she wouldn't give him a chance?

How would he go on without her?

It'd been darn easy to shrug and push forward after the last two mail order midwives hadn't worked out. He'd never met them, never heard a melodic voice, never glimpsed the spark of intelligence in sky-blue eyes.

He'd never kissed another potential bride.

Just Naomi.

By George, he wanted to keep her.

She sniffed. "I must confess—"

"Shh. It's all right."

She shook her head against his shoulder.

He couldn't let her go. She'd have her say, then somehow he'd convince her to stay.

She wouldn't leave him.

Not until she'd given them *every* chance.

"I'm not . . . He didn't . . ." She drew a deep breath. "He didn't die."

Joe blinked. *What?* He squeezed his eyes shut. He'd assumed—

How had the conversation gone? He'd asked if she'd ever been married.

He recalled her words, precisely. *"I was married, but . . ."*

Then he'd said, *"It doesn't matter."*

Was married, she'd said. As in *not* at the present.

Did that suggest she no longer loved her former husband? A wagon-load of good news. Yet something had prevented her from going through with the ceremony. "You're divorced?"

She lifted one shoulder. "I believe so. I *hope* so."

Ah, so that was the problem. "The preacher's question made you uncomfortable."

"You need to know my circumstances. I can't lie to you, Joe."

Warmth filled his heart. A very good sign, her choice to assure he knew the truth. "Thank you. Now, help me understand the problem." He pressed a kiss to her temple. "We'll figure this out together."

Her petite frame trembled. "On the twenty-first of June, my husband informed me he'd filed for divorce. His uncle is an influential judge in New York, so I'm certain the dissolution will happen." Her trembling worsened.

"It's all right." He *wanted* it to be all right. He'd do anything within his power to make it all right. "You can tell me anything, Naomi. *Anything.*"

She stilled, seeming to hover on the edge of disclosure,

trying to decide what she could trust him with . . . and what she couldn't.

He held her, silent and waiting. Wordlessly inviting her confidence.

"My husband," she whispered after several long moments, "my *former* husband, Ernest Walter Thornton the Third, kept a long-term mistress."

Fury swept through Joe, and he fought it back. With his bride cuddled in his lap, she'd know if his muscles clenched. She might misinterpret. This conversation was too important to mess up by reacting strongly. He had to earn her trust, and earn it he would.

"I saw them together, his mistress and him . . ." She trailed off, her voice pinched in pain. "She's pregnant, obviously third trimester. My former husband fathered a child with a woman he loves while married to me."

Joe had never met Ernest Thornton and his haughty Roman numeral three, but knew the type. And hated him. "You deserve so much better. I'm sorry, sweetheart."

"I assume he divorced me in order to marry his lover before his child is born."

Probably. The fool.

"He . . ."

Joe soothed with gentle words and a kiss to her hair.

"He told me he'd initiated divorce proceedings, but I've not actually seen paperwork. The man's a liar, obviously. I don't know what to believe. It's possible I'm still legally his wife."

And there it was. The issue that brought her to interrupt the simple ceremony that would join her to him in matrimony and ask to speak to him in private.

The only bright spot in this mess was her determination to treat him, Doc Joe, a simple country doctor who never would've known the difference if his bride were entering a bigamous marriage, with honesty and fairness.

Yeah, Naomi was the gal for him. "I want to marry you. I'll say that right now. But a divorce is so, so—"

"I don't care." Yeah, the stain of divorce had ruined more than one good name. "New York is more than half a continent away. No one needs to know."

"I don't know if I can... if *our* marriage would be..."

...legal?

Part of him didn't want to care. Not at all. She was as good as divorced, two thousand miles from a man who'd thrown her away. She deserved a fresh start.

If he had to guess, most folks west of the Mississippi had left big secrets back at the homestead. Some no doubt left rightful names behind.

But not Naomi. She answered to her name too easily. The woman had an honest streak a mile wide.

"It's legal," he insisted, "as long as we want it to be. Whether we say our vows before a man of the church or justice of the peace, marriage is an agreement between man and wife."

If they lived together, shared everything, built a life together.

Yeah, he wanted God's blessing but figured the Almighty would see things fairly.

She seemed unwilling to answer. He nudged her. "Naomi? What do you think?"

A little shrug. She seemed so small, so fragile—in stark difference to the confident woman he'd met in his surgery. She'd seemed six feet tall and near bulletproof when those talented surgeon's hands joined his, fighting for a wounded man's life.

"I think..."

He counted to ten. Then twenty.

Ultimately, all that mattered is that she was comfortable with it. If she didn't want to marry him, he'd wait.

Naomi was a gal worth waiting for.

Please, want me . . . eventually.

She shifted, her lips brushing his cheek. "I'm not accustomed to a man wanting my opinion, nor expecting to hear my ideas on any subject."

"You'll find I do." He wanted to kiss away her uncertainty. Banish it forever. And smack Ernest with his Roman numeral three for his idiocy. "That was before, Naomi. *He* was before. This is now. Let's move forward, you and I, and build a good life together."

"I like the sound of that."

Scads of uncertainty and angst melted away like ice in summer's heat.

"Me too. Ready?"

"Ready."

Ten

On the one-week anniversary of their wedding, Naomi walked home from the clinic, hand in hand with her husband. The sun had begun its slow descent, taking with it the oppressive heat of the day. Shadows lengthened.

Already, the depth of intimacy between them astounded her. One year and eight months with Ernie and she'd never felt so close, so well-known, so . . . *cherished.* The growing tenderness between them was sweet, and Joe's lovemaking reached her heart.

Ernie had been desperately wrong about many things, including their tepid romance. He'd blamed it all on her. Now, she had no difficulty seeing where the fault lay.

They turned the corner, and their own little house came into view. *Home.*

The clapboard structure could easily fit inside the front parlor of the brownstone in New York, but was much more a home than that austere structure.

Let Ernie keep the townhouse. She didn't want it.

This tiny three-room cottage was the *right* place for her. Here, it was easy to believe no other life existed.

"Do you like the new sign?" her husband asked.

"I love it. It's perfect."

He'd hung the shingle outside the clinic. *Dr. Joseph Chandler, MD, and Dr. Naomi Chandler, MD*. The town had long called him Doc Joe, and since he'd introduced her around, virtually everyone addressed her most informally as Doc Naomi.

Somehow, it fit. And she adored the connection to Joe.

The inhabitants of Evanston and surrounding settlements weren't only accustomed to women casting votes, they showed most open-minded acceptance of her as a female physician. She had plenty of patients of her own. Women who were anxious—and apologetic to Doc Joe—to have her care during pregnancies and deliveries, illnesses, and injuries. Many confided, in private of course, they simply felt comfortable with another woman. Her patients weren't all female. Men sought her professional advice too. All in the space of one week.

Joe put an arm about her waist as they climbed the porch stairs.

In no hurry to go inside, she moved to the porch swing, and he followed. The ropes squeaked at his greater weight.

He pushed off the floorboards to set the swing in gentle motion.

She eased her head onto his shoulder and marveled at the many ways he'd shown her love, affection, acceptance, appreciation—in every little thing. So much more than the new shingle. He'd made her his full partner in every way. He'd gone so far as to ask her opinion on financial matters. They'd visited the bank, and Joe had instructed the bankers to allow Naomi full access to their joint accounts.

Never had she felt more loved, more valued, more trusted.

She wanted their union to last the duration of their lives.

She wanted forever.

Joe kept the swing moving with gentle motions.

Her heart overflowed with a powerful emotion that must be love. Sure, she'd loved Grandfather and remembered, distantly, loving her parents. But she'd never been in love with a man, a lover, a husband. Until Joe.

More importantly, she'd been falling *in trust* with him as well. The man's heart couldn't be more giving, more genuine.

He loved her. Obviously. But he'd yet to say the words. No problem there. Ernie had never said the words, either. But her former husband wasn't welcome in her thoughts, nor in this marriage, so she banished him yet again.

Joe didn't need to say those three little words. She *knew*.

Never had any wife known with such utter certainty how very much in love her husband was.

But the thought of disclosing the inner workings of her heart, handing over that last bit of control, giving him the power to wield over her by confessing love—it just seemed too early. *Only one week.*

Her heart rate escalated, weighing the risk. Did she dare voice the significant changes in her heart?

Surely he knew how much he'd come to mean to her. He must know.

Opening her mouth wasn't necessary, was it?

She didn't want to ruin a good thing, so she held her tongue and snuggled closer. She draped an arm about his toned middle.

He caressed her arm, raising tingles of awareness in his wake. "I have something for you."

He'd surprised her with little gifts all week. First, he'd shown her his extensive medical library at the clinic, including subscriptions to many medical periodicals. He'd shared all those resources. Another day she'd accompanied him home from work to find he'd had several new blouses and skirts made for her, the dressmaker having slipped patterns off one blouse and skirt he determined too threadbare to be of use any longer.

Every day he gave her the gift of full partnership in medicine, the freedom to practice as his equal. They discussed cases and treatments and diagnoses. He asked her opinion. And listened. She asked questions, and he answered without a glimmer of condescension.

"You've given me so much. I can't think of a thing I need." He'd seen to her every need and most of her wants. Until Joe, she'd never known how very little she needed to be happy.

He pressed a quick kiss to her lips but all too soon pulled away. He pushed his long fingers into his trouser pocket and came up with something small that caught the waning rays of summer sunlight.

A ring?

Whether out of tradition or expectation or yet some other unknown motivation, Joe dropped to one knee on the porch floorboards. He held a gold ring between thumb and forefinger, the setting encasing a sparkling gem—far larger than the diamond ring Ernie had presented her at their highly celebrated engagement.

How had her humble country-doctor husband afforded such a magnificent piece?

Joe chuckled, his joy infectious. He kissed her twice in quick succession. "May I?"

She nodded even as he slid the ring onto her third

finger. A most impractical piece for a physician. She'd no doubt remove it many times a day—

Her husband loved her. And he'd given her an obscenely expensive ring she didn't need as a symbol of that growing, newfound love. How could she not treasure it?

"It's beautiful." And it fit perfectly. How could he know her ring size?

"I know phalanges."

Bones of the fingers? "Which range in size."

"I've held your hand a time or two. I'm an observant man. These stones perfectly match your eyes. I saw this and immediately knew it belonged on your finger. I like the idea of a ring on your finger, so men know instantly you're spoken for."

She touched his jaw. "I'm yours."

"You're mine."

She chuckled, meeting his gaze. "How? You know I don't need this." But her gaze fell to the glistening jewels, mesmerized by the fracture of light into a million sparkling rays.

"Evanston's fine jeweler, William Parpe, heard of our marriage and called me in from the street."

Because of his trust and generosity, she knew the state of his finances. They'd never be wealthy, not by her former life's standards. This purchase seemed unnecessary. "It's lovely, but you needn't spend this much. A simple band will do."

"It was paid for long ago." Joe's eyes twinkled, proud of himself for adorning her finger.

She had no difficulty imagining kindly Mr. Parpe slowly increasing a tab with the good Doc Joe and finally having an opportunity to settle the debt. Joe hadn't use for Parpe's wares until now.

"Thank you," she whispered. "I'll cherish it always."

The depth of Joe's love, *for her*, shone in his hazel eyes.

Her love for him brimmed, overflowed. So much for the early attempts to prevent entangling her heart in this new marriage.

She trusted him, completely. How odd, and how completely wonderful, to trust a man again, so very soon. A miracle she'd never imagined possible. "Thank you."

"You're welcome. Thank you for coming to Evanston."

"Thank you for waiting two long years. For me."

"I'd nearly given up hope."

Where would she be without him? "I'm glad you didn't."

"Come to bed, Mrs. Chandler." He helped her to her feet. "I'm tired."

She couldn't help but chuckle. The title of missus was indeed welcome. She didn't need to be addressed as doctor. Not all the time.

Eleven

Joe jammed the stack of newspapers, periodicals, medical journals, and letters beneath his arm, shoved his bowler back upon his head, and pushed through the post office door.

Outside, he fought for air. The news had hit him with the force of a locomotive at full speed, tearing through his version of reality. He hadn't even heard the iron beast approaching.

Did Naomi know? With all the mingling she'd done, calling on patients at their homes, visiting with the ladies at church, entertaining the women who'd stopped by the clinic to meet her—she very well might.

He couldn't lose her.

Anxiety strangled him.

He stood in the middle of the dirt-packed street and turned in helpless circles. Hopelessness threatening to drag him under.

Where was Naomi? He'd seen her at noon, when they'd eaten lunch together. She'd kissed him goodbye, heading out to visit patients.

He must find her.

She could be anywhere by now. Hours had passed, and the only sane thing to do would be to head to the clinic and hope she returned . . . or go home. But the haven of their home would make him crazy.

Her scent, everywhere.

Their bed, neatly made.

Who would make the bed after she left?

It would stay made. He'd *never* sleep in that bed again—*not* without her.

He headed to the clinic, his stomach churning, heart rolling over, and thoughts out of control.

The exercise felt good, helped marginally to clear his mind, but the images of the New York paper headlines had burned into his memory.

He'd fallen in love with a woman who hadn't trusted him.

He clutched the newspapers to his side as if wrestling the headlines into a headlock. If no one saw the condemning words, if no one found out . . . If Naomi didn't know yet, he might—

No. If she didn't know yet, she would, soon enough. He must be the one to tell her.

The conversation must take place.

Even if she left him.

Finally, he neared the clinic, perspiration trickling down his back. The oppressive, dry heat had worsened throughout the afternoon until he thought he'd go mad. He needed a drink. A tall glass of cold well water—

Two people ran for the clinic's entrance, threw open the door, and charged inside.

Raised voices within.
Trouble.
He ran.

Joe took in the flurry of action within their clinic in one sweep.

The town's new attorney, Eduard Sperry, lay on the table, his shirt ripped open and blood seeping from a shoulder injury. His right arm lay at a most awkward angle, the humerus fractured, the skin torn and bleeding with the bone stabbing through.

Neighboring shopkeepers darted between Joe and the unconscious attorney, heeding orders from Naomi.

Who had shot the attorney?

"Wash your hands, Mrs. Drescher," Naomi ordered, "and bring a tray from that cabinet, top right-hand side." In her element. Powerful. Beautiful. A vision.

Blood had splattered her pale blue blouse and ran down the right sleeve.

Abigail Drescher blocked his view of his wife.

"Doc Naomi." The preacher stuck his head in the entrance. "The men have the other wounded fellow. Where do you want him?"

Another wounded? Joe shook his head to clear it, dropped the offending mail on top of the glass-fronted surgical cabinet, and took charge of their second patient.

One quick scan of this one—likely a miner in his middle years—revealed an apparent gunshot wound to the right thigh, bleeding profusely. Thank God the poor sot had lost consciousness. His clothing, rank with sweat and dust, carried the distinct odor of sour mash.

"What happened?" Joe demanded of the two shopkeepers helping his wife.

Naomi met his gaze. "They found you. Good."

Somehow she'd caught a bleeder—the left sleeve of her new blouse now soaked with blood.

A hole in that sleeve caught his eye, like it might have—

He left his patient and grabbed his wife by her uninjured arm.

She flinched. "Help me set the bone. Take his shoulder."

He tested the hole with a fingertip. "You've been shot." Nausea crested, threatening to turn his stomach inside out. "*Naomi.* What happened?"

"I'm fine." Steel lined her voice. "On the count of three."

He barely secured the joint, provided adequate counter pressure while she twisted. The maneuver required exactness, precision, and somehow she had the control. Perhaps she hadn't been shot.

He couldn't risk it. He couldn't think straight, much less give his patient adequate attention, until he knew Naomi was unscathed.

He grabbed a scalpel from the surgical tray in his dominant hand and the sleeve of her ruined blouse in the other. With one careful slice, he cut away the saturated cotton, tearing the last bit.

The sleeve fell away, revealing an oozing wound.

The bottom of his stomach dropped out.

His knees nearly telescoped.

Sheriff Lloyd Preston chose that moment to charge through the doorway, issuing orders.

Joe ignored the lawman, focusing his attention on the entrance wound marring his bride's delicate skin. A bullet had lodged in her biceps brachii. No exit wound. She'd been facing her attacker. If the strike had come just a few inches to the left—

She'd just set a broken bone with a slug buried in her muscle. The wound bled, but not as profusely as it had when fresh.

All that blood—*hers*.

"Where else are you hit?" he shouted above the cacophony. He searched her person, conducted a hasty examination. No further sign of injury. But her dark skirt, bustle, and petticoats could hide much. "What happened?"

"I was simply in the wrong place at the wrong time." She cupped his face, forced him to look her in the eye. "Joseph, I'm fine. Help me with these two. They're far worse off than me."

She pulled away and returned to work.

He stood immobile, terror rendering him useless. Time slowed, stretching and distorting.

"Sheriff," she ordered, "get out of my surgery. *Out.* You're in the way and preventing us from doing what we must. Everyone but Doc Joe and Mrs. Drescher, *out.*"

Most complied, but Sheriff Preston muttered loudly about securing the troublemakers' weapons. He made a nuisance of himself, searching holsters, boots, pockets—

Joe glanced at the bloody shirtsleeve in his hand. Naomi's blood. He turned away, fighting bile and nausea.

Compassion redoubled. For every person who'd ever stood in his shoes, emasculated, guts in terror's clutches because his wife, his daughter, or his son lay on the surgery table, bleeding.

Love hurt.

Life, fragile and impotent.

Love for Naomi—true, pure, and alive—throbbed like a thumb smashed between hammer and nail. She could have died this afternoon, having never heard the words. Because he'd been afraid of pushing her too far, too fast.

He'd had hundreds of opportunities to tell her so, but it had taken 'til now to realize just how deep the emotion ran. Until faced with her leaving him, forever.

"Joe!" Naomi's clear voice.

His head snapped up. His gaze locked on his wife.

Stay. Stay with me. He wanted to beg, plead with her, promise her anything—

"I need you." Her stripped right arm bled in a trickle. "*Now.*"

He nodded, turning to the sink to wash his hands. "I'm here. I'm with you."

Twelve

Much later, when their two gunshot victims were stabilized, bones set and splinted, sutured, medicated, and lying in recovery, Naomi finally allowed Joe to treat her arm.

He hated the pain he caused, rooting with forceps to finally snag and remove the lead buried too near bone. He prayed she wouldn't suffer nerve damage.

A surgeon *needed* sensation and control.

She winced as he pulled the ball free. It thudded onto the floor.

He fought to relax his jaw and stop grinding his molars. Exhaustion dragged. He didn't know when he'd last been so emotionally exhausted.

He couldn't wait another moment to address the news he'd learned at the post office. He glanced at the newspapers and periodicals he'd tossed onto the cabinet. She'd want to read the articles, certainly, and weigh her options.

Though he already knew she'd return to the city.

He swallowed a sharp lump of grief.

With her uninjured arm, she gently cupped his face. Her slender, magnificently talented fingers curved about his jaw, and he leaned into her touch. Oh, how he'd miss her.

He'd fallen in love with his wife.

They'd shared a marriage bed for more than a week, and he'd likely been in love with her from the first. He wanted to rail at her, inform her of his love in a fit of anger, ensure she knew she'd caused his pain. He wanted to stack the odds in his favor, prey upon her humanity.

But he couldn't do that to the woman he loved.

He wouldn't complicate her decision. He would not beg her to stay.

If she stayed, it had to be her own choosing.

But no one with Naomi's uncommon capacity would choose rural Evanston when her legacy, the fine hospital in New York that bore her name, awaited her return. She had property there, money, prestige. A place to reclaim.

She wouldn't stay.

The good people of Evanston relied on him. He couldn't go.

"I don't know the miner," he heard himself say, "but I know the new attorney, Eduard Sperry." Stalling. This wasn't like him. He'd never had trouble getting to the point, saying what must be said.

Another casualty of losing his heart.

"The miner drew on Sperry in the street."

Had she been there? Witnessed it? Who had shot her? Lawyer or miner? For the first time, he wanted to see a patient suffer.

But not Naomi.

He'd bet she felt the pain now, in spades, if she hadn't before.

He glanced up from his work, met her gaze for the slightest of seconds. Pain seared through the vicinity of his heart. He fought to draw a deep breath.

He struggled against tears that threatened to fill and overflow. He couldn't let that nonsense start. So he blotted oozing blood from the stitches as he set them.

She covered his hand with hers. So warm, *so Naomi*.

His gut seized, even as the tightness in his chest ebbed. He *needed* this woman. Needed her more than he could believe.

He thought he'd been lonely before she'd arrived. He figured he didn't yet comprehend what lonely meant. Once she read the two articles and returned to her life in New York, he'd truly understand loneliness.

She squeezed his hand, preventing him from focusing on the final stitches. "I shouldn't have stepped between them."

Fear lanced, sharp and hot. "You stepped between two feuding men?" He heard himself yell, hated himself for raising his voice. But terror had him by the throat. "Two inches, Naomi. Two inches off, and he could have killed you."

"I won't do it again." She released his hand but wrapped smooth, cool fingers about his jaw, forcing him to look at her. "Men carry guns in New York City too. I've seen plenty of men draw on one another. I've treated victims countless times."

"Things are *very* different here."

He must've yelled again because she arched one brow and withdrew the warmth of her touch.

He scowled. Hard. And focused on the remaining stitches.

He wrapped the wound in a fresh bandage, tied it off,

and wished he could hide the reminder of her injury beneath a sleeve.

"Joe?" She searched his face, no doubt witnessed his agony. "You're scaring me."

No easy way to say this, no simple way to disclose what he'd learned.

He couldn't hide the rending pain tearing through his heart, his mind, his soul. His beloved wife deserved to make her own choice, to do what she needed to do. This was her life, her career in medicine, her future.

How would he survive saying goodbye?

Thirteen

"Joe?" Naomi repeated, palpitations inducing lightheadedness. Something far greater than a little gunshot wound had him troubled.

She'd glimpsed a stack of newspapers and mail he'd tossed on top of the surgery cabinet. Unless she was badly mistaken, her past had come calling.

By the look in his eyes—betrayal, anger, pain—

He knew.

All of it, at least as far as the newspaper's far-flung accusations went.

He deserved to know of her innocence.

Did you anticipate a reprieve, Naomi? Ernie's taunts echoed. He'd escaped from the drawer she'd mostly managed to lock him in over the past week. *You're stupid to think he wouldn't learn of your treachery.*

Eight days.

Not nearly long enough.

The honeymoon had come to an abrupt halt.

All she could do was survive the interrogation, pray he listened to her side of the story, and try to explain. She *wasn't* guilty.

Joe had proved a fair-minded man. Honest. Caring. He'd never said the words, but she'd seen the proof: he loved her. But that love was newly born. It wouldn't take much to uproot it, and like a tender plant, their love would wither and die in the harsh sun of reality.

Slowly, he gathered the scattered newspapers and mail from the top of the tall surgical cabinet, sorted the envelopes and medical journals from the newsprint.

Right there, in full-color, the *New York World*, June twenty-second. The edition she'd sought, twelve hours after fleeing the brownstone, and verified Dr. Krenn's threats.

She knew precisely all she'd been wrongly accused of ... and now, so did Joe.

Her husband's gaze burned into her face, and she had to summon every ounce of strength to meet his glare.

"I'm innocent of all charges."

His expression remained stoic.

At least he hadn't shut her out or marched her to the sheriff's office.

While he listened, she'd better say all she intended to.

"My former husband wanted me out of the way, and I told you why."

She'd grieve later. Right now, she must defend herself.

"Dr. Krenn is director at Fairchild Memorial. He worked in conjunction with my husband, my *former* husband—"

Joe held up a hand, insisting she stop.

The words poured out. He must hear her.

"I don't know why he'd accuse me of such horrible, dastardly deeds, but I didn't do it. I never met the mayor, never—"

Joe shuffled through the newspapers. He'd stopped listening.

If she could summon an ounce of comportment, she'd cease prattling. She knew how a man's mind worked. Joe had decided. That was that.

The thought of him *believing* such drivel, *believing* she'd done all they'd accused her of—she couldn't bear it.

She slashed at the tears streaking down her cheeks, angry at her loss of control. She'd come close but never lost control around Ernie or Krenn. She'd never been able to contain feminine, tender emotions around Joe, not from the beginning. The inability had worsened since she'd fallen in love.

How could she feign indifference even as he passed judgment that destroyed his affection for her?

Joe may be nothing like Ernest Walter Thornton, the-*pompous*-Third, but he was a man. And men made up their minds, she knew from sorry experience, often without listening to reason. Certainly without listening to her.

She should save her breath.

But love for *this* man, her husband, wouldn't allow her to quit easily.

The brush of newsprint against her hands, clutched tightly at her waist, opened her eyes to the newspaper Joe offered.

He'd clenched his jaw.

His pain sliced sharp and deep, tearing her heart from its moorings.

Her throat closed. Either focus on the paper he wanted her to see—maybe, if she were lucky, wanted her to explain—or witness his agony.

Like a coward, she focused on the paper.

Tears blurred her vision. She reached for the hankie in

her sleeve, remembered Joe had cut the garment away, tried her pocket, came up empty.

Joe pushed a clean handkerchief into her hand.

His considerate nature, midst suffering, stole her breath.

Loneliness yawned bleak and stark before her. She'd miss him, ever so much more than she'd thought to miss Ernie.

Joe's warmth, his love and acceptance and equity should have been hers forever.

He tapped the headline with a blunt forefinger. No anger, no righteous indignation. Her gaze flicked to his face, but the torment registered still as pungent. She wanted to put her arms around him to offer comfort.

Fear of rejection kept her from reaching for him. Two wounded men recovering in separate rooms, in case one regained consciousness before the other and attempted murder—*again*—prevented her from suggesting they discuss this at home, in private.

At last she read the headline. *THORNTON, KRENN IMPLICATED IN MAYOR'S DEATH! FAIRCHILD EXONERATED.*

Shock struck her heart, kicking the already overtaxed organ into triple-time. Perspiration trickled down her back, dampening her combination, corset, and blouse.

Implicated.

Exonerated.

When had this paper released? Not *The World, The Sun.* July first.

She'd been on her westbound journey to Doc Joe when this paper had hit the streets of New York City. News had traveled quickly, reaching Joe with his many subscriptions to medical journals and newspapers.

Evanston, apparently, wasn't far enough from New York.

The lead story's headline stood a full four inches tall, obviously important. The article ran well below the fold. Later, she'd read it in detail.

All that mattered now was rescuing her marriage.

She let the newspaper slide to the floor. Overwhelming relief nearly stole her balance. "I'm *innocent*."

Joe nodded. "I know." He stood statue-still.

"Joe. This is good news."

Realization hit her with the force of a left hook. She hadn't told him about the accusations or the whole nightmare in New York. Yes, the mistress and coming child, Ernie throwing her out—all reason enough to leave. Yet she would have stayed in the city if not for the threat of imprisonment or incarceration in the madhouse.

That, she'd withheld.

The New York World had filled him in on all the sordid details.

Joe's acute pain made ever so much more sense, now: she hadn't trusted him.

The day of her arrival, he'd emphasized how vital openness and honesty was. A dozen moments paraded through her memory—recent opportunities when she might have easily confided secrets.

She did trust him and yet committed an enormous lie of omission, heaped upon others and stacked atop a stretched bit of truth.

No one needed Joe's understanding more than she, and *no one* deserved him less.

Fourteen

"I'm sorry." She'd never been sorrier in her life. "I should have—"

He managed a shrug. A half step away from her turned his sturdy frame to an angle.

"Yeah," he said, just loud enough for her to hear. "You should have."

"I didn't know you then." Fresh tears filled her eyes. "Look at me."

Pride or anger or *maleness* wedged itself between them, and he refused.

"Look at me." She forced her voice to remain soft, gentle, persuasive.

Seconds ticked past. His wonderful, tender, lovely hazel eyes finally met hers.

I love you, she wanted to say.

He knew, of course, just as she knew he loved her. His posture telegraphed now was not the time to say it for the first time.

She'd have to meet him logic for logic, in language a male could comprehend.

"I couldn't tell you every reason the day we met, Joe, though I tried. You'll recall I tried to explain, gave you many reasons. I would have told you myself, eventually."

He rolled one thick shoulder. "Doesn't matter now."

She could have screamed. Of course it mattered—if they would save their marriage, all of this mattered.

"You have your life back." He swallowed hard. She watched his Adam's apple slide down his lean, tanned throat. "You'll go back to New York City, I assume."

"I have no interest in returning."

"The newspaper you're standing on explains the Administrator's role in killing Mayor Brown. It seems the mayor's wife hired a Pinkerton, two weeks before the man's untimely death to pose as his driver and determine where a long line of threats originated."

Joe's voice reminded her of the metronome on Grandfather's piano. And her many long hours of rehearsal. Monotonous. Stating facts. Rigid. Unyielding. Devoid of emotion.

Without so much as a glance at her, he continued, "Once Krenn and Thornton had the mayor in the hospital, they falsified records to implicate you. All so they could put their own man on the ballot and see him elected. It would have worked, if not for Mrs. Brown's suspicions."

Didn't he care?

She hadn't been made for the piano, couldn't tolerate a metronome, and had no patience for his lack of passion. "I don't care. I don't care about anything but you and me and our marriage."

"Your fancy life awaits you."

"Joseph Henry Chandler, look at me."

"If it's all the same to you, madam, I respectfully ask that you not expect that of me." He turned his back, his shoulders slumped.

Her heart broke for him.

She closed the distance, wrapped her arms about his middle, and hugged him tight, pressing her cheek to his back. And held on.

"I love *you*, Joseph Chandler. I *love* you."

He tried to move out of her hold, and he could have, had he truly wanted to. She held on tighter. The stitches in her wound pulled, burning and complaining loudly. Let them tear out.

She kissed him over the scapula. "More than the solid, life-altering reason that I love you, I need this town almost as much as this town needs me. You can't deny it."

He didn't answer.

No sense retaining a scrap of pride. "Nor can you deny that *you* need me."

His posture softened, just a little. The warmth of his big hand settled over hers.

She could have wept with relief. "What can I do to convince you?"

When he didn't reply, she asked, "What must I do to keep you?"

Joe hardly dared believe he'd heard her right.

He turned in her arms, cupped her face, the better to see the truth in her eyes. Love radiated from the blue depths. He'd seen this expression on her beautiful face over the past many days, but it took her saying the words for him to truly see.

He smoothed a thumb over the wet tracks on her cheek. "You realize I can't leave Evanston. The people here—"

"I concede they need you, as much as—or more than—they need me."

He searched her dear, familiar face. "You're sure, about me?"

"For a doctor, you aren't very bright."

The teasing lilt in her tone made it easy to chuckle along with her. "Forgive me, but it's hard to believe you want me, *love me,* more than the city, more than your career, more than the hospital your grandfather founded. It's all waiting for you."

"You believe I want that more than all I've found here, with you?"

Yeah, he had believed so.

Only dolts like him left the comfort and convenience of a city for the wilds of Wyoming Territory and *liked* it.

And maybe this one *highly* unusual woman.

"Oh, Joe." She pushed up on her toes and kissed him. "Anyone can take care of business in the city, see the hospital run honestly. I'm needed here. You might not admit it, but—"

"I admit it. I *need* you."

This amazing, wonderful woman wanted to stay. With him. In Wyoming Territory. In a tiny house wholly dissimilar to all she'd grown accustomed to her in her privileged life. The article spelled out how rich she'd been before her ill-fated marriage to Thornton.

His formerly wealthy wife would rather be paid in produce, meat, and traded services than cash.

She could have it all once more.

Her shocking choice pleased him beyond reason.

And made it easy to admit he loved her and wanted her to stay.

"I need you."

A little grin teased her kissable mouth. "That's a start."

He kissed her again, this time lingering. "I love you, Naomi. I think I've loved you from the day we met, from our first kiss."

"You withheld such important information?" She poked fun at herself, the choice to keep the falsified accusations secret.

"I admit it."

"What do you mean, you think you loved me from our first meeting or first kiss?"

He kissed the tip of her nose. "I've never been in love before. Guess I didn't recognize the signs and symptoms for what they were. Therefore, I couldn't diagnose the condition."

"Never?" She blinked. "You've *never* been in love? You, who love so fully, so completely, so naturally, *must* have been practiced and proficient."

"I know love of parents, brothers and sisters. But I've never loved a woman, not 'til you." He kissed her forehead, the tip of her nose, her lips. "I never knew it was possible to love with this depth and meaning."

"I've witnessed your love in so many ways, Joseph Chandler, but I do like hearing you say it."

"I love you, Naomi. With all my heart."

He cupped the back of her head, cradled her against his chest, and slowly rocked her in his arms.

Ah, yes. This felt just right. Her nearness, her determination to remain with him, at his side. The pair of them working together in medicine and in life.

To think he'd found her, when advertising for entirely someone else, astounded him. Luck had been on his side, during those long years when no one had followed through on his advertisement. Luck had graced him when Ernest Thornton proved himself a fool.

He'd never been so blessed as that moment, the love of his life snug within his arms.

"Doc Naomi?" A harried male voice yelled from the front walk. Footsteps pounded. "Come quick. The babe's coming."

Joe pressed a kiss to his wife's temple. This type of temporary goodbye he could handle.

The frantic father-to-be, recognizable now as the grocer, leaned heavily on the door frame. "Sorry to interrupt, Doc Naomi, Doc Joe, but you gotta come quick." He addressed the plea to Naomi.

She slipped out of Joe's arms. He handed her the prepared doctor's bag and stole a kiss.

Joe tucked his hands deep into his pockets as he watched his wife pick up her skirts and charge after the grocer.

Bright sunlight cut through the clouds, streaming in slanted, blazing swaths. Amazing, that such natural brilliance could not compare to the radiance in his heart.

He paused, considered, then followed his heart up Front Street. He wouldn't make a pest of himself, but simply wanted to be near Naomi and enjoy watching her deliver the new baby.

Babies. He picked up his pace, not wanting to miss the little one's entrance into the world.

Now that he'd secured a perfect wife in Mrs. Naomi Chandler, he couldn't wait for babies of their own.

He grinned as he made his way around back to the grocer's residence and heard Naomi's soothing voice instructing the laboring mother.

Wanted: Midwife. Check.

Wanted: Babies.

ABOUT KRISTIN HOLT

I recall the winter of my first grade year, basking in the heat from our fireplace in Kalamazoo, Michigan. Dad read aloud Madeline L'Engle's A WRINKLE IN TIME and Mom peeled orange segments for us to enjoy. That was the definitive moment I fell in love with fiction. I write sweet (wholesome) romances set in the 19th Century American West.

Find Kristin online:
Website: www.kristinholt.com
Facebook: Kristin Holt Author
Twitter: @KHoltAuthor

The Sound of Home
by Annette Lyon

OTHER WORKS BY ANNETTE LYON

Band of Sisters
Coming Home
The Newport Ladies Book Club series
A Portrait for Toni
At the Water's Edge
Lost Without You
A Midwinter Ball
Done & Done
There, Their, They're: A No-Tears Guide to Grammar from the Word Nerd

One

New York City, 1887

When Marilyn was called down from her room in the boardinghouse to meet a visitor, dread filled her middle. Her caller had to be Victor Hallows. No one else had visited her in nearly a year. And after she'd rejected his proposal of marriage last week, she'd hoped to never see him again.

She grudgingly descended the stairs and entered the parlor, where, sure enough, Victor stood waiting for her. The moment she cleared the threshold, he closed the door. Marilyn wished she could keep it open—privacy was the last thing she wanted with this man—but he'd block the door if she tried something, so she merely walked to the couch and sat down.

"I thought I made my wishes perfectly clear last time, Mr. Hallows," she said.

"Oh, but I'm quite sure you didn't think through the various possibilities that an acceptance would bring you." Victor sat on the couch opposite her and set a newspaper and a pair of gloves onto the glass end table beside him. "Someone in my position—with money and a reputation—could raise one's status quite remarkably. You'd never have to work another day of your life. You'd have servants and luxuries you can only dream of now."

If he genuinely believed that money and status could convince her to marry a man she loathed, he was sadly mistaken. "I'm sorry, but the answer is still no. I will not marry you."

Victor eyed her for several unnerving seconds before smiling with half of his mouth and cocking his head to one side. "I suppose I'd be amenable to a different type of arrangement, if you'd rather. You would still have wealth and luxury, without taking my name or wearing my ring on that pretty little hand of yours."

She could sense a trick hiding up his sleeve. "But?" she prompted. "What price would I pay for such a life?"

"Nothing. Nothing more than giving me the pleasure of your company several nights a week."

He wanted her to be his *mistress*? The very idea of his hands touching her—any part of her body—made Marilyn sick. She shook her head and swallowed back her disgust.

"Never," she said. The concept of a mistress—of *her* becoming one—sent shivers down her spine.

"Sweet, naive Marilyn, you don't understand how this world works," he said. "You would be a fool for giving up the chance to be taken care of by someone with wealth and influence such as myself."

"Then I will happily live my life as a fool." She rose and walked to the door, hoping that would be enough to make him leave.

To her relief, he stood and followed her. But he didn't leave. Instead, he leaned in so close that the curled ends of his greasy mustache tickled her cheek. She tried not to react outwardly in spite of feeling as if cockroaches were crawling all over her.

"Remember," he whispered with heavy breath, "you have nothing—no name, no money, no relations, no reputation—nothing but a pretty face to tempt a man, and your looks won't sustain you forever. If you aren't careful," he added, "you'll end up living on the streets, selling far more than flowers, in not many months' time."

Was he right? *Would* she end up on the streets? He was right that she had nothing and no one—no education, and not even skills beyond what she'd learned working at the Pricketts' bakery. She'd gotten by, thanks to her position there. But the Pricketts were old, and the store lost more money every day. It would have to close in a matter of months, a year at best. Then how would she support herself?

After Victor's last visit, she'd spent the night considering his offer, lying in her rented bed in a house stacked with other women in similar circumstances. He was a vile, vile man, granted. But perhaps she could endure his presence from time to time if doing so also meant never being hungry, having a soft bed each night, and never having to worry about replacing worn clothing with so many holes that it could no longer be mended. But no. She couldn't abide being his wife. And she absolutely couldn't abide being a mistress.

"I suggest you leave." Marilyn straightened her back—picturing her spine filled with strong, un-rusted iron. "I have nothing more to say to you." She reached for the doorknob, but Victor stopped her hand. His mouth slowly curved into a sickening smile that set Marilyn on edge.

"But I do have more to say. After you hear it, you may well have something more to say to me."

She lacked the strength to ask what he meant, so she simply swallowed against a dry throat and waited, unsure of what to brace herself for. What it would be like to live in a household where one had platters of food brought to you, where you could buy new shoes without squirreling away coins for months in advance. Her right boot had a hole in the bottom, currently patched with layers of newsprint. What would he think if he knew that?

"An . . . *associate* of mine has met an untimely end," Victor said, his eyes sparkling with amusement. He clasped his hands behind his back and began walking around Marilyn in large, slow circles.

"Wh—what kind of associate?" Marilyn asked, hating her mouth for betraying her nerves with a stammer.

"A business associate . . . of sorts." His step paused, and he turned to face her. "It would be most unfortunate if the police were to think that a young woman might have had something to do with his death. After all, the doctor who arrived at his bedside declared that he was most likely poisoned—something all too easy for a young woman of questionable morals to do without expecting to be caught." He paused and looked at her, his face wearing a lecherous expression as his eyes wandered over every inch of her, taking in every curve as if she were some feast he planned to partake of.

"Wh—what are you saying?" Marilyn asked in a voice so quiet that it was barely more than a whisper.

"What if," Victor said, continuing his speech as well as his circular path, "Mr. Fletcher's poisoning wasn't an unfortunate accident? What if the poison, intended for mice in his apartment, didn't simply fall into his coffee but was placed there? What if a young woman, perhaps jealous of Mr. Fletcher's attentions toward another young lady, had mixed the powder into his drink and then knowingly served it to him?"

He paused, looking at Marilyn, who stood stock-still. He made a contented noise that sounded amused. "And what if several eyewitnesses were willing to vouch that the young woman who visited Mr. Fletcher's apartment the very day he died was none other than one *Marilyn Davis*?" He stopped and looked at her, his head cocked again.

A cold chill went through her. She shook her head once, twice, and then several times rapidly. "No," she said. "You can't possibly do such a thing. No one would believe—"

"No? Who would believe an orphan desperate to improve her status in the world, over the word of a respected businessman?" He chuckled outright this time and smoothed his mustache, curling the ends just so. "Oh, I think we both know whose word would be trusted, especially if that man has influential friends . . . and material evidence." Victor returned to her, standing so close she could feel his breath on her face. "Do I make myself clear?" His airy tone had deepened into a far more serious one.

Marilyn's mind raced, trying to find some way to escape his clutches. She could think of nothing. If she married Victor, she would lead a life of luxury and privilege but would despise her husband and never trust him around her children. How could she ever bear to be anywhere near a man who'd obviously committed a murder?

I cannot choose such an existence. But what else can I do?

If she refused, he would go to the police with whatever "evidence" he'd concocted, framing her for the murder of a man she'd never even met. She suspected that the situation involved a gambling debt of Victor's—or worse. If he went to the police, they would believe him. Why wouldn't they? Who was she but a poor orphan with no connections to recommend her? How could she expect to contradict his statements and have anyone take her seriously when he had friends in powerful places throughout the city?

The Sound of Home

He stared at her still, his face having lost all trace of joviality and amusement.

"You've made yourself crystal clear," Marilyn said, hardly able to unclench her teeth enough to speak.

"Then it appears you have a decision to make," he said. "Think on it. I'll pay a visit on Friday evening to hear your decision. I'll even bring with me a pretty ring to put on that finger of yours, and we can take a carriage to a justice of the peace that very night." Victor placed his hat on his head. "I've always preferred to complete negotiations and contracts and such as quickly as possible. A timely resolution is much more pleasant for everyone involved. I'm sure you'd agree."

He leaned toward the end table and picked up his gloves and newspaper. "You enjoy reading," he said, slapping the newspaper onto the coffee table, folded to show a specific article. His finger tapped a black circle that encompassed a bit of text. "This should provide you with some diversion," he said. "I imagine you'll find it most . . . interesting." As he spoke, his voice dripped with sweetness like pastry glaze.

From where Marilyn stood, she couldn't make out the words, not even in the headline. Victor nodded with a partial bow, then left the sitting room and let himself out of the boarding house altogether. The outside door shut with a thud. A moment later, she heard his footsteps and watched his shadow move across the window. He was gone, for now. Yet Marilyn still couldn't move, for her feet felt glued to the rug.

Victor was far worse a human being than she'd ever suspected. He was a murderer. Simply thinking the word made her knees weak; she went to the couch and sat on it before they unhinged altogether. But then she was within arm's reach of the paper, and she felt compelled to read it. As if steeling herself against a poisonous viper, Marilyn closed her eyes and reached for the newspaper. She kept her eyes shut at first, unwilling to look but knowing in her heart that she couldn't resist. She would read it, if for nothing else than to be properly prepared.

Marilyn licked her lips, took a deep breath, and settled her gaze on the article Victor had circled in dark ink. The short write-up gave only the barest of details regarding the death of one Mr. Harvey Fletcher: the date, how he'd been found in bed, and that the cause of death had yet to be determined, as the responding physician believed the circumstances to be suspicious.

The article continued beyond the fold, so Marilyn had to open the paper some more to read the rest. Fletcher had long been suspected of various illegal activities, but police hadn't been able to gather enough evidence to arrest him. His shady background only strengthened the possibility that he was murdered. After all, the author pointed out that Fletcher had scores of enemies.

Many enemies, indeed, Marilyn thought. With shaky hands, she lowered the paper to her lap and stared at the flickering gas sconce on the wall. She knew—*knew*—that Victor had killed Mr. Fletcher. She also knew with utter certainly that if she didn't accept Victor's proposal, he would see to it that she was arrested for Fletcher's murder. Then she would be put on trial and painted not as a poor bakery worker but as a woman of questionable morals. She knew that Victor had enough pull in local society to see to it that she spent the rest of her life in prison.

She reread the article then forced herself to look elsewhere, but all she managed was to lower her eyes to the bottom of the page. There they landed on a different headline, or rather, on the bolded text of an advertisement. How she picked that one notice from among dozens,

The Sound of Home

advertising tooth powders, buttons, miracle battery cures, and millinery shops, she'd never know.

Perhaps it was the lack of pictures in this block of text that drew her eye. Whatever the reason, she found herself engrossed by the headline of a personal advertisement: *Wanted—Mail Order Bride.*

In spite of herself and her long-standing opinion of such arrangements as being foolhardy, ridiculous, and built on a foundation of sand, she kept reading.

> *Respectable American bachelor of thirty-three years of age, intelligent, sober, graceful, and affectionate, is desirous of immediately finding a neat, pretty, hardworking wife between the ages of twenty-five and thirty. Orphan preferred. Reply to Elayne Williamson, Union Square Post Office, New York. Ms. W. will provide the chosen applicant with train passage already paid for by said bachelor.*

Marilyn calmly folded the newspaper so Victor's article was hidden and the advertisement was on top. She smoothed the creases, careful not to get ink on her fingers. Only then did she realize how steady her hands had become. She felt utterly calm because she knew now how to live free from Victor, free from prison, and, hopefully, free of poverty and hunger. She would bind herself to a man she knew nothing of, not even his name.

He sounds educated, at the very least, she thought, which was some comfort. *But why does he prefer an orphan? I am one, but why should that matter?* The bachelor on the other end of the advertisement might be a brute in his own way, but anything was better than Victor.

Decision made, Marilyn stood, clutching the newspaper.

She marched up the stairs to her room and packed all of her belongings, even though she hadn't yet written to Ms. Elayne Williamson and had no train ticket.

This must work, she thought, laying a petticoat in her trunk. *It simply must.*

Two

Diamond City, Wyoming

If steam could truly come out of one's ears, then Thomas Yardley would have resembled a locomotive as he strode out of the bank toward his horse. He took fast, angry steps and nearly crushed his hat in one hand in spite of the sweltering heat of the afternoon sun. That dag-blamed brother of his.

How did Harry know how much money we have in the bank? Rather, used to have, he thought. They needed a new plow, and they needed to pay the mortgage for the farm. They needed a lot of things, quite frankly, including a new horse and especially some hired hands now that Harry was about as much help as their aging cat. Harry kept it for companionship, though it had long since lost its usefulness as a mouser.

And now the money was simply gone—all but five dollars out of almost a hundred. Poof, into thin air, like a magic trick.

Why had Frank, the cashier, given it to Harry? Everyone in the tiny Wyoming town of Diamond City knew better—knew that, while Harry would always be the elder brother, alcohol and an accident had stripped him of his ability to think like an adult. Thomas did all of the work now, nearly breaking his back to bring in a yearly crop, maintain the house and stables, plus cook, clean, and do everything else that Harry, Thomas, their father, and mother had once done. In short, Thomas did the work of four—or tried to.

He'd done his best, and so far, hadn't lost the farm. But apparently, he had lost all of the money he'd scrimped and saved in hopes of keeping the farm.

Then again, he did live in a place named after a mythical diamond mine that had never materialized, though many locals still had faith that it would someday be found. Maybe the banker and the rest of the town were as ridiculously optimistic about other things, too, like Harry's reasoning capacities.

Thomas shoved his hat on his head, mounted his old horse, and turned toward home at a fast trot. He would have preferred to gallop, but the old mare couldn't tolerate such speeds.

Maybe Harry hadn't yet spent the money, and there would be time to make everything right. Thomas prayed his heart out for the fifteen minutes it took to reach home. Then he pulled the horse to a stop beside the hitching post at the back door. After making a quick knot with the reins, he bolted inside.

Putting the horse up can wait, he thought. *This cannot.*

"Harry?" he called, shoving the door shut with his boot. He didn't bother cleaning his boots on the brushes by the door as his mother had taught him to do—a habit he'd continued after her death. *No time for that, either.* Steam kept building inside Thomas, needing an exit, as he stomped through one room after another, quickly covering the entire main floor with no success—including Harry's bedroom.

Where was that brother of his? "Harry? Where are you?"

No answer. Thomas hurried up the steep steps and suddenly worried over something other than the money. What if his brother had hurt himself again? Harry was forbidden to go upstairs ever since he had fallen down them in a drunken stupor. That's why he now slept on the ground floor.

That man is no better than a child, Thomas thought. *He'll always get into mischief and will end up pushing us into abject poverty.*

At the latter thought, Thomas gritted his teeth. He and Harry weren't homeless or destitute yet. Keeping the farm and keeping their parents' dream alive was his duty now that he could no longer share the responsibility with his brother.

The stairs ended in the small room that Thomas called his own. Harry used to claim the other room upstairs—the larger of the two and the one that had the most privacy, seeing as how no one had to pass through it to get to another, as was the case with Thomas's room.

If he's up there, he's safe, Thomas thought in an attempt to calm his nerves. *Unless he tries to fly by jumping from the window.* Thomas wouldn't put such a thing past Harry. Once, the man had left the chicken coop open, which allowed raccoons to get in and kill them all. On another occasion, he'd nearly burned the house down. He'd even almost cut off his own hand while trying to chop wood.

Thomas went through his room to the closed door on the other side. He knocked while turning the knob. "Harry?"

While he hadn't known what he would find, Thomas

certainly didn't expect the sight that met him: Harry, lying on the spare bed, smiling dreamily at what appeared to be a photograph.

"Harry," Thomas said again, walking over to sit on the edge of his brother's bed. "What are you doing?"

His anger yielded to the relief that his brother wasn't sick or hurt, and his curiosity got the better of him, for Thomas couldn't remember his brother ever looking so happy. He pointed to the paper. "What's that? Harry, do you hear me? What's in the picture?" Thomas leaned over, trying to get a glimpse.

Harry pulled the photograph to his chest. "Not *what*," he said as he glared at Thomas. "*Who*."

These childish games tended to wear thin when day after day of heavy work pressed on his shoulders. Yet Thomas tried to remain patient and sympathetic. "Very well, *who* is in the picture?"

Harry sat up suddenly, grinning widely, the photo still held to his heart. "Our new mother. Surprised, aren't you? I found a notice in the paper that said you can order brides, so I asked for a wife."

"You did *what*?" Thomas demanded.

"See, she'll already be married and know how to take care of us. She arrives on the morning train. You'll pick her up, won't you? Her name is Marilyn Davis. She'll cook for us, and sing us songs, and read us books and . . ." In spite of Harry's tough exterior, his eyes welled up with tears.

The only times Thomas had ever seen Harry cry were when he broke a leg at the age of seven, and again two years ago at their mother's funeral. Now his tears looked ready to spill onto his leathered cheeks.

Understanding and frustration slowly dawned on Thomas. In the face of his brother's hopes and dreams, the

The Sound of Home

anger ebbed. It would return—certainly when he couldn't make the next mortgage payment—but for now, Thomas couldn't curse his brother. He looked at the photograph: a young woman in a simple yet well-kept dress.

Quite pretty, Thomas thought. *She looks pleasant enough.*

"You sent her our money," Thomas said.

"I sent *Ms. Williamson* the money," Harry corrected. "She arranged it all." He counted on his fingers as he said, "The fee for the ad, Marilyn's room—"

"We paid for her *rent*?"

"Just for five days," Harry said. He stared at the gabled ceiling as he thought. "Oh, and some new clothes."

Thomas's stomach sank further. "You wired all of it?"

"If our new mother needs a new dress or boots, she gets them," Harry said soberly.

"Of course," Thomas said bitterly. What kind of scam woman would cheat a disabled man who had the reasoning powers of a ten-year-old? Thomas tightened his fists and tried to come up with a solution.

The money was gone—spent on dresses and ruffles and who knew what else. Where else did the money go? Train ticket. Food. Surely other costs he hadn't thought of, all of which cost more back east than it did in Wyoming.

"Ms. Williamson sent the picture with a business partner," Harry explained. "He brought it as far as Iowa then mailed it so I'd get it before she arrived." He gazed at the picture again, and his gentle smile returned.

But Harry's happiness didn't erase the fact that Thomas wished he'd taken Harry's name off the bank account. After the accident, someone at church had suggested that it would be a wise idea, but he'd figured that having Harry's name on the account couldn't hurt. At the time, he viewed the gesture as one their parents would have approved of.

Now they're probably shaking their heads at my stupidity.

His brother yammered on about how he'd gotten the idea after hearing about Joe Hutchins's mail order bride, and how Miss Faye at the telegraph office had helped him write the letter and send the money to New York. Thomas nodded absently, hearing only small pieces.

Thomas had two problems: this Marilyn woman and the mortgage. The woman was more immediately pressing. He might let her stay a night or two, just long enough to purchase another ticket and head back to where she came from. Maybe he'd insist she leave the new clothes behind, so he could sell them and get at least some money back.

He'd have to be firm. No female wiles of sad eyes above full, frowning lips would sway him. She'd be yet another mouth to feed. She'd probably expect to be doted on. Thomas wouldn't get much work done with a woman about. And that was aside from the gossip such an arrangement would create. A single woman living with two men? He had no stomach for that.

"Come downstairs," Thomas said. "I'll make some supper." Harry followed and went to his room, where he petted the cat on his bed as Thomas made dinner.

Thomas put water on for boiling potatoes then gathered several russets from the cool storage below the floor. As he scrubbed them, he missed how his mother used to work in the kitchen, making three hot meals a day for her men, as she'd called Pa and the boys.

The place definitely felt different now. Thomas set the scrub brush and potato down and looked about the kitchen and the sitting room beyond. The place lacked warmth without Ma's touch. *It could really use a woman's influence,* he thought.

The Sound of Home

He sighed and turned back to the sink, grabbing a potato with dirt clods covering it. One of these days, he'd like to court a girl and have a family. Unfortunately, that day would be long in coming, for his first priorities rested in keeping the farm and caring for his brother.

Three

As the train approached her stop, Marilyn peered out the window, trying to get some sense of her new home. All she could see were low hills, sagebrush, and buildings that looked ready to collapse, as if they might as well have been built of matchsticks.

A longing for home came over her. She wished this were a dream, that she could wake up in New York. She'd buy a hot dog from a street vendor, then stroll past decorated shop windows displaying clothing she could only dream of owning. She even missed seeing young boys on street corners, shouting headlines as they peddled papers. She used to buy one whenever she could. Many of newsies were orphans too, so she knew some measure of what they had lived through. Even now that she was a grown woman, the smallest acts of kindness from strangers warmed her heart. When she was a child, such moments kept her going another day.

The Sound of Home

Perhaps a life out West would have been easier, she thought, *easier than finding scraps to stay alive back east.*

As the landscape slid past slightly slower now, Marilyn even missed the crowds, bustle, and coal dust of the city. The train windows were open, and even breathing the fresh air felt different. The air was still hot, but something was missing—moisture. That was it. This feeling came from a dry heat that seemed to bake her lungs. She suddenly yearned for a big glass of water.

The train finally came to a stop. At the sight of the platform, Marilyn's insides went completely mad. She peered out the window even more intently. Watching the landscape had been more a matter of curiosity and comparison before, but seeing the face of the man she would spend the rest of her mortal days with meant something else entirely.

Let him be kind, she thought, praying she hadn't jumped out of Victor's frying pan and into Mr. Harry Yardley's fire.

"Are you quite all right?"

Marilyn turned to the young mother who'd sat on the aisle for the hundreds of miles of their journey—Betty. They'd talked a bit here and there, and Marilyn had helped with her baby at times.

"I'm—I'm quite well, thank you," Marilyn said, determined to at least pretend that her words were the truth.

"Good luck." Betty looked out the window toward a sign that read *Diamond City Station* in big white letters. "I hope your life here is as wonderful as diamonds."

"Thank you," she said. "The same to you and your boy."

With trembling knees, Marilyn stepped into the aisle, not wanting to get off. During her days on the train, she'd felt perfectly safe. Granted, her neck had developed quite a crick, and her back ached from sleeping upright, but she had remained out of Victor's clutches. For a moment, as she stood in line, standing tall to stretch her back, she imagined traveling back and forth across the country—never having to see Victor in New York, never having to settle in Wyoming as the wife of a man she knew almost nothing about.

For aside from Harry Yardley's name, age, and occupation, she knew nothing about him, which seemed highly unfair, especially because he had a photo of her taken in Ms. Williamson's office, but Marilyn had none of Mr. Yardley.

The man ahead of Marilyn in line stepped from the train, and it was now her turn to disembark. For the first time in days, she looked outside without a glass partition in the way. A sea of bobbing faces seemed to extend before her, even though the number of people here couldn't possibly have come close to the throngs she used to pass daily.

The press of passengers from behind encouraged her to grip the handrail and take the two steps to the platform. Once there, she breathed in deeply—the desert air would take some getting used to—then moved to the side to be out of the way. Would Harry Yardley recognize her from the photograph?

The ribbon! she thought, remembering the agreed-upon detail by which her husband-to-be would recognize her. People jostled her as they passed in both directions, but Marilyn opened her carpetbag and searched for the telltale red ribbon. Finally, under a copy of *Dickens's Dombey and Son* and her gloves—which, come to think of it, she should probably put on if she wanted to be taken seriously as a proper young woman—and under other assorted belongings, she spotted the ribbon.

How should I wear it? Ms. Williamson hadn't said. Marilyn guessed that tying it about the brim of her hat might be most effective, as it would be easily spotted at a distance by someone taller than an average-framed woman. But without a table or other support, securing a ribbon to her hat would be difficult at best. She settled on tying the ribbon into a circlet and slipping it onto her wrist like a bracelet.

The crowd had begun to thin. With a large cloud obscuring the sun, the day wasn't overly bright at the moment, but she raised her left hand to her brow anyway. She hoped that the gesture looked natural and that the ribbon on her wrist would allow her to be easily identified by Mr. Yardley, wherever he was.

A full minute passed. Then two. She cursed whatever fates had brought her to this godforsaken place of tumbleweeds, heat, and dust. If she couldn't have a photograph of her intended, couldn't Ms. Williamson at least have given Marilyn a more complete physical description? Better yet, couldn't she have avoided meeting the infernal Victor Hallows?

A movement in the corner of her eye made Marilyn freeze with anticipation, her senses heightened. Heavy footsteps sounded, moving toward her, probably from a man's boots. She wanted to turn her head to get a good look at Mr. Yardley—wanted it more than a long drink of cool water.

What would she find in his face? Compassion and kindness? Or would he be a Victor of another stripe? Unwilling to appear too forward, she forced herself to pretend not to see or hear him until he drew much closer and stopped about five feet away—quite a distance, considering the fact that she was his fiancée.

"Are you Miss Marilyn Davis?" His voice sounded deep and warm, and his pronunciation sounded educated.

A literate husband is good. She lifted her head and gestured toward her beribboned hand.

Summoning every ounce of manners, she said, "Indeed I am."

However, any sign of her good breeding was probably eclipsed by the fact that her eyes quickly locked on to the most handsome face she'd ever seen. Quite simply, she couldn't have pulled her gaze away if the train conductor had promised her free passage to anywhere she chose. A moment passed in silence. His forehead wrinkled with apparent concern, and Marilyn tried her best to recall how one's mouth formed words. At last she bobbed a curtsy and tried to speak.

"And you—" She cleared her throat and hoped he wouldn't notice just how pink her cheeks were turning. They had to be fuchsia if the heat in them was any indication—the early morning warmth could not account for it. Again, all words fled from her mind. She stared at him and, in a small corner of consciousness, hoped he didn't think her utterly daft.

She gaped because, goodness, the man was handsome, with a full head of deep brown hair, broad shoulders, and a trim waist. His shirtsleeves were rolled up part way, showing defined muscles in his forearms. Surely the sleeves hid equally defined biceps.

Farming builds nice figures.

Good thing he'd said nothing about his features to Ms. Williamson; a hundred girls if one would have clamored into her office with applications. Or was he unaware of his looks? Maybe he didn't want such things to matter to a wife. Either way, she smiled at her good fortune. Her risky venture as a mail order bride had taken a nice turn.

"You are Mr. Yardley, I presume?"

There, she thought with a bit of triumph. *Coherent speech. I'm not daft at all.*

The Sound of Home

But he shifted uncomfortably. He removed his hat, wiped his brow with his forearm, and replaced the hat. "I'm Yardley," he said, but both his tone and face were unreadable. "Or rather, I'm a Mr. Yardley, but the name's Thomas. You're looking for Harry, my older brother."

"Oh." Anticipation drained from Marilyn like water down the bakery's sink. She hoped her disappointment didn't show as she tried to hide it with a wide smile and a particularly peppy tone. "You are my future brother-in-law, then. Where is your brother?" She looked about the station, which seemed to have cleared rapidly.

"He's nearby," Thomas said vaguely. For someone who appeared as strong as an ox, he certainly seemed unsure of himself. He wouldn't even look her in the eye. "Let's go find your trunks and get them into the wagon," he said. "We'll pick up Harry then drive to the farm. It's not far." He turned around and took a step toward the luggage area, but Marilyn hurried forward and grabbed his arm, making him turn around.

"Wait," she said. "Is something wrong?" They stood awfully close now. Marilyn held his bicep and could feel its warmth through his shirt. It did indeed seem to be every bit as strong as she'd guessed. A small thrill went through her as she imagined what his arms must look like without a shirt covering them. Then she had to quickly tamp down her emotions. She couldn't let herself think or feel such things about someone other than Harry.

Harry may be just as handsome, she reasoned.

Thomas licked his lips, staring at the wooden slats at their feet as if trying to find a way to explain, so she jumped in. "Has Mr. Yardley—Harry—changed his mind? Is he ill? Has something hap—"

He shook his head, cutting her off. "Nothing as simple as any of that, I'm afraid."

"Then what?"

"You must be tired and hungry," Thomas said, finally looking at her with piercing hazel eyes. "Let's get you fed and rested, and then we'll talk."

She nodded and walked alongside him. "We'll talk," she repeated a moment later, "meaning the three of us—Harry, you, and I?"

His step came up short. He glanced at her and then away. "We'll see."

Thomas clamped his mouth shut after that, speaking only when necessary, such as confirming which trunk was hers and that she had only one. He and a station attendant loaded the trunk into the wagon as she climbed onto the seat. Thomas said nothing more, even after joining her.

We'll see? Marilyn thought. She looked at Thomas out of the corner of her eye. He still had his jaw set firm, and his eyes were narrowed as if he was puzzling out a problem.

She settled in, knowing that she'd have to be satisfied with his maddeningly vague response—at least until she met Harry.

Four

For Thomas, the ten-minute drive to Miss Faye's apartment felt like an eternity. He sat on the buckboard with a pretty city girl next to him, but the poor woman had no idea what a mess she'd stepped into. He still had no idea what in tarnation he'd do about the woman—send her back, he supposed. Her single trunk didn't give him much hope that she had many fancy silk dresses to sell, though, and he doubted he could afford another train ticket. Even if he could have, paying the bank seemed to be the higher priority.

So should he keep Miss Davis around to avoid spending the money on a train ticket? That might help him save the farm, but he doubted he could live with himself if he forced a woman to stay against her will. She'd come to marry, not to become a mother to two grown men.

Such a mess, Thomas thought as they approached the restaurant above which Miss Faye lived.

Miss Faye was a spinster who'd been friends with their mother. Every now and again, she cared for Harry when Thomas needed the help. The last two years had been hard on Thomas. He constantly worried over Harry—how best to care for him, and whether he belonged in a hospital. No wonder that Thomas had already noticed visible worry lines turning into wrinkles, especially along his forehead. He wasn't a vain man, but, each time he shaved, the creases in the mirror seemed deeper and reminded him that life on the frontier had aged him faster than the years had passed. Thomas let the buckboard roll to a stop.

"Is this your place?" Marilyn asked, looking confused. "It's . . . nice. I thought Harry was a farmer."

"Our farm's out of town a ways." Thomas hopped to the ground then secured the horses on the hitching post. He reached for Marilyn's hand to help her down. It felt soft, but not the kind of softness that came from a life of luxury. Whether it was from her firm grip, hinting at her physical strength and willingness to work, or from the feel of small calluses—slightly rough in some spots but nowhere near as leathery as his own—he wasn't sure, but Thomas could tell that she knew how to work. This was no weak, simpering woman who expected to be pampered, as he'd assumed any woman coming west for the adventure of being a mail order bride would be. He liked how she seemed both competent and confident.

Once on the ground beside him, Marilyn smoothed her skirts, wiping away the dust from their journey. She nodded toward the house. "May I ask why we're here?" Her cheeks flushed slightly, and he suddenly realized what she must be thinking a split second before she said, "Does the minister live here?"

"Not at all," Thomas said. "Miss Faye lives up there." He

pointed at a window above the restaurant. "We're here to pick up Harry."

Thomas kicked a rock into a fence post, wanting to put off the inevitable. *Better to tell her all now, before she sees for herself.* He supposed it would be the decent thing to do. He didn't like the idea of making a woman uncomfortable or upset, especially one who looked at him with such trusting, hopeful eyes—green, with a touch of gold. Did they change shades, depending on the color she wore?

Why am I suddenly thinking of ladies' fashions? A fever must be coming on.

Marilyn raised her eyebrows. "Why is your brother spending the morning with this Miss Faye?"

She seemed somewhat at ease, and Thomas dreaded undoing that. The moment he explained, she'd probably tense up again. He didn't want to see her countenance change from this hopeful expectation to sadness and disappointment.

Bet she's every bit as pretty with tears in her eyes.

Stop that.

He cleared his throat and turned to face the restaurant so they stood side by side—and so he wouldn't be tempted to keep looking at her, taking in every feature—then dove in without preamble.

"Harry is . . . well, Harry isn't right in the head." *Blunt, but the truth.* In spite of himself, his gaze slid in Marilyn's direction without turning his head. He tried to gauge her reaction.

Marilyn let out a frustrated breath. "Mr. Yardley. You don't really think your brother has lost his mind simply for seeking a mail order bride, do you?"

"No," Thomas said. And he didn't. If all mail order brides were like Marilyn, every bachelor in the county should sign up for one.

She's strong and intelligent. Not the type to wilt into a sniveling mess at the first sign of things going awry. He sighed. *This whole thing would be much easier if she would complain or if she had a temper.*

"Our family moved here ten years ago—Harry and me and our parents," Thomas explained. "We had a dream of making a comfortable living off the land. Things went pretty well until . . ." Why had he been about to tell her all of that? She wouldn't be around long enough to need every bit of their history. Yet he found that he wanted to tell her everything: about the past ten years. About his own hopes and dreams. About his frustrations and disappointments. He'd never felt an urge to confide in another person, at least, not since Ma's death.

"Everything went well . . . until . . . what?" Marilyn's tone sounded soft and concerned, something he never would have expected from a virtual stranger.

"Until our parents died," he said. "First our father, and then, a few months later, our mother. Harry and I managed for a few months, but then he . . . well, he turned to the bottle."

Marilyn furrowed her brow as if she knew exactly what that meant. She pressed her hand to her heart and shook her head sadly.

Thomas couldn't keep his eyes from finding the little hollow above her breastbone, visible between her thumb and first finger. He suddenly had a strange hankering to kiss that spot, which was probably even softer than her hands.

What is wrong with me? I'm trying to tell her about Harry's problems, and I'm thinking of kissing her neck?

"Alcohol has changed many a man," Marilyn said. Worry seemed to cloud her eyes, and Thomas knew that he'd better finish explaining so she wouldn't grow anxious; she didn't yet know that there would be no marrying his brother, so she needn't worry about Harry drinking himself into oblivion or beating her while drunk.

Thomas forced his gaze away from her lithe fingers, her soft skin, her pink lips . . .

"One night, after drinking heavily, Harry fell down the stairs," he said. "Hit his head hard on the way down and then against the floor—so hard the doctor didn't think Harry would live through the night."

"But he did," Marilyn said.

Thomas nodded. "The physical recovery took time, but his mind . . . well, it's never been the same, and the doc says it never will be. Harry's a different man now with a different personality. He has the understanding and behavior of a child of nine or ten. And that's not likely to ever change."

Marilyn's worried expression changed to one of confusion. "So how did . . .?" Her question hung in the air.

"How did he arrange all of this?" With a finger, Thomas made a circle, encompassing Marilyn, the town, and himself. "Every so often, Harry has flashes of maturity and insight. He must have had one of those and decided that he wanted a wife to come here to take care of him." Thomas kicked at some more pebbles. "He thinks you're already married and coming here to be a new mother to him."

"Oh. I see." Marilyn folded her arms as if closing herself off from him or, at least from the world.

Thomas wanted to reach out and pull her into a comforting embrace. He couldn't very well do that, of course; he was little more than a stranger to her.

Marilyn went on slowly as if piecing the puzzle together herself. "Harry wired a response to Ms. Williamson's advertisement and didn't tell you about it?" She looked up at him then as if waiting for confirmation. Her arms were still folded, and the very hurt he'd wanted to avoid showed in her eyes, along with welling tears.

Yep, he thought. *Every bit as beautiful with tears.* But the pain in her eyes made him hurt too.

"I didn't find out about any of this until yesterday," Thomas said. He almost explained how he'd found out from the banker, but closed his mouth again. She already had enough to worry about. It wasn't as if his financial situation mattered to her.

"So . . ." Marilyn pursed her lips in thought. "Will I be staying on as your housekeeper in separate quarters?"

I wish. Thomas had to shake his head. "We can't afford to pay a housekeeper right now. Things are . . . well, tight." He might have to elaborate on the bank and farm situation after all.

"I understand," Marilyn said, and the slight rounding of her shoulders spoke volumes.

She *did* know about having financial worries; he could tell. She might even know something about outright poverty. What did she know about such things, specifically? What had Marilyn Davis been through?

She sighed and looked up at Miss Faye's window. "If Harry isn't of sound mind, I don't suppose we could go through with the marriage, even if it's in name only."

"Don't suppose so." Although Thomas had known from the start that a marriage between Marilyn and his brother was about as likely as a coconut tree growing in Wyoming, even the mention set his teeth on edge. Why, he couldn't say; it wasn't as if he needed to protect Harry from women.

Because I don't want Marilyn Davis marrying anyone else? That's silly. Soon enough, he'd shake off the pull she had on him, and after that he wouldn't mind if she went off and married whomever she pleased. Where this feeling had come from, he'd never know. But he did *like* Miss Davis. A lot.

The Sound of Home

"I can't very well live with you if I'm not married or employed," Marilyn went on. "Oh, goodness, the talk that would create."

"Wouldn't want to hurt your reputation," Thomas agreed.

"What am I to do?" She seemed to be posing the question to herself and pondering how to solve the problem.

Marry me instead. The thought popped into his head without provocation, and the words nearly slipped right out of his mouth. Thomas forced his teeth to clamp together just in time. When he could trust himself again, he said, "I suppose you'll want to go back to New York. But I can't help you. Harry took out almost all of our money from the bank to get you here."

"Oh, no." She grimaced, groaning so quietly that he almost missed it.

"Do you have anything you could sell to buy a ticket back?"

"No." Her face went pale, and her unshed eyes built up again and finally spilled over. She wiped at them and sniffed. "I can't go back," she said. "Please don't make me."

There is definitely more to be learned about Miss Marilyn Davis. The thought was one part thrilling but four parts infuriating because the idea of going back clearly terrified her. Anything—or anyone—responsible for causing that kind of fear in a gentle woman needed to be run out of town on a rail.

Marilyn gestured toward the house and faked a smile. "Maybe I could live with Miss Faye for a spell," she said at the same moment that the very woman appeared in the window and waved.

"She has just one small room with a bed," Thomas said. "We can ask around to see if there's another room for rent."

From above, Miss Faye opened the window and called out, "Thomas, there you are."

"Thank you for sitting with Harry a spell," he said. "I'll take him off your hands now."

"Oh, stuff and nonsense," Miss Faye said, wagging a wrinkly finger at him. "Come on up, and introduce me to your lady friend. Harry has been telling me all about her."

A brief yet powerful surge of panic shot through Thomas's chest. He didn't want to explain while sitting around the same table as Harry, Marilyn, and Miss Faye—not until things got ironed out. Harry's silhouette appeared, lumbering past the window. He never had regained his coordination. He bumbled about like a baby learning to walk.

"Miss Faye," Thomas said, "this is Miss Marilyn Davis. Marilyn, this is Miss Faye."

The two women exchanged pleasantries, and then Miss Faye called, "We'll be right down." A minute later, Miss Faye appeared with Harry tagging along behind her.

He held out a hand to Marilyn. "I'm Harry."

She hesitated for only a moment before reaching out and shaking it. She smiled at Harry. "Pleased to meet you," she said.

"You're really pretty." Harry grinned.

"Why thank you," she said. "You're quite handsome yourself."

Harry stumbled toward Thomas, dragging his feet in the dust. "I told you she'd be pretty and nice," he tried to whisper, but his voice surely carried to both women. "Did you hear? She called me handsome."

A little twinge of envy went through Thomas, although he knew logically that she'd been acting kind toward his brother and that her words meant nothing more.

The Sound of Home

Does she think me handsome too? He tried not to think too hard about how much he hoped so.

"How about we go home and make supper?" Thomas suggested.

"Yes!" Harry said with a clap. He shuffled over to the buckboard, almost bouncing with excitement, but clearly couldn't get up by himself.

Marilyn watched him, and Thomas wished he knew what thoughts were going through her head. At least he knew one thing: Miss Davis was, as Harry said, kind. She didn't ignore him or brush him off as so many townspeople did, people who'd known Harry for a decade before the accident. She treated him with respect.

For the moment, Thomas was mighty glad that there was no money for another train ticket because that meant she would, of necessity, be in town for a spell.

"Thanks again, Miss Faye," Thomas said.

"I'm always nearby if you need anything," she said, and went back inside.

Thomas went to his brother, who was trying to climb into the buckboard but was unable to get his footing. "Let me help you, Harry." Thomas hefted his brother and supported his weight until Harry regained his footing and sat on the bench. Then Thomas turned to help Marilyn up. In comparison, she weighed next to nothing and soon sat beside Harry.

"Tell me about yourself," she said to him.

Harry picked at splinters on the bench. "Like what?"

"Well, like your favorite foods or games or books to read."

Thomas watched the interchange, marveling. How did she feel so comfortable with Harry, and so quickly? How did she know that the best way to handle him was to actually speak *to* him?

"I like spiders," Harry said, a bit of drool dripping out of the corner of his mouth. Without saying a word, Marilyn pulled a handkerchief from her bag and wiped his chin as if she'd done so a thousand times.

"Spiders," she repeated. "I don't know much about them, but they frighten me."

"Oh, I know so much about spiders," Harry said. "And I like them."

Thomas laughed to himself as he untied the horses, rounded the buckboard, and got in, knowing that Harry would launch into a long speech about all spiders—ones he'd caught, the different varieties and their names, which were poisonous, and on and on.

Once in his seat, Thomas flicked the reins, and they were off, Harry sitting between them and regaling Marilyn about all things spiderish. The moment felt right—even happy—in the oddest way. The only thing that would have made it better for Thomas was if Marilyn could have been sitting right next to him.

Five

All things considered, Marilyn found the drive to the Yardley farm surprisingly enjoyable. Much of that was thanks to Harry's chattering, although she could have done without hearing about the various sizes and shapes of webs, or about the spiders he'd tried to keep as pets.

Yet instead of such talk making her shudder and have nightmares, she couldn't help but get drawn into Harry's yarns and finding her heart softening toward this man who, as Thomas had said, seemed to be a child in a man's body. How could she feel anger or hurt over something this innocent, well-meaning man had done, even if it had upended her life?

Upended in a good way, I think. It might have saved my life. If I hadn't left when I did, I'd have been arrested by now.

Where she would end up from here, she didn't know. But the raw terror that Victor had sent through her was gone. Here in the West, the sheer expanse of land and space stretched on for miles without a single building reaching higher than two or three stories. There were also no swarms of people, where you had to move among thousands of strangers in a sea of anonymity—a sea of loneliness, really.

Since leaving the train station, she'd seen perhaps a few dozen people total and not a soul since leaving town fifteen minutes ago. But somehow she didn't feel lonely anymore, not while sitting on this bench of the buckboard with the Yardley brothers, listening to stories about eight-legged creatures. She almost seemed to belong there.

"Did you know that some spiders have a red picture on their backs?" Harry said. As usual, he didn't wait for an answer. "They're called black widows. I found one in the barn, and it was sure pretty. I wanted to be nice to it because I figgered widows must be sad and all, but Thomas wouldn't let me." Harry turned to Marilyn and added, "He can be strict, so ya know."

Marilyn couldn't hide a laugh; she leaned forward and stole a peek at Thomas. He shook his head with a grin.

"I'm afraid that I agree with your brother about the black widow," she said. "Those kinds of spiders may be pretty, but they're dangerous, too. Thomas just wants you to be safe."

"You think so?" Harry said in a tone that seemed to say that he'd never considered such a thing.

She nodded. "He cares about you."

"Huh," Harry said, and he pursed his lips. "Is she right?" he asked, elbowing his brother.

Thomas edged away from the elbow but patted Harry's back, holding the reins in one hand. "She's exactly right. I'm not trying to snuff out your fun. Just want you to be safe."

Harry leaned forward, resting his arms on his thighs, giving Marilyn a very good view of Thomas—something she hadn't had since they'd all gotten onto the buckboard. She'd forgotten just how handsome Thomas was, and the sight was a welcome reminder.

"She's nice," Harry declared, as if Marilyn weren't there at all. "Told ya that Mama would send us a nice lady to take care of us."

Thomas turned his head and looked right at Marilyn then, his eyes softening. She felt herself flush. It was one thing to note a good-looking man, but it was quite another to have such a man look right at you with a smile that made his eyes crinkle and his cheeks dimple. Her insides felt all warm.

"She certainly is nice," Thomas said, keeping his eyes on her for a few more seconds as if studying her before turning his attention back to the horses.

"Then I won't go looking for no more black widows," Harry said.

"Good." Marilyn patted his knee as if commending a schoolboy. "I'm glad to hear it."

As they rounded a bend in the road, a farmhouse and trees stood out in the distance. A thrill shot through Marilyn, for she knew without being told that this was the Yardley farm.

Home. We're almost home, she thought, though logic told her that it was not her home and never would be. *Wyoming is my home now*, she told herself. She might be able to make that much true.

For the last bit of the ride, Marilyn said little. Harry talked about jumping wolf spiders, but Thomas, too, seemed to have grown pensive as they neared their home. He pulled into the drive and stopped the buckboard at the back of the house.

"You two go on in," Thomas said. "I'll get the horses brushed down and fed and your trunk brought in. Harry, you get Marilyn a drink of well water and then show her the house. All right? I'll be in soon to cook us some lunch."

Harry stood up quickly, nearly knocking Marilyn off the buckboard. "My room is the biggest in the house," he said. "That's on account of how it used to be our Ma and Pa's room. Go on now." He made a pushing motion with both hands, hinting for her to get down. "I'll show you."

To Marilyn's relief, Thomas shushed Harry and got down himself, then went around to her side and helped her down.

"Wish I could say that the accident made him forget what it means to be a gentleman," Thomas said quietly. "But Harry never did learn manners as he should have."

He exchanged an amused look with Marilyn then released her. She felt the loss of his strong touch immediately and wished she had an excuse to keep her hand in his.

He'll be back soon, she reminded herself.

"Come, Harry," she said, hooking her arm through his. "Show me the house."

As the two of them moved toward the porch, Marilyn could practically feel Thomas's gaze on her back. She wanted to turn around to see if he really was staring at her, but she didn't dare. When she opened the door and stepped inside, the wagon wheels creaked as the horses moved forward again.

Once inside, Harry did exactly what he'd promised to do—he took her on a tour of the small two-story house, an excursion that took much longer than Marilyn had anticipated. He stopped to point out every knickknack, crack, and nail and tell a story related to it. By the time they returned to the kitchen, she sorely wanted that drink of water.

"Is there fresh water in the house?" she asked Harry, hoping he'd remember his brother's instructions.

The Sound of Home

He gestured toward the stove, on which, sure enough, sat a pail of water. But he didn't move toward it. Instead, he sat on the couch and scowled.

"Shall I get you a drink too?" Marilyn asked, slowly grasping how Harry's mind worked—and didn't work.

"I don't care."

"I'll get some for both of us then." First, she poured herself a tall glassful and drank it down in a matter of seconds. It seemed to soak into her parched throat, cooling her from the inside. She eyed the glass and then Harry.

He's likely to break glass, she thought. She found a metal cup in a lower cupboard, filled it with the ladle, and crossed to the couch, where he sat with folded arms, glaring at the door. Marilyn sat on the other end of the couch, holding the cup in both hands.

She hoped to say the right thing. "Harry, is something wrong?"

His jaw tightened, and for a moment, Marilyn worried he might strike her—intentionally or not. Though childlike, he was much bigger and stronger than she. But then his chin began to tremble.

"I want a black widow," Harry said. "I don't care what Tommy thinks. I'd take care of it. I wouldn't hurt it. He's just mean."

"Here's some water," Marilyn said, holding the cup out and hoping she'd be able to redirect his attention as she used to do with children at the orphanage years ago. He looked at the cup but didn't take it. "Harry," she tried again. "Some water might make you feel better."

He eyed the cup suspiciously for a moment then took it from her. He just stared at its contents. Then he threw the cup across the room, spilling the water in an arc.

"Oh!" Marilyn said in stunned surprise, unsure what to

do. Should she get up, find a dishcloth, and dry the mess? Or would that only enrage Harry further?

Harry burst into tears and leaned forward, putting his face in his hands. Marilyn's mind raced in circles. Was he upset over the water, or over not having a black widow as a pet? Had her presence upset him, or had this simply been a long day? Was he upset over Miss Faye somehow? And what should she do?

Again she thought back to the orphanage and to times when she'd comforted children younger than herself. She scooted closer to Harry, and, after a moment's hesitation, put her hand on his shoulder. His hiccuping cry hesitated, and he turned his head slightly in her direction.

"I'm sorry you're sad." She patted his back gently as she had comforted young Doyle long ago.

Harry's expression changed; he still cried, and he was still clearly upset, but the anger seemed to drain out of him. He sat up slightly, so Marilyn leaned to the side in an effort to look into his eyes. Instead of looking back at her, Harry threw himself her direction, practically draping his tall form around her as he sobbed into her shoulder.

After her initial shock—and after righting her balance—she realized that he was indeed behaving like young Doyle had. *He wants comfort, not solutions or platitudes or distractions.*

She patted his back again and whispered into his ear. "Go ahead and cry," she said. "Let it all out. There's a good boy."

He willingly did exactly that, his large frame shaking with sobs as he wailed even louder. If he could have fit onto her lap, he probably would have tried to get on it. A sense of maternal protection came over her. Harry seemed to be a child in every way that mattered, and he needed the kind of comfort his mother would have given him if she were alive. That's what he thought Marilyn had come for.

She found herself stroking his hair, saying things like, "Sh—there, now," and, "that's better."

After several minutes, Harry took a shuddering breath, then another, and then a third more controlled and even breath. Marilyn slipped the handkerchief from her pocket and handed it to him, still patting his back. He held the cloth with both hands, pulled back, and blew his nose so loudly that it sounded like a trumpet. Then he sat back and looked at her, rubbing one eye with the back of his hand and then the other eye, and smiled sheepishly.

"How about you go lie down in your room?" Marilyn suggested. "I'll get you some more water, and then you can rest for a spell."

"I don't wanna take a nap."

She smiled at that; he really was a child in so many ways. "You don't have to," she said. "Just lie down and think of stories you can tell me about the farm. I'd love to hear about the kinds of things you and your brother used to do together."

His face lit up. "Like the time we were killing chickens, and one ran in circles, and Tommy fell on his face, and the chicken ran right over his back?"

A light laugh escaped her. "Yes. Things just like that." She stood and pointed toward his room. "Go lie down, and think of more stories. When you've remembered ten stories you think I'd like, come tell them to me."

"I can do that," Harry said, standing. His face was still splotchy from crying, but he seemed happy. "Ten stories," he said as he waggled both hands in the air and shuffled to his room. He closed the door, leaving Marilyn in silence.

She waited where she stood in case he came back out.

She had a suspicion that Harry was indeed tired, and that lying still for any amount of time would be enough to send him to sleep. She'd used a similar tactic on Doyle and others many times. The door didn't open, so she turned and bent over to retrieve the spilled cup.

As she straightened, she startled at the sight of Thomas standing by the open back door, staring at her.

"Goodness, you frightened me." She held a hand to her chest to calm her heart.

"Sorry 'bout that," Thomas said, stepping farther into the room and closing the door behind him with a quiet click. He looked in the direction of Harry's closed bedroom door, clearly having seen some of what had transpired.

"How—how long were you standing there?" Marilyn clutched the metal cup between her hands.

"Long enough," Thomas said in an inscrutable tone.

Goodness, she thought, *how my face insists on heating at the slightest provocation.* This time, she wasn't entirely sure whether the blush stemmed from the surprise of seeing someone at the door, or from the fact that the person at the door was Thomas, who seemed to make her blush just by being nearby.

When Harry's crying bout had first begun, she became so focused on calming him that she hadn't noticed anything else. The tender, private moment between her and her charge now seemed intruded upon.

Thomas walked to the stove and, without another word, got to work lighting it and chopping vegetables for lunch.

Six

Thomas stirred the potatoes, onions, carrots, and bits of bacon in the frying pan. He added salt and pepper and a little more butter, working with his back to Marilyn. He didn't trust himself to keep his eyes away from her, and he needed to think through their situation with a clear head. Nothing about her made thinking easy for him, especially not the scene he'd walked into.

She'd only just met Harry—didn't know how his personality had changed since his accident. She had no reason to care about him. Yet she'd shown him compassion and kindness in a manner Thomas had never seen, save from their mother.

Perhaps Harry was right, he thought. *Maybe Ma did send someone to watch over us.* If so, and if Ma intended to give her sons another mother, she might have at least sent someone older and matronly, not a young slip of a thing, whom Thomas wanted to hold and protect and maybe even steal a kiss or two from. But what was he to do about her?

She'd come from back east at great expense to marry his unmarriageable brother.

She needs to go home. But the idea made his stomach feel as if a stone had settled somewhere inside it.

"Lunch is ready," he said, carrying the frying pan to the table. "It's not much to look at, but it's tasty."

"Smells delicious," Marilyn said as she took a seat. Then she glanced over her shoulder at the bedroom door. "What about Harry? Should we wake him?"

"Nah." Thomas shook his head as he sat down. "He'll be up soon enough. Best to let him wake on his own. He tends to have a decidedly unpleasant temper otherwise."

"I see," Marilyn said, and she scooted closer to the table. She clasped her hands and bowed her head, eyes closed.

Consarn it. She expects me to say grace. After Ma's death, Thomas had fallen out of the habit of praying. But he didn't want to disappoint or embarrass Marilyn, so he closed his eyes and rested his elbows on the table with his hands clasped like hers. He murmured what he hoped sounded like an adequate expression of gratitude then ended it with *amen.*

Ma wouldn't be pleased to know that I'm rusty at praying. He pushed away a twinge of guilt and offered to dish up some of the meal for Marilyn.

As Thomas had predicted, Harry woke up minutes later, likely from the smells wafting into his room. He livened up the conversation considerably. Afterward, Marilyn helped Thomas with the dishes.

Thomas would have enjoyed spending the time in such close proximity to her a lot more if Harry hadn't talked for the duration about various scrapes and mischief he and Thomas had been involved in as children. With the last fork dried and placed inside the utensil basket, Thomas draped his dish towel on the back of a chair to dry.

"Time for me to go out and finish up some chores," Thomas said. "Do you think you'll be okay with Harry for a spell?"

"Could I come along?" Marilyn asked. "And Harry, too? I'd like to help."

"You don't need to do that," Thomas said. "Remember, I can't pay—"

"I want to help," Marilyn interrupted. "It's the least I can do to repay your generosity." She smoothed back some stray wisps of hair and added, "Besides, I'd rather like to see what life on a farm is like. My only experiences are from the big city—a lifestyle quite different from yours, I'd wager."

"Indeed." Thomas eyed her, wishing that he knew what made her tick. She pulled out a hairpin, adjusted the twist, and slipped it back in to hold the hair in place. With her arms raised so, he had noticed something on her right wrist. She lowered her arms, but he walked over and gently reached for her right hand. She flinched slightly but didn't pull away. She hardly seemed to breathe as he turned her hand over, revealing a dark bruise around her wrist. Now that he looked closely, he could see that it went all the way around. He traced the purple and green marks gently with a finger, but she still sucked air in through her teeth.

He looked at her, searching her face for an answer to the question that made him feel both protective of her and furious toward whomever had laid a hand on her. "Who did this?" he asked quietly.

For several seconds, she avoided his gaze and even tugged at her hand briefly, but then stopped, as if she didn't really want to free herself. Slowly, she raised her eyes from their hands. Their gazes met, then held, for several seconds, during which they ignored Harry's rendition of "Cotton-Eyed Joe" and made the cat dance in his lap to the beat.

Marilyn's face had paled, and she looked away from him, her face a mask of pain and fear.

Thomas softened his tone further and tried again. "Marilyn. Please. Tell me who did this to you."

She didn't answer at first. But eventually, she licked her lips and nodded toward her carpetbag. "I'll show you."

She waited, then looked down at her wrist, still in his gentle grasp, until he came to his senses and released her arm. She rubbed her wrist then went to her bag, returning a moment later with a folded newspaper.

"I found Harry's ad in here the same day that I was threatened by another man." She laid the paper on the table and pointed to a dark circle drawn around an article.

Thomas leaned over to read it—a short notice about the suspicious death of a man. "I don't understand," he said. "Did you know him?"

"No." She smoothed her skirts, lifted her chin, and went on. "A man named Victor Hallows demanded that I marry him, and I refused." Her gaze drifted to the newspaper. "He and Mr. Fletcher knew each other in some capacity—something illicit, no doubt." She shuddered slightly then went on. "Victor claimed to have evidence to implicate me in Mr. Fletcher's death."

"What evidence did he have?" Thomas asked, certain even without hearing the words that Marilyn was innocent of any wrongdoing.

"A tin of arsenic that he would claim belonged to me," she said. "I've never purchased arsenic for anything. I've used it at the bakery to get rid of mice, but that poison belonged to Gerald and Ruth, and—"

"You didn't kill anyone," Thomas said.

She looked up at him in wonder. "How can you be so sure? You hardly know me."

"I don't know how I know," he said. "I just do." Thomas crossed his arms and leaned against the counter. "I suppose this Victor is responsible for killing Fletcher?"

"I believe so," Marilyn said. "Though I have no proof. I simply couldn't marry a murderer. But Victor said that if I refused him, he would have me arrested and tried for the murder." She reached for the table and turned the paper over so the article lay face down, as if that would somehow keep Victor Hallows at a distance. "He has connections in business and government," she continued, hands clasped so tightly that her knuckles turned white. "And I don't know where else. He is highly respected, so his word, unfortunately, would have been believed over that of a poor orphan girl, especially if he had managed to plant a tin of poison in a place that I could have had access to."

So many thoughts and emotions rushed through Thomas—among them a desire to find one Mr. Victor Hallows and throttle the very life out of him. But that didn't seem like the right thing to say now. "That's horrible," he said instead.

"But then I found Harry's advertisement on the same page," she said. "So fortune smiled on me and gave me a way to escape."

"I suppose so." Thomas now understood why Marilyn had looked so afraid at his suggestion that she should return to New York. No wonder she wanted to stay out West, even if it meant living in a tiny room like Miss Faye's.

Marilyn waved a hand as if shooing the subject away and turned to face Harry. "Come along," she told him. "We're going outside to—" She paused to consult Thomas. "What will we be doing, exactly?"

"Repairing a few holes in the fence," he said, a bit confused.

"Right." Redirecting her attention to Harry once more, she said, "We're going to repair a section of fence. I'm sure you can be a great help with that, right?"

Harry nodded enthusiastically. "Yup. Let's go," he said, and he lumbered for the door. Halfway there, his boot caught on a knot in the wood floor; he stumbled and would have ended up landing on his face if Thomas and Marilyn hadn't both reached out to steady him. In the process, Thomas's hand found hers, as they both supported Harry's back. Thomas would have been happy to keep his hand on hers indefinitely.

"I'm fine," Harry said, stepping forward, out of their reach, and heading outside. Marilyn exchanged a look with Thomas, smiling shyly, then followed Harry.

The three of them spent nearly two hours in the back pasture. Marilyn asked all kinds of questions about things Thomas hadn't given much thought to before, such as why barbed wire was shaped as it was, why cows tried to escape, and how long had it taken to build the fence. She seemed to genuinely want to know the answers, and she didn't shy away from the work. She knelt in the dirt right next to him. She held pieces of wire as he cut, hammered, or twisted, as the case required. She found tools he needed from the bag he'd brought along. She continued to ask him questions.

And in between all of this, she also kept Harry occupied and close by, so he wouldn't wander off or hurt himself. She gave him assignments that he happily carried out—to gather ten stones shaped like hearts, to count the trees along a nearby mountain ridge, and to find pictures in the clouds overhead.

Thomas worked on the fence the entire time, but he remained keenly aware of everything Marilyn did and said. He noted how she didn't complain, even when a barb poked her finger and drew blood. How she held the wire in awkward positions until her arms trembled. All the while, she never complained about the heat or dirt and never said a word about wishing she'd stayed behind with Harry.

Somehow, Harry had remained more well behaved and agreeable today than in any time in recent memory—a veritable miracle in and of itself. Marilyn seemed to have a way with Harry.

Just the type of caring woman Harry needs, Thomas thought. She'd proven herself to be a hard physical worker, too. *If she stays, she could be an asset to the farm.*

She was both pretty and kind. But what Thomas remembered most vividly were the times their arms had brushed against each other and how, when Marilyn's hair had been only inches from his face, he smelled lavender.

She's just the type I need, too. The thought popped into Thomas's head before he knew it. His skin almost prickled with Marilyn's nearness. *Stop it,* he ordered himself.

He finished hammering in the last nail then quickly stood and began collecting his tools in hopes of chasing off thoughts of pretty, kind, smart, and hardworking Marilyn and of what life would be like if she did stay. She followed his lead, gathering his hammer and nails as he carefully wound the spare barbed wire into a loose coil.

She is just the type of help the farm needs. This statement appeared in his mind suddenly in a tone that almost sounded like his mother's voice. He didn't chase the thought away this time. Instead, Thomas walked slowly to his leather satchel and worked there silently, packing up tools, trying to think.

Ma, did you send her? he thought. *Because if you did, you might be on to something. Maybe Miss Davis could help both of your boys—help Harry along and help me keep the farm. She works hard, and she seems to like it here. If you were around, I wouldn't be so far behind on everything. No one could take your place, but a woman like her...*

Marilyn came over and knelt across from him. She slipped several tools into his bag then looked up at him. "What now?" she asked. "Are there more chores to do? I've always wanted to learn how to milk a cow."

"Stay," Thomas said suddenly.

Her brow furrowed as she seemed to be trying to follow his train of thought. "Stay here," she guessed, "with Harry?"

Thomas shook his head to tell her no as well as to chide himself for being so harebrained in his approach. Somehow, the brother with the injured brain seemed to have more finesse in wooing women than Thomas did.

Harry probably had help contacting Ms. Williamson in the first place, Thomas realized with a start. And then he smiled.

"What?" Marilyn asked, leaning back slightly with a suspicious air. "You suddenly have a mischievous expression, and I'm not sure I trust it."

"We live in a small town without a lot of people," he began.

"Yes . . ." she said, her voice trailing off in obvious confusion.

"News—and gossip—tend to travel quickly," he said.

"Yes . . ." she said again, her tone shifting to one of caution.

Thomas nodded at his brother, who was blowing away the white globe of seeds from a dandelion. "If I were a wagering man, I'd bet that most of the townsfolk think Harry sent the telegraph to Ms. Williamson on an errand—that I sent him to do it." He scuffed a rock with the toe of his boot. "They probably think that I was the one looking for a bride."

"That makes sense," Marilyn said. "Although that would

mean—" She stopped suddenly, and her eyes widened as if she just now understood what he was suggesting. That they make the rumor true. Matching pink spots bloomed on her cheeks.

"Would that be so terrible?" he asked with a shrug, hoping to appear casual, though his heart was hammering in his chest. "As you said before, it could be in name only between the two of us, but a marr—*that kind of arrangement*—would certainly prevent townsfolk from talking."

Why was speaking to her suddenly so hard? He could hardly look at her for nerves as he went on. "You'd be able to stay in the house, lend a hand with the work—which would be a great help, if you're willing—and keep an eye out for Harry." He snuck a glance at her. While her shock seemed to wane, the lively expression in her eyes earlier had also dimmed.

She smoothed her hair back—there was that dodgasted bruise again—and said evenly, "That sounds wise, all things considering." Then she lowered her face and stared at her hands in her lap. "I suppose the sooner the better," she added, "if we want to avoid gossip."

"Agreed." Thomas hated that she sounded disappointed. He was offering her a permanent home and a way to remain out of Victor's clutches, were he to ever track her here.

I've been decent to her, haven't I?

Or am I so awful that the very thought of marrying me is enough to depress a woman, even if it means her safety?

He waited for her to look up, so he could see her eyes again, hoping to see something in them besides disappointment. When she didn't lift her face, he went on. "The farm always has chores that need doing. You're welcome to help tonight. Then I'll get some supper on, and I'll go to fetch the preacher." He paused, hoping for some kind of reaction. "Is that all right with you?"

She nodded but said only, "Yes, thank you."

Seven

After several more hours of work—irrigating fields of alfalfa, thinning rows of corn and carrots, mucking out the horse stall, feeding the cows—the three of them walked back to the house in silence, the Yardley brothers flanking her. For herself, Marilyn felt more bone-deep fatigue than she could remember feeling ever before, and her muscles hurt all over, many of which she hadn't even known existed. She could only imagine how she'd ache come morning.

And I thought that bakery work was hard because of the early morning hours.

She eyed Thomas as he walked at her side. "I could make something to eat, if you'd like," she offered, "so you can leave to fetch the preacher sooner." Truth be told, she didn't relish the idea of cooking—she had appreciated Thomas's skill in the kitchen earlier—but she felt indebted to him, and she certainly couldn't repay him with money. Besides, getting the marriage settled before she spent a night under the Yardley roof seemed prudent. If Thomas had guessed correctly at the town's gossip and assumptions—and she had no doubt that he had—then the preacher would likely be expecting a visit anyway.

"Good plan. Thank you." He sounded perfectly mannerly and cordial.

And therein lay the problem.

Every minute that Marilyn had spent in town, she'd come to find Thomas more and more attractive—physically, of course, but over the course of their day together, he seemed as amazing in other ways too.

Would that he saw something more in me than a lonely, poor woman in need of a home like a stray puppy.

Thomas Yardley had proven to her that goodness ran through his very core. Many men in his shoes would have sent Harry off to an asylum, sold off the farm, and drunk the proceeds. Many men would have turned a woman like her around and sent her back east, regardless of the fate she'd face there. Instead, Thomas had welcomed her into his household and treated her well.

He was nothing like the men she'd known in New York, who'd turned to ladies of unseemly character. She suspected he was nothing like most men in the West; she'd heard stories about brothels and such. And she knew in her bones—every bit as deeply as she now felt weary of body—that Thomas Yardley had never, and would never, do such a thing.

He didn't have a temper like Victor's, either. Instead, Thomas had shown indignation over how Victor hurt her. Thomas had invited her to stay under his roof, and he'd even agreed to fetch the minister to make her an honest woman under the circumstance. Thomas had a gentleness that complemented his strength and intelligence. Put together,

The Sound of Home

those characteristics created a man she could only have dreamed up before.

She had one remaining wish: that he'd see her as more than a poor girl in need of rescuing. Her heart felt dangerously on the verge of falling headlong in love with this man. It was the fear—of living near him but not *with* him, of not being a part of his life and heart the way he'd already become a part of hers—that had cast a shadow over her otherwise good fortune.

Inside the kitchen, Thomas showed her where to find pantry items, and then he headed out to saddle up his horse. Marilyn stood by the back window, looking out at the stables until he left. Only then did she turn to light the stove.

Be glad, she thought. *He's a good man, and you came west without ever expecting your future husband to be anything close to Thomas Yardley's equal. Stop moping and be happy.*

She made a simple meal of biscuits and sliced ham. An hour after she'd expected Thomas to return, Marilyn and Harry ate together in silence. After she and Harry had eaten their fill, she set some food aside for Thomas and did the dishes while Harry got ready for bed.

Still no sign of Thomas. Night fell, another hour passed, and a twisting worried her middle. Where was he?

She helped Harry get to bed. She taught him how to say prayers then tucked him in and sang a lullaby. With the sun down, the summer heat faded quickly, and a nipping chill came over the house, so Marilyn lit a fire in the fireplace. She selected a novel from the small collection on the mantel, then sat in the rocking chair, which likely used to belong to Mother Yardley. Rocking back and forth with a comforter across her knees, Marilyn read about a boy named Huck, who sought adventure, and a slave named Jim, who sought freedom. She related a bit to both of them.

When the fire had died down, making it hard to read, she debated whether to add more wood. *Perhaps I should go to bed,* she thought. *What time is it, anyway?* She yawned and walked over to the clock on the mantel. It was nearly eleven. Worry gnawed at her again.

Thomas is a grown man, she reminded herself. He knew this area, and she didn't. If something had gone wrong, she couldn't go for help until morning anyway. So she might as well go to bed and assume that Thomas would return safely in the interim.

But what if something *had* happened to him? What would she do then? She had no rights to this house, and Harry would be sent only God knew where, and . . .

Marilyn went to her trunk to distract herself as she'd distracted Harry earlier. *Better to keep myself moving so my imagination won't get the better of me.*

She bent over to find her nightclothes, but at the sound of clopping hooves, she froze and listened, thinking she'd imagined the noise. There it came again—definitely horses, and more than one.

Was it Thomas and the preacher? Or could Victor have possibly found her? She silently backed into the shadows by the stairs, snatching a poker from the fire as she passed it. She didn't want to use the weapon, but would if the need arose.

Now she heard voices. *Definitely two men.* But nighttime and distance seemed to distort them, so she couldn't determine whether one of the voices belonged to Thomas. As the horses came to a stop and the men dismounted, she could hear them walking on the gravel outside. Her hand tightened around the poker as she waited. The back door opened, and Marilyn gritted her teeth, bracing herself.

The Sound of Home

A man in a black suit stepped inside and removed his hat. At the sight of his priest's collar, Marilyn leaned against the wall in relief. Thomas came in a moment later, all smiles. He hadn't been hurt, and Victor hadn't found her. With each realization, she felt a bit more light-headed, and realized a second too late that she'd been locking her knees. She felt herself going limp then heard Thomas curse and run to her, catching her just before she could hit the floor.

"Marilyn. Marilyn!" he said. "Can you hear me?" But Thomas's voice seemed far away as if he were yelling from the other end of a long tunnel. "Please, no. Stay with me. Please." She felt him patting her cheek, but when she couldn't wake up at that, he cradled her head between his hands and laid it on his lap. "Father?"

Another voice spoke—the priest? If only she could open her eyes to see.

"I believe she's had a fainting spell," the other man said.

A moment later, a damp cloth pressed against her forehead, cool against her hot skin.

Finally, Marilyn had the wherewithal to make her eyes flutter open. Thomas gazed down at her, his brow furrowed deeply with concern. She managed a smile, and he sighed with relief, smiling back—a sight she would never tire of.

Perhaps I will be happy, she thought, *married to the man I love, even if he doesn't love me back.*

Thomas helped her into a sitting position and then propped her against the side of the couch. "You scared me something terrible," he murmured.

"Sorry," she said. "I didn't know if it was you or . . . or someone else."

"Victor?" he asked.

She nodded, ordering her fear to stand aside for the moment. *Thomas doesn't need to see me quivering like a kitten.*

"He won't be bothering you ever again," Thomas said. "I promise you that."

"I hope so." She wished his promise could be true.

"I'm sorry I was gone so long," Thomas said. "I didn't expect to be so long at the telegraph office."

"I don't understand," she said. This time she looked at the priest for help.

"Father O'Malley's my name. Your fiancé did something remarkable tonight," the priest said, kneeling beside her and placing a hand on her shoulder. "Got the telegraph operator to open up after closing time, and he sent some urgent messages. Turns out that the police in New York stay up even later than Thomas does."

Marilyn's tired mind still seemed filled with cobwebs. She looked at Thomas, who slipped a supportive arm around her shoulder. She sighed into his form but asked, "What does he mean?"

"He means that I exchanged several messages with the police. About twenty minutes ago, we got word that Victor Hallows was arrested for Mr. Fletcher's murder." Thomas lifted one shoulder in a half shrug. "I told them about his threats to you and asked them to look for a tin of arsenic in his living quarters," he explained. "They found one."

One hand flew to her mouth. "He's in jail?" she said. "He's really in jail?"

Thomas laughed with happiness. "He is, and I'm quite sure he'll be there long after a trial."

Renewed energy coursed through Marilyn's veins. She had to move, had to stand up. Thomas and Father O'Malley helped her to her feet. Once upright, she found herself still needing to lean on Thomas to stay on her feet, but she didn't mind being steadied by the embrace of his strong arms one bit. In fact, for the first time in her memory, she felt perfectly safe.

The Sound of Home

"This young man just had to clear things up for you back east before tying the knot," Father O'Malley said.

Marilyn had to lean her head back quite a ways to see Thomas's face. "Why?" she asked. "Why did you do all of this—and tonight?"

"Because you deserve to have a choice," he said. He reached up and brushed her hair from her forehead. She closed her eyes and drank in the fluttery sensation. "Marilyn, if you'd rather leave town, find work and a home elsewhere, you're free to now. You don't need to marry me to escape Victor."

"Oh," she said. That was kind of him, definitely. But, did this mean that he wanted to be rid of her?

"Or," he went on, pulling her a bit closer, "you can choose to stay here and make a life with me." He glanced at the bedroom door. "And with Harry, of course, but I'm hoping that I hold the greater appeal." He chuckled then reached for her hand and held it, stroking her palm with his thumb. The feeling was so heavenly that she could have fainted straight away again.

When he spoke next, Thomas looked right into her eyes. "I'd *really* like you to stay," he whispered, making it feel as if they were alone. "I—I've come to care for you, Marilyn Davis. If one day is enough to feel more than general affection, I might say that I'm starting to feel something much, much more than that. But if you don't feel the same way..."

"Oh, but I do," Marilyn said, laughing through sudden tears. "I definitely do. I was afraid that you didn't, and I was loath to entirely muss up your lives or stay on as nothing more than a caretaker for Harry."

Thomas released her hand and gently wiped her tears from one cheek and then the other. "I can assure you," he said, "that you'll be far more than Harry's caretaker. I truly hope you'll be my wife—and *not* in name only."

To her left, Marilyn heard Father O'Malley give a contented sigh, reminding her that they were not, in fact, alone. She and Thomas separated slightly, both clearing their throats.

"Oh, don't stop on my account," Father O'Malley said, grinning. "I'll be ready whenever you are. Take your time."

Thomas looked at Marilyn and lifted one eyebrow as if in question. She knew what he meant without words and stood on tiptoe to reach him as he placed a gentle kiss on her lips. It lasted only a second or two, but that was enough to cause a flurry in her middle. She wanted to be able to kiss him for longer and any time she wanted to—to be able to be held by him throughout her life. But they couldn't do either under Father O'Malley's amused, watchful eye.

Marilyn turned to him and said eagerly, "We're ready."

"We'll need a witness, won't we?" Thomas asked. After the priest's nod, Thomas took a step away, still holding Marilyn's hand, and knocked on Harry's bedroom door.

"Won't he be terribly upset?" Marilyn asked, remembering the caution from earlier that day.

"Not for this, he won't," Thomas said. "He'll be happier than a weasel in a henhouse." Sure enough, Harry cheered when he heard the reason for Father O'Malley's visit. He performed his job as witness solemnly, standing there in his long nightshirt and bare feet.

The ceremony was a bit unorthodox—Marilyn didn't know a soul who'd had a wedding that resembled this one in any way—but it was perfect for her and Thomas. When Father O'Malley pronounced them husband and wife, Thomas kissed her again, this time so thoroughly that she wondered if her feet would ever touch the ground again.

The Sound of Home

Harry went back to bed, and Father O'Malley said good night before mounting his horse and trotting off. In the distance, Marilyn heard howling. "What's that?" she asked Thomas.

"Just coyotes," Thomas said, wrapping his arms around her from behind and holding her securely. He kissed her cheek and murmured, "They're far away. No need to worry."

"Oh, I'm not worried." Marilyn turned in his arms until she faced him, wrapping her arms about his neck. "I just wanted to know because that's the sound of home."

ABOUT ANNETTE LYON

Annette Lyon is a Whitney Award winner, a three-time recipient of Utah's Best of State medal for fiction, and a four-time publication award winner from the League of Utah Writers, including the Silver Quill Award in 2013 for *Paige*. She's the author of more than a dozen novels, almost as many novellas, several nonfiction books, and over one hundred twenty magazine articles. Annette is a cum laude graduate from BYU with a degree in English. When she's not writing, knitting, or eating chocolate, she can be found mothering and avoiding the spots on the kitchen floor.

Sign up for her newsletter at AnnetteLyon.com/contact
Find her online:
Website: AnnetteLyon.com
Blog: blog.AnnetteLyon.com
Twitter: @AnnetteLyon
Facebook: Facebook.com/AnnetteLyon
Pinterest: Pinterest.com/AnnetteLyon

For Better or Worse
by Sarah M. Eden

OTHER WORKS BY SARAH M. EDEN

Seeking Persephone
Courting Miss Lancaster
The Kiss of a Stranger
Friends and Foes
An Unlikely Match
Drops of Gold
Glimmer of Hope
As You Are
Longing for Home
Hope Springs
For Elise

One

Greenborough, Colorado, 1879

Following his brother out West had been Gerald Smith's first mistake. Staying had been the second.

"We'll have an adventure," his brother had said.

"We'll be pioneers," his brother had said.

"I didn't find near enough gold in Colorado; I'm going to Dakota Territory," his brother had eventually said, leaving Gerald to pay off all the debts they'd accrued over the previous two years while they'd been busy *not* finding gold.

Prospecting was no more certain than gambling. Gerald had given it up the moment his brother's no-good, traitorous rump disappeared over the horizon. He'd spent the two years since digging himself out of the hole, both figuratively and literally. He had enough of a crop to eat year-round, a good milk cow, two fine horses, a roof that only leaked in one particular spot, and a growing herd he hoped to one day turn into a growing profit.

He wasn't necessarily comfortable, but he wasn't starving. Still, a man could only eat eggs and biscuits so many days in a row without feeling a touch deprived. He hadn't the time for making anything else.

His nearest neighbors regularly took pity on him, inviting him over for supper and sending him home with extra. Bob Attley and his mother were more than generous. Their attentions leaned heavily toward smothering.

"Thank you kindly for the meal, Mrs. Attley." Gerald grabbed his hat off the rack by the door. "I always look forward to your cooking."

"What you need isn't my cooking. You need someone to cook for you." Mrs. Attley said that often.

As always, Bob shot Gerald an apologetic look. Gerald had long since learned to ignore the heavy hints Bob's mother tossed at him at the end of every meal they took together. He simply plopped his hat on his head and pulled open the door. This time, however, Bob followed him out.

"I ain't meaning to pry," the man said, "but why is it you never found someone to cook and clean for you?"

"What woman's gonna want to come work for a surly man like me?"

Bob shook his head. "I hadn't meant hiring someone on. I was talking about finding yourself a wife."

"So was I."

Gerald knew perfectly well the life he had to offer any woman. Long days. A lot of work. No luxuries, sometimes not even all the necessities. Still he couldn't help wondering what it would be like to have someone nearby, other than the Attleys.

He thought on that as he made his way home. He would like someone to talk to, someone to share the load. His brother didn't seem likely to return, so he had resigned himself to doing the work alone. He was tired and, though he didn't like to admit it, more than a little lonely. Living as he did, so far from civilization, there was little hope for relieving the long, quiet hours in any way other than finding himself a wife.

Though he'd dismissed the possibility any number of times, that night he lay awake, wondering what it would be like to have someone else in the house. If he were to send for a wife, would that make things better? Would she talk his ear off? Or be more inclined to listen as he spoke his thoughts? He would come home from the fields to a warm meal, instead of needing to make himself another pan full of fried eggs. That'd be a fine thing.

Who was to say they wouldn't at least get along, perhaps even learn to love each other? He wasn't, after all, such a gruff, unlikeable fellow that no woman could ever grow fond of him.

And he wouldn't be so lonesome.

That, alone, made the prospect very, very tempting.

"It seems to me that this Mr. Smith you've agreed to marry is not at all the sort you ought to marry."

Mary Hill had listened to the same argument again and again from her landlady in the three days since she had accepted a much needed, though secondhand, offer of marriage. A man who would send for a stranger to marry likely had something so wrong with him that no one he knew would agree to be his wife, her landlady had argued. He would likely mistreat her, had been the further argument. It was a good one, truth be told.

But Mary had no family, no home, no secure job. The world was a difficult place for a woman in her situation.

Accepting a mail order marriage was far from ideal, but, then again, so was starvation.

"This may not be the romantic love of a lifetime most girls dream of," she said, "but that does not necessarily mean it will be miserable. I have no doubt Mr. Smith has chosen a mail order bride for the same reason most Western men do: there are no other options. That area of the country is not exactly overrun with women, you know."

Her heart dropped at the less than enthusiastic argument. Even she couldn't make the prospect sound entirely hopeful.

"I have heard disheartening things about these Western men," her landlady said. "Very rough around the edges. No tender feelings or sensibilities whatsoever. The wives they order aren't worth much more to them than their cattle, sometimes even less. I can't imagine that's what you want."

What I want and what is possible are no longer the same thing.

She reminded herself of that as she packed her meager belongings. She was not a pessimist, but she had learned to take a logical view of the world. She was tired of moving from house to house, tired of never being qualified for a decent job, tired of being alone.

This was her only option. The *only* one.

The realization didn't prevent her from hesitating when the time came to board her train. It didn't stop her from chewing her fingernails during the entirety of that day's ride westward. It certainly didn't stop her heart from dropping clear to her boots at the sight of a tender, loving young couple across the aisle in the passenger car.

Her decision made sense. In fact, she firmly believed it had been the right one. That didn't stop her from worrying.

She closed her eyes as the miles flew by, resting her head

against the back of her seat. What if her landlady had been right after all? This man she was marrying might very well be an absolute terror. There'd be no escaping, no changing her mind, and she likely wouldn't know the truth of his character until after they were married.

Mary didn't know what awaited her in Greenborough, Colorado. But she could make the best of whatever it was. She would be the hardest working, most determined optimist Mr. Smith had ever met in his entire life. And she would hope—desperately hope—it was enough.

Two

"You'd best throw in another bag of flour," Gerald said. His woman'd be doing a spell more cooking than he did. He'd stopped by the mercantile to purchase supplies. What else would a woman need? "A bar of that lavender soap, as well."

Mrs. Barnett, who, along with her husband, ran the mercantile near the train depot, watched him with wide eyes. "Lavender soap? I've never known a bachelor to ask for lavender soap."

He picked up a small jar of dried herbs. "Might send some to m'aunt. It'll be her birthday soon." Lies seemed a safer course of action than the truth. If he let spill he'd sent for a woman, every female within miles'd be knocking down his door wanting to socialize with the new arrival. He'd really rather spend their earliest days together getting to know one another rather than hosting the entire valley.

Mrs. Barnett placed the paper-wrapped soap on the

counter beside the tin snips he was purchasing. "Anything else?"

It'd be a bit late by the time he and Miss Hill—Mrs. Smith she'd be by then—reached home. He ought not expect her to make dinner. "Have you any of your meat pies?"

"I do, indeed." Mrs. Barnett smiled proudly. She was quite famous in these parts for her meat pies. "One? Perhaps two, if you're particularly hungry."

"Three."

Mrs. Barnett's surprise only slowed her down for the briefest of moments. "Three? You must be quite hungry today."

"I am." Actually, he hadn't had much of an appetite all day. Few things made him nervous, but this day's business did.

He paid for his purchases and tucked his newly acquired items under his arm. He dipped his head in Mrs. Barnett's direction before moving to the door.

He knew nothing of his coming bride other than her name, that she was coming from Nebraska, and that she was a woman. While he wanted to insist he wasn't bothered by all the empty spaces in his mental picture, it did weigh on him more than a bit.

So long as this Miss Hill was an improvement over the Miss Hill he'd known in Ohio in the years before he and his brother had left for the West, he would be satisfied. She had been only a year or two younger than Gerald and had fancied herself the third member of their little band, despite both Gerald and Tommy telling her otherwise any number of times. She'd been a pebble in his shoe for two years. A wife ought not to be a pest.

He tossed his smaller items into a basket tied to the bed of the wagon, then checked to make certain the Barnetts had loaded the correct amount of flour, sugar, and lard. Satisfied that all was well, he hopped up and onto the front bench. He set the horses in motion and tooled his way down the street to the depot.

This one wasn't a busy stop on the rail line. Very few people ever came to Greenborough. Gerald preferred it that way. He knew he shouldn't've followed Tommy, but if he was to make his home here, he'd prefer it be a peaceful one.

He found a shaded spot not far from the depot and tied his horses up there. The sun was nearly at the midway point in the sky. Miss Hill's train was due a little before noon. Soon, then. Gerald leaned against the side of the wagon and waited.

Though he knew it was pointless, he spent some time wondering about his coming bride. Was she short or tall? Pretty or plain? Soft-spoken or outspoken? He'd told the matchmaking company that he needed a woman who could cook and work hard. Other than that, he hadn't the slightest idea what to expect.

The sound of an approaching train whistle pulled him from his distraction. This was the moment of truth. She was here.

He stood up straighter as the sleek, black steam engine ground its way to a halt in front of the depot. The screech of metal on metal never had been a pleasant sound, but he found it almost welcome in that moment. Fetching himself a bride hadn't exactly been a dream of his, but now that the time had come, he felt a pulse of anticipation pounding in his neck. Things were going to change now; he hoped for the better.

The train stood utterly still. Passengers looked out of the soot-stained windows, eying the tiny place with equal parts confusion and dismissiveness.

The man who ran the depot didn't step outside to greet the train. He likely wasn't even in today. There was little point being there unless a large delivery was scheduled. Only Gerald met the train. And only one train door opened.

A porter hopped out of the second passenger compartment, a trunk in hand. He set down his armful, then turned around and held a hand out in anticipation of a passenger.

Gerald stepped closer, eying the empty doorway. Tall? Short? Pretty? Plain? How would the woman turn out?

The quickest flutter of yellow skirts skimmed the edges of the doorway before disappearing once more. Yellow? That was not a very practical color.

He moved closer still, wanting a better view when Miss Hill finally made her full appearance.

"I almost forgot my bonnet." A woman's voice emerged in the exact moment the yellow dress reappeared. In the next instant, she stepped out into the light.

"You're Miss Hill?" he asked.

"I am." She looked back at the train as she answered him, then down at her traveling bag. "I don't suppose you have brought a wagon. Even if the porter were to allow me to carry my trunk, I don't imagine I could get very far with—"

Her words stopped the moment she looked directly at him. Her blue eyes pulled wide. Her dark eyebrows shot upward. "Gerald? Gerald Smith?"

He narrowed his gaze. She did look familiar, though he couldn't identify her.

"No." She shook her head and stepped back. "You can't be my Mr. Smith."

"If you're Miss Hill, I'm your Mr. Smith." He studied her even as he spoke. Heavens, but he was certain he knew her.

A terrible suspicion entered his thoughts. He'd known another Miss Hill; he'd been thinking of her only a moment earlier. If this Miss Hill looked familiar, and he'd known only one Miss Hill, then this woman was...

"Ah, blasted, doggone—"

Miss Hill—Mary—spun on her heels and stepped back toward the train. It, however, began moving in the very instant she approached, having completed its brief business in Greenborough.

Mary stood with her back to him, watching the train pull away. She didn't say a word; he suspected he knew exactly what she was thinking and feeling. An arranged marriage to a complete stranger was one thing. An arranged marriage to a person one already disliked was quite another entirely.

"This must be some kind of gull. I've been hornswoggled or something," Gerald said.

Mary snatched the handle of her traveling trunk and dragged it along the train platform toward the small one-room building that served as the depot office.

How had this happened? Of all the women in all the country who might've been picked to come West and fill his house, why had he been sent this one? They'd not cared for each other as young people; they'd certainly not do so now. It was Bob Attley's fault. He'd been the one to put the idea in Gerald's head. Without that prodding, he'd never have found himself in this mess.

Mary, having tested the door and found it locked, had resorted to knocking on the window. "Hello?" she called out.

She could knock all afternoon for all the good it'd do her. The building was empty and likely would remain so for days, perhaps weeks.

Gerald set his hat on his head once more and stomped

back to his waiting horse and wagon. The sooner he returned home and put the entire ordeal behind him the better. He would simply write to the marriage-arranging company and tell them to send someone else. Anyone else.

He climbed onto the wagon bench and took up the reins. No one could expect him to do anything other than return home.

But he made the mistake of looking back at the depot. Mary stood there, a look of worried confusion on her features as she peered up and down the railroad tracks, one hand on her hip, the other brushing a stray bit of brown hair away from her face.

I can't leave her here. But neither could he take her home with him. Doing so would require they be married. Nothing else would do. He might've been rough about the edges, living in the uncivilized West, but he was no scoundrel. But marry her? Mary Hill, of all people. Mary Hill, who'd driven him mad and pestered him clear out of temper for years.

He rested his elbows on his legs and leaned forward. He'd once resorted to hiding in an outhouse for more than an hour, waiting for her to give up searching for him just to be free of her for one blessed afternoon. She'd followed him through their small town, into his family's fields; anywhere he went, she was there.

The experience might've been a flattering one if she hadn't been so blasted pestery. "What are you doing? Why are you doing that? May I see? May I help? What should we do today? Why won't you do what I want to do?" Ceaseless questions.

And now she's meant to be my wife. I'll never escape. Not ever.

Nope. He wouldn't go through with it. Mary'd simply

have to fend for herself. She was a woman grown; she could manage that.

He looked over at her again, apparently not one to learn from his mistakes. She sat on her traveling trunk, facing the empty track. Hers was a posture of waiting. Did she mean to simply remain until a passenger train stopped in Greenborough? Heavens, she might be sitting there for weeks.

He muttered to himself as he climbed down once more. For four years he'd been free of Mary Hill dogging his heels. Now he was responsible for pulling her out of another scrape. Why was it the fates hated him so much?

His boots hit the planks of the platform with a forceful rhythm borne of frustration and disappointment. He'd let himself imagine pleasant things about the woman he'd been sent. He ought to have imagined the worst outcome possible. Then at least he wouldn't have felt so misled.

"You can't sit here forever, Mary," he said. "You'll have to be coming along with me."

She shook her head firmly. "I'll simply wait for the next train."

"The last time a train stopped to take on or let off passengers was well over a month ago. You'd be a fool to sit here for weeks on end."

She folded her arms, lifted her chin, and turned her head in the direction her train had come. "I'd be a fool to marry a man whose poor opinion of me I remember very clearly."

"Who said anything at all about marrying you, woman?"

"That is why I am here. We both know that."

She'd be in for quite a surprise if she thought he meant to move forward with that plan. "I ain't marrying a woman

I'd likely throttle in the first week. But I also ain't leaving you here all by yourself."

"If you are suggesting I live in your house without—"

He pushed out a frustrated sigh. "I'm taking you to the preacher's house. He'll know what to do you with you until you can find a train back to Ohio."

"I haven't lived in Ohio for years. You aren't the only one who has had adventures."

Adventures. He shook his head at the poor fit of that word. His time in Colorado had been a lot of things, but an adventure wasn't one of them.

"A train back to wherever in the world you'd be heading back to," he amended. "It don't matter a lick to me. Come on, then."

She must have gained some sense over the years since he'd last seen her. With no more argument than her small bit of protest from a moment earlier, she began dragging her trunk toward his waiting wagon.

He took it from her and hefted it into the wagon bed. She climbed up on the wagon bench, hugging the far side, leaving a canyon-sized gap between them. Gerald held a rather neutral position on religion, but in that moment he thanked the heavens for Reverend Carter.

Three

Mary prided herself on being clever, but she'd been a fool this time. The security of a home of her own, the call of the West, the hope, however vague, of being cared about had spoken to a deep need in her. She'd known the decision was a gamble, that there was no guarantee the stranger she'd pledged herself to would prove kind or loving or good. But there'd been nothing for her in Nebraska.

Colorado had been her promised land and "Mr. Smith" her last thread of hope.

Gerald. Why did he have to be *Gerald* Smith? She knew perfectly well how little the man thought of her. He'd disliked her when they were younger. He'd told her the day he and Tommy had left to seek their fortunes that he wouldn't miss her for even a moment.

She'd mourned his departure, though not for the reasons he would likely have assumed. Mary knew full well that Gerald believed she'd dogged his heels in order to make a nuisance of herself. He'd thought her little more than an irritant—he'd told her as much often enough. It was far more than that, however. Far more.

Her uncle Bill had come to live with them not long after they moved to Ohio. He had made her life a nightmare. But Bill kept away when Gerald was around. Something about the younger man had intimidated him. She had, therefore, kept close to her neighbor for years, despite knowing he rather hated her, because when she had been with Gerald she had been safe.

For two years she'd spent hours every day with Gerald. Sometimes she'd talk; sometimes she'd listen. She had, for two years, spent more time with him than any other person, and he'd never stopped disliking her. Spending a lifetime with him wasn't likely to change that.

"Either you've stopped being chatty over the past four years or I've lost my hearing." Gerald always had been a touch grumpy. That much hadn't changed.

"I'm rather tired is all."

Her stomach chose that exact moment to loudly protest its empty state. Mary set her gaze on the horizon, hoping Gerald hadn't heard the telltale rumble.

He gently pulled back on the reins and brought the team to a stop. Mary could see no reason for him to do so. No home sat nearby. No church. This wide-open area hardly seemed the place to find the preacher.

Gerald reached behind the bench and pulled a small paper-wrapped parcel from the back. He set it on the wagon beside her. "Here," was all he said.

"I don't understand."

He clicked his tongue at the horses and flicked the reins, setting the wagon in motion once more. "They're meat pies," he said, tipping his head in the direction of the parcel between them. "It was meant to be dinner tonight."

"Dinner for you and your wife," she countered. "Since that is not going to be me after all, I won't take your food away from—"

"Stubborn and prickly. You've not changed."

"Unfortunately," she muttered, "neither have you."

They continued on in stony silence as the minutes passed. The parcel sat, unopened, the contents uneaten, all the way to a turn in the road where a small church sat beside an equally small house. Both were tinted with the thinnest layer of white as if there'd not been enough paint to do the full job.

Gerald stopped the wagon directly in front of the buildings, but didn't immediately hop down. "There're enough meat pies for the both of us, as that'd been my plan. So it does me no good to keep 'em all to myself. You'd do well to eat one while the preacher sorts things out."

"Eating in front of people would be rude," she pointed out.

"Requiring Reverend and Mrs. Carter to feed you when they hadn't been planning on doing so would be ruder." He shot her a look of tried patience. "Eat, woman."

"I would far prefer you call me Mary."

His shoulders dropped. "Eat, *Mary*," he corrected. "Please."

The "please" was unexpected and, if she wasn't entirely deceiving herself, sincere.

She took up the parcel and offered a quiet, "Thank you."

A moment later they were standing at the preacher's front door. Gerald stood with his hat in his hands. It might have been a humble posture on anyone else. He had been intimidating even at seventeen. Now twenty-three, he likely could be quite frightening when he chose to be.

The door opened, and a woman, her salt-and-pepper hair pulled back in a loose bun, greeted them.

"Ah, Gerald. And—" Her eyes darted from one of them to the other. "I don't believe I met your—?"

Apparently, he hadn't told anyone his plans to bring home a wife.

"Is the reverend about?" Gerald asked.

"Of course, of course." She stepped back, motioning them inside. "Come in, please."

Gerald met Mary's eyes and pointed his chin in the direction of the house. That, it seemed, was his way of offering to allow her to step inside first. She kept the paper-wrapped meat pies close to her. They were no longer warm and, more likely than not, would leave grease marks on her dress. But having something to cling to—*anything* to cling to—brought a certain comfort.

Their hostess stepped into a simply furnished parlor. "Dearest, Gerald Smith has arrived."

Mary looked at Gerald, unsure how he meant to go about explaining their situation. She would have gone about it herself, but he actually knew these people. It made far more sense for him to undertake the explanation.

"We've a problem, preacher," Gerald said. "I sent for a wife, a mail order bride, but they sent me Miss Hill here."

That was one way to summarize the situation.

"And you object to Miss Hill?" the preacher asked.

Gerald nodded. "Things won't work out between us."

Reverend Carter looked up at last, his heavily wrinkled brow pulled deep. "You've realized this in the short time required to drive from the train depot?" He shook his head. "That seems a rather drastic conclusion, especially from two people who willingly agreed to marry complete strangers."

"I'd've married a complete stranger," Gerald said. "But I know Mary. Knew her when we both lived in Ohio."

"You are acquaintances?" Mrs. Carter clapped her

hands together, a wide smile touching her maternal features. "What a joyful coincidence."

"No, dear," Reverend Carter said. "Gerald has declared he hasn't come here to be married. That is hardly joyful."

"Why in heaven's name would you rather marry someone you don't know than someone you do?"

Mary felt it time and past that she spoke on her own behalf. "Because we had two years in which to decide if we cared for each other. We discovered we didn't."

"But you might now," Reverend Carter insisted. "You would both have been quite young all those years ago."

"Some things don't change," Gerald said. "But now I don't know what to do with her."

Reverend Carter's expression turned immediately stern. "'What to do with her'? Gerald, you've brought her all the way to Colorado on the promise of a home. You had better do right by her."

Mary was no wilting flower, shriveling at the thought of not having a man to look over her. "I would really rather not marry a man who clearly does not wish to marry me."

"My dear, you agreed to marry a stranger. The time for being picky has passed."

She didn't want to admit that the preacher was likely right, but he was. Frustration bubbled anew. This had been a bad idea from the beginning.

"What, precisely, were you hoping to accomplish here, if not a wedding?" Reverend Carter asked Gerald.

"Mary needs a place to stay and food to eat. She can't sit at the train depot for days on end, hoping a train stops."

Reverend Carter began shaking his head before Gerald had even finished his explanation. "We do not have the room for nor the provisions to feed another person. Ours is a poor community with little to give. Mine and Helen's circumstances are no better than most."

Mrs. Carter set an arm around Mary's shoulders. "Come, let's step into the lean-to and leave the men to discuss their business."

"As that business impacts my future, I would like to remain and participate in their discussion."

Mrs. Carter was, apparently, not expecting that. She sputtered a moment before trying once more. "The men can manage this. We'll just step away and give them a moment's privacy."

"I would prefer to stay."

"She's stubborn as a polecat, Mrs. Carter," Gerald said. "You'll be wasting your breath by arguing."

Stubborn? Did he truly think her insistence on having a choice in her own future was merely a matter of being stubborn?

"Perhaps, Gerald, you might step into the lean-to with Mrs. Carter to discuss something mundane while I decide what is to be done. I will be certain to let you know what path I have decided you ought to walk."

"Retract the claws. I wasn't going to insist you leave." His attention returned to Reverend Carter. "There must be someone nearby who needs a woman to do some work, who has room enough for another body and food enough for another mouth."

It wasn't the most personal appeal for her well-being. Besides, she'd spent enough time as a servant. She'd come West to find a home.

"You sent for a wife, Gerald. And you've received one." For a man with a stooped posture and quiet, unassuming demeanor, Reverend Carter was proving unmovable. "Now it's time for you to fulfill your commitment."

"Reverend," Mary stepped into the conversation. "He doesn't wish to marry me. He didn't like me when we were younger. There is little reason to believe he could learn to do so now."

The Reverend's eyes narrowed on her in a studying manner. "This is the second time you've told me *he* doesn't want to marry *you*. The only objections I've heard from you are the result of his. How do you feel about marrying Gerald Smith? Do you dislike him as much as he dislikes you?"

That was a sticky question. "He disliked me first, so I can't say how much of my opinion of him is merely a distaste for being rejected so out of hand."

If her answer surprised Gerald, he didn't let it show. She likely hadn't been subtle about her interest in him when she was quite young. Her fifteen-year-old self had been quite smitten with seventeen-year-old him when she'd first arrived in that small Ohio town. Her starry-eyed infatuation hadn't lasted terribly long; Gerald had been far too obvious in his distaste for her company. Still, he had apparently seen it and hadn't forgotten.

Mary refused to be embarrassed by those long ago feelings. They'd quickly died, to be replaced by a simple appreciation for his intimidating demeanor. He'd unknowingly protected her from the unkindness of her uncle, and for that reason she would do her best not to think too ill of him.

"You seem an honest and forthright young lady," Reverend Carter said. "I have known Gerald these past four years, and I can assure you he is a hardworking man of integrity. While you may have disliked one another as children, I have yet to hear an unaddressable obstacle to your success now."

"We weren't children," Gerald muttered. "And I never said she was a scoundrel or any such thing—she wasn't. We're a bad match is all."

Reverend Carter shook his head. "You had fully intended to make the best of whomever you were matched with. You can simply do so now. Both of you."

"But if he is determined not to like me—"

"That could have just as easily happened with a stranger, Miss." For a preacher, Reverend Carter was not terribly empathetic. "What the two of you need right now is a little determination."

"But—"

"No one here has the means of hiring you on. Few have the means of feeding another person even if they wished to. There may not be another train for weeks. This is your situation, and you need to make the best of it."

One look at Gerald told her he was coming around to the preacher's way of seeing things. "You've nowhere to stay except with me. And we'd none of us allow that if the two of us weren't married."

"Gerald—"

"We accepted a mail order marriage knowing the risk, knowing the chances of failure, intending to make the most of it. I think we'd best do just that."

Reverend and Mrs. Carter nodded their agreement.

"Everyone is very unconcerned about this." She couldn't possibly be more concerned than she was. "He has already told me he doesn't like me. He told me for two years. The day he left Ohio he told me he wouldn't miss me for even a moment. How can you not be concerned about that being the basis of a marriage?"

"That does not sound like the Gerald I know," Mrs. Carter said.

"Sounds far more like Tommy, if you ask me," Reverend Carter said. He looked over at Gerald. "My apologies if speaking ill of your brother brings offense."

"It ain't nothing I don't already know."

"You agreed to this," Reverend Carter told her once again. "For better or worse, you've nowhere else to go. This is your only option."

While Mary knew they were right, she couldn't rid her mind of worry. This was the rest of her life, after all, her chance for happiness. She had to have some reason to believe that chance hadn't vanished the moment Gerald had appeared on the train platform.

"May I speak to you a moment, in private?" she asked him.

He agreed with a nod and motioned her a bit to the side of the room.

She rallied her courage and pressed forward. "I know you dislike me. I know you always have. But will you—*can* you—promise that you'll at least try to make this a happy marriage? At the very least try to make it not an *un*happy one? I have to go forward with some reassurance."

"I ain't never been the courting kind," he said. "Sweet words and flowery speeches . . . that's not me."

"That's not what I'm asking."

He studied her a moment, though what he was looking for she couldn't say. "Have you ever known me to be unkind, Mary? Truly unkind?"

Of course she hadn't. It was one of the reasons she'd turned to him to escape the cruelty of her uncle. Though Gerald hadn't liked having her about and had made no secret of that dislike, he had never been cruel.

"Do you think we can make this work?" She was asking herself as much as him.

He shrugged the tiniest bit. "There are worse things than marrying someone from my growing-up years. You could've turned out to be a murderer." His gaze narrowed on her. "You're not a murderer, are you?"

"Not yet," she muttered.

A smile tugged at one corner of his mouth and brought a twinkle of humor to his brown eyes. He hadn't smiled much, even when they were younger, but she'd never forgotten the change it wrought in him. The man was inarguably handsome when he smiled.

"Any other requests?" Gerald asked.

She had one—she had a very crucial one—but she couldn't force herself to speak it out loud.

Gerald stepped closer and lowered his voice. "What is it, Mary? I can see there's more."

"Will you promise—" No, she couldn't say it.

"Promise *what*?"

"Will you promise not to—" She had to finish her question. Knowing the answer would change things. "Will you promise not to hit me?"

Gerald's mouth dropped open, and his brow creased. "Hit you? You think I'd—? Good heavens, Mary. What kind of a person do you think I am?"

"That's what I'm trying to discover," she said. "And it's far easier to face down the monster I know than the one I don't." She'd stood firm before her share of them. No one had been permitted to see vulnerability in her since the day she'd left home.

Gerald set his fists on his hips and narrowed his gaze on her. "I ain't never hit a woman in all my life. I don't mean to start now."

The surge of relief she felt took her by surprise. She'd been more worried about that than she'd allowed herself to admit. An arranged marriage was a risk, no matter how one looked at it. And she knew better than most the misery a man could inflict on the women in his life. But she'd had no other options. None. It had been a risk she'd had no choice but to take.

Maybe being accidentally matched to Gerald Smith wouldn't be such a terrible thing after all. Maybe.

Four

Gerald had fully expected some awkwardness the evening of his wedding. A stranger would be in his house, trying to make herself comfortable there. But having that stranger be Mary Hill only added to the discomfort.

She'd not said a word during their long drive from the Carters' home to his. She sat stoic and emotionless. He hadn't the slightest idea whether or not she was happy about how things had turned out for them.

Will you promise not to hit me? That question hung heavy in the back of his thoughts. Had she asked because she felt he, in particular, was likely to be violent toward her? Or had the question arisen because someone else had beaten her?

He hadn't been part of her life the past four years. Anything might've happened to her in his absence. Perhaps her mother had remarried, choosing a man who had treated his new stepdaughter with unkindness. Perhaps Mary, herself, had attached herself to someone violent.

She had been a pebble in his shoe, yes, but much of that had come from naïveté, from her inherently trusting nature. He had recoiled at her constant, pestering presence, but he'd never wanted anything bad to happen to her.

He pulled the wagon to a stop in front of the house. Mary sat as silent as ever, looking up at the home that would now be hers as well. He saw it with a critical eye for the first time: the small size, the sparse kitchen garden, the greased-paper windows in need of glass.

"It ain't much to look at," he said.

"Your family's home in Ohio had green shutters as well."

He hadn't really given that much thought, but she was right. That was likely why he'd chosen green shutters for this house. "My ma'd be pleased to know I brought something of home this far away."

"Have you not written and told her?"

"I write to Ma regularly, but I can't say I've mentioned the shutters."

She looked up at him. "Will I get a mention in your next letter? I daresay she'd be rather shocked."

"She and Pa, both." Although they'd both rather liked Mary. They, in fact, were the reason he had endured Mary's constant presence.

"She's such a sweet thing, and so fond of you," Ma had said. "Be patient with her."

"She needs your kindness," Pa had said. "Be gentle with her feelings."

What would the two of them say to hear he'd done more than be patient and gentle, but had actually married her?

"They were always so kind to me," Mary said, a wistfulness in her tone. "I think I was happier at your home than anywhere else."

He watched her a moment. She had seemed happy when she was with his family, but he hadn't thought she'd seemed unhappy at other times. He'd seen her at church on Sundays, and she'd been fine. He'd seen her walk home from school the first year he'd known her, before she'd finished her schooling, and she'd smiled and laughed as much as ever.

"I can see I am trying your patience," she said, "as usual." She slid to the far end of the wagon and climbed down. "Point me in the direction of the kitchen, and I'll start supper."

"We do have the meat pies yet."

She reached back up and pulled the parcel of pies off the wagon bench. "I'll warm them up."

Mary was showing herself a logical sort of person. If she'd also developed a strong inclination toward work, she'd do well in the wilds of the West.

Gerald climbed down and wrapped the horses' reins around a porch post. "C'mon in." He motioned her up the porch and to the front door and let her inside.

Why in heaven's name was he holding his breath? He'd not cared before what anyone thought of his home. Why should he now?

"It's humble," he told her. "I've not been here enough years to make much in terms of money, and I'm determined not to mire myself in debt trying to gather fancy things."

"I lived in the back room of a boardinghouse before coming here," Mary said. "Even the humblest of homes would be an improvement over that."

She stepped inside and pulled off her shawl, hanging it on a hook near the door.

"Why were you in a boarding house? Surely your mother—"

"Mother died some time ago. I didn't choose a mail

order marriage for the excitement of it, Gerald. I'm quite alone in the world, and that is a dangerous position for a woman." She turned about, pies tucked under her arm. "Which direction is the kitchen?"

He wasn't so easily satisfied with her explanation. "What about your uncle? What was his name? Burt? No, Bill. What about your Uncle Bill?"

She shook her head. "I haven't seen him in four years."

Four years? "He must have left Ohio shortly after Tommy and I did."

"*He* didn't leave." She crossed to a door, pulling it open. "Closet." She pulled open another. "Corridor." She turned back to face him. "Where is the kitchen?"

"If he didn't leave, then you must have." It was the only other explanation. "But why?"

She held his gaze a moment before answering. "Did Tommy never tell you?"

"Tell me what?" Obviously something about her.

"Hmm." She opened another door, the right one this time. "The kitchen, at last."

He followed her into that room. "What didn't Tommy tell me?"

She set the pies on the table. "It doesn't matter now."

What in heaven's name had his brother kept from him? Something that might explain her leaving when he did. "Were you—" He felt stupid even asking the question, but he wanted to clear things up if he could. "Were you in love with me?"

She smiled a little. "No, Gerald. I didn't confess to your brother an undying passion for you."

"Then what?"

She shooed him out. "Go see to your horses and your evening chores. I'll have the pies warmed and ready when you return."

Mary pulled open a couple of drawers, then snatched from one of them a kitchen towel and tied it around her waist like an apron. She met his eyes once more. "Go on," she said. "I'm certain you have plenty to do."

He never had been one for giving up a mystery so quickly. "How soon after I left home did you leave?"

She pulled open the firebox of the cast-iron stove. "About two weeks."

She had insisted she wasn't following him, but that seemed rather like. "Where did you go?"

"At first to different towns in Ohio." She added kindling to the firebox. "I had finished school, so I was able teach in a few places until they found a qualified teacher. Then I was a girl-of-all-work for a few families here and there."

Gerald had known a few girls and women who'd filled that thankless, back-breaking role. He didn't at all like the idea of her living that life. "Your mother didn't go with you?"

"She stayed at home with Uncle Bill." Mary found the flint box and made quick work of lighting the fire. "He wrote a few months ago and told me she'd passed on and had left him the home and land and not to bother returning. Apparently, he thought that was something I wished to do."

"But you didn't?"

She looked up at him from her position at the stove. "Home is not always where the heart is." She closed the firebox and began searching the cupboards, clearly intending to get straight to work.

She'd been a pampered girl in the years he'd known her. Nothing about her fit that description any longer. There'd not been even a moment's hesitation when the time had come to work. She'd learned to light a fire, to cook a meal. And she'd spent years on her own, away from her family, away from those who might have coddled her. "Pampered" was clearly not the life she lived.

There was a different air about her now. Before, she'd seemed forever on the verge of bursting, taking in the world with wide eyes and hopeful enthusiasm. Those eyes were now wary. Her steps seemed measured, her very posture one of readiness for some disaster or another. Life had not treated her well these past years.

"I am sorry about your mother," he said.

She didn't look back from her search of his kitchen drawers. "I mourned the loss of a mother years ago, when I first left home. While I still miss her, the pain is not so acute as it once was."

He didn't like the pain and suffering he continually heard behind her quick explanations of her life. She'd been a pest, yes, but he'd cared about her. He still did.

He hadn't chosen her, and she certainly hadn't chosen him, but this was what life had handed them. While he'd never intended to mistreat his new bride, he felt an unexpectedly strong surge of determination to make his home a safe harbor for her.

Over the next fortnight, Mary came to a firm realization. Gerald had sent for a mail order bride not out of a wish for courtship and romance, but out of a need for someone to work with and someone to talk with. There was no better way to explain their days than that.

He quietly went about his work, returning for meals. While they ate, he spoke of the land, the neighbors, the plans he had for securing a dependable income. He welcomed her thoughts and asked after her day. At night, he thanked her for the work she'd done, told her he'd enjoyed her company, then went to bed. In his own room.

He never put an arm around her or held her hand. He'd certainly never kissed her. And while she wanted to believe that this was how he'd intended his marriage to play out even before recognizing her on the train platform, she had watched over the past two weeks as the room she now called her own had slowly emptied of his clothes and books and other belongings.

She had hoped that her arranged marriage would eventually lead to true affection, perhaps even real love. She suspected he had as well. Did he never mean to try? Were there never to be any loving glances or fond caresses? She had spent years as a girl-of-all-work, resigned to laboring in a home that never would be her own for people whose feelings for her never went beyond indifference. She didn't like the idea of continuing on that way for the rest of her life.

But what could she do about it?

She looked up from her sewing and out the front window. Life was not perfect, but she did have a lovely view. A view that, at the moment, was revealing a small cloud of dust, distant on the road. She rose and stepped closer to the glass.

Was someone coming? In the two weeks she'd been in Greenborough, she'd not had a single visitor. Gerald had told her that the residents were few and scattered, and they didn't often see one another.

She set aside her mending and hurried from the house and across the yard to the barn. The dim interior was lit enough for her to see Gerald's broad frame hard at work dropping hay into the animal stalls.

"Gerald?"

He turned at the sound of her voice. She thought she saw a flicker of pleasure when he looked at her, but she couldn't be at all sure. Perhaps she was only seeing what she hoped to see.

"Someone is coming," she said. "I can see the dust they're kicking up down the road."

He leaned against his pitchfork. "I wonder who that'll be."

"I haven't the slightest idea." She hadn't met anyone after all.

"I'll come have a look." He set his pitchfork against the wall of the loft and climbed down the ladder.

She likely should have gone back to the house—he probably expected her to—but she waited and watched his approach. How little had changed since they were younger. She still hoped and silently pleaded for him to notice her there, to put a reassuring arm around her. Her reasons during those years had been a bit different than they were now, but they were every bit as strong and heartrending.

He'd come to the place where she stood. His gaze slid over her face. "Are you unwell, Mary?"

She shook her head. "I'm a little weary, I suppose."

"Are you working too hard? I'll not have you wearing yourself to the bone and growing ill. This is meant to be a good life for you, not a burdensome one." He said things like that often, thoughts just tender enough to make her hope there was more beneath them than a tentative friendship.

"My thoughts were too full last night for sleeping well is all. I'm not working too hard, I assure you."

He didn't seem satisfied with that answer. "Do you need to lie down?"

"No."

His gaze flicked to the barn door. "Are you nervous about the visitors?"

He was attentive, just not in the way she needed.

How would she ever receive the things she needed, or at the very least know that those things were out of her reach, if she never spoke of them? She simply had to find the courage to do so.

"Gerald?" Her voice emerged quieter than she'd expected and far less certain. She swallowed and pressed forward. "Would you—?"

He didn't look away, didn't seem the least put out by her bumbling attempt at a request.

"Would you hold my hand?"

His brows pulled low immediately. "Hold your—? You said you weren't afraid of the visitors."

"I'm not."

"Then why do you need me to hold your hand?"

Because I need a moment's affection. Because the young girl who once adored you would like to know you don't resent her now. Because I can't live the rest of my life entirely unloved.

She couldn't find words she was willing to speak out loud to explain this aching need in her. She wasn't asking for him to fall desperately in love with her or to suddenly be all tender affection. She simply needed something from him. Anything. The tiniest reason to hope things would get better.

"Never mind," she said, stepping back toward the door. "It was silly."

His longer strides caught up with her quickly. She didn't turn back or stop walking.

"Mary, please." His hand, gentle on her arm, stopped her at last. "Do you want me to hold your hand?"

She wanted to say no, that it didn't matter. But she couldn't lie, so she simply nodded.

"May I ask again why?"

She took a deep breath. "Because I always imagined that someday, when I was married, my husband would hold my hand. My father held my mother's hand. It was how I knew they were happy and that she was cared for. I know ours is not the ideal marriage they had, but I'd like to have at least that small piece of it."

It was a far more vulnerable explanation than she'd intended to offer, but it was the truth.

His warm, calloused hand, slid down her arm, and his fingers wrapped gently around hers. "Mary Smith, I promise you here and now that I will hold your hand anytime you wish for it. Only, please don't run away from me when you're needing something. I can be prickly and rough and difficult, I know that. But I don't want you to be unhappy."

"I don't want you to be unhappy either." She dropped her gaze to his hand, engulfing her own. "And I know you didn't want to marry me, of all people."

His thumb rubbed a slow circle along the back of her hand. "There is one advantage to marrying a childhood playmate as opposed to a stranger."

"What's that?"

"Well," he said, "for one thing, you've seen me at my worst, so you aren't likely to be shocked when my charm starts to wear off."

There was just enough cheek in his words to add a bit of welcome humor. She found she could even smile. "Oh, have you been trying to be charming all this time?"

"I've been at my most charming. Hadn't you noticed?"

"Oh, dear," she said dryly. "You may have to work on that."

"And that's another good thing about being previously acquainted," he said. "You're already comfortable enough to tease. A sense of humor's an important thing out here where life can be hard."

She held fast to his hand, reveling in the warmth and reassurance he exuded. "Life can be hard no matter where a person is. I've found it usually is, in fact."

His gaze turned to the horizon and the cloud of dust growing closer. "I'd wager you are about to meet our nearest neighbors. Brace yourself, Mary. The Attleys are exhausting."

She leaned her head against his arm. "You may have to hold my hand through the entire ordeal." Though she made the comment in jest, the idea appealed to her more than she'd expected it to.

He squeezed her fingers. "Come on, then, Mary. Let's introduce you to your neighbors."

He didn't release her hand as he walked with her to the new arrivals' wagon, or as they invited the Attleys inside, or sat on the sofa, visiting. She knew he kept her hand in his only because she'd asked him to, but it was a kindness she very much needed, and in that moment it was enough.

Five

*G*erald found he rather liked holding his wife's hand. He was, in fact, discovering that he rather liked his wife, something he'd not have thought possible only a few short weeks earlier. Much of Mary's worry and wariness had eased over the almost-month since she'd arrived in Greenborough. She talked more. She laughed often. Those lighthearted bits of her personality that had grated on him as a young man were quickly becoming the highlight of his day.

Though he'd not realized it when he'd sent for a wife, he needed more than mere companionship and a helping hand. He needed a reason to smile and something to look forward to during the grueling hours of work. Mary had proven to be exactly that.

A nasty turn in the weather brought him in early. He sat on the sofa, not planning his next day or thinking about his plans to prepare for the upcoming winter as he'd have once done but, instead, listening to Mary working in the kitchen.

She hummed as she moved about. He didn't remember

her doing that when they were younger. He likely would have found it obnoxious—he'd found almost everything she did obnoxious. He'd been rather unfair to her all those years earlier.

"The stew won't be ready for another hour." Mary stepped out of the kitchen as she spoke. "You're in from the fields earlier than I'd expected."

"I'll not starve in the next hour."

She smiled. Heavens, he was coming to love that smile. "Mrs. Attley tells me that I'll never have the slightest hope of earning your affection if I let you go hungry. This next hour might undo all the goodwill we've built this past month."

"It hasn't been a terrible month for you, then?" He could hear the uncertainty in his tone and wasn't sure he liked it. While he did want her to be happy and worried that she wasn't, he wasn't used to being rendered so desperate for another's good opinion.

Mary sat beside him on the sofa. "The two years I spent pasted to your side were among the happiest I've known. Being in your company again has been lovely."

"I don't know why it is you enjoyed spending time with me back then. I was a bit horrible to you."

"Even when I annoyed you, you weren't unkind. That meant a great deal to me then. It still does."

He threaded his fingers through hers. "Your hand is warm."

Another of her smiles made an appearance. "I've been slaving over a hot stove."

"And I've been outside in the wind and rain." He pressed her warm fingers to his face, intending to show her how much colder he was. But the touch sent a shiver of awareness through him, and he couldn't find the words to finish his tease.

"You're freezing, Gerald." Mary hopped off the sofa, pulling her hand free of his before he could make the slightest protest. She pulled open the cedar chest beneath the far window and took out a quilt. "You did change out of your wet clothes, didn't you?"

"I did."

She returned to the sofa, quilt in hand. "You're still so cold, though."

"Colorado is a cold place, dear. I've been chilled through many times before."

Her cheeks reddened instantly. She pressed her lips together and lowered her gaze.

"Did I say something wrong?"

She silently shook her head, still not looking at him.

"Mary?"

She pulled the folded blanket up against her. "No one's called me 'dear' before. I know you didn't mean anything by it. I just . . ." She bit her lips closed once more, still not looking at him.

He hadn't meant anything by the endearment. But if using it would make her color up so adorably, he'd pull it out more often. He'd never considered himself a flirt. Perhaps he'd simply never had the right partner. Imagine if, rather than prickle up at her and insist she leave him alone, he'd spent their two years together teasing and flirting with her? Those years would've been a vast deal more pleasant.

"So, did you mean to give me the quilt or did you fetch it so you could hug it?"

She bit back a smile. "Of course. I was distracted."

Oh, yes. Teasing her was far more enjoyable.

Mary unfolded the quilt and laid it across his lap. When she stood, clearly meaning to go see to something or other, he took hold of her hand once more. She gave him a questioning look.

"I'd be far warmer if you stayed here with me," he said. "You do have an hour before the stew'll be ready."

She slowly, warily, lowered herself to the sofa once more. She watched him, clearly unsure what to expect. He hadn't intended to make her nervous. He'd given her all the space she could want the past month. Truth be told, that distance had been harder to maintain with each passing day. But, if she wasn't comfortable being close to him, he wouldn't force her to be.

He held her hand, but didn't draw her nearer. And he chose an impersonal topic in the hope that it would ease the uncertainty he saw in her expression. "The mercantile down by the depot has some seed still. I thought we ought to decide what we mean to plant in the kitchen garden come spring. If we have the seed already, we can begin planting as soon as the ground thaws."

She took up the topic, and, as they discussed the importance of various herbs and vegetables, she relaxed by degrees. By the time they settled the question of carrots, she'd wrapped her arm around his and leaned against him. The gesture was a quiet and simple one and, he quickly discovered, one he hoped she would adopt regularly.

"You didn't plant any beets this year, I noticed," she said from her position curled up against him. "I think that would be a useful addition."

"Ma used to pickle beets each fall. I looked forward to it all year."

"I'll pickle beets for you next fall, Gerald. I'm quite good at it."

He leaned closer and kissed the top of her head. "And what can I do for you, dear? What piece of home would you like to have here?"

She moved ever nearer, her side pressed to his. "You are

the only part of home I've wanted these past four years, and I have that now."

"Me?" He shook his head at that. "I made life a misery for you."

"I never felt terribly wanted when I was with you, I'll confess that much." She didn't look up at him, which only added to his growing guilt. "But I also never felt unsafe. That meant a great deal."

It was not the first time she'd spoken of craving the security she'd felt with him. "What was happening in your home, Mary? What was it that meant safety was a novel experience?"

He felt her shake her head. "I'd rather not talk about it. I'd really rather not even think about it."

He slipped his arm free of her embrace and set it around her shoulders. He wanted to ask questions. He wanted to know so many things about her. But he sensed that her trust in him was fragile. If he pressed, she'd simply pull away.

She tucked herself into him and set her hand on his chest. He set his free hand on top of hers. He'd meant to offer *her* comfort, but found that sitting there with her beside him was bringing *him* comfort as well. Maybe that was part of the magic of a marriage: even small gestures of kindness brought healing to both people.

Gerald closed his eyes, letting the perfection of the moment settle over him, from the smell of her lavender soap to the warmth of her nearness. How easily he could imagine spending his future this way. Theirs hadn't been an ideal beginning, but they were finding their way, slowly but surely.

A heavy, pounding knock at the front door broke the spell. Mary startled and sat upright once more. Another knock followed, just as loud and impatient as the first.

"Who could that be out in this weather?" Mary's gaze was riveted to the door.

Gerald shook off his distraction. Mary was clearly nervous. He meant to see to this visitor and set her mind at ease.

He tossed back the quilt and stood.

"Be careful," Mary said.

He gave her a reassuring smile. "I doubt someone's come to murder us or steal all our valuables."

She shook her head at him. "Well, just in case they have, I'll ask you again to be careful."

He gave a quick nod, then pulled open the door. It wasn't a band of bank robbers or a desperate stranger with shifty eyes. It was, in fact, the last person on earth Gerald would have expected to see on his front porch: Tommy.

Mary couldn't see the new arrival, but the stiffening of Gerald's posture told its own story. Someone—or some*thing*—unpleasant had arrived at their door. Gerald had offered his support time and again in her hour of need. She could certainly do the same for him.

She joined him at the door and slipped her hand in his, looking up at him with as much reassurance as she could muster.

The new arrival spoke first. "You've a woman here?"

She looked at him for the first time and nearly stumbled backward. "Tommy?"

His eyes pulled wide. "Mary Hill?" His gaze returned to Gerald. "Why's she here?"

"She's Mary Smith now. And it's your presence, not hers, that's baffling, brother."

Tommy laughed long and loud. "You married her?

Ain't that a lark. The girl you called 'The Plague' is now your wife."

The Plague. That was far from flattering. But it fit. Gerald hadn't much cared for her when they were younger. And Tommy hadn't much worried over other people's feelings. His jests had often come at other people's expense— at *hers* much of the time. It seemed that much hadn't changed about him.

"I'll go check the stew." She made to walk away, but Gerald didn't release her hand.

His searching gaze met hers. "Mary?"

"I'm fine," she said quietly. "You see to your brother."

He let her hand slip from his but with obvious reluctance. She could feel his gaze on her back as she crossed the room. She'd not yet reached the kitchen when Tommy's voice echoed from the doorway.

"Seems you didn't need to beg me to leave Gerald behind all those years ago. You sniffed him out in the end. You always were a persistent little thing."

Though his words weren't truly unkind, there was something smug and belittling in his tone.

Mary didn't look back, didn't speak. She slipped into the quiet sanctuary of her kitchen. Why had Tommy chosen that moment to invade their lives? Before his arrival, she'd been sitting in Gerald's embrace. She'd felt safe and cared about and almost . . . almost loved.

Six

Gerald turned from the door and stepped in the direction of the kitchen.

"You're going to leave me standing out in the rain?" Tommy asked.

"Do whatever you must. I've far more important people to see to than you."

He heard the front door close behind him. "Mary? Mary Hill? There must be an amusing or horrifying story behind *her* being here."

Gerald spun back around and pointed a finger of warning at his brother. "She's Mary *Smith*, and if you dare to speak to her again as flippantly as you did a moment ago, I will beat that information into your thick skull."

Tommy held up his hands in a show of innocence. "No need for threats. I didn't say anything to her that you didn't on a daily basis four years ago."

The guilt Gerald felt at the admittedly accurate accusation only further fueled his temper. "This is her home,

Tommy. She has only to say the word, and I'll toss you from it."

He didn't wait to watch the impact of his declaration on Tommy. If Mary was hurting or upset, that was far more important than his brother's sensibilities. It wasn't that he didn't care about his brother—he certainly did—he simply couldn't clear his mind of her expression when she'd told him how much she appreciated the feeling of safety she had with him, that she felt secure and looked out for when he was nearby. He wouldn't fail her in that now.

Mary was at the kitchen window, looking out at the storm. Either she didn't hear him step inside or chose not to acknowledge him there.

"Tommy shouldn't've said those things to you." It was not the most eloquent way to break the silence, but flowery speeches had never been his specialty.

She didn't turn back. "He didn't tell me anything I didn't already know. Except the part about you calling me 'The Plague.' I was aware that you referred to me as a pest and a pebble in your shoe, but 'The Plague' was one I hadn't heard."

"I was seventeen, Mary. I was young and foolish and selfish."

She shook her head. "And I was a pest and a pebble and a plague. I know that. I even wondered after you left if I'd pushed you to it, if you had crossed the country simply to be away from me."

"It wasn't you at all." How he wished they could have back the moment of closeness they'd shared earlier, rather than this awkward distance he couldn't seem to span. "He spoke so convincingly of adventure and making our fortune. As you can see, that didn't exactly turn out to be true."

"Perhaps he's come with more promises and opportunities."

"He likely has." Tommy was forever coming up with schemes.

She looked at him at last, though her expression was strained. "Then you had best go hear him out. And while you do, try to make certain he doesn't leave a water mark." Her smile was fleeting and noticeably lacking in actual joy.

"You don't think I would actually take him up on another of his schemes, do you?"

"I don't know what to think, Gerald." Did she really doubt him that much?

What reason did she have not to, though? He'd nearly left her at the train station, after having left her—at least in her view—all those years ago in Ohio.

"I'm not going to abandon you," he said. "You can trust me on that."

"Will you ask Tommy if he means to stay for supper?" Mary asked. "I'd like to know how many places to set at the table."

This, then, was his new task. Not counting place settings, but showing Mary that he was dependable, that he wouldn't fail her, that she needn't fear his desertion. It was a tall order to fill considering their past. But he had never been one to shy away from a task simply because it was difficult.

He pushed the kitchen door open once more and stood in the threshold facing the outer room and his brother, dripping at the other end. "Are you staying for supper?" he demanded.

"You wouldn't toss me out without at least a meal, would you?"

Gerald looked back at Mary. "He's staying."

She gave a quick nod as she stirred the pot of stew.

He left her to her work and the peace of the kitchen. "Do you have any dry clothes?" he asked Tommy.

His brother shook his head. "All my belongings are in a wet bundle on your porch."

"You can change into something of mine. C'mon." He motioned him down the hallway.

"I'm touched by your concern for my health."

Gerald didn't look back; he could hear that his brother was following him. "I'm not overly worried about you catching cold. But I'll not have you dripping mud and water on Mary's clean floors and making extra work for her."

"What happened to you, Gerald? I'd've never imagined I'd see you so easily whipped by a woman. And Mary, of all women. I don't know how it is you got stuck with her."

Gerald threw open his bedroom door. "I didn't get stuck. What I got was lucky. And if you'd like your luck to hold, you'd best rein in that tongue of yours." He jutted his chin in the direction of the small bureau on the far wall. "There's a few things in there. Hang your wet things on the nails so they'll dry."

"I'll be on my best behavior," Tommy promised. "Wouldn't want to upset the little lady."

Gerald pulled the door closed behind him. He'd all but forgotten what a pompous windbag his brother was. It was, he feared, going to be a long night.

"And this fellow's cousin has already made a fortune in cattle down in Texas." Tommy had finished his second helping of stew and was filling his bowl with a third. "It's the greatest opportunity of our generation, Gerald. All we need is a few head to start a herd, which I know you have, and we could be rich."

"Where've I heard that before? 'Colorado is set for a

boom. We'll be rich.' And, 'The Dakotas are dripping in gold. I'll be rich.' In case it's slipped your notice, Tommy, neither of us is rich."

Tommy was undeterred. "But this is just the thing. You've already learned about cattle, and I know the right people in Texas."

"This fellow's cousin?" Gerald made no attempt to hide his disbelief. He'd heard similar promises before.

"I know you've become domestic"—Tommy spoke the last word as if it were a bit of vulgar profanity—"but I can't let you pass this up. This is a sure thing."

Nothing with Tommy was ever a sure thing. "I'm happy where I am with what I have."

Tommy wagged a finger at him. "I'll convince you. I always do."

"I'm done following you around," Gerald said. "So save your breath, eat your supper, and make plans to set out on your own."

"Help me convince him, Mary." Tommy grabbed Mary's arm and tugged it a bit. Before Gerald could object, Mary snatched her arm free. "Just say"—he put on a high voice—"'Dearie, I'd like to be wealthy. I want you to buy me fancy things and pamper me.' C'mon. We'll talk him around."

"No, thank you." It was the first thing Mary had said all night, and she spoke without enthusiasm and without looking up at either of them.

"Now isn't the time to turn wishy-washy, Mary Contrary," Tommy said. "Nag him like you used to do."

"Do not call me that," she said firmly.

Tommy shot him an amused look, though why the man thought he'd enjoy a jest made at Mary's expense, Gerald couldn't say. "We'll convince her."

For Better or Worse

"Eat your supper," Gerald muttered. His brother was driving him mad.

"I'll convince you both." With that declaration, Tommy tucked in to his stew.

Gerald attempted to catch Mary's eye, wanting to convey if he could that she needn't worry about Tommy, that he'd find a way to take care of the problem. But she didn't look up. Her posture spoke of both worry and defeat.

Gerald didn't like it one bit.

Seven

"I talked all night, and he wouldn't budge." Tommy stood beside Mary as she hung the wash on the line. He hadn't given her a moment's peace since Gerald had left to tend the herd. "And though he said he wasn't interested, I know him better than that. Though he acts the part of staid and prudent husband, he has the Smith blood in his veins. He's itching for an adventure, I know he is."

Mary refused to believe it. Gerald had promised her he wouldn't walk out, that he wouldn't abandon her as he'd done four years earlier. He had promised.

"But he would listen to you," Tommy said. "If you told him it was a good idea—"

"I won't lie to my husband, Thomas Smith."

"It's not a lie." His voice snapped behind his usual jovial tone. "This is his opportunity. He left home for this. He's been working toward this for years."

She pinned a long bed sheet to the clothesline. "It seems to me he has invested in his land the past two years. Perhaps that is why he isn't taking you up on this grand opportunity."

"He'd leave this place in a heartbeat if he were free to do so," Tommy said.

She glanced at him. "What are you implying?"

"Nothing. Nothing." He shrugged a little. "I think it's odd, though, how hard-nosed he's being about this. Even when I left for Dakota, he spent some time thinking about coming with me. He won't even hear me out this time."

"He's put down roots," she said, grabbing her empty laundry basket and moving back toward the house.

"The Smiths don't put down roots. We've been wanderers for as long as anyone can remember." He followed her into the house. "Keep us trapped in one place, and we go mad."

We go mad. She had been a plague in Gerald's life once. She hated the thought of being that again. "Gerald may decide to go with you, but he'll do so because he wants to, not because I pressure him into it."

"Come now." He leaned against the table, his arms folded across his chest. "You can't convince me you didn't 'pressure him into' marrying you. The way he celebrated being free of you four years ago, I can't believe he jumped at the chance to have you back."

"He wasn't exactly overjoyed." She set her basket down and crossed to the sink. "But things have worked out well. He hasn't complained."

"Saint Gerald wouldn't complain. Not out loud."

She looked back at him. Her heart lodged firmly in her throat. She forced her voice past it. "He seems happy."

Tommy shrugged a single shoulder. "Maybe he has been. But he's trapped here, working land he didn't want and supporting a wife he didn't choose. I'd hate for him to come to resent either one."

He wouldn't resent her. Would he?

"Your uncle felt trapped. I saw it in his face all the time. I don't have to tell you what that resentment did."

Uncle Bill had hated living with them but had refused to leave. He'd insisted Mother needed him, Mary needed him, everyone needed him. He'd stayed because he had to; that's the way he'd explained it. And the 'having to' made him hate them. That hatred had quickly turned to unbearable bouts of anger.

"Gerald isn't like Bill," she insisted.

"I doubt Bill was always like Bill." Tommy's look was a pitying one. "I don't want to see you hurt again like you were before. Think this through. I don't want either of you to regret any of this."

With one backward glance, Tommy left the kitchen. *I don't have to tell you what that resentment did.* Again and again she heard those words. Uncle Bill had stayed because he'd had to, or at least felt he did, and she had paid the price for that for years.

She wrapped her arms around her middle in an attempt to comfort and reassure herself. Tommy's declaration was replaced by one from Gerald the night before. *I'm not going to abandon you. You can trust me on that.*

But wasn't refusing to abandon her exactly the problem Tommy was pointing out? He would stay because he felt obligated, but he would feel trapped and stuck and resentful. He had also promised on the day they were married that he wouldn't hit her. He had promised.

"You can trust me," Gerald had said.

She wanted to. She truly did.

Gerald hated to leave Mary with Tommy, but heavy

For Better or Worse

rains like they'd had the night before had been known to wash out the fences at the upper pasture. He had no choice but to check on them. He saw to the barest, most essential chores around the place, then returned to the house.

Tommy was on the sofa. "You've been gone for a while."

"I was working." He didn't see Mary. Maybe that meant Tommy hadn't been bothering her. "What've you been doing?"

"Mostly waiting for you. I did watch Mary hang up the wash. That was as dull as expected."

Gerald peered out the small side window. The wash was still hanging on the line, and Mary was nowhere to be seen. "Did you at least offer to help her?"

"I was too busy helping *you*."

That sounded ominous. He turned back, bracing himself.

"I don't want you to be trapped here, and I don't think she wants you to be, either."

"What did you say to her?"

Tommy assumed his most innocent expression. "Nothing, really. We just chatted about life and opportunities. We spoke a little of her uncle and what being tied down to his female relations had done to him."

"Her uncle?" The very man Mary refused to talk about. "What about him?"

"I got to know him a little back in Ohio. He was a lowlife. All he ever talked about was how much he hated being stuck there, but he needed the money he hoped her mother would leave him when she died."

Which was exactly what had happened in the end.

"He was why she followed you around everywhere," Tommy said. "Bill Carlton was short-tempered and violent, but he was a little afraid of you."

"What do you mean 'violent'?"

"He didn't beat on her when you were around, so she stayed close." Tommy spoke so casually about this, as if he wasn't undoing every assumption Gerald had made about Mary, as if he wasn't revealing information Gerald ought to have been told four years ago. "It's why she begged me not to take you away. With you gone for good—"

"—she would never be safe." Good heavens. It was little wonder she'd clung to him so much. She'd been beaten, hurt. She'd asked him the day they were married if he would promise not to hurt her. He'd thought it a reflection on him, but it was a plea from her past. "And you told her that I would treat her the same way her uncle did if I didn't go with you to Texas?"

"No. We simply talked about the importance of not being . . . trapped."

"So help me, Tommy—"

Shock filled his brother's expression. "I didn't do anything. We talked."

"Where is she?"

Tommy shrugged. "I don't know. She left about a half hour ago."

Gerald pulled open the door to the kitchen. She wasn't in there. He moved down the hall and opened the door to her bedroom. Empty. She really had left.

"Did she say anything? Where she was going or when she would be back?"

Tommy shook his head. "I don't think she's going to stop you from going to Texas, so that's good news."

"I don't want to go to Texas. I have never wanted to go to Texas." He opened the front door. "And if you have driven Mary away, you had better pray you reach Texas before I reach you."

"What has crawled under your skin, brother? She's a mail order bride."

"She's Mary." He yanked open the front door. "She's my wife, and I—"

"Good heavens, you love her."

He buttoned his coat up once more. "Of course I do. And we have a chance at happiness. I am not going to let you take that away."

Tommy sputtered a moment. "I didn't know. I—"

"If you need a place to stay, you remember where the sod house is. You're welcome to stay there as long as you need. But I am going to find my wife and bring her home, and it would be best if you weren't here when I get back."

"Do you want me to help you look?"

"No." He stepped out onto the porch, the wind picking up. They were in for more weather, it seemed.

Mary, where are you? If only he could find her and reassure her that he was nothing like her uncle, apologize for not realizing her situation when they were younger, promise to never let Tommy back in the house again, if need be. He would settle for begging her to give him another chance.

He'd told Tommy the truth: he loved her. It was a new and fledgling sort of love, but it was real. She was the best part of his life. He wanted her back.

She'd been gone thirty minutes or more. Even on foot she could have covered a considerable distance in that amount of time. He would reach her faster if he took the horse. Chances were good she'd made for the train depot.

He rushed to the barn, then pushed the door open. If he hurried, he might catch her in time to convince her to come back before the clouds burst. He could—

She was there, feeding his horse a carrot and rubbing its neck.

"Mary?"

She looked up at him and smiled. "You're back early. Did the rain wash out the fence like you feared?"

She hadn't left. Mary hadn't left.

She rubbed the horse's nose, then slipped from the stall. He stared—he couldn't help it—he'd been so sure she'd left him.

"Did something else happen? You look worried."

"Tommy said you left."

She snatched a basket from nearby and hung it over her arm. "I came out to fetch eggs, but your horse looked so lonely. We visited for a while."

He stepped closer to her. "I didn't know about your uncle." It was not the most elegant introduction of the topic. "I didn't know what you were living with."

Her smile was a little sad. "We worked very hard to keep all of that hidden."

"I should have noticed. I should have realized something else was happening. I shouldn't have left you."

She reached out for his hand. "You're here now."

He held fast to her fingers. "Tommy tried to convince you I wouldn't be."

"I trust you far more than I trust him."

He brushed the fingers of his free hand along her cheek. "I swear to you I will live worthy of that trust. I will do all I can to ensure you are safe and happy. Only, please, give me a chance to earn a bit of your love as well."

She leaned in to his touch. "Oh, Gerald. I have loved you since I was fifteen years old."

"Oh, Mary. My Mary." He pulled her up to him, pressing his forehead to hers. "My dearest, loveliest Mary."

"That is a vast improvement over your response to seeing me on the train depot all those weeks ago."

He cupped her face in his hands. "I was an idiot. I have been an idiot about so many things."

"It is a good thing I love you anyway."

He sighed. She loved him. His Mary loved him.

She set her hands on his chest and closed her eyes. He leaned closer and brushed his mouth over hers. Her breath tiptoed warmly over his lips.

"Oh, Gerald," she whispered.

He kissed her fully, deeply, holding her tightly to him. She clung to him with equal fervor. He'd lost her once to his own blindness, a mistake he did not mean to repeat. Fate had given him a second chance. Mary had given him a third. He wouldn't need a fourth.

"I love you, Mary Smith," he said as the rain pelted the barn roof. "I'll love you forever."

ABOUT SARAH M. EDEN

Sarah M. Eden is the author of multiple historical romances, including the two-time Whitney Award Winner Longing for Home and Whitney Award finalists Seeking Persephone and Courting Miss Lancaster. Combining her obsession with history and affinity for tender love stories, Sarah loves crafting witty characters and heartfelt romances. She has twice served as the Master of Ceremonies for the LDStorymakers Writers Conference and acted as the Writer in Residence at the Northwest Writers Retreat. Sarah is represented by Pam van Hylckama Vlieg at D4EO Literary Agency.

Visit Sarah online:
Twitter: @SarahMEden
Facebook: Author Sarah M. Eden
Website: SarahMEden.com

An Inconvenient Bride
by Heather B. Moore

OTHER WORKS BY HEATHER B. MOORE

Heart of the Ocean
The Fortune Café
The Boardwalk Antiques Shop
The Mariposa Hotel
Timeless Romance Anthologies
The Aliso Creek Series

OTHER WORKS BY H.B. MOORE
Finding Sheba
Lost King
Slave Queen
Beneath (short story)
Eve: In the Beginning
Esther the Queen
The Moses Chronicles

One

Boston, 1885

Carmela Domeneca Rosalia Callemi placed her hands on her hips and restrained herself from yelling at the two flour-covered boys in the tiny kitchen. The young boys blinked up at her, their large brown eyes wide with fear. Their dark mops of curly hair were speckled with the flour, and the white stuff also covered their faces, arms, hands, and likely other parts of their small bodies that were not currently visible to Carmela. She should yell; she should swat their behinds, but instead, her mouth twitched. Then laughter bubbled up.

The boys glanced at each other and grinned, looking like matching ghosts. They would not get a walloping—that they knew now—for their auntie was laughing too hard.

Carmela wiped the tears from her eyes then sighed. "You two. Will you ever live a day in which you don't create some sort of chaos?"

Although, life is chaos, Carmela thought. Absolute chaos since she'd arrived with her widowed brother and his two boys in America. When Paulo's wife had died of smallpox on their little vineyard in northern Italy, Paulo had said that he couldn't live in Italy one day longer and breathe the air his dead wife should be breathing too. Then he'd begged Carmela to come with him, to start anew and look after her nephews.

Carmela hadn't needed much convincing. She loved her nephews, yes, but the small village she'd lived in her whole life had been absolutely stifling. Her three friends were all married with babies on the way.

But it was like Carmela had the plague: not one man had ever turned his eye toward her. No man had ever proposed. She was plain. Outspoken. Laughed too loud. And was perhaps a bit strong-willed. All attributes that leant one to be an excellent childminder, but perhaps not attributes that made up a sweet, biddable wife.

"Auntie," Simon said, tugging at her skirt, imprinting the well-worn cotton with a bit of flour. *"Zia, abbiamo fame."*

Carmela smiled down at Simon. "English please," she said. They'd been in America six months, and Carmela had insisted that the boys learn English with her as quickly as possible. At home, and especially around their father, they often resorted to Italian.

"We're hungry," Simon repeated.

"I'll bet you are," Carmela said, feeling another laugh bubble up. "Is that why you wanted to make bread?"

Simon glanced over at his brother then nodded.

"Well, let's clean up, and then we'll go out and buy a loaf," she said. She didn't know if they had enough flour, anyway. She'd have to buy more on the way home. The thought of spending precious coins made her wince.

Simon's eyes widened at Carmela's suggestion. It would be a treat indeed.

Quicker than she had thought possible, the boys helped her clean up, and they were out the door, stepping onto the bustling streets of Boston. The day felt stifling, though it was almost sundown. The boys skipped ahead, laughing and teasing each other in a mixture of English and Italian that Carmela was sure only they understood.

As they passed along the wooden sidewalk, every so often, the boys would stop to watch a pair of horses pulling a wagon or a carriage. The boys loved horses and missed them from the vineyard. But this wasn't a luxury their father could afford. Besides, there was nowhere to keep a horse.

Then the boys stopped at a shop window and pressed their hands and faces to it, entranced by the window display of candies and baked goods. The smells emitting from the bakery were heavenly indeed.

Carmela caught up with them. Cookies and sweet rolls and pies and cakes were sitting prominently in the window, enough to make anyone's mouth water. In the lower corner of the window, she noticed that someone had pasted an advertisement that read:

> *MAIL ORDER BRIDES! The Seymour Agency is seeking women of intelligence and good moral character, educated, and thoroughly versed in housekeeping. We have select men of good appearance and substantial means, who are in want of a wife to share their western homesteads with. Please inquire at the Seymour Agency on Thursdays between the hours of 1:00 and 5:00 in the afternoon. Approved applicants will be permitted to open correspondence with a gentleman.*

Carmela found herself laughing at the audacity of the advertisement. Did the agency think that a woman would agree to marry a man over a few exchanged letters—sight unseen? she wondered. What happened when the woman climbed off the train to find that her intended had a crooked nose and broken teeth, not to mention a huge mustache and unruly beard?

"Carmela!" a woman's voice singsonged its way into Carmela's thoughts.

She turned, knowing it was Ruthie, the red-headed, blue-eyed Irish girl who was mad about her brother. *Good thing he doesn't go for the short, freckled type of girl,* Carmela thought, *not to mention the one girl in all of the world who had a laugh louder than herself.*

"Hello, Ruthie."

"Oh, you've got Paulo's boys," Ruthie said, stating the obvious. She ruffled both of the boys' heads, and they ducked beneath her touch. But Ruthie didn't seem to notice.

"Going to the bakery?" Ruthie asked, again stating the obvious.

"Yes," Carmela said. "We've seemed to have run out of flour." The boys giggled, and she hid a smile.

"I'll come in with you," Ruthie said, linking arms with Carmela.

Carmela supposed that she should think more kindly of Ruthie, but the woman was too bossy. And, with Carmela being bossy as well, it just didn't work.

She quickly bought a loaf of bread then hurried out of the shop. But Ruthie was right behind them.

"Oh, is this what you were reading?" Ruthie said, tugging on Carmela's arm. Slowly, she turned to see Ruthie pointing to the poster. "A couple of my friends have gone through that agency, and now they live in huge mansions in Montana."

Huge mansions, huh? Carmela thought as she folded her arms. "Do their husbands have all their teeth?"

Ruthie screwed up her face. "What?" Then she laughed. "Oh, you're trying to be funny. Paulo told me about that."

Paulo had told Ruthie what? Carmela wondered.

"It's a viable option," Ruthie said.

Carmela wasn't sure what viable meant, but she could very well guess.

"I mean, how old are you now?" Ruthie narrowed her eyes as if she were trying to guess Carmela's age. "Aren't you older than Paulo?"

"She's twenty-eight," Simon spoke up.

Maybe I shouldn't have taught him English after all, Carmela thought.

But Ruthie's bright blue eyes grew brighter. "Oh. You're on your way . . ." She smiled down at the boys. "I mean . . ." For once, Ruthie was at a loss for words.

Carmela took full advantage of this. "Come along, boys," she said. "We best get home and fix supper before your father returns."

Two

The night was blacker than usual when Carmela awakened. The moon that had shone into the tiny bedroom must now be covered with clouds, she decided. What had awakened her? Then she heard scuffling and a ... giggle?

Carmela was wide awake in an instant. She climbed out of bed, her heart pounding as she clutched her nightgown closed at the neck. She heard another giggle, followed by a sound of hushing.

Carmela's stomach tightened. If this was what she thought it was . . . She opened her bedroom door and stepped out into the short hallway that led to the kitchen. The oil lamp was on in the kitchen, creating a cozy glow. It took only three steps to come into full view of Ruthie, perched on the edge of the table with Paulo standing in front of her. Ruthie had wrapped her arms about Paulo's neck, and Paulo was kissing Ruthie—on her lips, on her neck—and was moving down to her gaping bodice.

"Carmela! Holy heavens! You scared me!" Paulo said, pulling away from Ruthie so quickly that she almost fell off the table.

Carmela's mouth opened, and a dozen reprimands fought for a way through, but nothing came out. She was speechless for, perhaps, the first time in her life.

"It's not what you think," Ruthie said, sliding off the table, smoothing her skirt, and buttoning her bodice.

"Don't treat me like a fool," Carmela said, her words coming fast now. "You are a fool, Paulo Callemi. You have two little boys, who think the world of you. You are in a new country with barely a cent to your name, and now you are with this . . . hussy!"

Ruthie gasped, her face growing as red as her hair. "Paulo, don't let her call me that."

Now Paulo's face was turning red, and he folded his arms, which were made strong by the mill work he did six days a week. "I'm going to marry Ruthie," he said. "And nothing you can say will stop me."

Ruthie gasped again then practically threw herself at Paulo, wrapping her thin freckled arms about his tanned neck. He turned his face and kissed her.

Carmela's stomach roiled. Ruthie was so . . . so different than Paulo's beloved first wife, Francesca. Francesca had been tall, willowy, dark-haired, golden-skinned, and soft-spoken. Carmela turned away, her eyes burning with tears of shame. If her brother was happy, who was she to interfere? Yet, her heart ached with a fierceness she couldn't explain. Had she thought she would live the rest of her life with Paulo and his two boys in this tiny apartment?

She turned away from the kissing couple, now completely oblivious to her in their new rush of felicitations for each other. Then she walked back to her room and burrowed under the thrice-patched quilt, her mind oddly turning to the advertisement pasted to the bakery window. When she'd first read it, she had thought mail order marriages were only things for desperate women—and perhaps they still were—except for now, Carmela was desperate herself.

Three

Leadville, Colorado

"God rest his soul," Reverend Stanley said, then he replaced his black hat and stepped back from the gaping hole that now housed the coffin of Gideon Butler, the older brother of Samuel Butler.

Samuel blinked his eyes against the dry wind. His brother was good and buried now, and Samuel should be grieving, but he wasn't. Gideon Butler had been a hard-drinking, foul-tempered man as long as Samuel could remember. At Samuel's age of twenty-five, there seemed to be a mile between him and his brother, Gideon, who had been thirty-five on the day of his demise two short days ago.

His death had involved a drunken brawl, three pistols, one woman, and—as rumors had circulated—a bag of silver. Although, the silver had never surfaced. Yet, Samuel wouldn't discount the rumors of silver. After all, Leadville was a booming silver-mine town, filled with men coming from the East and the West to find their fortunes. Ownership of a bag of silver was something you could live . . . and die by.

Samuel snorted at this thought, drawing the attention of the handful of mourners at his brother's graveside. One man sported a shiner, and two of the women looked like they'd spent all night in the tavern. And, knowing the company that Gideon had kept, Samuel could readily assume that these women lived in the nefarious quarters above the tavern.

The reverend crossed to Samuel and stuck out a large, beefy hand. "So sorry, Mr. Butler. Will we see you at services tomorrow?"

The reverend's words were about as subtle as Samuel had ever heard from the preacher. And, with all the effort that he'd put into this respectable ceremony for such a disrespectable man, perhaps Samuel owed the reverend something. It wasn't that Samuel was against churchgoing folks but he knew if he shut down his blacksmith shop for even a few hours on Sunday, he'd lose too much business. He had to be open when the customers demanded it.

"I'm training an assistant," Samuel said. "So, that will give me more time to see to things such as church services by and by."

"Good to hear," the reverend said in a soft voice, patting Samuel on the shoulder as if he were a small child needing the comfort. "We'll look forward to that day soon."

Samuel just nodded. *The sooner this farce of a service is over, the better,* he thought. He would never proclaim that he was even near perfect, and he certainly wasn't a churchgoing man. But, wasn't there something against a rotten-through-and-through sinner being buried on holy ground?

Of course, Samuel thought, looking over the lumps of dirt and grass that made up the Leadville Cemetery, *this ground doesn't look too hallowed.*

The distant sound of a train whistle brought Samuel's mind back to the present. He'd spent enough time away from his shop for this death business, and he had to get back. The arrival of a train from the East always brought the Leadville citizens into town—and their horses. He couldn't afford to miss any opportunities . . . not if he wanted to turn his two-room shack into an actual home.

Granted, his place was better than a shack but not much bigger. He'd put in for another acre of land as well. He just had to wait until the bank approved the loan. Samuel figured that, by this time next year, he would be the owner of a decent parcel south of town, would have an apprentice or two, and would live in a home—something that his older brother Gideon had never aspired to.

Five years ago, when the brothers had found themselves orphans and when Gideon had followed Samuel from Boulder, where they had grown up, Samuel had tried to be patient, hoping that Gideon would change his ways in a new town. Although Gideon was hired at the Dawson Silver Mine, his employment was always on the verge of being terminated due to his perpetual drunkenness.

The only misgiving that Samuel had now about his brother as he walked away from Gideon's lonely grave was that, just a few weeks ago, Gideon had told Samuel that he had a surprise for him, that he was changing his ways, and that he was going to become respectable.

Samuel shook his head at the memory. He never did find out what Gideon had meant or if the man had even been serious. *Perhaps it was just one of Gideon's many drunken promises*, Samuel thought. Although, at the time, Samuel had heard sincerity in Gideon's voice.

The walk from the church house to his blacksmith shop was short. By the time Samuel arrived, he spotted a tall, red-haired man waiting for him. Mr. Brown was his name, although it belied his appearance. Brown had a filly with a crude rope tied around its neck, which looked like she'd been wild just moments ago. The gray coat of the horse shone in the midday light, promising that a good brushing down would make her a beauty.

"Where'd you get this beauty?" Samuel asked, walking up to the filly and stroking her nose.

"Bought it off Parker," Brown said, showing a gap-toothed smile. "Need to get her shoed."

"I'll get right to it," Samuel said. "You can pick her up in an hour."

Brown nodded. As he left, Samuel took a few minutes to stroke the horse, calming her down and assuring her that he'd take good care of her.

"Mr. Butler?" a woman said, her accent sounding foreign.

Someone from off the train, Samuel thought, *probably asking directions.* Without looking up, he answered, "That's me."

"Mr. Gideon Butler?" the woman said again, her voice more insistent this time.

Samuel looked up and met a pair of hazel eyes beneath the darkest lashes he'd ever seen. The woman wore a deep green satin dress, dusty at the hem, with a too small bodice . . . not that he was noticing. These types of women were off-limits for him. He wouldn't be distracted by members of the opposite sex with rosy cheeks and painted lips. Maybe one day, when he had his acres, his finished home, and his thriving business, he'd consider finding himself a wife. It might be easier now without the constant presence of his drunken brother.

"Uh. Gideon's my brother," Samuel said.

The woman brought a handkerchief to her nose as if she couldn't bear the stench of the blacksmith's quarters. Samuel knew that the stench wasn't him or, at least, not all him.

"Oh," the woman said, lowering her handkerchief, her face breaking out into a smile, a smile that froze time.

Then Samuel's heart restarted. So, he wasn't immune to a beautiful woman. This one, though, must have missed Gideon's funeral . . . probably *engaged* elsewhere.

"It's very nice to meet you," the woman said, blinking up at him.

She was tall for a woman and not in the least demure, he decided. He supposed that she'd have to be quite congenial for her line of work. But, when she stuck out her hand to shake his, he paused. This was new.

"D—do I know you?" Samuel had never stuttered a day in his life.

"Not yet," the woman said with a laugh. "But I'm looking forward to getting to know you better."

Samuel fought for normal breath as he briefly shook her hand. Leadville, Colorado, was high in the mountains, yet he'd become accustomed to its thin air within days of their arrival. But it seemed that this woman had brought an extra dose of thin air with her. Should he cut her off now, or let her down gently? With the demise of his brother, she was probably short a client now.

"I'm afraid that I can't help you, miss," he said, although the woman did look older than the young things that Gideon had usually spent his time with. She tilted her head, the first look of confusion crossing those beautiful . . . those eyes.

"Is Gideon not here, then?" she asked. She took a small step to the side and peered around Samuel as if she expected to see Gideon inside the blacksmith shop.

The thought of it made Samuel laugh. The woman gave

him a strange look, but Samuel couldn't help it. He didn't think that Gideon had even known where his shop was when he was alive, let alone ever worked in it. Gideon was about as comfortable around horses as a child was with a set of straight pins.

"You're looking for Gideon?" Samuel said slowly, his words trying to catch up with hers.

"Yes. Isn't that what I said?" The woman's gaze returned to Samuel, and the only way he could describe her expression was *perturbed*.

"And you are?" he asked.

Then the woman's smile was back as if she had been hoping he would ask her that very question.

"Why, my name is Carmela Domeneca Rosalia Callemi," she said.

Her smile was almost angelic, Samuel decided. He kept his eyes firmly on her face as she took a deep breath in that too tight bodice. Then she added, "And I'm Gideon's mail order bride."

Four

*I*f Gideon Butler were half as handsome as this brother of his—who must be a bit younger than Gideon's professed thirty-five years—Carmela would be very pleased indeed. Although Gideon had written to her of his description, she knew that men tended to be all mouth and no trousers.

As it was, Gideon's brother had the bluest eyes she'd ever seen, and the slightly long hair beneath his hat was the color of golden wheat—something she'd seen plenty of outside the train window.

She couldn't quite make out the character of Gideon's brother. Though, perhaps he was teasing her, or perhaps, like Gideon had said in his letter, the town was devoid of proper single women. Thus, he needed to correspond with a woman back East who was interested in marriage and in starting a new life out West.

Carmela had been interested in both. She'd written three men over the past few months as Paulo and Ruthie mooned over each other. The day after their wedding, Carmela had shown them her train ticket and kissed her nephews good-bye. Now wasn't the time to think about the howling and clinging that had ensued. *The boys will be perfectly happy with their new mother,* she told herself.

She blinked up at the man before her. Though she still didn't know his first name, that didn't matter so much. But, why was he staring down at her with a look of utter confusion and . . . disgust? The intensity of his gaze caused her to take a step back and her stomach to twist itself into a tight knot.

Something isn't right, she thought, but she had no idea what it could be.

The man cleared his throat and shifted away from her as if he could no longer stand near her. "Gideon died two days ago," he said in a quiet voice. "I just returned from his funeral services."

Carmela stared at him. She wasn't sure if she had heard right. "*Gideon* Butler?"

"Yes," the man said, his voice growing fainter as his face paled.

"You mean . . ." She brought her handkerchief to her nose. This time, it wasn't to ward off the pungent smells of horses in too-close quarters but because she suddenly couldn't breathe. In fact, her hands were shaking, and there was a strange noise coming from her chest. Then she realized that she was gasping.

Gideon's brother gripped her arm gently and guided her to some sort of crude bench, telling her to sit down. Then he was pressing a tin cup into her hands and telling her to drink.

She obeyed, but what she had expected to be cool, sweet water was actually warm and foul-tasting. Carmela promptly spit it out.

"Hey, watch it," the man said, jumping out of her way.

She wiped her mouth with her handkerchief. *This can't be happening. There must be another Gideon Butler.* "Are you sure he's dead?" she asked in a raspy voice that didn't sound like her own. "Is there more than one Gideon Butler in Leadville?"

"No, I'm sorry," the man said, venturing closer now that it was apparent that she wasn't going to spit out any more water. "My brother is the only Gideon Butler in Leadville, Colorado, miss."

A distant train whistle sounded, and Carmela snapped her head up, her pulse pounding. "Do you think there's time to get back on the train?" She stood, although she still felt a bit shaky, and looked around for the carpet bag she'd brought. She hadn't brought much since she didn't have a lot and because Gideon had told her that he earned a fine wage at the mine.

"Not unless you want to go to California," the man said.

"Oh," she said, although it was more like a wail. She looked into the very blue eyes of Gideon's brother. "When will it turn around and head back to Boston?"

The man drew his brows together. "I don't know the train schedule by heart, but I figure it will be three or four days before it's heading back this way."

If someone had punched her in the stomach, it couldn't have knocked any more breath out of her. "Well, then," she began, her voice trembling. "I'm sorry to have bothered you, and I'm . . ." She stopped, realizing that she had to do this right. "Would you mind so terribly taking me to Gideon's final resting place?"

Was that a flash of annoyance on the man's face? she wondered.

"If you can wait a bit," he said. "I need to shoe this

horse, and then, as long as there aren't customers waiting, I can take you to the cemetery."

Carmela blew out a breath. She felt shaken up, annoyed, hungry, and, to tell the truth, completely put out. She wanted to grieve over Gideon, but mostly she wanted to grieve for her own misfortune.

"You're welcome to sit on the bench," the man said. "Would you like another drink?" Both of them looked at the half-filled tin cup still on the bench. "I suppose not," he continued with a chuckle.

Carmela lifted a brow at him, for there was nothing funny about any of this. But he didn't seem intimidated at all by her.

"By the way," the man said, "Name's Samuel, Samuel Butler, kid brother of the infamous Gideon." He turned away then, and Carmela was shocked to hear another soft laugh coming from him. This man—Samuel—had just come from his brother's funeral, and he was laughing?

Perhaps it is a nervous habit, she thought, *how he copes with tragedy.*

She eyed the gray horse that Samuel had started working on. She'd ridden horses, of course, back in Italy. The horse eyed her, watching her as she was watching it. Samuel seemed to have an easy way with the horse, and Carmela couldn't help but notice that the superb strength of the horse was quite matched by that of the man shoeing it.

Samuel said nothing while he worked, and exhaustion crept its way into Carmela. There was nothing she could do now but wait. So she pulled out from her handbag the sheaf of letters that she'd saved from Gideon. She'd read them several times on the train, and now it felt fitting to look at them once more before going to the man's graveside.

Gideon's penmanship was beautiful, almost feminine in

nature, and his words seemed cultured and refined. That was what had first drawn her to Gideon and had made him seem above and beyond the other gentlemen she'd exchanged a couple of letters with. She had been surprised that Gideon was a miner—with such educated writing. But she had supposed that this was where the money was out West: in mining. She'd heard stories, of course, of men striking the right vein and becoming wealthy overnight.

"What do you have there?" Samuel asked.

Carmela pressed the letters to her chest, feeling a distinct invasion of her privacy at his question. "Letters from your brother."

Samuel shook his head and gave a half snort.

"What?" Carmela said, her face growing hot. "Not every man needs to be a romantic, but did you think I'd come all this way without knowing anything about the man I intended to marry?"

Samuel turned from his bench, facing her head on with those blue eyes of his. "I'm beginning to think that you don't know a thing about my brother," he said. "For starters, he was illiterate."

It took a moment for this word to translate for Carmela. Her English was more than fine, but not every word came easily. "He couldn't read or write?" she asked.

"Exactly," Samuel said. "If he did write those letters . . ." he began to say, looking pointedly at the letters still clutched against her chest, "he must have hired someone to do it for him."

Carmela slowly lowered the sheaf of letters. This information made a terrible sort of sense. The handwriting was very flowery, not exactly what one might expect from a man. *But the words were still Gideon's, right? I couldn't have been duped that completely.*

"Can I see one?" Samuel asked.

Carmela stiffened. "*You* can read? How is that you can read and your brother can't?"

Samuel lifted a shoulder. "Gideon didn't go to school much; I did. He was interested in other, uh, pursuits."

What could it hurt? she asked herself. If Carmela were to properly grieve her almost husband, perhaps she could allow his brother to enlighten her on Gideon's character.

She handed the most recent letter to Samuel. He read through the words quickly, laughing a time or two, which only made Carmela's face flush, then handed the letter back.

"He calls himself 'a man who is fiercely loyal and willing to protect his lady'?"

"Yes," Carmela said. When she'd first read those words, they'd sent heat directly into her heart—for, was there anything more important than a loyal man?

Samuel turned back to the horse, finishing off the last shoe.

"What?" she asked. "What's wrong with your brother's statements?"

Samuel shook his head, which only made Carmela feel more put out. The man had asked to read the letter, and now he wouldn't even talk about it?

Well, she could ignore him as much as he was ignoring her. Once she'd paid her respects at Gideon's grave, she'd rent a room at the hotel until the next train came through, that is, if this town had a hotel. A knot of worry worked its way into her stomach, but she could just be hungry as well. She dreaded returning to Boston so soon. She would have to spend the last of her money for another ticket—the money that Gideon had sent to her for a new dress and a ticket. She'd found a secondhand dress in order to save some money for when she arrived in Leadville. She'd hoped that her frugalness might have impressed Gideon.

But now, there was no one to impress.

And Carmela was, once again, unattached.

Five

Samuel dreaded breaking the news of his brother's sullied ways to the woman walking alongside him. At one point, when they had passed the taverns of questionable repute, Samuel had tucked her arm inside of his in order to stave off the gawking of several foul-smelling men.

"This place is quite wild," Miss Carmela Callemi had murmured.

When they reached the open road just past the bakery, she immediately freed her arm from his.

So much for my gentlemanly act, he thought. At least she was generous enough to let him continue carrying her carpet bag. He was frankly surprised that she didn't have a couple of large trunks.

Yet, Samuel could only guess at what was going through her mind. He found it quite incredible that she'd believed a man would write such elaborate prose in a letter. Samuel suspected that she must have had only trustworthy men in her life to be so taken in with one of Gideon's schemes. He had no idea how Gideon had planned to pull off taking in a wife and keeping her happy.

In fact, an unconscious glance at Miss Callemi's profile told him that, although she decidedly had a sharp tongue, she was frightfully innocent to be traveling all the way from Boston on her own. If Gideon had lived and had brought her home, Samuel knew that it wouldn't have been long before Samuel would be defending the honor of Miss Callemi and punching Gideon square in the jaw.

"What are you shaking your head about?" she asked, her voice breaking through his thoughts.

Samuel startled at the sound and said, "Just wool-gathering, I suppose."

"Memories of your brother?"

Samuel chuckled. "Not exactly. More like future scenarios that I won't have to worry about now." At noticing the crinkle in her brow, Samuel had the oddest urge to pull her to a stop and run his finger over the lines to tell her to not worry over someone as rank as his brother. Instead, he looked up at the clouds, racing across the sky, their hurry matched by the pace of his heartbeat.

Women, he thought. He wasn't any good around them. Never had been. He'd stayed well clear ever since Gideon had brought that hussy to their place in Boulder, and Samuel had been forced to kick them both out.

So, Samuel was more than grateful when the church house came into view—and the cemetery behind it. He could get this task over, finish out the day in his shop, and blot Miss Carmela Callemi from his mind's list of things to concern himself over.

"Oh, it's . . . quite barren here," Miss Callemi said as they rounded the church and stopped before the cemetery.

Gideon's grave was covered over, and someone had left a handful of already wilting wildflowers on top.

A nice gesture, Samuel supposed and gave himself the tiniest prick of guilt that they hadn't been from him.

"Leadville is more concerned with silver than with schoolhouses or churches," Samuel said. He tugged off his hat, letting the newly cooled wind blow through his hair.

"What's your favorite memory of Gideon?" Miss Callemi asked.

No question could have surprised Samuel more. Trouble was, it made him have to think—hard. He felt her hazel eyes watching him. And, despite the air turning cooler, his body was warming up. He had to think of something—fast—then get back to town.

"When I was about five," he said, "I remember thinking that Gideon could do anything. A circus came to town that summer, and my parents were too busy with chores to take me. So Gideon took me, and my eyes were opened to a world that I previously didn't know existed. He even bought me my own bag of boiled peanuts."

Miss Callemi released a small sigh, and, for a moment, Samuel was caught up in that sigh as well. Gideon's life had ended too soon. That was true, but perhaps Samuel could remember the good things about him. *Every man has redeeming attributes,* Samuel thought. *Didn't he?*

"There's that expression again, sir," Miss Callemi said. "What are you thinking about? I don't think I've ever seen a man with such earnest mysteriousness as yourself."

Samuel tilted his head and studied the brunette standing mere feet from him. Her hair had been tugged free from a couple of pins, and loose strands blew about her neck. "Has anyone ever told you that you're a busybody, Miss Callemi?"

Her mouth twitched, those pink lips that he'd thought

were painted with makeup only to realize that they were part of her natural coloring. Then her lips turned up, and she lifted her chin and laughed. Laughed!

Samuel found himself smiling, quite dumbly, for he had no idea why she was laughing. But he liked it, liked it very much indeed. She took a deep breath and stepped toward him, laying her hand on his arm. Surprise shot through him at her touch. It was as if he were rooted in place, unable to speak, unable to move.

"Mr. Butler, I'll take that as a compliment. I've been called much worse."

Again Samuel's eyes dipped to her bodice. *Did she mean . . . ?* No, he decided, and he wouldn't do her the dishonor of suspecting her of it.

"Thank you for showing me Gideon's grave," she said, continuing in that charming accent of hers. "Can you direct me to the closest hotel?"

Samuel nearly dropped the hat he'd been holding in his hands. If he could trust his instincts, then this was a virtuous woman. The hotel rooms across from the tavern would not be an appropriate place for her to spend even one night, let alone the three or four nights it might be until the train made its return trip to Boston.

But, what was her other option? Mrs. Smith, who rented the two rooms above the bakery to women, already had them occupied with the school teacher and the secretary of one of the mine owners. So there wouldn't be additional room to put up Miss Callemi. He supposed that he could speak to the reverend and see if he had any ideas. And then another idea formulated in his mind. Before he proposed it, he turned his face upward toward the sky. It was windy, yes, but not a cloud in sight.

"What on earth are you doing now, Mr. Butler?" she asked, her voice cutting into his tumbling thoughts. "One moment, I think you are quite intelligent, and in the next..."

He lowered his gaze and stared at her pinked cheeks. "Continue."

"Uh, I think I'm being too much of a busybody." She smiled, looking chagrined. "If it's too much trouble, I'll just walk back into town and ask for directions there. You've already done enough for me, and I certainly appreciate it." She stuck out her hand.

Samuel could only stare at her hand now. What was wrong with him? Had this woman been about to call him daft? *She might be quite correct,* he thought.

"Mr. Butler," she said again. "Good-bye and thank you again." She turned and started to walk away.

"Wait," Samuel said. "Your luggage."

She rotated. "Oh, yes."

"But—" He held up a hand, finally able to put his thoughts into words. "You can't stay at the hotel in town."

She said nothing and just raised that infernal eyebrow.

"I—I mean, it's not a good place for such a fine lady as yourself," Samuel said, walking toward her. He lowered his voice as he continued. "The tavern is directly across the street, and the men can't be entirely trusted. Miners can be a rowdy lot. And, seeing as how it's Saturday night and that the miners will have tomorrow off, there could be quite a bit of celebrating going on."

Miss Callemi's gaze remained steady upon his, but she'd clasped her hands tightly together.

"I checked the weather," he said, glancing again quickly at the blue sky, "and it seems that it's a good night to sleep under the stars."

Her hands snapped to her hips. "I know we're in the Wild West, sir, but you can't expect me to sleep outside."

"No," Samuel said with a laugh. "*I* will sleep outside, and *you* will sleep inside my house."

Her eyebrow lifted quite high at this. "I don't think so," she said in a slow voice. "I've only just met you. And, if you're so worried about my reputation, then staying in your home seems quite inappropriate." She reached for her carpet bag.

"Hear me out," Samuel said, grasping her arm gently. Surprisingly, she didn't pull away but merely waited for him to continue. "Once people in town discover that you were planning on marrying Gideon, you'll be laughed at."

Her face slowly bloomed red. "And, why is that?" she whispered.

Samuel hesitated, but he'd come this far, and he absolutely had to convince her to stay at his house until the train came. He admitted to himself that he liked this woman—her frankness, her courage—and he didn't want to see her embarrassed. But he didn't relish destroying the image she'd had of his brother.

"Mr. Butler," she said. "I asked you a question, and you'd better stop toying with me."

Now it was his turn to redden. He hadn't meant to toy with her. Releasing her arm, he said, "My brother was an unscrupulous and immoral man." Samuel rushed on, trying to get it all out in a few breaths. "The women at the tavern all know him by name, and he probably owes gambling money to most of the men. He hasn't been sober for more than a few hours for as long as I can remember. And, if anyone in town knows that you arrived here as his mail order bride, I'm afraid they'd never let you live it down."

Her lashes lowered as she looked away from his desperate gaze. "I understand now why you laughed at me when I showed you Gideon's letter."

Samuel could only nod because, in truth, his chest hurt from the ache that was growing there. His brother had wronged this woman, and now, it was Samuel's responsibility to make it up to her. *One more thing,* he thought, *to clean up after my brother. But, at least this will be the last of it.*

She lifted her head, her cheeks stained with the embarrassment that Samuel had hoped to prevent. "I will stay in your home, Mr. Butler. And, when that train arrives, I will leave and never look back."

Six

At first, the drops of rain sounded like a faint melody upon the roof above Carmela's head. And then, the melody crashed together into a full symphony, drowning out all of the comfortable night sounds of the ticking clock and the low, crackling fire, which Samuel Butler had built before heading outside.

Carmela jolted upright as the tempo of the rain increased. Suddenly, the small bedroom flashed bright like a noonday sun, followed moments later by a boom of thunder. Carmela shrieked and pulled the covers over her head. It was strange enough to be sleeping in a man's bed, let alone inside his house, and now, this wild storm had awakened her.

Samuel! He was outside, having sworn that the weather would hold long enough for him to spend the night beneath the sky.

Setting her mouth into a grim line, Carmela threw her covers off and grabbed the robe she'd laid at the foot of the bed. Pulling it on, she headed for the door that Samuel had told her to bolt after he left. The man seemed quite protective, if Carmela had to say so herself, not that she had minded. It reminded her of something that her brother might do.

She pulled open the door and stared out into the driving rain. The wind was pushing its drops nearly sideways. Carmela searched in vain for a light or any sign of Samuel. She had no idea if he'd gone behind the house or, perhaps, to the lean-to, which looked like it had been built for a horse, although any beast was absent now. There was only a hen house with a couple of chickens.

Then another dagger of lightning threaded the sky, lighting up the homestead for a few short seconds. But this was long enough for Carmela to catch a glimmer of white beneath the lean-to.

"Samuel!" she cried out. "Get in the house! You're going to get soaked!"

Miraculously, he must have heard her, even over the now rumbling thunder. The white figure moved, and, before she knew it, the man was running toward the house. Carmela stood aside, holding the door, and Samuel brushed past her, coming to a halt in the entry way.

Too late, she thought. He was completely soaked. His white undershirt was plastered to his chest and arms, while his hair dripped, dark with water.

Without thinking too much about it, Carmela shut the door, turned to Samuel, and grasped his arm. "You're wet all the way through," she said. "I thought that you said it wasn't going to rain."

Samuel rubbed his hand over his wet face then shook his head, sending droplets flying.

"Ah!" Carmela said as she stepped back, out of the way. "Just because you're soaked, doesn't mean that I want to be too."

"Sorry," Samuel said, although he didn't sound too sorry.

It was then that Carmela noticed that he was trembling with cold. How long had it been raining before she'd awakened? And, how long had he been soaking in the rain? Her instincts from taking care of two motherless boys took over.

"You've got to get out of these wet clothes," she said. "I'll stoke up the fire and heat up some water. Do you have tea or coffee around here?"

"I'll be fine," Samuel said, his deep voice filling the small space between them.

Carmela met his gaze, his blue eyes looking dark in the dim light of the open hearth. Then he drew back and sneezed.

"Oh! You will not be fine, sir," she said, her hands on her hips. "Get out of those clothes now, and let's get you warmed up."

He wiped his face again and sighed. "All right, Miss Callemi." His tone might have sounded serious and contrite, but Carmela didn't miss the upturned edges of his mouth.

"Very well. You change while I see to the fire and the tea," she said, turning away, feeling that this room couldn't possibly seem smaller.

"Can you bring me a pair of dry trousers from my bedroom?"

His voice stopped her, and she felt the heat rise in her neck. "Of course." She hurried to the bedroom, forgetting to light a candle and bring it in with her. So, instead, she shuffled through the bureau, feeling her way along his clothing, trying to determine which items were shirts and which were trousers. Then she realized he'd need both, grabbed what she could find, and returned to the front room.

Stopping dead, she clamped her mouth shut. He'd pulled off his wet shirt and stood there, the light of the fire dancing along his muscled chest, as if this were the most ordinary occurrence. Something bubbled in Carmela's stomach, telling her that this was far from ordinary. Samuel Butler was a handsome man with a strong physique. Naturally, it was a bit surprising to see him partially clad, but she shouldn't be caught staring.

With a determined exhale, she stepped forward, staying as far away from him as possible while extending the dry clothing toward him. "I'm not sure what I grabbed. The bedroom was dark."

Again, the sides of his mouth lifted, and Carmela turned away with haste, sure that her cheeks were aflame. She busied herself with stoking the lazy orange flames while one part of her was listening to Samuel's movements as he changed his clothing. *He is in the same room . . . undressing*, Carmela thought.

If Carmela had been a cursing woman, she would have cursed at herself, if only to steel her mind against the image of Samuel's bare torso. As it was, she let one tiny curse slip into her mind. Thankfully, this seemed to jolt a bit of sense into her mind, and she said, "You didn't answer my question about the tea or the coffee."

"Both." Samuel's voice rumbled from the other side of the room. "The tea might be quite old, though." He gave a soft chuckle. "You can turn around, Miss Callemi. I'm decent now."

There were two ways to read into that comment, but Carmela decided she wouldn't read into it at all. She turned from the now well-kindled fire, which had brightened the room. Samuel was indeed dressed in dry clothing: another white shirt, she saw, and dark trousers.

"I'm surprised that you wear so much white out here in the country," she said before she could think better of it. *Well, it isn't like my nosiness comes as a surprise any longer.*

"I was sleeping in my undershirt," Samuel said, his eyes capturing hers, even from all the way across the room. "And this is my Sabbath shirt."

"Oh, I'm sorry," Carmela said immediately. "I didn't mean to—"

"It's all right," Samuel said. "I haven't been to church in a while. It's about time I put this shirt to good use."

He hadn't buttoned it all the way, Carmela noticed, and the sight of the exposed triangle of his upper chest brought back the memory of his full torso.

"I can go find another," she said.

Samuel took a step toward her. "This is fine. I'm more interested in that tea you keep mentioning."

She was very aware that they were alone together in the house and that it was the middle of the night as the rainstorm pounded the windows and roof all around them. The fire and Samuel's presence heated up the room well enough, and Carmela didn't need to add any of her additional thoughts—of Samuel being a handsome and considerate gentleman—to the warmth inside the place.

And, she realized, she was in her robe. Although it was plenty modest, her robe was still her sleeping attire and not meant for public viewing. And Carmela certainly considered Samuel as part of the public.

She walked past him, ignoring her thumping heart. "Sit by the fire. I'll have tea ready soon. It will warm you right up." Was he chuckling again? she wondered. If he was, she decided to ignore it.

Not much later, she had the water boiling over the fire and two teacups ready. Samuel had leaned back in his chair and had closed his eyes, which was a good thing so that Carmela didn't have to deal with his blue-eyed gaze as much. Another flash of lightning, followed by thunder, sent her heart skittering again. It wasn't that she was entirely afraid of storms but that this house felt so exposed on such a large bit of property.

"Are you all right?" Samuel asked.

Carmela opened her eyes, unaware that she'd flinched and closed them. Samuel stood not two steps from where she clenched the tea tin in her hand.

"I am," she said. "I suppose I'm not quite used to—"

Lightning jagged across the room, followed immediately by thunder so loud that it vibrated the wooden floor beneath her feet. "Oh!" she cried out, practically leaping at Samuel.

Thankfully, he was sturdy, and, instead of knocking him off balance, he grabbed onto her and wrapped his arms around her.

"Sorry," she whispered, still feeling the thunder's quake throughout her body. But she didn't pull away; somehow she couldn't. Samuel didn't release her either and kept his arms around her, strong and comforting.

Her head rested against his warm chest, and her heart seemed to thump in time with his. She didn't want to move, but she knew that the longer she stayed in his arms, the harder it would be to draw away.

Another roll of thunder sent a shudder through her body, and Samuel tightened his hold, for a moment, then released her.

"Here," he said. "Sit by the fire." She let him lead her there then accepted the teacup he gave her. Finally, he draped a quilt over her shoulders.

"I'm supposed to be taking care of you," she murmured. "You're the one who was soaked in the rain."

But Samuel merely sat across from her, the fire burning merrily next to them. Thankfully, the thunder had subsided, growing more distant with each occurrence, although the rain kept up its pounding on the roof.

"Does it rain like this often?" she asked.

"We get some pretty good storms in Leadville," Samuel said. "I hear that Boston has quite fierce winters."

"I haven't experienced one firsthand," Carmela said. "We sailed over in April. Gideon said that you get quite a bit of snow here too." She hadn't meant to bring up Gideon. But, this time, Samuel didn't refute what his brother had said. Perhaps Gideon hadn't deceived her about everything.

"Tell me about your homeland," Samuel said, peering at her from his chair.

So Carmela did. The coziness of the room, with the fire's orange glow while it rained outside, made her feel like the outside world was far away and that she could easily talk to Samuel. She told him of the vineyard her father ran, how her brother had wanted a new start in America after his wife had died, and how she'd decided to travel with him to help with his two boys.

Samuel told her of his experiences growing up in Boulder and how he was always like an older brother to Gideon, even though Gideon was older in years. He also told her of his dreams of running his own business and how he loved to work with horses.

Carmela didn't know how long they talked into the night, but she couldn't ever remember speaking to a man like Samuel, who actually seemed to listen to every word she said.

Seven

Samuel hated to wake Carmela, but dawn had come and gone, and he had to get to his blacksmith shop to be ready for business. He pushed open the bedroom door where Carmela slept, a streak of sunlight falling across the bed. Her dark hair tumbled about her face, and her long lashes rested against her cheeks, making her look like a dark-haired angel with her creamy complexion and rose-colored lips. It was a marvel to see her so peaceful and quiet. The Carmela he'd gotten to know was not one to shy away from giving her opinion or asking any question that sprang to her mind.

He smiled as he recalled their conversation from the night before. He'd learned a lot about her, and he surprised himself by sharing quite a bit about his own life. He'd never been so talkative with a woman before—or with a man, for that matter. And Samuel had been more than content just being his own man.

All of a sudden, Samuel realized that Carmela had opened her eyes and was now staring at him.

"Oh, sorry," Samuel said, straightening from where he was leaning against the doorframe. "I didn't mean to wake you."

She didn't say anything for a moment, merely blinking a couple of times. Then she gave a little gasp and tugged the quilt high against her neck. "How did I get here?" she asked, looking about the room then back to him, her dark eyes wide.

Samuel felt his neck heat up. "You fell asleep in the chair, so I . . . carried you in." She stared at him, and he raised his hands. "I slept out in the other room," he explained.

Carmela exhaled, looking relieved. "I didn't mean to take over your house," she said, and her face pinked. "Thank you for taking care of me last night." She pushed up onto one elbow. "How are you doing? Did you ever warm up?"

"I did," he said. And he was plenty warm now, in fact. "I . . . uh . . . need to get to the shop, but I didn't want to leave you here by yourself. So you're welcome to come with me. Although, I'm not sure that you will want to face the questions from the townspeople that are sure to come by."

Carmela stifled a yawn. "I would prefer to stay here."

Samuel nodded. "Help yourself to whatever you need. The food pantry isn't as well stocked as it probably should be, but there are plenty of apples out back."

"Thank you," Carmela said, a smile lighting up her face.

Samuel took a step back, knowing that the sooner he left, the better, or he might be tempted to stay here and spend the day with her, learning more about her home country and listening to her talk about her family.

So he bade her farewell and hurried out of the house.

The rain had stopped that morning, but the mud was unavoidable. He trudged along the muddy road that lead into town. As the sun broke through the clouds, he thought of what might have happened if Carmela had arrived just one week earlier. She could have been married to Gideon already, and she would have become his widow. It was strange to think that his brother might have been married to such a hardworking, beautiful woman.

Samuel had never envied his brother anything. But, if Gideon had lived and if Carmela had become his wife, Samuel realized that he would have envied Gideon one thing: Carmela. He shook these thoughts away. Gideon hadn't married Carmela. Gideon wasn't even around anymore. But, it was hard to reconcile this reality yet. Samuel half expected his brother to stagger out of one of the taverns as he passed or to show up at the shop today, asking for a few cents.

A customer was already waiting for him as he reached the shop. Samuel hurried to help Mr. Kirkpatrick. The man was tall, thin, and wore spectacles. But his poor eyesight didn't prevent him from being an astute horse dealer. He'd probably sold most of the miners in Leadville their horses.

"Sorry to hear about your brother, Mr. Butler," Kirkpatrick said, as always, erring on the formal side by calling Samuel by his last name.

"I appreciate it," Samuel said, then closed the topic. "What are we doing today?" He grasped the reins of the horse Kirkpatrick had brought in and began to stroke the top of her head.

"She needs a shoe adjustment," Kirkpatrick said. "You know, Mr. Butler, Mr. Christensen backed out on purchasing this mare."

"Oh?" Samuel said, stopping mid-stroke. He wasn't entirely surprised that Christensen had backed out. The man was the jovial type and rarely serious.

"I told you I'd give you a fair deal," Kirkpatrick continued.

"Thank you," Samuel said. "I'll think about it." He resumed stroking the mare's head. She was a fine horse, muscled and healthy. It would save him time in a lot of things, especially when he started expanding his homestead. His stalwart stallion had died just a few months ago, and he hadn't had time to purchase another animal.

As he began shoeing the mare, Samuel wondered if Carmela rode horses. Surely she had, if she'd grown up in a vineyard. He imagined bringing the mare back to his house today and showing her the horse. Maybe he'd ride with her for a bit if she were skittish about it. He was sure that the woman would make a pretty form riding a horse—her hair flowing behind her, the wind tugging at her clothing . . .

"Where did you go?" Kirkpatrick said, cutting into Samuel's thoughts.

Samuel looked up from his task. "Sorry?"

Kirkpatrick chuckled and raised his brows above his spectacles. "Didn't know where you went for a moment. Woolgathering, I suppose?"

He was waiting for an answer, but Samuel wasn't going to provide his true thoughts. "Didn't sleep much with the rainstorm, I guess."

"That thunder was something else," Kirkpatrick agreed.

Samuel straightened and looked over at Kirkpatrick. "How much for the mare?"

A slow smile started on Kirkpatrick's narrow face. "A year of shoeing all the horses I bring to you, and she's yours."

Samuel stuck out his hand. "You have a deal," he said, and they shook hands.

The rest of the morning passed quickly as customers came to him with their horses and for wagon repairs. The clouds had dispersed as if last night's rainstorm had never happened, and the sun seemed to have baked away every last water droplet, for his shop was plenty hot.

Well after the lunch hour, Samuel could no longer ignore his hunger. The tavern usually sent a boy around to the local businesses to deliver sandwiches. But Samuel hadn't had any interruptions today. So he decided that he'd walk to the bakery and buy something from Mrs. Smith.

Just as he stood up to close up shop for a short time, someone stepped inside.

"Carmela?" Samuel said, taking a moment to register that she really was here, in his shop. He'd been picturing her back at his home, maybe searching through his food pantry for a decent meal. She wasn't wearing the fancy green dress from the day before but a simple blue cotton dress that fit her better. She'd tied her hair back with a ribbon, and she carried a wrapped parcel in her hands.

"I thought that you might be hungry," she said, stepping forward. "You didn't leave the house carrying a lunch." She began unwrapping the parcel, and a heavenly smell struck Samuel.

"What is it?" he asked as she set the offering on the bench.

"Apple tarts," she said. "I made them myself. And a couple of egg sandwiches."

Samuel stared at the baked goodness. "You made apple tarts?"

"Yes," she said. "And I used the rest of your flour, so you'll need to resupply. That, and you'll need more sugar."

He was stunned and didn't know what to say. He couldn't remember the last time a woman had fixed him a meal.

"While you're eating that, I'll get you some fresh water,"

she said, moving her hands onto her hips. "Do you need anything else?"

Samuel shook his head. "You didn't need to do all of this."

"It's the least I could do," she said, lowering her voice, although they were the only ones in the shop. "You took care of me last night, when I should have been helping you."

Samuel flashed her a smile, and, when she smiled right back, he felt his heart expand. He couldn't believe that his brother had persuaded this beautiful woman to come out West. There were two sandwiches, so he offered her one.

"I've already eaten," she said. "I'll go refill your water bucket. I saw the pump on the side of the building."

Before he could protest, she'd taken the bucket and sailed out of the shop. Stomach grumbling, he bit into the egg sandwich and moaned at the goodness. By the time Carmela returned, he'd finished a sandwich and an apple tart.

"The streets are quiet this morning," she said.

"They usually are on Sunday mornings." Samuel brushed off his hands and rose.

"Don't mind me," Carmela said, flashing him another smile. "I'm just going to snoop. That is, if you don't mind."

Samuel chuckled. "I don't mind," he said, and he realized that he didn't. He enjoyed the second sandwich and second apple tart while she did just that—inspecting his shop and checking out the blacksmithing equipment. When she reached the table where he kept his account ledger and correspondence, she shook her head.

"How do you find anything in this mess?" she asked.

"It's meant to be confusing," Samuel said, "in case someone breaks into the shop and wants to review my accounting methods."

She arched a brow, her mouth starting to lift in a smile. Then her smile froze. "You have quite a bit of unopened mail here." She reached for a letter and picked it up. "To Gideon?"

"Oh, that," Samuel said. "One of his . . . *friends* brought it over. I haven't taken the time to go through it yet."

"Lydia Weathers," Carmela said. She held up another letter. "Jessica Brown. Are these relatives?"

Samuel was surprised at her interest, but Carmela had been planning on marrying Gideon, so maybe that accounted for her curiosity. He packed away the remains of his lunch and crossed over to her. Then he took the first letter from her hand.

"I had no idea that my brother was such an avid correspondent." Perhaps Gideon was writing to more than one mail order bride. Now, he was as curious as Carmela. Picking up a letter opener from the table, he slit open the letter and withdrew the folded, glossy paper. It was thick like a photograph.

Turning it over, he realized that it was a photograph, but one that he wished Carmela wouldn't witness. It was too late to hide it from her, however, since she was standing right next to him.

"Oh!" she said, sounding as shocked as Samuel felt.

Although, Samuel shouldn't have been entirely shocked that his brother was ordering photographs of naked women from who knew where. He slipped the photograph back into the envelope and carried it over to the forge. Tossing it in, he said to Carmela, "I'm sorry you had to see that."

She didn't say anything for a moment and just watched the flames turn the envelope into black ash. Samuel moved around her and gathered everything else addressed to his brother, tossing the envelopes one by one into the fire, making sure that they caught fire and burned completely.

"You are so different from your brother," Carmela said in a soft voice. "It's a wonder that you're related at all."

Samuel didn't really know how to answer that, but he was pleased at her observance. He'd spent his life trying to live differently than his brother—and someone had finally noticed.

"Mr. Butler," Carmela said, her hand sliding into his.

Her touch startled him, but he welcomed it. "I think you should call me Samuel," he said, looking down into her eyes. "I feel that you know me quite well, at least better than anyone else."

She continued looking up at him, and he wished he could know what she was thinking. Ever since she'd arrived in Leadville, she'd had one setback after another.

"I'd be honored to call you Samuel," she said. "But you must call me Carmela."

He nodded. "Carmela."

She smiled as his poor accent didn't translate so well to say her beautiful Italian name. Then she seemed to move closer to him, just as he leaned down. He couldn't take his eyes off of her lips, and he lowered his face toward hers, not sure that he was thinking straight but feeling that instinct had taken over.

"Mr. Butler?" a female voice said behind him.

Samuel released Carmela as quick as lightning and spun around. "Mrs. Smith," he said, sure that his face was bright red.

"You never picked up your bread order yesterday," she said, carrying a paper sack. "I was sorry to hear about your brother," she added, her eyes widening as Carmela stepped out from behind him.

"Oh, I didn't know you had company." Mrs. Smith's eyes nearly popped out of her head as she stared Carmela up and down.

Here it is, he thought. Samuel would have to say something, and, whatever it was, it would be all over town like a flash.

But before he could make introductions, Carmela stepped forward, her hand outstretched. "Hello, ma'am. I'm Carmela Domeneca Rosalia Callemi," she said. "I'm awaiting the next train to Boston, and Mr. Butler here is a friend of someone who was once dear to me."

Mrs. Smith's mouth rounded into an O. But she quickly recovered and said, "I'm Mrs. Smith. I run the bakery down the road. If you're in need of refreshment, I can oblige you."

"Oh, thank you so much," Carmela said. "I appreciate the offer. I am perfectly all right." Carmela turned to Samuel. "Thank you again, S—Mr. Butler. I'll just be on my way." Then she left the shop, leaving Samuel to face Mrs. Smith.

Eight

He had been about to kiss me, Carmela thought as she hurried away from the blacksmith shop. And that Mrs. Smith woman would have walked in on them. *Wouldn't that have been something for the town to gossip about?* Although, Carmela wasn't sure why a kiss between her and Samuel Butler would be fodder for gossip in a mining town that, apparently, had two taverns and plenty of tavern women.

The town seemed to be finally coming alive as she walked down Main Street. A couple of the shops had opened, and music floated out from one of the taverns. Loud laughter erupted, and a man burst out of the front door, staggering to keep his balance. His efforts almost worked until he ran right into Carmela.

"Sorry, miss," the man said, slurring his words. He grasped Carmela's arms to steady himself. It was all she could do not to slap him. His breath was foul, and his clothes looked like they'd been slept in for several weeks in a row.

She drew away from him, peeling his fingers off of her skin. Then she stepped back and turned toward the road. She'd rather walk in the muddy street, she decided, than on the boardwalk next to the tavern.

But then a strong hand latched onto her arm, stopping her. "Where ya goin' in such a hurry?" the man asked.

She turned to face the drunk again. "Let go of me now, or I'll scream!" she warned.

The man only chuckled, his foul breath puffing into her face. "Never minded a bit of screamin'."

Carmela slapped his cheek with her free hand. The man cried out, releasing her. And suddenly, another man stepped out of the tavern.

This man was sober and looked well-dressed. "Johnson!" he barked as he latched onto the man's collar and tugged him toward the doors. "We're going to sober you up then kick you out for good." He gave a quick glance at Carmela. "Are you all right, miss?"

"I am," she said, brushing off the front of her dress, feeling like she might have caught some disease.

"I hope Johnson's poor behavior won't stop you from visiting my establishment." Then the man had the gall to smile at her.

Carmela could only stare at him in disgust. "I don't ever plan to step foot inside your place."

The man only smiled again and tipped an imaginary hat. "If you change your mind, you'd be very welcome."

Carmela turned from him and walked back the way she'd come. She wasn't thinking now about where she was going, just that she had to get away from the tavern owner and the drunk. She didn't know who was worse. Walking briskly, she arrived at the blacksmith shop once again. She could hear the pounding of metal—Samuel was inside working.

Taking a few deep breaths, she tried to calm her racing heart. But this didn't help, and tears budded in her eyes. Finally, she stepped into the shop. Just seeing Samuel made her feel better.

He looked up from his work bench, and a smile broke out on his face at the sight of her. "You've returned," he said with obvious pleasure.

If she hadn't still been so upset, this sight would have made her melt.

"What's wrong?" he asked, his face sobering. He stood and crossed to her, his expression seeming full of concern. The thought that Samuel might care, might truly care, brought her tears to the surface. "Carmela?" he asked in a worried tone.

She stepped closer and wrapped her arms about his waist. He didn't move for a moment, but then his arms came around her, feeling sure and strong.

"What's happened?" he asked again.

Carmela finally found her voice. "There was a man who grabbed me. He was coming out of the tavern and—"

Samuel drew away. "Did he hurt you?"

"No," Carmela breathed. "He just . . . scared me. Then the tavern owner came out, calling the man Johnson. But the owner wasn't much better."

Samuel's jaw clenched. "Wait here. I'll be right back."

"What are you going to do?" she asked.

He looked back at her as he strode to the door. "Make sure neither of them bother you again."

"But—" Carmela started to say, yet Samuel was already gone. *What if Samuel gets hurt?* she worried. She hurried out of the shop after him, but he was already halfway down the boardwalk. Before she could call out, he disappeared into the tavern.

Carmela felt ill. *I've caused a lot of trouble for Samuel already. And he'll probably praise the heavens the moment I get back onto the train.* Just as she neared the tavern, two men burst out. She recognized the first as Johnson immediately, for he staggered, nearly falling, then steadied himself and took off running, albeit in not quite a straight line.

The second man was Samuel. He seemed unharmed, although he looked a bit roughed up. "Samuel!" she cried out just as several other men came out of the tavern. Some of them pointed in the direction Johnson was running, but others seemed more intent on watching Carmela.

She took a deep breath and gained command of her emotions. It wouldn't do to start crying with relief in front of all these strangers. Samuel watched after Johnson for a moment, then he was apparently satisfied, and he turned toward her. He looked surprised to see her, but didn't say anything to that effect. Instead, he walked to where she was standing and touched her lower back, steering her away from the gathering crowd.

"What did you do in there, Samuel?" Carmela whispered as they walked along.

"First, I told the tavern owner that if he ever spoke to you again, he'd regret it," Samuel said. "Then I took care of Johnson. He won't be showing his face anytime soon." He slowed as they arrived back at his shop. "Look, Carmela, it's best that you don't walk through town unaccompanied. There are very few unmarried women here, and most of those are ladies of ill repute."

Carmela's face felt hot. She'd gathered as much. "Thank you for defending me," she said. "But I feel terrible that you went to all that trouble." She felt the tears burn in her eyes again, but she refused to let them fall. She was strong, not some whimpering female.

"Have you ridden horses?" Samuel suddenly asked.

"I have," she said. "Although it's been a while."

"Then I'll close up and take you home on my new mare," Samuel said. "Riding her back will take no time, and you won't have to sit in the heat of the shop all afternoon."

"Your new mare?" Carmela was more interested now. "Where is she?"

"Behind the shop, probably eating all of the grass there."

Carmela followed him around the shop. A beautiful mare with a dappled brown coat grazed on the nearby grass as she stood tied to a tree.

"Oh, she's beautiful," Carmela said, stepping up to the horse and holding her hand out for inspection. "What's her name?"

Samuel leaned against the side of the shop. "I don't know exactly. What do you think it should be?"

"I can name her?" Carmela asked, turning back to the horse. "Hmmm. How about Cinnamon or Nutmeg? She reminds me of sweet spices."

The horse lifted her head and let out a soft snort. Carmela laughed. "I think she likes her new name."

"Which will it be?" Samuel straightened, crossed to the horse, and gently stroked its head.

"Cinnamon."

"All right," he said.

Carmela fixed her wide eyes upon him. "Really?" Samuel smiled, and something fluttered in Carmela's stomach.

"Really," he said. "Now let's get going." He helped her onto the horse then climbed up behind her. As they rode down Main Street, she noticed that the crowd from the tavern had dispersed. Carmela decided that anyone who saw her with Samuel could speculate all they wanted. She didn't know them, and she was more than happy to be under Samuel's protective care.

With one of his arms wrapped around her, she realized that she had never felt so protected and energized at the same time as she did now. She had not expected Gideon to have a brother and one who had all the qualities that she had thought Gideon himself would have. *If he had never duped me into coming out to Leadville, I would have never met Samuel.* Perhaps fortune had smiled on her after all.

Nine

Samuel was still feeling upset as he rode with Carmela back to the homestead, but he hoped that he was hiding it well. It had taken every bit of his resolve not to challenge Johnson to a gun duel. Leadville wasn't exactly the Wild West, but women should be able to walk down Main Street and not worry about being harassed. Samuel's heart still pounded at the thought of the treatment this innocent woman had received at the hands of a drunken man.

He wanted to pull Carmela into his arms and comfort her again. But he would have to settle for having one arm wrapped loosely around her waist as they rode on the newly named Cinnamon. He found himself relaxing as Carmela's dark hair brushed against his neck, and he inhaled her scent of wildflowers and fresh soap.

As they passed the train station, Carmela turned her head. A notice had been posted on the outside of the station about the next train's arrival from the West. Even from his position, Samuel could read it. There was no denying that tomorrow the train would come through at noon.

Disappointment rushed through him, and Samuel had to shake it off as Carmela said, "Oh, the train is coming tomorrow—at last."

This meant that, by tomorrow at this time, she would be gone from Leadville forever, on her way back to Boston. Samuel wondered why he was suddenly so melancholy at the thought of her leaving. He barely knew her, and she'd had nothing but disappointments since she had arrived.

"I can pay for your ticket," he said. "It's the least I can do about the . . . uh . . . mix-up." He regretted offering this because he didn't want her to get on that train.

She shook her head and then turned slightly so that she could look up at him as they rode. "You are too kind," she said. "But I have enough for the ticket. I wouldn't want to put you out any more than I already have."

"You haven't put me out," Samuel said, knowing that these were the truest words he'd ever spoken. He had enjoyed helping her. He wished they could spend more time together, for he wanted to know everything about her.

All too soon, they reached the homestead. Samuel climbed off the horse then helped Carmela down. As she slid off the horse, she slipped into his arms, and he had the sudden desire to touch her hair and her cheek, to lean in and breathe.

"Thank you for the ride," she said, looking up at him, that sweet smile on her face.

"You're welcome." Neither moved for a moment, and then, at the same time, they both stepped away from each other. "I'll return before sundown," Samuel said.

She nodded. "I'll have something prepared for supper when you return."

Samuel supposed that his mother might have said this to his father, but no one had ever said this to him. He'd always fixed his own suppers. And, on the times when Gideon came staggering to his door, broke once again, Samuel had fed his brother too. So, he couldn't help the grin that spread across his face. He wanted to grab Carmela and swing her around. Instead, he mounted the horse and settled onto its back.

"That would be a treat," he said.

She smiled back at him, and his heart thudded hard against his chest. What would it be like, he wondered, to come home every day after work and be greeted by that smile? Internally shaking away his imaginings, he urged the horse around and rode back to town.

If someone had asked him later what he had done the rest of the afternoon, Samuel wouldn't have been able to give an accurate account. After he had closed up shop and mounted the horse to ride back home, he didn't even pay much attention to the gathering clouds that promised another rainstorm. The cooling wind also did nothing to interrupt his thoughts, which were full of Carmela: the stories of her childhood that she'd told him the night before by the fire, the way she'd breezed into his shop and delivered lunch, and how she'd sought him out for comfort after the run-in with Johnson.

Every thought was dominated by this woman, who was at his home right now, preparing him supper. How could he not think of her? He'd never been so grateful to ride a horse home after work in his whole life. This would cut down the time he would have normally taken. And, that meant having more time with Carmela before she would catch her train the next day.

He could smell supper before he had even entered the yard, which must have been because the aroma was foreign to him and because he'd been thinking about supper for the past few hours.

As Samuel dismounted Cinnamon, Carmela came out of the house. She had a linen dishcloth tucked into her waistband, acting as an apron, and her hair had come loose, sending stray tendrils about her face. She was even more beautiful than he had remembered. He took a deep breath and tried to organize his thoughts so that he wouldn't say something foolish. She'd already been put through enough with Johnson and the tavern owner.

"You're back," she said. "Supper's just ready. I'll set the table while you wash up."

Wash up? Samuel faintly recalled being told this by his mother many years ago, but he hadn't heard it since then. He smiled to himself as he led the horse to the lean-to, fetched the mare some water and grain, and then washed up at the water pump.

When he walked into his home, he was struck by the transformation. Carmela had been busy during his absence. A jar of fresh flowers sat on the small kitchen table, the place had been swept and dusted, and everything seemed to gleam in the glow of the setting sun. In addition, the place smelled heavenly, like fresh bread and simmering stew.

"I hope you like vegetable stew with dumplings," Carmela said, bustling about the place as she arranged bowls and spoons. "There wasn't much in your storage by way of meat, and I didn't think you'd appreciate me using one of your hens."

"It smells delicious," Samuel said, hanging his hat on the edge of the chair. Then he sat down, his stomach tightening in anticipation.

Carmela ladled stew from the pot into the bowl in front of him, and the steam warmed Samuel's face.

"Do you say grace in your home, Mr. Butler?" she asked in a sweet, almost teasing voice.

"I do now," he said with a wink. He bowed his head and closed his eyes. Then he offered what had to have been the shortest prayer ever sent up to heaven.

When Carmela had said amen, Samuel wasted no time in digging into the soup. The stew tasted even better than it had smelled. He looked up at Carmela after swallowing the first spoonful. "Will you marry me?" he asked.

She laughed, but her face pinked, and Samuel realized that he was more serious than he had thought. Carmela had been willing to marry his brother sight unseen. So, perhaps a marriage proposal from himself wouldn't be so out of the ordinary.

"You're just hungry," Carmela said, her laughter fading into a smile. "Hunger will do strange things to a man."

Samuel could only nod since he'd shoved another spoonful into his mouth. The dumplings were something else. "All I can say is that, if you opened your own café, you'd give Mrs. Smith some tough competition."

"She seems like a nice lady," Carmela said, starting to eat her own stew.

"She also takes in lady boarders like the school teacher, Miss Delany, and Lydia Stone, the secretary of the mine owner."

Carmela arched her brow. "Single ladies? I would think they'd be married in no time at all in this town."

"Perhaps they will be," Samuel said. "Although, none of them are as sweet and as pretty as you." He didn't know why he was laying it on so thick, but it was as if his mouth was running faster than his mind.

Carmela's face pinked again. "You are certainly complimentary today, Samuel."

He felt his own face redden and wondered whether she would laugh if she knew his true thoughts—about her. He continued eating, wishing that he could keep this moment wrapped up so that he could open it later, when she was gone, and relive it.

"I wouldn't mind having you sleep in the house tonight, Samuel," she said in a soft voice. "It appears that we'll have another rainstorm."

He looked up at her in surprise and saw that she was gazing out the windows. The clouds had darkened, and the tree was bent with the wind.

"Although, I'll be comfortable enough out here," she continued. "You should have your room back."

Samuel shook his head as Carmela met his gaze. "You will need your sleep if you're catching a train tomorrow." He held her gaze and almost wished she'd say that she had changed her mind. Just then, the rain started. Carmela laughed, and Samuel joined in.

With his stew and dumplings finished, Samuel helped Carmela clean up, even though she tried to shoo him away. Then he built a fire to keep out the damp air, which was seeping now into the house. He figured that he needed something to do. Otherwise, he might find himself following Carmela around.

Ten

The thunder rippled overhead, and Carmela nearly jumped out of bed to run into the front room. *But I am a grown woman, not a little girl, scared of a storm. And besides, Samuel is probably sound asleep.* She'd never had anyone enjoy her food as much as he had, not to mention the compliments he continued to pay her throughout the night. For a few unguarded moments, she had even thought he might be interested in her . . . really interested.

But she had talked herself out of getting such foolish notions, which would only break her heart. When morning came, she'd have to say good-bye and would never see him again.

The small bedroom flashed bright with lightning, and Carmela braced herself for the thunder that would surely follow. When it did, it sounded as if it were directly over the house. She gave a little yelp and burrowed more deeply into the covers.

"Are you all right?" a voice said from the doorway, startling her yet again. "Carmela?"

"I'm fine," she said, but she knew that her voice sounded weak and unconvincing.

"Come here."

This wasn't really a command or a request, but Carmela didn't need to hear it twice. She gathered the quilt about her and climbed off the bed, following Samuel into the front room, where he'd stoked the fire into a nice blaze. She stood in front of the hearth, feeling the heat radiating on her face. Then she closed her eyes, relishing in the warmth and comfort the simple fire brought.

"Better?" he asked, standing behind her.

She didn't know how close he was standing, but his voice was low and mellow. She imagined him wrapping his arms about her waist and how she would lean back against him. *But that wouldn't happen*, she thought. She was leaving the next day for Boston, and he'd remain here, on his Colorado homestead.

She released a sigh at the turn of events that had brought her here. She had been so focused on Gideon that she'd never considered that everything might change. But changed it had.

Then Samuel rested his hand on her shoulder, and she nearly startled again.

"Are you warm?" he asked.

"Yes." This response came out as a whisper. He lifted his hand, and the pressure and warmth from his touch was gone all too soon.

She didn't want him to step away but wanted to remain in the cocoon of his presence. How could she have come to desire this man after such a short acquaintance? she wondered. As the fire crackled before her, its popping sounds mimicked the thumping of her heart. Another crash of thunder came, but this time she didn't jump, and she only pulled the quilt tightly about her.

What would Samuel do, she wondered, if she confessed that she was coming to care for him? That, despite the unsavory run-in with Johnson, everything else about this stop in Leadville had been made wonderful . . . because of Samuel? She had enjoyed talking to him, had relished in his interest, had blushed at his compliments, and had felt valued and cherished for her opinions and forthright nature.

What would he do if she told him she didn't want to leave on that train?

"Do you want something to drink?" Samuel's voice echoed in the quiet room.

He was still there, standing close to her. So she turned to face him, wishing she had the courage to tell him of her growing feelings. But, what if he rejected her, laughed at her? Why would any man want a woman who'd been fool enough to agree to marry a man such as Gideon?

"All right," she said. "But I'll get the tea. It will give me something to do."

She turned toward the kitchen area just as he tried to step to the side. So Carmela bumped into him, and, because her arms were bundled up in the quilt, she swayed off balance. Samuel reached out to steady her, grasping her by the shoulders.

She couldn't help her next actions, being so close to him that she could feel his warm breath touching the top of her hair. She raised up on her feet and whispered, "Samuel."

He didn't speak but merely tightened his grip on her shoulders and lowered his face until his lips brushed against hers. This was the barest of kisses, but it felt like a fire had been lit inside of her, burning hotter than the fire in the hearth only a couple of paces away.

She released the quilt, and, as it fell to the floor, she wrapped her arms around his neck, pulling him closer. Samuel's lips met hers again, taking possession of hers as his hands moved to her waist, drawing her body flush with his.

She kissed him back, knowing that he might think less of her now. First, she was willing to marry his brother sight unseen, and now, she was kissing him. But her worries spun away as Samuel moved his mouth against hers, seeming to want her as much as she wanted him.

"Carmela," Samuel said in a breathless voice, breaking away from her.

It took her a moment to open her eyes and gaze up at him. Was he angry? Disgusted? Or embarrassed? she wondered. But she saw nothing in his eyes except for the same intensity that she felt in her heart.

"I'm sorry," she said. "I wasn't thinking. I'm not a wanton woman."

"I know," Samuel said in a whisper, tracing her cheek with his finger. "You're a beautiful, kind, and intelligent woman, but we need to talk."

She lowered her eyes, unable to gaze into those blue eyes of his. Had she just ruined his opinion of her? Was it too good to be true that he might possibly return her affections?

"Carmela," he said, grasping her hands gently. "Look at me."

She exhaled and looked up, dread pounding through her body. He would lecture her, and then she'd be on the train tomorrow, making Leadville, Colorado, a surreal memory.

"I know that how we met was unconventional," he began.

She wanted him to rush through his speech, to get it over with, and then she could return to the bed and curl up under the quilt until daylight arrived.

"But I don't want to you go back to Boston," he continued.

Her head snapped up, and she stared at him. "What?" she breathed, hardly daring to believe that he was saying what she had hoped for.

"Stay here with me," he said in a rush. "Marry me, Carmela Domeneca Rosalia Callemi, and make me a happy man. I know I don't have much of a home yet. But, with the two of us, we can accomplish great things."

She placed her hand on his chest. "You remembered my full name?"

"I remember every word you've spoken to me," he said, covering her hand with his.

"And . . . you want me to *marry* you?" she asked. It was almost impossible to believe. "Why?"

His brows furrowed slightly. "Because I adore you more than I ever thought it would be possible to adore a person. And, I haven't slept all night for the dread of sending you away forever."

Her breath caught. "Are you in earnest, truly?" she asked.

That smile of his was back, and he leaned forward, resting his forehead against hers. "I've never been more serious about anything," he said. "We could have the reverend marry us tomorrow. What do you say, my sweet Carmela?"

Her heart thudded once—then twice. She knew she would always be safe with this man, and she realized that she too adored him. So she placed her hands on his shoulders and tilted her face up. "I will marry you, Samuel Butler."

He laughed, pulling her against him, kissing her forehead, her cheek, her neck, and, finally, her lips.

ABOUT HEATHER B. MOORE

Heather B. Moore is a USA Today bestselling author. She writes historical thrillers under the pen name H.B. Moore; her latest is Finding Sheba. Under Heather B. Moore, she writes romance and women's fiction. She's one of the coauthors of The Newport Ladies Book Club series. Other works include Heart of the Ocean, The Fortune Café, The Boardwalk Antiques Shop, the Aliso Creek series, and the Amazon bestselling Timeless Romance Anthology series.

For book updates, sign up for Heather's email list: HBMoore.com/contact
    Website: www.HBMoore.com
    Facebook: Fans of H.B. Moore
    Blog: MyWritersLair.blogspot.com
    Twitter: @HeatherBMoore

The Price of Silver
by Siân Ann Bessey

OTHER WORKS BY SIÂN ANN BESSEY

One Last Spring
The Insider
Within the Dark Hills
Cover of Darkness
You Came For Me
Deception

One

Idaho Territory, April 1880

Caleb Walker stared at the older woman sitting in front of him, his initial disbelief rapidly developing into full-blown anger.

"You cannot be serious, Mother," he said.

Eliza Walker rose from her rocking chair beside the cabin's stove. "I'm completely serious, Caleb. The young lady arrives in Birch Creek by train this afternoon." She raised the letter in her hand. "See for yourself."

Giving the letter's cream stationery with its decidedly feminine penmanship nothing more than a passing glance, Caleb ran his fingers through his thick, dark hair and forced himself to take a deep breath. Taking out his frustration on his mother would not help; wringing his younger brother's neck, however, might solve a great many things.

"Does Jake ever think before he acts on any of his harebrained ideas?" he asked, still trying to come to terms with his brother's latest activities.

"This idea wasn't completely without merit," Eliza said, placing a placating hand on Caleb's arm.

"Mother!" Caleb could barely contain his exasperation. "No good man should begin a correspondence with a woman, offer to marry her sight unseen, send her a ticket to the middle of nowhere in Idaho Territory, and then, less than two weeks before she arrives, leave town to make his fortune at a silver mine hundreds of miles away."

Eliza frowned, concern lining her weathered face. "I daresay you're right. But he only had a couple days' notice on the silver mine claim, and I'm pretty sure he wrote to tell her he was leaving. Perhaps, with the winter storms as bad as they've been this year, his letter got held up."

Caleb stared at her incredulously. "So, you've known about this mail order bride of his all along?"

Eliza moved over to the cupboard on the other side of the small room, took out two mugs, and placed them on the wooden table. "I knew he'd placed an ad in one of those newspapers back East," she said, lifting the coffee pot off the stove and beginning to pour. "I confess, I had my doubts that anything would come of it. But, seeing as how there's not too many eligible young ladies hereabouts and that the few who do live close enough to consider courting seem to have settled on other suitors, I understand why he did it."

She glanced over at her son with an expression of sympathy, and an all too familiar ache filled Caleb's chest. Despite his best efforts to prevent the lingering hurt from showing, his mother must have seen something in his face because she quickly looked down and resumed talking.

"He has exchanged one or two letters with this girl," she said.

Caleb rolled his eyes. "You don't decide to get married after sharing only one or two letters!"

"I know it's not what you would have done," she said, "but Jake's always been the more impulsive of the two of you."

"Yeah. And from his hauling home that brown bear cub, when he was five, to heading off on this latest wild goose chase at the newest strike-it-rich silver mine in the territory, I always get to be the one left to deal with the problems his lack of common sense leaves behind."

Caleb began pacing back and forth, his long stride crossing the room in five or six steps. "I won't do it again," he said. "Jake's on his own this time. He created this mess; he can fix it."

Eliza waited until Caleb had reached the table again before handing him a mug filled with steaming coffee. "I know you're mad at your younger brother right now, and I understand your reluctance to get involved," she said, picking up the discarded letter and opening it. "But, there's someone else we have to think about this time. You and I both know that we can't leave that innocent girl sitting at the train depot all by herself."

Caleb tried to block out the pitiful image his mother's words had evoked. But it was impossible. No matter how he felt about his brother's poor judgment, he knew that abandoning a young woman to the train depot's frigid nighttime temperatures or its unscrupulous male visitors was not an option. Stifling a groan, he wrapped his fingers around the mug and took a gulp of the scalding liquid. Over the rim of the cup, he met his mother's knowing brown eyes. She gave him an encouraging smile, and, with a sinking heart, he knew he'd lost the battle almost before it had begun.

"Fine," he said with a defeated sigh. "What do you suggest I do with the unfortunate female when I find her?"

The Price of Silver

"Her name is Katie," his mother said, glancing at the paper again. "Katie Spencer. And I suggest you take her to the mercantile, to pick up a few items we need, then hurry back up here before it gets too dark."

Caleb stared at his mother. "You want me to bring her here to the cabin?"

"Well, where else would she go?" Eliza asked, looking at him as though he were addled. Truth be told, Caleb was beginning to wonder if he was.

"What about putting her back on the train to her own home?" he suggested.

Eliza pursed her lips. "You can give her that option, I suppose. But we'll have to take from the money we've set aside for the new calves to pay for the ticket." She started to move toward the jar on the top shelf, where their precious savings was kept.

"I'll bring her back here until we can get word to Jake," Caleb said, interrupting her progress. "He can either put an end to his mining adventure and come back home to claim his bride, or he can send the money so that she can go back to where she came from."

Eliza nodded her agreement. "That sounds very sensible."

"Right," Caleb muttered as he took his hat off the peg by the door and smashed it onto his head. "It seems I got Jake's portion of that virtue along with my own." He wasn't sure if his mother had heard him, but her lips twitched as though she were fighting a smile.

"I'll write Jake while you go hitch up the wagon," she said. "That way, the letter will get off today."

Caleb gave a resigned nod and opened the door. He would do what his mother asked, which meant coming to Jake's rescue yet again. But that didn't mean he had to like it.

Two hours later, Caleb drove the wagon out of the canyon. The afternoon sun was lowering in the sky, and, in the distance, the strident sound of a train's whistle filled the air.

"Dang it, Titus," he said, giving the reins a light flick. "We're going to be late after all."

As the uneven dirt road widened and smoothed out a little, the large, brown horse quickened its pace, and soon the cluster of buildings that made up the small town of Birch Creek came into view. A white, clapboard schoolhouse sat on one end of Main Street, right across from the church. Older homes filled the gaps between the blacksmith's shop, the tannery, the town mercantile, and the barbershop. On the other end of the street, the Grand Hotel, with its accompanying saloon, proudly claimed its prime location, directly across from the newly constructed train depot.

Two wagons rolled away from the depot's entrance as Caleb pulled up. He raised his hand in greeting to the drivers, both of whom he recognized as distant neighbors. A group of men entered the Grand Hotel's front doors, their carpetbags in hand. After a quick look to ensure that no women were among them, Caleb jumped off the wagon, tied the reins to a nearby hitching post, and walked onto the railway platform.

At first, the area appeared to be empty. A single wooden handcart stood beside the ticket office, but there was no movement from within the tiny room. Caleb walked toward it, turning as the sound of labored footsteps reached him.

"Afternoon, Mac," he said, when the town's part-time conductor shuffled out from behind the signal box. "I was hoping you were still here."

The Price of Silver

"What can I do for ya, Caleb?" the gray-haired man asked.

"Can you tell me if any young ladies got off the train this afternoon?"

"Well, now," Mac said, scratching his head through his thinning hair. "It jus' so happens there's a nice young thing sittin' all alone 'round the corner. But, if her ride don't show up soon, I'm fixin' to ask her home with me." He gave an almost toothless grin. "You're not plannin' to beat me to the punch, are ya boy?"

Caleb gave him a half-hearted smile. "Could be," he said. "I'll go talk to her."

Directing a muttered curse toward his absent brother for placing him in this difficult situation, Caleb rounded the ticket office and immediately spotted the one remaining passenger, sitting on a wooden bench with a small brown trunk beside her. His feet slowed to a stop, and he watched as the young woman suddenly became aware of his presence and hesitantly rose to face him.

He'd had over two hours alone in the wagon to imagine the various types of women who might respond to a mail order bride advertisement—and he'd come up with several very plausible possibilities. But none of the visions he'd conjured up in his mind came close to the one in front of him now.

She appeared to be in her early twenties and was of average height and slender build. Her dark brown hair was pinned up in an elaborate bun at the base of her head, beneath a hat of the same deep purple as her dress. A short, gray wool jacket and leather gloves were her only protection from the late afternoon's lowering temperatures. And, as she turned her startlingly blue eyes on him, he had the uncomfortable feeling that their shine was partly due to recent tears.

"Mr. Walker?" Her question brought him back to his awkward position.

"Yes," he said, moving forward again. Then, realizing what this admission would mean to her, he quickly amended his response. "Well, no. Not exactly."

A sudden wariness filled her eyes, and she took a small step back. "Are you or are you not Mr. Walker?" she said.

Caleb took off his hat and offered her his hand. "My name's Caleb Walker, ma'am. I'm Jake Walker's older brother, and I've come to pick you up. I apologize for getting here so late. The canyon road was in worse shape than I had thought."

"You're Jake Walker's brother?" she said, cautiously raising her hand to his.

"Yes, ma'am," Caleb said, trying to ignore the frisson of awareness that raced up his arm at her touch.

"I'm Katie Spencer," she said, releasing his hand. "It's nice to meet you."

"Likewise," Caleb said. He pressed his hat back onto his head and turned to point at the brown trunk. "This your only luggage?" he asked.

"Yes." She picked up a small reticule that was still lying on the bench. "That's everything."

Caleb nodded. Without another word, he bent down, hoisted the small trunk onto his shoulder, and turned to face the exit.

"The wagon's parked right outside," he said.

Two

For about the millionth time since she'd boarded the train in Saratoga Springs, New York, Katie wondered if she'd completely taken leave of her senses. A well-bred young lady simply didn't take off across the country, unaccompanied, to marry a man she'd never met before. It just didn't happen. And yet, here she was, following a complete stranger to a wagon that would take her who-knew-where, with nothing to fall back on but her instincts and a handful of coins in her reticule.

A year ago, she never would have believed that she'd find herself in a position like this. She'd been a baby when her mother had died, but she and her father had enjoyed a close relationship. He'd run a stable for the finest racehorses in the state of New York, and she'd filled her childhood with helping him care for those majestic animals. As she'd grown older, she'd accompanied him to many of the horse races, and she'd been readily welcomed into that high-society crowd.

But, when their prize-winning racehorse, Moonspinner, collapsed in his final lap on the Saratoga race course, everything had changed. Without an obvious cause for the horse's death, and with thousands of dollars on the line, accusations of neglect and mishandling were heaped at her father's feet. Within weeks, all but two horses had been relocated to other stables around the state, and her father's health had gone downhill as quickly as his fortune.

In the end, Katie had been forced to sell everything they owned to pay the legal, medical, and funeral bills. No one had cared enough to help. Her only visitor after her father's funeral had been her former beau, Bart Hansen, who'd simply come to reclaim his promise ring.

With no home, no income, no family, and no marriage prospects, she felt as though the tiny advertisement for a mail order bride, hidden among the "Wanted" pages of the *New York Times*, had been written especially for her. So she'd sent off a letter immediately, and Jake Walker had replied.

Over the last few weeks, she'd experienced more kindness through the letters of this unknown cowboy than she had from friends she'd known all her life. And it had motivated her to choose a different path: one that would take her out from under the dark cloud of gossip and censure; one that would give her a fresh start. Leaving behind everything safe and familiar, she'd taken the biggest risk of her life. And, as she watched Mr. Caleb Walker lower her trunk into the back of his wagon, she could only pray that she'd made the right decision.

Thus far, her limited interaction with Mr. Walker had been encouraging. After enduring over thirty minutes of despair, believing that she'd been forgotten at the train depot, his arrival had been an overwhelming relief. And she was grateful that, despite the odd circumstances that had brought them together, she didn't feel threatened by him. In fact, he had treated her with respect.

She wondered now how much he resembled his brother, Jake. Mr. Caleb Walker's broad shoulders and strong arms had made light work of carrying her trunk, just as his long legs had quickly eaten up the distance to the wagon. She guessed that he was usually clean-shaven, but the lateness of the hour had left an evening shadow on his chin. From where she stood, his dark curls were barely visible beneath the wide brim of his cowboy hat.

Suddenly, he raised his head and looked right at her. Embarrassed at having been caught staring, Katie felt her cheeks color. "I appreciate you coming to get me, Mr. Walker," she said. "But, would you mind telling me why it was you and not your brother who came?"

He made his way around the wagon to help her onto the seat.

"You can call me, Caleb," he said. "And I came because Jake's not here."

Katie frowned. "What do you mean, 'not here'? Where is he?"

"He headed up to Coeur d'Alene about two weeks ago," Caleb said. "Got word of a new silver strike up there, and left as soon as the roads were clear of snow."

Katie stared at him, trying to dampen her rising panic. "I don't understand. Why did he have me come if he's no longer here?"

"As near as we can tell, your letters crossed in the mail," he said.

Katie turned away from Caleb's perceptive eyes and swallowed hard. "A mail order bride with no groom," she whispered. "What's to be done with me now?"

She didn't even realize she'd said the words out loud until he answered her.

"Mother's written to Jake, explaining what's happened. And, while we're waiting to hear whether he's going to hightail it back here or send you the money for a return ticket, I'm to take you home."

"Home?" Katie prayed that she could keep her tears from falling in front of this man. Did he not realize that she had no home?

He nodded. "We have a place up the canyon. Didn't Jake tell you about it in one of his letters?"

She shook her head, and, for a split second, a look of irritation crossed his face. "Well, I'll tell you about it as we ride," he said. "And Mother will be sure to take care of anything I forget."

"Your mother lives there too?" Katie asked, experiencing the first glimmer of hope that her already shredded reputation may not, after all, suffer complete destruction.

"Mother, Jake, and me," he said. "Pa passed a few years back."

"I'm sorry," she said, only too aware of how much that loss hurt.

"He was a good man," Caleb said simply.

He helped her into the wagon, and they drove in silence as far as the mercantile.

"The post office is inside the store," Caleb said, bringing the wagon to a stop and withdrawing a letter from within his jacket. "I'll get this mailed off to Jake."

He jumped down from the wagon and tied up the reins. Then he moved to her side.

"Do you want to come inside?" he asked.

With the way Katie was feeling right then, she couldn't imagine anything much worse than meeting a curious shopkeeper or his customers.

"If it's all the same to you, I'll wait with the wagon," she said.

Caleb gave a small nod. "I'll only be a few minutes."

When Caleb exited the mercantile a short time later, there was no one in the wagon. Kicking himself for having left Miss Spencer alone, he hurried forward, scanning the road for any sign of his missing passenger. The street was unusually quiet. A couple of older men were talking outside the barbershop, and a wagon was parked down by the schoolhouse, but, with evening coming on, most people must have already headed home for supper. Where could she have gone? With rising concern, he rounded the wagon and lowered the small load of provisions his mother had requested into the back.

At the hitching post, Titus nickered, and Caleb heard a soft voice respond. He looked over in time to see Miss Spencer step out from behind his horse, and he watched as Titus lowered his head to gently rub his nose against her neck. Miss Spencer giggled and stroked the horse affectionately.

"It's just as I thought," she said to the horse. "You're nothing but a big softy."

Caleb raised his eyebrows, not sure which emotion dominated—his relief at having so quickly found his charge or his surprise at her fearless approach to his large workhorse. Before he could say anything, however, another voice reached him.

"Why, Caleb Walker! You weren't actually planning on leaving town without stopping to see me, were you?"

Caleb's heart sank. He turned to face a young lady,

who'd come out of the nearby store and was sashaying up the sidewalk toward him.

"Afternoon, Miss Skidmore," he said, closing the back of the wagon and purposely keeping the vehicle between them.

"Miss Skidmore?" She gave a pretty little pout. "And just when did you decide to get all formal?"

He shrugged. "'Bout the time you got yourself engaged to Billy Haskins, I reckon."

"That shouldn't make any difference at all," she said, an inviting smile on her lips.

"Actually, ma'am," Caleb said, walking over to Miss Spencer, who'd been silently watching the whole exchange from behind his horse, "it makes a heap of difference."

Without a word, he took Miss Spencer's arm and led her back to the wagon. With Amy Skidmore looking on with wide eyes, he helped Katie Spencer onto the seat and then climbed up beside her.

"Miss Skidmore," he said, giving a short pull on the rim of his cowboy hat in her direction. Then, with a gentle flick of the reins, he wheeled Titus around and headed down the empty street, increasing the distance between him and the young woman on the sidewalk as quickly as he could.

Once the town was behind them, Miss Spencer was the first to find her voice.

"That young lady was quite anxious for your attention."

Caleb grimaced. "She's claimed enough of that already. She won't be getting any more."

"I see," she said quietly.

But Caleb was quite sure that she didn't. And, for some reason, having Katie Spencer think ill of him did not sit well at all. Perhaps, if he explained himself now, the subject wouldn't raise its ugly head again. He took a deep breath.

"Up until a few weeks ago, I believed myself to be courting Miss Skidmore," he began. He sensed rather than saw Miss Spencer turn to face him. "Living up the canyon limited how much I could see her, but I'd go whenever I could steal a day away from my responsibilities at the ranch. It wasn't so hard in the fall, but winter came early this year, and we were snowed in for weeks."

He paused, remembering his shock when he'd finally made it to town and had seen Amy for the first time in a couple of months. "The canyon road finally cleared enough for me to attend the annual church spring social," he continued. "I arrived at Miss Skidmore's house, expecting to escort her to the dance. But, when I got there, her parents told me she'd already left—with her new fiancé." Caleb stared straight ahead, reliving that moment of shock. "I went to the dance long enough to see them for myself. Then I rode home."

Miss Spencer remained quiet. Caleb waited for a few minutes before glancing her way. She met his eyes and gave him a tentative smile.

"For what it's worth," she said, "I respect the way you behaved when Miss Skidmore approached you. Most of the men I know would have succumbed to her batting eyelashes."

It wasn't the response he'd anticipated, but, at her unexpected candor, Caleb chuckled. And when Miss Spencer realized that he wasn't going to take offense, her smile grew.

They lapsed into silence again, but something about their brief moment of camaraderie lifted Caleb's heavy heart and left him wondering if, perhaps, a pair of dancing blue eyes would have been harder to ignore than Amy Skidmore's sultry looks. Shaking his head to clear his thoughts, he reached down and pulled a blanket out from under the seat.

"Here," he said. "I should've given you this right off. Temperatures drop fast in the canyon."

Miss Spencer took the blanket from him and unfolded it, setting it across his knees along with her own.

"Tell me about your ranch," she said.

Caleb felt himself relax. This was a subject he was happy to discuss.

"Once you get me started, I may not stop," he warned.

"I won't be bored, I promise," she said.

Caleb hid a smile. He was coming to like the way Katie Spencer spoke her mind.

"Very well," he said. "I'll hold you to that."

Three

Twilight melted into darkness, and Caleb loosened the reins, giving Titus his head. The sure-footed horse pressed forward despite the lack of visibility and the steep, uneven terrain.

"Once daylight's gone, I reckon he can find his way home better without my help," Caleb said.

"How much farther is it?" Katie asked.

"Another two or three miles," he said. "The mouth of the canyon narrows quickly and becomes the Wilson Pass. It's a steep climb, but, once we're through, the canyon opens up with wide meadows on either side of the river. It's not the best land for growing crops, like the potatoes and wheat they plant in the Teton basin, but it's perfect cattle country. The grazing's good, and the mountains are rugged enough to make cattle thieves think twice."

"You have cattle thieves here?" Stories Katie had heard of the lawlessness out West came flooding back, and she shifted nervously.

"Rustlers come through every once in a while," Caleb said. "But they usually head over to Wyoming Territory, where the really big outfits make for easier pickin's."

"How many cows do you have?" she asked.

"One," Caleb said.

There was a long pause while Katie processed this information. She was glad that the darkness hid her shock. What kind of ranch had only one cow?

"Her name's Daisy," Caleb continued. "Mother looks after the milking and such, so Jake and I don't have much to do with her."

"Do you have any other animals?"

"Half a dozen chickens," he said. "Enough to keep us in eggs. Then there's a couple of pigs. One of them had piglets not long ago, and Mother's already working on fattening them up. We lost our old dog a while back," he added, "so we're looking to get a new one as soon as our neighbor's pups are ready to leave their mother."

The life she'd left in New York suddenly felt like it belonged to another world. "Do you have any other horses?" she asked, desperate to know there would be something familiar when she reached her final destination.

"Yep. Jake took his horse with him, but, along with Titus, we have my mother's mare, Echo, and my stallion, Mica. Echo's due to deliver a foal here in the next couple of weeks."

"Really?" she said. Even though Caleb's silhouette was all that was visible in the moonlight, Katie turned to face him, her excitement over the horse's birth temporarily eclipsing her dismay over Jake's family's unfortunate circumstances.

She saw the outline of his head nod. "Should be," he said. "And, if prices at the auction in Jackson Hole are good, we plan to add fifty young steers to our herd next month."

"Your herd?"

"We have about two hundred and fifty head right now," he said. "I'd like to get it up as close to three hundred as I can."

"But you said . . ." Katie stopped as Caleb began to chuckle for the second time in the last hour.

"Miss Spencer," he said, and she could hear the humor in his voice. "If you're going to be a rancher's wife, the first thing you need to do is learn the difference between a cow and a steer. A dairy farmer raises milk cows; a rancher raises beef cattle."

Katie was glad that it was too dark for Caleb to see her cheeks redden.

"You purposely misled me," she said with as much indignation as she could muster.

"I did nothing of the sort," he said. "You came to your own conclusions."

The wagon jolted over something on the road, and Katie clung to the edge of the seat as they lurched one way and then the other. To her frustration, it was remarkably difficult to stay in a huff when so much of her attention was needed to simply stay upright on her seat.

"Well, it's good to know that Jake's prospects aren't quite as bleak as I had first thought," she said, opting for honesty instead.

"So I imagine," he said drily. "And, who knows, perhaps he'll come back from the silver mine a rich man."

Caleb's words were an unhappy reminder of her untenable position. She honestly didn't care whether Jake came back wealthier. When she'd answered his advertisement, she'd set aside her lifelong dream of finding love. Her only hope had been that she could claim a relationship built on mutual trust and respect. But now, she had to face the fact that, unless Jake returned, even this might be out of reach.

She listened to the sound of the nearby river, wishing she could see the water, meadows, and mountains that Caleb had described. Instead, she focused on the majesty of the night sky above. Like a velvet backdrop, peppered with brilliant specks of light, the sight was both breathtaking and humbling.

They followed the river for a little longer before Titus veered left and took a path that led uphill again.

"The cabin's that way, just past the tree line," Caleb said. He raised his arm and pointed into the distance. For the first time, Katie spotted two lights, twinkling far below the stars in the sky. "Mother always puts candles in the windows to guide us home at night," he said.

Katie tightened her grip on the seat as a fresh wave of nervousness washed over her. How was a mother who obviously cared about her sons going to react to a mail order bride appearing on her doorstep? Would she treat Katie with indifference or disdain? With tolerance or acceptance? Suddenly, the answers really mattered. Katie had never known a mother's love, but she'd often longed for it. And now, as she faced her first night in this far away place, she prayed for it.

Titus shook his head and neighed as they rolled past the shadowy outline of a building to the right. An answering neigh told Katie that it was the barn. An owl hooted, and she watched it glide from a tall pine tree beside the barn across the open space before them. Up ahead, a door opened. In the flickering light, Katie saw someone step out onto the doorstep of a small log cabin. Caleb pulled the wagon a little closer before reining Titus to a stop. He jumped off the seat and walked over to the woman in the doorway.

"Sorry we're so late," he said, bending over to give her a brief hug. "I've never seen the road so bad. The spring runoff did some real damage."

"Well, you're home safely now," she said. "Did everything go all right?"

Instead of answering, Caleb walked back to the wagon and extended his arm to Katie. Hesitantly, she climbed down, and he led her over to his mother.

"Mother, this is Miss Katie Spencer. Miss Spencer, Jake's and my mother, Eliza Walker."

"Please call me Katie," Katie said. She looked over at the man at her side. "You too, Caleb."

Caleb gave her an accepting nod, but his mother reached out to grasp Katie's hands.

"Welcome, Katie," she said. "You must be awful weary after that long journey. Caleb will take care of the horse and bring in your luggage. So come on inside, and we'll have you settled in no time."

Katie blinked back her tears. It had been so long since anyone had offered her such kindness that she'd almost forgotten it existed.

"Thank you," she said.

"Of course, dear." Eliza turned to her son. "As soon as you're done, Caleb," she said, "I'll have some stew ready for you." Then she ushered Katie into the cabin.

Katie had never seen such a rustic home. The entire cabin was about the size of her former house's dining room and was divided into two sections. On one side, there was a kitchen area with a wooden cupboard and table, four simple wooden chairs, a rocking chair, and a large stove. Pans hung from the ceiling, and something that smelled divine was bubbling in a large pot on top of the stove. Two windows were cut into the log walls and were currently covered with blankets to block out the chill.

A log wall separated this area from what Katie could only assume were the bedrooms. There were two doors, hung with rawhide hinges, and Eliza led her to the closest one.

"We'll put you in here," she said. "It's the boys' room. But, seeing as how Jake's gone and how Caleb's just as happy sleeping in the barn, it should do just fine for the time being."

"That's very good of you," Katie said. "I'm sorry that Caleb will lose his bed because of me."

Eliza waved off Katie's apology. "With a new foal due any day, he'd be sleeping in the barn anyway." She moved back to the stove, took the lid off the pot, and gave the contents a stir. "Now, come get something to eat."

Katie couldn't remember when she'd eaten last, and her stomach had been growling from the moment the aroma of Eliza's stew had reached her.

"It smells wonderful," she said.

Eliza smiled. "Let's hope it tastes good too."

She handed Katie a bowl and was filling a second one when Caleb walked in with Katie's trunk on his shoulder.

"That was fast," Eliza said approvingly. "Go ahead and put Katie's things in your room."

Caleb raised one eyebrow and gave his mother a roguish look. "In my room?"

"Caleb Walker!" Eliza said, shaking her wooden spoon at him. "Watch yourself! You put that trunk in there, then take your stuff out to the barn."

Caleb laughed, and Katie was struck by how laughter lit up his handsome features. She studied the bowl of stew in front of her until he came out of the bedroom.

"Thank you, Caleb," she said, forcing herself to face him.

"You're welcome," he said. He raised the small bundle in his hand. "I'll take this out to the barn and be right back. Save me some stew!"

Four

Katie woke the next morning to the sounds of whistling and the creak of the cabin's front door opening and closing.

"Hush, Caleb." Eliza's loud whisper reached Katie from the other side of the log wall. "You'll wake Katie."

"Shouldn't she be up already?" he replied.

Katie threaded an arm free from the wool blanket that surrounded her and pulled up the animal pelt that lay across the window above her head. Bright sunlight streamed into the room.

"She must've been worn out," Eliza said.

"Wish I could use that excuse to stay in bed," Caleb grumbled.

Katie stifled a groan. How had she let this happen? Remaining in bed while others got up to do early morning chores was definitely not an auspicious beginning to her time at the ranch. She tossed the blanket aside and stood up, her breath catching as her bare feet touched the cold floor. Her trunk was right beside the bed. Within seconds, she'd dug out her light blue dress and her shawl.

Dressing as quickly as she could, Katie wove her long hair into a single braid and tied up her boots. Then, after glancing back once to make sure she'd left everything tidy, she opened the bedroom door and entered the kitchen area. Eliza and Caleb were sitting at the table, talking softly. They both looked up as Katie walked in.

"Good morning, Katie," Eliza said cheerfully.

"Good morning," Katie replied.

Caleb got to his feet and gave her a nod. Then he placed his empty bowl in a large metal tub and reached for his cowboy hat.

"I'll be down in the south pasture today," he said. "The fence needs fixing before we move the cattle in."

"All right," Eliza said, handing him a pail. "Here's your lunch."

"Thanks," he said. He opened the door and stepped outside. "I'll be back by sundown."

Then, with a click of the latch, he was gone.

"Come sit and have breakfast," Eliza said, turning to Katie again.

Glad to move closer to the warm stove, Katie took the seat Caleb had vacated. "I'm sorry I didn't get up earlier," she said. "I had no idea how late it was."

"Give yourself some time," Eliza said, passing her a bowl of oatmeal. "Every new place takes getting used to."

Katie accepted the oatmeal gratefully. "Can I help you with any chores today?" she asked.

"Well, I'm not one to turn down an offer like that," Eliza said. "As soon as you've eaten, I'll show you 'round. Then, if you're still of a mind to help out, I'll put you to work."

Two hours later, Eliza had given Katie a tour of the

chicken coop, the pigpen, and the barn. She'd shown her how to sneak up on the chickens to find their eggs and how to feed the pigs without being attacked by a dozen squealing piglets. She'd introduced her to Daisy, who was grazing peacefully not far from the barn, and had shown her where the milking was done. Then she'd taken her to the other side of the barn, where Katie had given Titus an affectionate pat before meeting Echo for the first time.

Echo was a beautiful chestnut mare with liquid brown eyes. Her round girth and labored movements all pointed to how close she was to her foal's arrival, but she ambled toward Katie and raised her nose to greet her.

"Oh, you are beautiful," Katie said, running her hand softly down the mare's long neck. Echo nickered and nuzzled Katie's cheek.

"She likes you," Eliza said.

"The feeling's mutual," Katie said with a smile.

They lingered a little longer with the horses before Eliza led Katie to a small clearing among the pines where a spring bubbled up through some craggy rocks and flowed in a small stream to join the river below.

"This is where we collect our water," Eliza explained. "Jake dug out a space between the rocks that we use as a cooler in the summer. The cold spring water helps keeps our milk, butter, eggs, and cheese fresh when the daytime temperatures go up." Eliza pushed a large slab of stone to one side to reveal a two-foot wide hollow. "It goes back about three feet," she said.

Katie was glad that Eliza had shown her something Jake had worked on. It made him seem more real.

"What does Jake enjoy most about the ranch?" she asked.

Eliza thought about that for a few minutes. "That's an

interesting question," she finally said. "I don't know that he really enjoys working with the cattle. Not the way Caleb does, anyway. Caleb loves the land and thrives on working it. Jake works hard but more because he knows the jobs need to be done," she explained. "Jake's joy comes more from trying new things. He got a lot of pleasure out of making this cooler. It was his own idea, and it works great."

Katie studied Jake's cooler again, feeling pleased that the man she was to marry could be so innovative.

Caleb lowered his shovel and tipped his hat back so that he could wipe the sweat off his forehead with his sleeve. Replacing fence posts was a brutal job. Even on a cool spring day, it was hot, dirty work. He looked down the fence line. Ten posts stood tall where, only a few hours before, a broken fence had rested on the ground. He had another six to go.

With resignation, Caleb pressed the shovel into the heavy, water-saturated soil again. He was pushing himself hard even though he'd gotten very little sleep the night before. It wasn't that he'd been uncomfortable in the barn. He enjoyed sleeping in a bed of hay. It was more that he couldn't get a certain young woman with deep blue eyes out of his head. Even today, no amount of work had taken his mind off her for long—and that was beyond frustrating.

He was used to treading carefully whenever he conversed with a young lady. He'd learned through painful experience that he needed to carefully navigate the treacherous waters of female subtleties and flirtation. So, he'd been on his guard when he'd picked up Katie at the train depot, not knowing what to expect. But she'd taken him by surprise. She'd been frank with her opinions and genuine in her interest. In short, she'd been easy to talk to. And, even though the canyon road had been rough and the potholes deep, the journey home had been one of the most pleasant he'd had in a long time.

He was filled with questions, and he'd spent all night telling himself that none of them mattered. After all, it wasn't his business why a pretty, young woman like Katie Spencer would feel it necessary to respond to a mail order bride advertisement. Was she running from something or someone? How did she really feel about her current situation? And, why should he care whether or not she appreciated this canyon the way he did? Those things should be Jake's problems, not his.

When he'd arrived at the cabin that morning to learn that Katie was still in bed, it had almost been a relief to believe he'd found a flaw in her. Laziness was not a trait he tolerated well. But, when she'd walked out of his bedroom with creases from the bedding marking her cheeks and her blue eyes still adjusting to daylight, he'd known that his mother had been right. Katie had been deeply asleep right up until her entry into the kitchen.

With a groan, Caleb tossed a shovelful of dirt onto a nearby pile. Perhaps, if he found out more about her, he could put his questions to rest. He'd done almost all the talking on their journey through the canyon. It was time he did some listening. For he was more than ready to sleep through the night again.

Five

By the end of her second week at the ranch, Katie's days had fallen into a fairly predictable routine. She rose at the same time as Eliza, and, while Eliza went to milk Daisy, she collected the eggs and fed the chickens and the pigs. When those chores were done, the two women returned to the cabin to make breakfast. Caleb joined them there after he'd finished taking care of the horses.

Katie listened for Caleb's whistle each morning. As soon as she heard him coming around the corner of the small cabin, she'd plate up his breakfast so that, by the time he entered and hung up his hat, it was ready for him. Caleb always left soon after he'd eaten, and that was when Eliza and Katie got to work on the more time-intensive chores. Some of these jobs were simple things like sweeping and dusting, but, more often than not, they were things that Katie had never done before.

Cleaning out the chicken coop was, by far, the nastiest, smelliest activity she'd ever undertaken. And, rather than be appreciative, the chickens squawked their disapproval at her intrusion and took it in turns to launch full-scale attacks on her legs. This disagreeable experience made the days that she'd spent mucking out her father's stables seem pleasant by comparison.

On another day, Eliza showed Katie how to use the butter churn. After churning for what seemed like hours, Katie's arms and shoulders felt as though they were on fire, but she was proud of the large pat of butter she had to show for her efforts.

The pain in her arms paled in comparison to the ache in her back after a morning of digging in Eliza's garden. Eliza was anxious to prepare the soil for spring planting, but the melting snow had left the soil wet and heavy. Weeds from the previous fall had already started to multiply, and rocks littered the large area, making their progress slow. It took them working together for three days to completely clear the ground, and, when they were done, Katie promised herself that she'd never take a potato for granted again.

Most days, Eliza encouraged Katie to put aside her work by the late afternoon so that she could spend an hour or so exploring the ranch. Katie came to love this time alone. Every afternoon, she'd set off on foot, not knowing exactly where she was headed or what she would see. She wandered the forests, loving the smell of the pine needles and the song of the birds. Sometimes, she'd follow the stream down to the meadow and watch the cattle as they grazed along the river. Wildflowers were already blooming, and she often gathered some, marveling at the variety of colors among the delicate blossoms.

She often saw squirrels and chipmunks, woodpeckers and blue jays. Once, she came upon a small herd of deer. As she approached, their heads popped up, their ears twitching nervously before they bounded off into the forest in unison.

Along with the wildlife, she also kept an eye out for Caleb. She was never sure where he'd be, but, occasionally, she'd spot him off in the distance in one of the meadows. Usually, he was riding his black horse, Mica, through the cattle or along a line of wooden fencing. Sometimes, she'd see him repairing a section of fence or clearing debris left by spring runoff. She never got too close, not wanting to interrupt him or to become an irritant. But, seeing him—even if it were only for a few minutes—made her day better.

Her favorite part of each day, however, was the evening, when Caleb was back, dinner was over, and they would all sit down together around the stove and talk. When Caleb and Eliza asked Katie about her life in New York, it was easy to tell them about her happy growing-up years; it was much harder to share her more difficult, recent past. Eliza obviously sensed her struggle, because she'd taken Katie's hand and given it a comforting squeeze.

"Whenever you're ready, dear, not before."

Katie had drawn courage from this little show of support and had opened up about her father's misfortunes, the unjustified slander that had been heaped upon him, his rapid decline in health and subsequent death, and the ensuing loss of her home, stables, and so-called friends.

When she finished her story, she was met with silence, and she experienced a pang of fear, wondering if, perhaps, she'd said too much. Would the Walkers not want to be associated with someone whose family reputation was so tainted? She glanced at Caleb and found his eyes upon her.

"Well," he said, "that explains your love of horses and their love for you."

Gratitude for his perspective warmed her heart. "I've been around horses for as long as I can remember," Katie said.

"I've never seen Titus act so much like a lap dog as he does around you," Caleb told her. "And, if I'm not careful, Mica will start thinking he's your horse."

Katie felt her cheeks color. She'd not known that anyone was aware of her daily visits to the horses in the barn. Titus, Mica, and Echo helped her feel grounded when everything around her was shifting. They gave her unconditional affection, and she reciprocated. The horses were her lifeline.

"I'd be willing to trade collecting the eggs and feeding the chickens and pigs in the morning for taking care of the horses, if you're interested," she said.

Surprise filled Caleb's eyes, quickly followed by something that looked suspiciously like humor. Eliza, however, couldn't hide her amusement. With a peal of laughter, she patted Katie's hand.

"Oh my stars," Eliza said. "The stories I could tell about Caleb and the chicken coop!"

Sensing an opportunity to learn more about the man in front of her, Katie turned to Eliza. "Please tell me," she said.

"Well," Eliza sat back and gave Caleb a mischievous look. "Where do I begin?"

Caleb rolled his eyes. "I'm sure Katie would much rather hear about Jake."

"I believe we can kill two birds with one stone," Eliza said. "Remember the raccoon catcher?"

With a groan, Caleb got up to pour himself a cup of coffee. "Fine," he said. "Just get it over with quickly."

Eliza chuckled and immediately launched into one of her many stories about the two boys. "When Caleb and Jake were young," she began, "they traded off weeks being in charge of the chickens—feeding them, collecting the eggs, and cleaning the coop. It was Jake's week, and he went out one morning to find all the chickens in a dither because some critter had dug a hole under the fence and stolen the eggs. There were eggshells on the ground outside the coop, and he found more by the trees, so he figured it was either a fox or a raccoon, sneaking in from the forest."

She glanced over at Katie. "I've already told you how much Jake likes to try new things. Well, he got to thinking about how he could catch this egg thief red-handed, and he came up with some elaborate trap that would be triggered the moment the wild critter crawled through the hole it'd dug into the coop," she explained. "He set the wires and showed Caleb how his slick invention worked, then left Caleb in charge because it had rolled over into being Caleb's week for doing the chickens.

"So, Caleb went out the next morning," she continued. "And, sure enough, there was some four-legged critter stuck in the chicken coop. Caleb put on his gloves and opened the gate, ready to take care of the thief, only to be hit square in the chest with skunk spray."

Katie put her hand to her mouth to mask her giggle.

Caleb shook his head. "The chickens went crazy," he said. "Our old dog howled every time he caught wind of me, and no one let me near the cabin for over twenty-four hours."

"So, you slept in the barn then too," Katie said.

"If I'd done that, I likely would've killed off the horses and the cow," he said. "I was stuck outside till Mother scrubbed me down with some awful potion."

"Hey, now," Eliza said. "You might still be sleeping outside if it weren't for that skunk-spray remedy."

Caleb gave a rueful grin. "I believe it."

Caleb returned to the barn after another evening spent with his mother and Katie at the cabin. The first few nights had taught him a great deal about Katie Spencer. Not only had she opened up about her background, she'd also revealed much about her character and integrity. Over the following evenings, his mother had shared stories about him and Jake and their father. Katie had listened to all her memories with rapt attention, openly sharing in the laughter and tears. If he hadn't witnessed it himself, he wouldn't have believed it. In under three weeks, Katie had become part of the very fabric of his family.

He moved toward Mica's stall and sniffed. The lingering scent of lavender still clung to the air: a sure sign that Katie had visited the horses recently. He was quite certain that she didn't realize how aware he was of her movements, how much he now looked forward to her handing him his breakfast each morning, and how he watched for her when she walked the hillsides in the afternoons. No matter how engrossed he was in his work, he somehow sensed when she was close by. Without fail, he'd glance up to catch a glimpse of her in the distance and would wish that she were close enough to exchange a few words.

In the stall next to Mica, Echo gave a snort. Caleb reached over and patted the chestnut mare's neck, studying her carefully as she moved closer.

"Not much longer, girl," he said, offering the horse a handful of extra oats. "Maybe, for your sake alone, it's a good thing I'm still not sleeping well at night."

Six

Katie had just finished buttoning her dress the next morning when she heard Eliza calling her name. She hurried into the kitchen, but Eliza wasn't there. Confused, she stood still, wondering if she'd imagined hearing the faint voice. Then she heard it again, and Katie realized it was coming from the other bedroom. Giving a light knock, she pushed open the door and peeked inside. A bed and a chest of drawers filled the tiny room. Eliza was lying in bed, her graying hair braided, her face pale.

"Is something wrong?" Katie asked anxiously.

"It's my darn lumbago," Eliza said, taking a sharp breath as she tried to alter her position in bed. "It hits me every once in a while just to remind me that I'm not as young as I used to be." She frowned. "I guess all that yard work has finally got to me."

"I'm so sorry," Katie said. "What can I do to help?"

Eliza gave a weak smile. "I won't be up for much today, I'm afraid. We'll put off the cleaning I had planned, and I'm quite sure Caleb can make a bowl of oatmeal without me fussing over it. But, if there's any way you could take care of milking Daisy, I'd be most grateful."

Katie's heart sank. Of all the requests Eliza could have made, this one was likely the worst. She'd watched Eliza milk the cow a couple of times, but that was the extent of her milking experience.

"I'll do my best," Katie said, hoping she conveyed more confidence than she felt.

"I know you will, dear," Eliza said.

"Can I get you anything before I go out?"

Eliza shook her head. "Don't worry about me. I'll try to rest a little longer. Take care of the animals first."

With a nod, Katie left the tiny bedroom, grabbed her shawl from the peg near the door, and stepped out into the brisk morning air.

She was halfway through gathering the eggs, when Daisy's plaintive mooing reached her.

"I'm coming, Daisy," she said, uncovering the last of the eggs hidden in the straw and adding them to her basket. "Sorry, piglets, you'll have to wait a little longer," she added as she raced past the pigpen toward the barn.

She entered the barn and made straight for the milking area. Daisy was already there, waiting for her. Katie put the basket of eggs in the corner. Grasping the cow's rope harness, Katie pulled her close enough that she could tie her securely to the stall.

"You're going to have to bear with me, Daisy," Katie said softly. "There's an awful lot I don't know."

She turned and looked around, mentally reviewing all she needed: pail, stool, clean rag, soap, and water. Thankful that she'd watched Eliza prepare for milking more than once, Katie gathered everything, washed out the milking pail, and cleaned Daisy's udder. Then she positioned the pail beneath Daisy's udder and took her place on the stool. Taking a deep breath, she grasped one of the teats and squeezed. Nothing happened. She tried again. Daisy turned her head and regarded her with doleful eyes.

"I'm sorry, Daisy," Katie said. "I'm trying. Really, I am."

Daisy shuffled her feet, and Katie readjusted her own position, pulling down as she squeezed. After fifteen minutes, Daisy gave a disgruntled moo, and Katie leaned her head against the cow's warm body.

"I don't know how to do this, Daisy," she said, trying to keep her voice from breaking. "I don't want to hurt you, but I have to get you milked."

"Slowly adjust the pressure on each of your fingers," someone said.

At the unexpected sound, Katie jumped up, knocking over the stool and the empty milk pail with a clatter.

"Caleb!" she gasped. "You scared me."

"Sorry," he said. "I was feeding the horses, when I heard your voice." He looked around quizzically. "Doesn't my mother usually take care of the milking?"

Katie nodded. "She's down in bed with lumbago."

He groaned.

"Does it happen very often?" Katie asked.

"More often than I'd like," he said. "She's been overdoing it again."

"We've been working on the garden for three days," she explained.

"That would do it." He reached over and righted the pail and the stool. "Sit down," he said. "Let's see if we can't help Daisy out of her misery, then I'll go check on Mother."

Katie took her seat again.

"Now put your hands like this," Caleb said as he

wrapped his fingers around one of Daisy's teats. He moved back, and Katie tried to follow his example. "That's right," he said. "Now, squeeze from the top to the bottom."

Katie tried, and a single drop of milk appeared. She turned to him with dismay. "I'll be here all day," she said. "And Daisy will hate me forever."

He laughed. "An hour at the most. And Daisy's a very forgiving cow."

She shook her head, tears of frustration blurring her vision. Caleb knelt down behind the stool.

"You can do it, Katie," he said gently.

He reached around her, placing his hands over hers and guiding them back into a milking position. Carefully applying just the right amount of pressure on each of her fingers in turn, he kept this fluid motion going until her hands were moving in unison with his. With a sudden hiss, a stream of milk shot into the metal pail.

"It's . . . it's working," Katie said, struggling to form a coherent sentence with Caleb's arms around her and her hands in his. She turned her head to find Caleb's face just inches from hers. His fingers stilled but did not release their grip. Their eyes met. Then, for a fleeting second, his gaze dropped to her lips. Beside them, Daisy shifted impatiently. Caleb blinked and leaned back, pulling his hands away. Katie felt the loss immediately.

"Try it on your own," he said, sounding a little out of breath as he got to his feet.

As if in a fog, Katie turned back to Daisy. Replicating the technique Caleb had modeled, she squeezed the teat, and, immediately, milk squirted out.

"That's it," he said, already walking toward the door. "Keep it nice and steady, and you'll be done in no time."

Katie simply nodded. She was still too shaken by her

response to Caleb's intimate proximity to trust herself to speak.

Caleb headed straight for the water barrel that sat to one side of the cabin. He took off his hat, lifted the lid, filled the pitcher that was hanging inside, and dumped the entire contents on his head. Shuddering against the sudden cold, he shook his head, spraying water droplets everywhere. After running his fingers through his hair, in an attempt to tame the curls, he smashed his hat back on and marched into the cabin. He may have chilled himself to the core, but at least he could think clearly again.

As he entered the quiet cabin, his steps slowed, and he closed the door softly. The kitchen felt empty without his mother and Katie bustling around to make breakfast. The thought brought him up short. How had he gotten so accustomed to having Katie around in such a brief period of time? Perhaps because she belonged here? Caleb gave an exasperated sigh. He'd felt that way for days. But what he still needed to come to terms with was that she belonged here with his brother.

A drip of cold water ran down his neck, and he shivered. Gathering some wood from the basket in the corner, Caleb added fuel to the stove then walked over to his mother's room and tapped lightly on the door. No one answered, so he peered inside. His mother was sleeping peacefully. Closing the door again, he retreated to the kitchen and filled a pot with water. Breakfast would have to be oatmeal today.

When Katie arrived back at the cabin, carrying a full pail of milk and a basket of eggs, Caleb was gone. A short note lay next to a pan of warm oatmeal on the table. She put down the milk and eggs and picked up the small piece of paper.

Gone to meet up with a neighbor to move cattle. Mother still asleep.

Katie dropped onto the nearest chair. Perhaps she'd only imagined the connection she'd shared with Caleb that morning. She glanced at the note again. It appeared that he was going to ignore whatever had occurred between them. Surely, she could do that too. She put a shaky hand to her forehead. For the sake of her future at the ranch, she would have to.

Seven

When Eliza awoke, Katie took her a bowl of oatmeal in bed. Once she'd finished eating, however, the older lady insisted on getting up. Her movements were slow and obviously painful, but she shuffled her way to the rocking chair and stayed there, seeming content to talk while Katie dusted and swept.

"It was so much harder to keep this place clean before the boys put in the wood floor," Eliza said.

Katie paused over her pan full of dirt. "When did they do that?"

"Last winter," she said. "Before that, it was a dirt floor."

Even now, the Walkers' cabin was the most primitive home Katie had ever seen. She could hardly imagine what it would have been like to live here without flooring.

Eliza pointed to the pans hanging from the ceiling. "Jake attached the leftover wood to the rafters then put in the hooks, so I could keep my pots and pans out of the way." She gave a small smile. "That boy's always thinkin' of something new."

Katie stilled the broom that she was wielding. Today, more than ever, she needed to focus on Jake. "When do you think we'll hear from him?" she asked.

Eliza looked thoughtful. "He should've gotten my letter by now," she said. "If the news that you're here brings him right home, he could be here any day. But, if he doesn't show up soon, Caleb should go into town to see if there's a letter waiting."

Katie's stomach knotted with nervousness at the thought of Jake's return and what that would mean, but she wasn't sure how long she could go on living with Eliza and Caleb without the propriety that marriage would afford. Her life here lacked the sophistication and affluence she'd once known, but she already loved the rugged beauty of the land and the simplicity of their everyday life.

Working alongside Eliza had also given Katie a purpose, and she cherished the older woman's kindhearted acceptance. Would Jake treat her the same way? Would he ever feel more for her than that? Unbidden, the memory of Caleb's hands around hers filled her mind. She pushed the image away and tightened her hold on the broom handle.

"I hope we hear something soon," she said.

"Me too," Eliza agreed.

After lunch, Eliza stayed seated while she talked Katie through the process of making biscuits. And, when Katie took the puffy, golden brown circles out of the oven, Eliza was full of praise for her first-time effort.

"They're as near perfect as I've ever seen," Eliza said, struggling to come to her feet.

Katie put down the towel in her hand and hurried over to Eliza's side.

"Are you ready to lie down for a bit?" she asked.

Reluctantly, Eliza nodded. "This fool lumbago's such a

nuisance, but I've learned that, if I rest up the first day, the pain's usually better the next."

"That sounds very wise," Katie said, offering Eliza her arm as they made their way slowly to the bedroom.

"Why don't you leave the biscuits cooling and go out and get some fresh air while I'm resting," Eliza suggested.

Katie gave her a grateful smile. "Maybe I will," she said.

The air felt damp as Katie made her way down the narrow path that led to the meadow. She tucked her shawl more closely around her shoulders and glanced at the sky. Patches of pale blue were still visible, but, to the south, a bank of dark gray clouds was rolling steadily nearer, portending rain by the end of the day.

The birds, which usually maintained a continual chorus, were silent, the sound of their voices replaced by a steady rumble that vibrated through the ground. Katie could hear the lowing of cattle up ahead, and, when she turned the bend, her feet came to an abrupt halt. The meadow, which usually rolled out like an expansive green carpet all the way to the river, was completely hidden beneath a mass of moving steers.

Katie slowly moved toward a nearby fence. She stepped onto the lowest rung and watched in wonder as two cowboys rode up from behind the herd, one on one side and one on the other, using their horses to guide the moving cattle toward the open gate of the south pasture. While the steers jostled for position, mooing loudly as they pushed and shoved against each other, the cowboys funneled the cattle through the narrow opening.

All of a sudden, a steer broke loose, bolting away from

the gate. With a warning shout, the cowboy that she recognized as Caleb turned Mica around and galloped after the escaping steer. His arm shot up, his hand swinging a circle of rope. Seconds later, the rope sailed through the air and slipped around the steer's neck.

The steer staggered to a stop as Caleb drew up beside it. With its head in a noose, all the fight left the animal, and it fell into step beside Mica. When they reached the gate, Caleb leaned down from his saddle and pulled off the rope. Without a backward glance, the steer ambled into the pasture to join his herd. Then the second cowboy moved from his position beside the gate, swinging it closed and latching it.

Katie stood on the fence for a few more minutes, watching the cattle milling around as Caleb conferred with the other cowboy. Then a large raindrop landed on her cheek. She looked up as a roll of thunder sounded, and, all at once, the rain started falling in earnest.

Jumping off the fence, she ran for the path that led to the cabin. Behind her, she heard the echo of hooves on the ground, then the hissing of something flying past her ear. Suddenly, a rope snaked down from her shoulders to her waist.

"Caleb!" she gasped, swinging around as he and Mica drew closer. "You roped me!"

"Yep," he said with a grin. "And you were movin' pretty quick."

"Take it off," she said, squirming to free herself.

He reached down and gently pulled at the wet rope around her waist, his touch quickening her pulse. The rope fell to the ground, and Katie stepped out of it and away from Caleb. With the speed that comes from practice, he looped the rope over his saddle horn, and then he stretched out his arm to her.

"The storm's coming in fast," he said, rain now dripping off the brim of his hat. "I'll give you a ride to the cabin."

Katie took another step back. She wanted to sit astride a horse again more than she could say, but she was afraid—afraid that if she put her arms around Caleb as he rode home, she wouldn't want to let go. To protect her arrangement with Jake, she knew that she had to keep her distance.

"I can run," she said.

Thunder rolled again, and Mica sidestepped nervously.

Caleb frowned. "You'll get soaking wet."

"I'm already wet," she said, backing up farther. "I'll see you at dinner." Then, before he could say anything more, she turned, lifted the hem of her dress, and hurried up the wet, muddy path.

Eight

Katie went straight to her room and stripped out of her wet clothes. Taking a towel, she dried her hands and face and put on her clean blue dress. Then she moved back into the kitchen and sat down in front of the stove. One by one, she pulled the pins out of her hair until it fell like a damp curtain all the way to her waist. She turned slightly, hoping the heat from the stove would speed her hair's drying time.

Suddenly, the front door flew open. She swung around, and Caleb stepped in, dripping water all over the floor and panting as though he'd just finished a race.

"I need your help, Katie," he said, his words coming out in gasps. "Echo's in trouble."

She stood up. "The foal?"

He nodded. "It's coming. But something's not right."

Katie ran to her room and snatched her wet shawl off the floor. Tossing it over her head, she raced back to the kitchen where Caleb had the door open again. Lowering her head against the driving rain, she sprinted toward the barn.

Caleb barely beat her there. He shut the door behind them and took off his hat, shaking the moisture from it onto the floor before hanging it on a nail beside some horse tack. Katie took off her shawl and did the same thing. Then they both moved quietly toward Echo's stall.

The mare was lying in the straw. As they drew near, the muscles across her torso rippled, and she gave an agonized groan. Katie fell to her knees beside the struggling horse.

"It's all right, Echo," she said, running her hand down the horse's neck. "It will be over soon." She looked over at Caleb. "What's wrong?"

Caleb was rolling up his sleeves next to a bar of soap and a bucket of water. "There's only one hoof in the birthing canal," he said. "No sign of the nose yet. But, if I can't get the other hoof and the head down in the next few minutes, it's going to be too hard to work against these strong contractions."

Katie swallowed hard. She'd seen this happen to a foaling mare once before, but that time there'd been a vet, her father, and three experienced stable hands available to help.

"Lubricate your arm as well as you can," she said. "Follow the one leg until you feel the foal's chest. That should guide you to its face, nose, and other leg."

"Can you let me know when she has her next contraction?" he asked.

Katie nodded and placed a gentle hand on Echo's abdomen. Almost immediately, she felt the muscles begin to tighten.

"It's coming," she said.

Caleb knelt at Echo's tail, placing his hand on the tiny, sack-covered hoof protruding from the horse's birth canal.

Echo groaned again, her eyes rolling, and Caleb's arm disappeared. Katie stroked Echo's neck, talking softly. Caleb closed his eyes, and Katie saw beads of sweat appear on his forehead as he leaned up against the horse's rump.

"The head's in position," he said through gritted teeth. "I've just got to get the other hoof."

Echo shook her head and raised her shoulders as if she were about to rise.

"Keep her down," Caleb urged. "I'm almost there."

"Lie still, Echo," Katie said. "Lie still."

Echo rubbed her nose against Katie's long hair before flopping back into the straw as her muscles tensed again.

"Another contraction," Katie said.

Caleb's grunt coincided with Echo's groan.

"It's through," he gasped as his hand reemerged holding a second tiny hoof.

Relief flooded Katie's heart. Caleb slid back on his heels, and, as the contraction peaked, he grasped both of the foal's hooves and pulled gently. Immediately, a little nose appeared. Moments later, the head and shoulders were through. Echo gave one more groan, and, with a whoosh, the foal was born.

Looking exhausted, Caleb got to his feet and walked over to the bucket. He washed his hands and arms then dried them on a towel. Katie rose from her position at Echo's head and moved to stand beside him. He reached for her hand, and she threaded her fingers between his, watching as the mare met her foal for the very first time.

"It's a miracle," she said. "Every time, it's a miracle."

She turned to look at him. As their eyes met, he raised his free hand to her cheek, and she leaned into it. He drew her closer and bent his head until his lips touched hers. Gently, he ran his fingers through her long hair, and, as she responded to his touch, his kiss deepened.

When they finally drew apart, Katie's legs felt as wobbly as the newborn foal's.

"Heaven help me—I've done this all wrong," Caleb breathed. Then, releasing her abruptly, he stepped out of the stall.

In a few long strides, he had his cowboy hat in hand and the barn door open. A gust of wind blew in, and the tack clanged against the post. He turned back to face her.

"I have to write Jake," he said.

Katie reached for the stall railing. "What will you tell him?"

The agony in his eyes now was as real as the tenderness she'd seen there just moments before.

"That I've fallen in love with his bride," he said.

The door closed behind him, and Katie lowered herself to the straw-covered floor.

"Perhaps you should tell him that she's fallen in love with you too," she whispered.

She had to leave. After tossing and turning in bed until the early hours of the morning, examining one heartbreaking scenario after another, Katie had come up with no other solution. If Jake were to walk through the cabin door tomorrow, she couldn't marry him—not when she knew full well that she was in love with his brother. And, if Jake didn't return for weeks, living and working beside Caleb while knowing they would have no future together would be torture for them both.

With almost no money to her name, her first priority would have to be finding a job. Then, once she'd saved enough for a train ticket, she'd have to decide on a destination as far from Walker Ranch as she could go. Saratoga Springs held little appeal. Even though there was some comfort in familiarity, she didn't want to return to the painful memories that New York held. She'd have to pick up the pieces of her broken dreams and patch them together somewhere else.

The most obvious answer to her financial difficulties was to go into Birch Creek to see if there were any positions available at the hotel or the mercantile. She didn't relish the thought of running into Amy Skidmore again, but Katie knew from past experiences that desperation enabled a person to face a great many unpleasant things. Asking Caleb to take her into town would be another of those. But it would have to be done.

Katie heard the shuffle of feet coming from Eliza's room and knew she had waited long enough. Slipping out of bed, she hurried to dress before the cold floor spread its chill any farther than her feet. She ran a brush through her hair, blocking out the treacherous memories of Caleb's embrace as she plaited her hair into a long braid and deftly wound it into a coil at the base of her neck. It could not be loose when she saw him again.

She entered the kitchen at the same time as Eliza. The older lady was walking slowly, but she didn't seem as stiff as she had the day before.

"How are you feeling?" Katie asked.

"No better than you, by the look of things." Eliza reached out to touch Katie's cheek. "You're very pale."

Katie gave a wan smile. "I'm afraid I didn't sleep very well."

"And no wonder," Eliza said. "You had a very eventful time yesterday."

Katie's heartbeat quickened. How much did Eliza know?

The Price of Silver

After Caleb had left the barn, Katie had stayed to do the afternoon milking and had lingered there late into the evening, waiting for the storm to pass and watching Echo and her foal. She'd missed dinner and had returned after Eliza had retired.

"Caleb told me he couldn't have managed without you," she said. "Said he's thinking of naming the foal Saratoga."

Katie's eyes widened. "Saratoga?"

"Yes. Fitting, don't you think? That young colt had to fight a mighty battle to get here," Eliza explained. "And you came all the way from Saratoga Springs to help him win it."

"It is a good name," Katie said, touched by Caleb's thoughtfulness.

Eliza looked pleased. "Well now," she said, tying on her apron. "I think this aching old body might be up for making breakfast if you'd be willing to take care of the milking again."

Thanks to Caleb, Eliza's request didn't fill Katie with the same panic she'd experienced the day before.

"I'm not as efficient as you," Katie said, "but I think I can manage it."

"Take all the time you need," Eliza replied, carefully reaching across the table for a bowl of eggs. "I daresay I'll be moving a mite slower than usual too."

An hour later, Katie returned to the cabin with a pail of milk and a small basket of eggs.

"The pigs and chickens are fed," she said. "And I let Daisy out into the meadow."

"Thank you, dear." Eliza handed her a plate of eggs and biscuits. "Now, come get some breakfast."

Katie glanced at the chair that Caleb usually occupied. "Is Caleb not eating today?" she asked, dreading their next meeting, yet aching to see him again.

"Oh, he's come and gone already," Eliza said. "I must say, I've never seen him be so anxious to go into town. Said he had business he had to take care of right away, and he left as soon as it was light."

Katie lowered her fork. He was sending his letter to Jake. "Did . . . did he give you any idea when he'd be back?"

"Can't say that he did," Eliza said, giving her a curious look. "But I don't suppose he'll be too long. Sometime early this afternoon, I'd wager."

Katie stared down at her plate, her appetite now gone. "I'm sorry, Eliza," she said, "but I don't seem to be very hungry this morning."

Concern filled the older woman's eyes, and she studied Katie's pallid complexion more carefully. "Are you sickening with something, child?"

Katie shook her head. "I'm fine," she said, feigning a cheerfulness that she didn't feel. "What chores do you have for me today?"

Eliza looked unconvinced. "I don't want you overdoing things," she said.

Katie leaned forward and placed a soft kiss on the older woman's cheek. "I won't, I promise," she said. Then, with a small smile, she added, "But you have to promise the same."

Nine

Caleb had ridden hard, giving Mica his head on the open meadows and pushing him upward on the steeper climbs. The buffeting canyon wind was a perfect reflection of the battering his heart had experienced over the last twenty-four hours, and he felt physically and emotionally spent. He rode into town, determined to have the letter, which he'd spent all night composing, on its way to Jake on the first available train. But, before Caleb could mail it, the postmaster handed him an envelope addressed to Katie in Jake's distinctive handwriting.

With a sinking feeling, Caleb accepted the letter, got back into the saddle, and started for home less than ten minutes after his arrival in Birch Creek. He didn't know what the envelope contained, but his gut told him that his future happiness would depend upon what was written within the folds of the papers now lying in his inside jacket pocket.

When he reached the ranch, Caleb dismounted and led

Mica into his stall in the barn. Grabbing a brush and a towel from a small pile in the corner, he began the horse's regular rub down. A hint of lavender reached him, and he groaned.

"Am I always to be tortured by that smell, Mica?" he asked.

The stallion snorted, pushing his nose against the empty water bucket.

"Don't give me that, you big phony!" Caleb said. "You may think water's more important right now, but I'll wager you'd feel pretty low if Katie were to stop coming to see you."

He gave Mica some water and feed then checked on Echo and Saratoga. Already the young colt was prancing around the stall, testing his legs and his mother's patience. Caleb smiled. Katie had been right: yesterday, they'd witnessed a miracle. He pulled Jake's letter out of his pocket and gazed at it. Was it too much to ask for another one?

When he entered the cabin, Katie and his mother were making cheese at the kitchen table.

"Goodness, Caleb, that was a fast trip!" his mother said.

Katie's hands froze over the cheesecloth bag she had been squeezing. She looked over at him, her blue eyes appearing troubled.

"I have a letter for Katie," he said, holding out the envelope.

Katie rose to her feet. "Is it from Jake?"

Caleb nodded.

She wiped her hands on her apron then reached for it. "Would you . . ." She looked from Caleb to Eliza. "Would you mind if I read it in the bedroom?"

"Of course not," Eliza said. "We're almost finished here anyway."

Katie gave her an appreciative smile and hurried out of the room. Caleb hung his hat on the peg by the door and reached for the coffee pot. He poured himself a mug of the hot brew, and glanced back at the closed bedroom door. How long did it take to read a letter? Was she going to stay in there all day?

Placing the mug of untouched coffee back on the table, he clenched and unclenched his fists. He walked to the stove, cut over to the corner of the table, then went back to the front door. After another quick look at the bedroom door, he paced the same triangle again.

"Caleb?"

With a start, Caleb remembered his mother. She was standing at the table, watching him, her brow furrowed.

"Is there something you need to tell me?" she asked.

Caleb ran his fingers through his hair. No matter what happened after this, he decided, his mother deserved to know his feelings.

"I've fallen in love with Katie," he said, the words coming out in a rush.

"Oh my." His mother dropped to her seat. "Does Katie know this?"

"Yes," he said.

"And, does she feel the same way about you?" she asked.

"Perhaps," he said helplessly. "I'm not sure."

The bedroom door creaked open, and they turned to see Katie, standing in the doorway. In one hand, she held two sheets of paper; in the other, some bank notes.

Katie took a deep breath, willing her trembling to subside. She'd read Jake's letter twice, but she was still no closer to understanding what it meant for her future.

"Jake isn't coming back anytime soon," she said. "The

silver mine's been more successful than he ever imagined. And, with new miners arriving all the time, he says he has to stay to protect his claim. He's sending money so that you can take on a hired hand to help at the ranch while he's gone."

She looked at Caleb, trying to gauge his reaction to this news. He was gripping the back of one of the wooden chairs, his eyes on her.

"What's his plan for you?" he said.

"He says the mining town's no place for a woman and that he doesn't want me waiting here alone since he could be gone upwards of a year," she said. "He's sending me back to Saratoga Springs."

Eliza gasped, and Katie fought back her tears.

"He's sent me money for the train with enough left over to find a place to live," she said, showing them the bank notes.

"What about your marriage agreement?" Caleb pressed.

Katie dropped her gaze. "He's released me from my obligation. He said that if another, better offer comes along, I should feel free to take it. And, if not, he'll send for me again when he gets back to the ranch."

At the sound of the kitchen chair being pushed aside, Katie looked up again. In three short steps, Caleb closed the distance between them. He reached for her hand, and her heart started to pound.

"All those sleepless nights, telling myself I had no right to feel the way I did about you," Caleb said. "All those long days in the south pasture, telling myself you could never be part of my future. And now, just when I thought I'd lost you forever, Jake's given me a chance."

He tightened his grip, his eyes never leaving hers. "There's only one thing I can offer you that Jake can't—and that's my heart," he said. "I think I started falling in love with you on the wagon ride back from the train depot, and those feelings have only grown stronger since then. Marry me, Katie. Say you'll stay at Walker Ranch as my wife."

There was nothing Katie could do now to stem her tears.

"Yes," she said. "There's nowhere in the world I'd rather be than here, married to you."

He pulled her closer, the joy in his eyes taking her breath away. With his free hand, he gently wiped the tears from her face. "I love you, Katie Spencer," he said.

"I love you too," she whispered.

The sound of another chair being pushed back from the table reminded Katie that they weren't alone.

"Well, Caleb," Eliza said, humor lacing her voice. "It seems like you might need to take back what you said about Jake making the most senseless decision of his life in sending for a mail order bride."

"You're right," he said. "I've changed my mind. Sending for a mail order bride was the second most foolish thing Jake's ever done."

Katie pulled back in his arms. "You still believe that?" she asked.

"Yep," he said. "But I've learned my lesson. I've always come down on Jake for following his heart and not his head. Now, he's finally tried to do the practical thing, and look where it's gotten him." His brown eyes twinkled. "I'm starting to think that being sensible isn't what it's cracked up to be," he added. "When it comes to being foolish, nothing will ever top Jake's decision to let his bride go."

Caleb lowered his head until his lips were inches from hers. "And I'll forever be thankful that Jake made both choices."

Katie heard Eliza's laughter just before the cabin door

closed behind her, and then there was nothing but Caleb's kiss.

ABOUT SIÂN ANN BESSEY

Siân Ann Bessey was born in Cambridge, England, but grew up on the island of Anglesey off the coast of North Wales. She left her homeland to attend Brigham Young University in Utah, where she earned a bachelor's degree in communications with a minor in English. She began her writing career as a student, publishing several magazine articles while still in college. Since then she has published historical romance and romantic suspense novels, along with a variety of children's books.

Although Siân doesn't have the opportunity to speak Welsh very often anymore, she can still wrap her tongue around, "Llanfairpwllgwyngyllgogerychwyrndrobwllllantysiliogogogoch." She loves to travel and experience other cultures, but when she's home, her favorite activities are spending time with her family, cooking, and reading.

Find Siân Ann on Facebook: Sian Ann Bessey—Author

Dear Timeless Romance Anthology Reader,

Thank you for reading *Mail Order Bride*. We hope you loved the sweet romance novellas! Heather B. Moore, Annette Lyon, and Sarah M. Eden have been indie publishing this series since 2012 through the Mirror Press imprint. For each anthology, we carefully select three guest authors. Our goal is to offer a way for our readers to discover new, favorite authors by reading these romance novellas written exclusively for our anthologies . . . all for one great price.

If you enjoyed this anthology, please consider leaving a review on Goodreads or Amazon or Barnes & Noble or any other e-book store you purchase through. Reviews and word-of-mouth is what helps us continue this fun project. For updates and notifications of sales and giveaways, please sign up for our newsletter on our blog: TimelessRomanceAnthologies.blogspot.com

Also, if you're interested in becoming a regular reviewer of the anthologies and would like access to advance copies, please email Heather Moore: heather@hbmoore.com

We also post announcements to Facebook as well: https://www.facebook.com/TimelessRomanceAnthologies

Thank you!
The Timeless Romance Authors

MORE TIMELESS ROMANCE ANTHOLOGIES

www.ingramcontent.com/pod-product-compliance
Lightning Source LLC
LaVergne TN
LVHW021755060526
838201LV00058B/3099